More praise for *Bombingham*

"*Bombingham* is an ambitious, unsentimental novel. It opens intimate perspectives on the violent history of racial segregation and human destruction. Here the American national traumatic experiences are vividly presented through the material sensation and the personal drama. Tony Grooms has written a rich book that has a big heart."

—HA JIN
Author of *Waiting*

"A taut, devastating novel . . . There is always poetry amid great pain, whether we care to acknowledge it or not, and Grooms finds it by balancing the horror with carefully chosen moments when heroism gains the upper hand. . . . *Bombingham* is masterfully paced as it leads readers through the exhilarating tumult of Walter's long, hot, and bloody summer. . . . A haunting reminder that the gains achieved in Birmingham and elsewhere were not cheaply won. Considering the years and tragedies that have since accumulated in our national memory, it may become easy to forget that there was always a price."

—*The Washington Post*

"Anthony Grooms is one of our finest younger writers, and this [is a] powerful, involving first novel about the single thing most obsessively wrong with this country, and the one thing that can defeat it."

—RICHARD BAUSCH
Author of *Someone to Watch Over Me*

"Riveting . . . Whether describing the daily indignities of life under Jim Crow laws or the ignorance and brutality of the men who enforce them, Grooms writes with grace and clarity. . . . [He] confronts this suffering head-on, showing that hope and dignity sometimes can be reclaimed in the process. This is a powerful, important novel."

—*Publishers Weekly* (starred review)

(Please turn the page for more reviews. . . .)

BOMBINGHAM

BOMBINGHAM

A Novel

ANTHONY GROOMS

ONE WORLD

BALLANTINE BOOKS • NEW YORK

A One World Book
Published by The Random House Publishing Group

Published in the United States by One World Books, an imprint of
The Random House Publishing Group, a division of Random House, Inc.,
New York, and simultaneously in Canada by Random House of
Canada Limited, Toronto.

www.oneworldbooks.net

Library of Congress Catalog Number: 2002105149

ISBN 0-345-45293-3

This edition published by arrangement with The Free Press,
a division of Simon & Schuster, Inc.

Cover illustration by William Low

Manufactured in the United States of America

First One World Edition: October 2002

12 14 15 13 11

To the children of "Bombingham,"

wherever that might be.

Acknowledgments

Special thanks to
Rudolph Byrd, Robert A. Boyd, Gray Stewart, and my wife,
Pamela B. Jackson, for their counsel and encouragement.
And to my teachers Merman Johnson, Erleana Mason, and
Cecelia Wright of Louisa; Louis Catron of Williamsburg;
and Susan Shreve and Richard Bausch of Fairfax.

In memory of my friends,
Raymond Andrews, Tori Impink-Hernandez,
and Alecia and Twyla Carlos Nelson,
and my mother, Dellaphine Grooms.

CITIES ARE WHAT MEN MAKE THEM

—motto above the door of the Birmingham City Chamber, 1963

BOMBINGHAM

1

IN FRONT OF US, about a quarter mile, was Thoybu, a complex of straw houses among the palms. Like so many of the villages we had run through, it looked tranquil at a distance, with felicific fronds waving above the thatch roofs. The silence, though, ought to have been a warning, but my head throbbed, a lump the size of a potato pressed against my anus, and I wanted to sleep more than anything. I didn't like being in the open, and the two platoons were strung out across the paddies. The sunlight hurt my eyes and made me dizzy, so I looked down and followed Haywood. He was over six foot and two hundred pounds. His deep tracks filled with brown water.

Vester walked beside me, elbow to elbow. His face was pearled with sweat. "Goddamn hot," he said. I didn't say anything. Maybe I gave him a half smile. "Okay, cool. Be that way if you want. Your 'Bama ass gone get plenty hot before this day is over."

"It's all a matter of mind over matter," I said.

"You full of shit."

"I don't mind and you don't matter."

"You tell 'im, Tibbs." Bright Eyes walked on my left. My name was Walter Burke, but I let them call me "Mr. Tibbs" after a character Sidney Poitier played in the movies.

"You don't matter, neither," Vester said. "That's why your black ass is here. And that rabbit over there?" He referred to Bright Eyes. "I wouldn't even bother scraping his pale-face ass off the sole of my shoe."

"I'm just on a Sunday stroll," Bright Eyes said. "Just like going to church on revival Sunday. Picnic on the grounds. Ham and chicken. Macaroni and cheese—"

"What the hell is he talking about?"

"Cakes and pies. Grandma makes this caramel cake and Aunt Claudia, she makes a squash pie. Ever heard of that?"

"Shut the fuck up, you Bugs Bunny-looking motherfucker. What the fuck you talking about, anyway? You see any goddamn squash pie out here?"

RTO's radio crackled and the squad leader talked into it. They were just on the other side of Bright Eyes. I looked at Bright Eyes. He smiled and pushed at his helmet.

"It's A-okay, a cruise," he reported.

"There no such thing as a cruise," I said.

"You've just got to put an edge on everything."

"He's just a edgy brother," Vester said.

"Hard-edged," Bright Eyes said. "Wouldn't you say, Tibbs? I mean, there's a difference. Edgy is jumpy like. But hard-edged is cool like."

"Cold-edged. Like a mama-san's tit," Vester said.

I didn't say anything. Mr. Tibbs would have found the conversation contemptible.

"What mama-san's tit have you been sucking?"

"The same damn one as you."

"Then you must have been sucking it the wrong way. Remind me to show you some technique. Tibbs got technique. Tibbs, you need to give your brother man a lesson in tit sucking."

"Keep cool, Harvey." I quoted a line from the movie, mimicking Mr. Tibbs's exacting elocution.

Haywood let us catch up to him. He squeezed in between Vester and me. "I got a uptight feeling about this one," he whispered. "There's got to be a Betty out here somewhere. I just feel it." The lump in my stomach turned over. Haywood was usually right about these things.

I slowed down and it seemed that everyone did, as if the line had run up against an unseen tension. I squinted and surveyed the flood plain, puzzled with paddies. The river was behind and to the left of us. Haywood pointed to a figure running away. "Who want this one?" he asked.

"Looks like a papa-san," Bright Eyes said. "I ain't for capping papa-sans."

"He's legal," Haywood said.

"Legal, my ass." Bright Eyes looked at me for support. "Fugazi! That's fucked up."

I lifted my rifle and sighted along the barrel. The man was dressed in the loose-fitting outfit we called black pajamas. We had been told it was okay to shoot anyone in black pajamas who ran because he was VC, running to give warning. The figure made slow progress across the paddies, fighting the suction of the mud with each leap. It appeared to be an old man, though from the distance it could easily have been an old woman with her hair up. I followed the figure with the point of the barrel.

"You got 'im, Waltie?" Haywood asked. There were perhaps thirty GIs closer to the figure than us.

"I got 'im." My heart fluttered and I squeezed off a round. Sporadic popping came from up and down the line, but I was first. The figure tripped and went down.

"What that make? Four or five for you?" asked Haywood.

"Who's counting?"

"You are counting. But I wouldn't count that one," Bright Eyes said. "I wouldn't count that one if I were you, Tibbs."

"You are not me," I said.

"Lord a mighty, don't get so testy about it. I'm not saying you did something wrong. I'm just saying I wouldn't count that one."

"Count what you want to count," Haywood said. "It doesn't change anything. The way it is, is the way it is."

"But the brother got style," Vester said. "He so cool, he scare me. A hundred degrees out here and he ain't even sweating. Just pick 'em off like—*pow!*"

Haywood looked at me and snorted. He and I knew better. He was my age, but seemed older. He already had his short-timer's stick. He knew how important it was to do what you had to do to get by.

"But I wouldn't have capped a papa-san," Bright Eyes said. "Not an old man."

"It wasn't an old man."

"What was it then? Looked like papa-san to me."

"It wasn't *your* papa," I said and moved ahead.

"Least you could have let somebody down the line do it. Maybe they could have seen it better."

"Whose conscience are you? You out of everybody," Haywood said to Bright Eyes. "You ain't got no room to talk with that ring of baby fingers hanging around your neck."

"Ain't no baby fingers on my chain." Bright Eyes pulled a chain out of his shirt. It had an ear on it from a kill he had made earlier in the week. The ear was beginning to mold.

"Goddamn," said Vester. "Throw that goddamn shit away. Walking around like a goddamn cannibal with that goddamn thing on your neck. It stinks."

"It's my power."

"Fuck your power. It stinks. This ain't Africa or something; we ain't no goddamn cannibals. It stinks."

"Y'all ease up," Haywood said, authoritatively. "Keep alert. I think we're in for some action."

"Uh-uh," Bright Eyes disagreed. "CO said, 'Contact unlikely.'"

Just then a snake shimmied across my path. I froze and held my breath. It was one of the slender, green, quick kind we often encountered in the bamboo thickets. A kind of cobra. It skimmed across a puddle and disappeared into the spring green shoots.

That's an omen, I thought, but I did not say it. I looked into the blue sky, and for a moment felt its weight. "We'll get through. We'll get through, all right," I heard Haywood saying. He had seen the snake, too. "Oh, Lord," I heard Bright Eyes say. "Goddamn, here we go," Vester said. Then I heard popping coming from out of the trees in the village. The men in formation closest to the village fell into the mud, and like a row of dominoes the line went down.

I threw myself into the mud and tried to spot the snipers through the sight of my rifle. The fire got heavy. GIs groaned and cried out. The radio crackled and word came down the line to dig in, but it was all I could do to lie still and hope to stay clear of the rounds patting the mud all around me.

The fire slackened after ten minutes, and we were ordered to move forward. By now I was not thinking about my head or my stomach. My senses were outside of me like the feelers of an insect, aware of every movement, every sound, and every smell. We all were insects, ground beetles testing the mud with each step lest we set off a mine. We gained a couple of hundred feet before we fell back in heavy fire. Haywood spotted an area in the trees just in front of the village. "Bust caps right along in there," he directed, and the four of us burned up a lot of ammunition concentrating on the one clump of trees. After ten or fifteen minutes, the fronds were dangling from the trees and our fire received no answer from that clump. I couldn't see our line anymore because the men were low, digging shallow holes in the mud into which to slap their bodies. Smoke wafted across the fields. After a while, a Chinook came across, headed toward a Medevac flare, but the chopper drew so much fire, it couldn't land.

"We need some air. Why don't they send us some air?" Vester asked.

"It won't be long," Haywood assured him. "Lieutenant's called for it by now. Just lay flat and we'll get through this."

"We need some air," Vester yelled across to the squad leader.

"It's on the way," the squad leader said. He was from Boston, and he sounded like it.

"When? Next Christmas?" Bright Eyes yelled.

"Be easy. Be easy," Haywood said. His voice was resonant, and Bright Eyes squeaked. Their voices reminded me of the drones and chirps of crickets. Vester whined. They were a jazz trio of insects. And I . . . I was the singer. I was Nat "King" Cole. Cool and mellow. Only I hadn't begun to sing yet.

The VC opened up with thirty-caliber guns, twenty or thirty of them, and jackhammered all around us. I looked at Haywood, and he raised his head and looked back. His eyes were round and bright. He opened his mouth to say something when a round peeled his head open just above the brow.

"Goddamn," Vester said, "goddamn, goddamn."

I closed my eyes and put my face down in the mud. For what seemed like a long time, I didn't think about anything, but felt myself loosen and drain over the paddies. Then a familiar uneasiness came to me as I began to pull together again. For a second I allowed myself to hope that Haywood was alive. I had seen the bullet catch him, but maybe it was only a flesh wound, the kind that cowboys get on TV.

"Goddamn, goddamn."

I raised my head and looked again. Haywood was dead, as dead as any dead man I had seen. I tried to swallow what that meant; it meant nothing to me. I gripped tighter on my rifle and tried to crawl ahead, away from Haywood, but the firefight kept me in place. I put the mud-slicked rifle stock against my shoulder and sighted at Thoybu. They kill us; we kill them. The sight passed over the place where the papa-san had fallen, and I thought that if I hadn't shot at the papa-san, then Haywood would be alive. It should have been me, since I shot at the papa-san, since I felt dead already, it should have been me.

I had imagined that it would be me before Haywood. After all, he was the one who dreamed about what he would do back in the world. He was going to go to college, to make something of himself.

I had promised Haywood that if I survived him, that I would write a letter to his mother and father. *Dear Mr. and Mrs. Jackson, I was with your beloved Haywood at the end, and I can assure you that it came quickly and without any pain. In his last breath he whispered about you, about home, about home sweet home. . . .* He had said he would write one for me, too. I told him not to trouble himself.

When the fire slackened, I slithered over to Haywood. Bright Eyes was already beside him.

"He's gone," Bright Eyes said.

Haywood didn't look too bad. Part of his head had broken open, but had fallen back into place, held by a flap of skin. They could have a funeral with him.

"Medic!" Vester screamed.

"Are you hit? Are you hit?" I screamed back.

He was crawling to Haywood. "Goddamn. Goddamn."

"Quit your damning," Bright Eyes said. "It's over. He's gone."

I looked where the RTO and the squad leader had been. They weren't there. Our line was still. "Just be quiet," I said. "Just be real quiet for a while." For a moment it seemed like a beautiful summer day. Blue sky. White billows of cloud. The rustle of a light breeze. It could have been Alabama. Alabama was "the Beautiful State." That is what the word meant. Haywood knew this. He knew a lot of what I knew. He was from Eufaula. I was from Birmingham. *Dear Mr. and Mrs. Jackson . . . Dear Haywood's Mother and Father . . . Dear Haywood. . . .* I closed his eyes, and now I had his blood on my hands. "Let's be quiet for a while."

The thirty-calibers picked up again; the mud became soupy with blood and piss; the sun became hotter, and the air filled with biting flies. There was the smell of open bowels, smoke, and oil. The guns whined and popped incessantly. I lay beside Haywood and nestled my face in the mud beside his torso. The mud was warm and smelled faintly of manure.

ABOUT THREE WEEKS EARLIER, the four of us were in our hooch at base camp near Da Nang, when Haywood asked me to tell him about Birmingham. He had grown up not one hundred and fifty miles away, he said, and yet, Birmingham could have been in another country. He had heard it was almost as big as New York City and had buildings fifty stories high. His father called it the Pittsburgh of the South because of the steel mills. From twenty miles out, you could see flares rising from a forest of smokestacks. And on a mountain overlooking the city was a giant statue, taller than the Statue of Liberty. "All that right in Alabama."

I lay on my bunk with my head and shoulders propped on my duffel bag and studied the dust and gnats that swam in a swath of daylight coming in through the door. We had our shirts and boots off, and were trying to relax and stay cool. Bright Eyes rolled a huge joint and passed it my way. Arm Forces Radio was playing Motown.

I toked on the joint and then sucked quickly at the burning end before I passed it on to Vester. When I exhaled, I told Haywood that I didn't want to talk about Birmingham.

"Why not?"

"It's not as cool as you think."

"But that's all I've heard. I mean, it's supposed to be the Magic City, and it's the cradle of the movement. That's all I ever heard about it. What a beautiful place it was and how we won our rights there. Did you ever see Martin Luther King?"

"I guess."

"You did?" Haywood sat on the corner of my bunk. "Man, that must have been something. I mean, a man like that."

"It's a shame what happened to him," Bright Eyes offered. King had been killed two years earlier.

"Did you march?" Haywood continued. "I heard children marched, too. I would have marched."

"I guess."

"You guess?"

I put my hands behind my head.

Vester sang along with the radio; a cloud of cigarette smoke came from his mouth. In the middle of singing he said, "He won't talk because of that rabbit over there. You afraid of that rabbit? You don't have to be scared no more, brother. We free now." He opened his mouth wide and laughed.

I looked at Bright Eyes without laughing.

"Hey Tibbs, you full of shit," Vester continued. "You trying to come off like a goddamn cool cat. You know Mr. Tibbs ain't nothing but the Man, a bona fide pig." Bright Eyes passed me a bottle of bourbon and I swigged. "How come you can't talk in front of a white rabbit? You scared you gone get him nervous talking about black revolution?"

"What fucking black revolution?" Bright Eyes said. "Your ass the same place as mine."

Vester slapped his thigh and laughed. "Black power, Mr. Charlie. Black revolutionary power à la my brother El Hajj Malik Al Shabazz . . ."

Bright Eyes had heard it before. "You mean the late El Hog deBuzz—"

"I mean I'm gonna knock you upside your knotty country-ass head, white boy. Don't speak ill of the great man."

"Shut up, Vester," Haywood said. "Can't we have just an hour without your motor mouth?"

"I was just trying to inform my white brother here about some of our black history since it's obvious he ain't never been in contact with no deep soul brother like myself. He's been hanging too close with you half-white colored brothers—"

I took a deep breath and began to mimic some Negro historians I had heard. "From the swamps of great Luxor, a mighty people arose—"

"Shut up, Tibbs—"

"Building the great pyramids and the city of Timbuktu—"

"Shut the fuck up! Over there pretending you be somebody. You ain't nobody." Vester began a bad imitation of Mr. Tibbs. "'They call me *Mister* Tibbs.' Who Mr. Tibbs but somebody's flunky-ass cop?"

"Shut up," Haywood said.

"Mr. Tibbs be a cherry-assed motherfucker and you a cherry, too. All y'all."

"Be quiet," Haywood said. We were quiet for a moment. Haywood had played football; he had been good enough to play in college but hadn't gotten a scholarship. When he was back in the world, he said, he was going to study engineering, maybe Alabama State. He had expressed this wish to me many times because he thought I was serious about school, too.

After a silent round of joint and bottle, Bright Eyes put on his boots. "I'm going out to the gate to look for girls."

"Wait up," said Vester. He scrambled to put on his boots.

"Hey, now. What's all this white rabbit shit? Now, you want to hang with the rabbits, my black-colored brother man?"

"You know I dig you. I mean, you more like a brother than a rabbit. Any motherfucker can see that. Look at them lips. Look at that nose. You got soul wrote all over you."

A BREEZE STIRRED and dust blew into the hooch. I closed my eyes and enjoyed the tingle of evaporation from my chest and stomach. For a moment, I was not in Da Nang, but in Birmingham. Haywood was not Haywood, but Lamar. I wanted to call Haywood, "Lamar" and hear him answer, giggling.

"They are gone now," Haywood said. "Do you want to tell me about it?"

I sighed. "Why? Why is it important?"

"It changed things."

"It changed the fucking world, didn't it?"

I heard Haywood fidget. I knew he was getting angry.

"I didn't march," I lied. I heard a gecko scuttling along the roof beam. It was hunting insects. "I didn't see King, okay? I might have seen him from a distance, but I didn't really see him, okay?"

"I thought I heard you had."

"No. But I did have a friend named Lamar. He was my best friend, like a brother. He was in the march." I swallowed. "It's not like one day you wake up and go downtown and march. You get pulled into it, or pushed into it."

"What pushed your friend to it? Freedom? I mean, he wanted his rights?"

I opened my eyes. Haywood still sat on the edge of his bunk, his knees a few inches from me. He looked eager for the story.

"Freedom? He's free as hell, now. And so are you."

Haywood looked disappointed. For all of his big frame and sinew and fuzzy hair around his collarbone, he looked like a baby. He could take a football team, or a fire team, into the field. He could fend off a tackle or lay an ambush for the VC. But he was still a baby.

"Man," I said, "you had better be careful."

"Why?"

"The way you think. It'll get you hurt."

"What? What about the way I think?"

I heard the lizard pounce and looked up at the rafters. I couldn't see the lizard, but I heard it tearing and crunching its prey.

"I'll tell you, later."

WITH THE NIGHTFALL, the tracers lit up the sky, leaving trails like slow meteors or momentary comets. "Make a wish on it, Waltie," a voice in my head said. The constellation of Scorpio lay peacefully, curled against the Milky Way. With the darkness, I knew the battle would get very close. Either we would move on them or they on us. Haywood had become swollen from lying in the sun all day. His skin was tight and his joints stiff. In the colored glow of the tracers, his face looked pleasant, though like a fat version of himself. I was ready to move away from him, but the mud cradled my body, and I was afraid to move. I wanted to be away, and I thought about Birmingham. "Make a wish on it." All of my time in Birmingham, I had been wishing, dreaming, and then I stopped . . . I let go of dreams. I became loose. So loose that I seemed to go in all directions at once, and nowhere at all. *Dear Mr. and Mrs. Jackson, There is a tracer in the sky over Birmingham. Dear Haywood . . . Dear Lamar. . . .*

2

"MAKE A WISH on it," Lamar said.

"You can't," I said. "You wish upon shooting stars—meteors—not comets. Besides, it's all superstition."

Lamar had spotted the comet first. I had refused to look, knowing for sure that he would say "April fools" the moment I glanced up, but he gesticulated with such sincerity that I risked a look and saw the faint streak above the eastern horizon. We had met at Center Street School to assemble and deliver the *Birmingham Herald*. The morning was clear and warm enough that we were comfortable in our light jackets. Above us, the stars glittered, and we were trying to place them in constellations when Lamar saw the comet.

He gave me a look that dismissed my opinion. He closed his eyes tightly.

"What did you wish for?" I asked.

"I'm not telling since it's superstition."

"Don't tell then." I went back to rolling the papers, but secretly I had made a wish, too. Like so many boys our age, I wanted to be an astronaut.

While we rolled and banded the papers, Lamar kept up an entertaining chatter about the comet. At first he said it was the Christmas star come a little late—or maybe it was a NASA experiment, some kind of new rocket that was in orbit around the Earth—

"Or a Russian rocket," I interjected.

Lamar considered and dismissed the thought. "If it was a Russian rocket, we would have destroyed it by now. If that's man-made, it's American. Waltie, you know what? One day, we are going to fly up there, too. You wait and see. It doesn't matter if you're colored. My mama said if they fly monkeys up there, they can—you remember the big cake?" I remembered because we had made such a to-do about it. As a part of the celebration for John Glenn's return, he was presented with a giant cake, as tall as a person, in the flask shape of *Friendship 7*. Lamar had talked for hours about how it must have tasted and how he wished he could have gotten a piece of it. Then my father said that probably no Negro in the country had gotten to taste it. A Negro might have helped to bake it, but he didn't get to taste it. Offhand though it was, the remark resonated with Lamar and me. If no Negro could even taste the cake, how much more difficult would it be for a Negro to become an astronaut? The realization didn't discourage us. We decided we would be the first Negroes on the moon.

"But, oh—it couldn't be—but, noooo—a flying saucer." Lamar mocked fear. "Suppose it was coming to take the Earth away from white people and to give it to the colored so we could run things for a while."

"That," I said, using my father's phrase, "is highly unscientific."

AS WITH MOST of our ventures, getting a paper route had been Lamar's idea. He had heard that the regular route boy, a teenager, had taken a job at TCI, Tennessee Coal and Iron, the largest of Birmingham's steel mills. "That's a mighty rough place for a teenager," my father had said when I told him why the route had opened up. Lamar knew the teenager since they both lived in Loveman's Village, and he assured my father that the boy was "as big as a man." He had gotten a girl "you, know"—as Lamar put it—so he needed to quit school and take the higher-paying job so he could meet his responsibility. "What a shame," my father said noncommitted and fiddled with an album cover. It had been a Sunday afternoon, after church, and my father was in the living room listening to jazz. His feet were propped on an ottoman and crossed at the ankles. He soaked in the opening bars of Nat "King" Cole's "Unforgettable." It was going to be a romantic afternoon. Already his breath was sweet with bourbon. Soon he would be grabbing my mother around the waist and making her dance in his imaginary jazz room. He deferred my request to my mother, who was in the kitchen basting a pot roast. She was not easy to convince. She said that she did not want me riding around Birmingham at the crack of dawn, especially with the KKK running loose. Recently a store on the periphery of the neighborhood had been blown up, and black people blamed it on the KKK or the police, if they made that distinction.

"Well," my father said lazily from the entrance to the kitchen, "when aren't the KKK running loose? We wouldn't cross the street if we worried all day about the KKK."

"You'd better worry," Mother snapped.

ROLLING THE PAPERS, Lamar and I took only the slightest notice of the headlines—a bus strike was threatened to begin that day. Later I learned that there were other matters afoot, matters in which we children would soon find ourselves at the very center. However, I did notice one small ad. It featured the face of a big-jowled, bespeckled white man, Bull Connor, who was the city's public safety commissioner, in charge of the police and firemen. To us children he was the boogeyman. I had heard my great uncle, Uncle Reed, rail against him. He said Bull Connor was a grand dragon in the Ku Klux Klan and his responsibility for public safety meant keeping the public "safe *from* Negroes." He accused Connor of having lynched colored men in his jails. He said Connor not only stood by while colored people's houses burned, but he even ordered his firemen to burn the houses.

I probably wouldn't have noticed the ad, busy as I was glancing at the comet before the sunrise washed it out, but the ad was repeated throughout the paper. Everywhere a reader turned in the paper, he came face to face with the pip-eyed Bull Connor. I pointed out the ad to Lamar, who made a sour face when he saw it. We held the paper in the light coming from inside the school. The ad complained about an editor of an Atlanta newspaper, and said that the "quisling Ralph McGill, who had integrated Atlanta" was "brainwashing you." The "you," followed by an exclamation point, was further defined as "the people of Birmingham." Even then, we realized that "you" did not include us—nor did the phrase "people of Birmingham." Lamar laughed at the banner at the foot of the front page that read, "Your vote could decide the outcome of tomorrow's election."

I wondered aloud what "quisling" meant, and Lamar answered without missing a beat that it meant "midget." He had learned the word in Mrs. Griffin's spelling bee, he said. I was not a speller, and did not participate in the competitions. "Yes, you see, this Ralph guy is a midget and if there's anything Bull Connor hates worse than colored, it's midgets."

"Why would he call the guy a midget in the newspaper?"

"He didn't call him a 'midget,' he called him a 'quisling,' which is a bad word for midget. It's a fighting word."

I took a deep breath and put an armful of papers in my bicycle rack. When I turned back to Lamar, I saw him struggling to keep a straight face. "You a lie."

"A-pril fools!" He rolled on the pavement, laughing, and pointing at me as I coolly gathered more papers. I knew that this would be just the first of Lamar's pranks. At every chance, right up until a bedtime telephone call, he would try to fool me. Looking back on it, I'm ashamed to admit that he was too often successful. I was not naive in those days, nor particularly gullible, but I did have a wide-eyed openness to things, especially things wondrous. Lamar played my curiosity: Mrs. Griffin was wearing a wig; Joe Brown had a pet monkey; Arlene Spencer's father was decapitated in a car wreck; Mr. Edwards, the vice principal, found a rattler by the swing set. I knew I shouldn't have believed him, but I wanted to. I studied Mrs. Griffin's hairline for some clue of a skull cap; asked the hulking Joe if I could play with his monkey; dipped my head in sympathy and morbid fascination every time Arlene passed me in the hall; and sneaked out to the swing set to look for the four-foot diamond back with its crushed head and six-inch rattle.

With our route marked out on a paper, we set off on our bikes through the neighborhood. We both had Sears Flyers, simple three-speeds, and both geared to the hilt with handlebar tassels, front baskets, and trumpet-shaped horns. Lamar took one side of the street, and I the other, and we paced each other. This arrangement took us a few minutes longer than dividing the route, but it suited Lamar to a tee. He loved being able to talk as we flung the papers toward the door stoops, or slipped them into paper boxes that some of our clients had affixed to their mailbox posts. Though there were a good mix of professions from doctors and lawyers to factory workers, the most common profession in Tittusville was schoolteacher. Next door to where I stayed on Tenth Avenue were the Jeterses, both retired from teaching. Across the street was Mrs. Rucker who taught at Center Street. Her reputation for surliness and hard work made us grateful she was not our teacher. Next to her, the Dobsons—he, a factory worker and she, a high school teacher; and, across from them, the Mannings, another teaching couple. My father, too, was a teacher. He taught science at Ullman High School. He could teach any branch of science and so was called on to teach the ninth grade general courses, but his specialty was biology. Father had studied a year at Meharry Medical College, the only medical college for Negroes in the country, and so he garnered great respect from his students and fellow teachers. He had dropped out of college in order to support his family; I was well on the way by the time my parents married. If my father regretted leaving medical school, he never said it.

Though it was just at the other end of Center Street, Loveman's Village was across busy Sixth Avenue from Tittusville. It was a complex made of rows of barrackslike brick buildings, two units per building, each marked with a concrete stoop in front and back. A narrow lane named for a president separated each row. Lamar lived on Wilson Way.

When I first made friends with Lamar, in the first grade, my mother wouldn't allow me to go to Loveman's Village. She said that the projects were dangerous. Too many drunks. Too many knife fights. After a year of Lamar visiting our house, she relinquished. Nothing ever happened to me at Loveman's Village. In those days, it was much like any other black neighborhood in Birmingham, though poorer than most. Sure, there were the drunks, and dope-heads, and a heroin addict or two, but all together they weren't so mean. If I went quickly by the corners where they congregated, they hardly noticed me.

Mother Thompson lived next door to Lamar. A wiry but grand-motherly woman, she was active in Reverend Shuttlesworth's church. Shuttlesworth was Birmingham's most outspoken civil rights activist. Mother Thompson dared to advertise the activism by placing posters on her front door, notifying people about mass meetings of the Alabama Christian Movement for Human Rights. As children we paid little attention to the posters or to the dozens of pamphlets we found at the bottom of the rank, damp garbage cans in her backyard.

One afternoon, the week before we started our paper route, Lamar's mother, Mrs. Burrell, and Mother Thompson had a con-

Lena's mother!

frontation that focused our attention on the civil rights movement. Lamar, Josie—my sister—and I were playing on the back stoop with a microscope Lamar had gotten for Christmas. Since it was a Wednesday, Mrs. Burrell's day off from domestic work, she was very dolled up. She wore a bright blue dress that pinched her waist and flared out below her hips. Her face was powdered and rouged and brightened with lipstick and she was holding her hands, wrist limp, in front of her and shaking them to dry her nails.

Mother Thompson greeted Mrs. Burrell with an approving grunt. "You looking sharp, gal. You must got a beau on the string tonight."

"Naw, Mother," Mrs. Burrell chuckled and dipped her head in an instant of mock embarrassment, "it ain't nothing like that. Just a friend."

"Must be a mighty good friend." Mother Thompson threw out wastewater from a pan into her square of lawn, and put the free hand on her hips. "Y'all young girls can . . ." she made a grinding motion with her hips, not meant to be witnessed by the children, though we were only a few feet away. I caught a glance of her, but did not look up. "Y'all be wheeling them in!"

Mrs. Burrell protested by waving both hands, but she smiled in a way to show her pleasure at the compliment.

"I'm too old for that stuff, myself," Mother Thompson went on. "Naw, Mr. Thompson was one too many for me!" she said of her long-dead husband. "I only got two somebodies now, me and the Lord. Any man-fishing I be doing now, I be doing for the Lord." Then she turned serious. "There's fixing to be another mass meeting, now, Mrs. Burrell, and I want to extend an invite to you. Before you say no, I want you to think about what we trying to do. You know, this time we got Reverend King coming in, and it's going to be different—"

"Now, now, Mother, you know I don't take no stock in all that mess."

Mother Thompson's silence was abrupt, and caused us children to look up. She had both hands on her hips, the pan dangling from one. "I sure get tired of triflin', Mrs. Burrell. This ain't no mess. This is serious business—and it's the Lord's work, too."

Mrs. Burrell forgot about her nails, put her hands on her hips, too, and dipped a hip, to boot. "It might be the Lord's work, but it's still a mess. Look around front, Miss Thompson. Now, I don't mean no disrespect—I was raised to respect—but when you got all them posters and signs tacked all over your front door, what am I supposed to think? That reflects on us all. Building look like a bulletin board! Now, I don't care what you do—but you got to keep it inside."

Mother Thompson took a step backward, stopped, and wagged her finger. "You *better* care what I do. I'm trying to help *you*. You got a child to raise. You ought to be doing it, too!"

Mrs. Burrell turned her profile to Mrs. Thompson. The heat had passed. "I know that. I just can't do everything. I'm doing the best I can with what I got."

"Girl, you just need to get some more—and I mean *get*, 'cause Mr. Charlie and Miss Ann ain't giving." Mother Thompson went in and slammed the door behind her.

Mrs. Burrell remembered her nails, blew on them, looked a moment at Lamar. "She ain't going do nothing but get us blowed up." She went in and let her screen door slam, too.

When Mrs. Burrell mentioned bombing, Josie slipped her hand inside of mine and squeezed. She was nine; we liked to say nine going on ninety-nine. With her head full of thin, well-greased plaits, our mother's meticulous handiwork, she looked quite the little girl, but our Grandmother Pic sometimes referred to her as "an old soul." I took my hand away and patted her on the back and took my turn looking in the microscope.

The slide was simply labeled "blood." Lamar wondered if it could be human blood. I didn't think so. I said it was against the law to sell human blood.

"Not if it's in the interest of science." Lamar cocked his head confidently. "Besides, it ain't even a whole drop of blood. It's not enough to hurt anybody."

"That's easy to say, if it's not your blood," Josie said.

"I think they took it from animals," I said. "Probably from a cow. Probably they got it from the slaughterhouse. Besides, if a person gave enough blood for all the microscopes Sears sold in one year, it would bleed him to death."

Josie took her turn peering into the microscope. "It's pretty," she said. "Looks like the windows at a church."

"Does not," Lamar said and took his second look. "Looks like old lady Thompson's blood to me."

"Be quiet," Josie said.

"I'll sell Sears plenty of blood after I kick her ass."

I laughed, but Josie stood up. "That's mean."

Just then Mrs. Burrell called Lamar from inside the screen door. Her tone was scolding. He went in and a minute later came out and told us we had to go home.

THE PAPER ROUTE ended at Sixth Avenue, the thoroughfare between Tittusville and Loveman's Village and downtown. A few blocks from where the route ended was the burned-out shell of Williams's store, the neighborhood grocery that had been bombed a few weeks earlier. We had not heard the blast, only heard about it the next morning when Mr. Jeters interrupted our Sunday breakfast. "Th-Th-They bombing in T-Tittusville, now," he said. We children called him "Jittery Jeters" because of his stutter. True to his nature, my father invited Mr. Jeters to have a seat. If the news excited my father, he never showed it.

"Was anyone hurt?" my mother asked.

"J-just ruined the store."

"Now, that's a shame," Father offered. "And just on the outskirts of Tittusville. I didn't know Williams was doing anything political. Is he a race man?"

"You don't have to be a race man," Mother interjected sharply, "you just have to be colored."

After church, we took a family outing to survey the damage at the store. Mother wouldn't let us get out of the car, so we drove around the block slowly, just one of several carloads of sightseers, black and white.

Already, my head was filled with images of bombings and lynchings from the stories I heard my uncles tell at family gatherings. Later, I would realize that those stories, as terrifying and brutal as I imagined them, could never describe real violence. Violence has odors, both loud and subtle as the heightened senses pick them out. The stories my uncles told about lynchings always happened at a great distance—in Tuscaloosa or in Albertville, or "over in Georgia"—but never in Birmingham. Birmingham's stories were about bombings, but never in Tittusville, until the store bombing. It seemed the Birmingham Klan was too sophisticated to toss a rope over a tree limb. It preferred the blast and rumble of dynamite, or the flash of a gasoline bomb—so much so that Fountain Heights on the north side of the city, a white neighborhood where blacks were beginning to buy houses, had so many bombings and fires it was called Dynamite Hill. Bombings were so common that black people had nicknamed the city "Bombingham."

But on that beautiful April Fools' morning, with the wind whistling around my ears as I headed home from my first delivery, my first real job, what news those papers contained—the affairs of adults—were far from my mind. I was, for a moment, in a suspended time. Freewheeling down Center Street hill toward home, I could think of nothing but wonder in the world.

3

THE NEXT SATURDAY, coming home a little late from the paper delivery, I saw Father in the yard squatting beside the tiller and the toolbox. Though we lived within the city limits, like most of our neighbors we kept a garden. If my father had had his druthers, he wouldn't have bothered. But my mother liked the garden for its fresh tomatoes, so he obliged her.

I stood at the edge of the garden and watched Father pull weeds out of the tiller's tines. The air was ripe with the smell of the damp ground. Mrs. Jeters's azaleas made a crooked, crimson fence between the side yards. It was the first time that week I had found him alone, and I had wanted to ask him about my mother.

Earlier in the week, Mrs. Rucker had called to ask us to join Reverend Shuttlesworth's boycott against the downtown merchants to force them to integrate their staffs. I had answered the phone and passed it to my father. Father was very polite, saying, "Yes, ma'am" to Mrs. Rucker, but he was also rolling his eyes. Politely but firmly, he said, "Clara," referring to my mother, "isn't very well, Mrs. Rucker. She just won't be able to help with any organizing. And I—well, frankly, I'm just not interested." He hung up, mumbling as he walked away. "What does she think, that we can just quit working and sit up in jail?"

My father tugged at dried morning glory vines, tangled around the tines. The crackling and snapping made a musical noise. He sighed with satisfaction as they unraveled, and I ventured the question.

"Daddy, is Mama sick?"

He stopped pulling at the vines, stood, and put both hands on my shoulders. Suddenly my anticipation leapt. From the moment his hands gripped my shoulders, I knew that what he would say was serious. He looked beyond me and was quiet. His lips trembled, then calm came over his face. "You will have to be very strong for us now. First of all, you mustn't tell anyone. Not even Lamar. You must respect your mama's privacy. Promise?"

I promised, but my mind was suddenly busy as I imagined the worst right away. My mother was going to die. I shuddered and my father's hands gripped my shoulders more firmly. He asked me if I wanted to sit down. We sat on the grass and he kept one hand on my shoulder, a steady weight holding me in place, absorbing the wave of trembling that had overcome me. I couldn't tell at first whether the trembling was coming from inside of me—my stomach or my spine—or from the ground.

"Your mother has a cancer."

The trembling stopped. My eyes blurred, but I did not cry, even though it occurred to me that I should. There was nothing to cry about. There was only disbelief. I sat for a moment as quiet and still as the shrubbery, and our dog Bingo came up and licked me. I stroked his head.

"Are you all right, son?" Father asked.

I tried to jump up just then, I don't know why, to run to my mother, I guess. I wanted to see how she looked, though I had seen her just that morning at breakfast, and she had looked fine.

Father held me in place. "Listen," he said, "I know this is a shock, and I'm sorry this is happening to you." His speech was practiced, measured. "From now on, things are going to be different. You won't be able to depend on your mother for the things you used to. She'll need her rest if she is to get better. And you are going to have to take on a little more responsibility, I'm afraid." He stopped, and I understood that though he had practiced this little speech, it wasn't easy for him. It was a full minute before he could continue, stopping to swallow, to clear his throat. "You are going to have to take care of your sister more. And don't tell her. Please. Don't tell her a thing. You are a big boy, and I know I can count on you." He moved his hand to the base of my neck and patted me softly. "Can I count on you?"

I answered slowly. I had heard every word, and yet I had understood nothing. I knew very well everything he had said—every instruction—and yet it all seemed hinged on the most improbable of all premises, that my mother may not live.

"Yes, sir," I said.

"Want to shake on it."

His hands were broad and angular, unlike my own, which were round like my mother's. He enclosed my hand in both of his. He squeezed a bit, but he did not shake. I felt he wanted to say something more. I wanted him to. I didn't care what. Suddenly he let go of my hand and stood. I remained seated. His soiled khaki knees were at eye level. Looking up at him, he looked like a dark tower set against the blue sky—lean and angular. Clouds passed behind his head.

Bingo and I sat for a long time and watched my father work. He seemed to ignore me as he steadied the tiller back and forth across the garden. Bingo turned his head to one side and let an ear flip up. He let out a quizzical ruff and purred like a cat when I stroked his head. He licked me and rolled over, persuading me to scratch his stomach. Later, Josie came with word that our mother wanted me to come in for lunch.

SEVERAL TIMES during lunch I wanted to say something to my mother about her sickness. It seemed to me that she knew I knew about it. I watched her move back and forth through the house, her graceful movements belying so serious a sickness as cancer.

Josie sat next to me, humming to herself and swinging her legs as she ate peanut butter and jelly.

"Stop swinging your feet," I said to her.

"Swing them if I want to."

"Stop." I felt I needed to control her, least she disturb Mother. I knew nothing about what kind of illness cancer was, or at that moment, what kind of cancer my mother had. But I knew that it meant death. On visits to the country, I had heard Grandma Pic announcing in a fatalistic tone that someone she knew had "the cancer." She had led me to understand that cancer was beyond the powers of doctors to cure. Only God could cure it, if he chose to—and he never seemed to choose to. Quiet was necessary now. Quiet, in everything we did. No television or radio. No loud playing, inside the house or out. Bingo couldn't bark when strangers approached. He couldn't howl at night. The ringer on the telephone must be turned down. "Please don't swing your feet," I admonished softly. "It's noisy."

Josie stopped and gave me a quizzical look. I knew I would eventually have to tell her. She would never cooperate without knowing the truth and besides, we never kept secrets. For the time being, she stopped. She cocked her head seeming to know that something was amiss and that she needed to cooperate in order to learn what it was. Outside, the tiller backfired and Bingo yelped.

When she came into the kitchen, Mother asked if we wanted more milk. "I'm fine, thank you," I whispered.

"And you?" she asked Josie.

Josie looked at me, and then at Mother and answered likewise.

"Okay. What's up, you two?" Mother asked. She sat down. She took Josie's hand and then mine. "Did Daddy talk to you?"

I opened my mouth and a grunt escaped. I began to shake and lose my breath and my eyes watered—but I held back the sobs.

"Now, baby," Mother said. She dropped Josie's hand and pulled me close to her. "It's all right to cry."

"But I can't—I don't . . ."

"Go ahead and cry."

I felt like crying; I could feel small heaves in my stomach trying to turn involuntary, but I tightened my belly and held them in place. I did not want to cry and I would not. Crying was when something was wrong and there was nothing wrong with my mother. Crying was when somebody was dead. And my mother was not dead. She was looking just as she always looked.

Josie had gotten down from her chair and had come around to Mother's side. I pushed away from Mother and struggled to gain my composure. I was a big boy, I kept telling myself, and big boys don't cry.

"What's the matter?" Josie asked and Mother let go of me and pulled Josie into her lap. She held her like a baby and Josie went limp and laid against Mother's breast, and Mother began to rock her slowly.

"Honey, things are going to be a little different for a while because Mama is sick."

"I know," Josie said.

"You do? Did Daddy tell you?"

"Daddy didn't have to tell me. I figured it out because I heard you tell Daddy you went to the doctor. You are going to have a baby. I'm going have a little sister or brother."

"Shut up," I said to Josie. "You don't know anything."

"That's okay," Mother said. She let out a little chuckle. "You kids really are something else. Nosey. Where did you get that noseyness from? Born with it."

"I just notice things," Josie said, pleased with herself.

"Will you shut up," I said and stood. "Just shut up."

"Walter," Mother said firmly. "Sit down. It's going to be all right. Truthfully." She paused. "What did Daddy tell you? Word for word."

I sat down. My stomach heaved again and my breath caught in the back of my throat. "Daddy said you were sick and that you might—you might . . ." I was set to say "die," to come to face the facts like a good scientist. My father had said many times that a good scientist must see what is real, not what he hoped or expected to see. "Hope" was not in the scientific vocabulary.

She didn't wait for an answer. "He said I might die?" She let out a soft chuckle. "Honestly, Walter, your father was just preparing you for the worst possible situation. My chances are very good. Honest."

"Is the baby going to be a boy or a girl?" Josie asked.

Mother and I were quiet. My head was spinning and the world spinning, and my heart was about to jump in my throat. Mother was not going to die!—and then I let out a laugh at Josie, but it didn't come out as a laugh, but a bark. It startled us—there was another quiet moment and Josie said, "You sound like a dog," and we all laughed.

Then my mother put her arm around my neck and pulled me over to her and kissed me beside my mouth. She kissed Josie and then me, again, and then Josie. We heard my father on the back steps and Bingo's wagging tail banging against the screen door. Suddenly, Mother pushed Josie from her lap and stood. She looked dazed, scared, not sure which way to turn. She walked quickly away from the table, half running, and then the bedroom door shut crisply.

MY FATHER came into the kitchen and fixed himself a peanut butter sandwich and a glass of sweet tea. He didn't say anything until he sat at the table and then he asked if I had brought home a newspaper. He seemed casual, considering the drama of that morning and I wondered if somehow he had forgotten that Mother was sick. I mentioned to him that she had run to the bedroom. He looked over the top of the paper. "Is she all right?"

"I think so."

Crossing his knees, he leaned back in the chair that Mother had occupied only minutes earlier. He took a bite of his sandwich, shook the newspaper to straighten it, and washed the peanut butter down with a mouthful of tea.

"She looked all right," I said.

"She was going to cry," Josie said.

Father gave me a sharp look like I had done something wrong. He got up and went to the bedroom. The door shut very softly.

"You shouldn't have said she was going to cry," I said.

"But she was. I could tell."

AFTER LUNCH, we began our chores from a list that our mother had taped to the refrigerator. Being that it was a warm day, she had asked us to bathe Bingo, a job that Josie and I liked doing. Before we had finished setting up, however, Lamar appeared. He wanted to play, and so began to rush us through the chore.

Bingo was always reluctant to get into the tub, but he never resisted Josie. I believe it was because we had gotten Bingo just after Josie was born. Baby and puppy, they seemed to have become twins. Bingo spent so much time outside Josie's bedroom window that my father eventually moved his dog house there. Sometimes he came in through the window and curled into bed with her.

As we rubbed soap through his coat, Lamar raised the improbable idea that wet white people smelled like wet dogs. This was just one of a slew of reports about white people that filtered down to us from adults. We had heard that white people never washed their hands, kissed their dogs on the mouths, never seasoned their food, and ate fried chicken with knives and forks. As curious as I was, I accepted such reports dubiously.

"You ever smell a wet white person?" I asked.

"I didn't say I had. But my mama has. She said that when the old white woman she works for comes in out of the rain, her hair smells just like a wet dog."

"I like the way a wet dog smells," Josie said and took a long sniff of Bingo. "Smells like flowers."

"You're just smelling soap," Lamar said. He proposed we do an experiment in which we compared a strand of Bingo's hair to that of a white person's under his microscope.

"Where you going to get a white person's hair?" I asked.

"I'll get Mama to bring one home from her old white woman."

"That's not going to be enough to smell," Josie insisted. It was hard to tell if she was being serious or sarcastic.

"We're not going to smell it. We're going to look at it under the microscope."

"How's looking at it going to tell you how it smells?"

Lamar sighed with exasperation, but did not admit the lunacy of his idea. He never would.

Bingo remained still until we rinsed him, his clue to shake. Josie led him out of the tub and onto the lawn and we ran to take cover while Bingo shook. I had run down to the corner of the house, under the windows of my parents' bedroom.

Inside I heard their voices. Tight. Tense. My father's tone had a high pitch to it, but he wasn't yelling. Though my mother was holding her own, she sounded like she was crying. My parents didn't argue much that I knew about, so this tense mumbling worried me, especially coming after learning about Mother's sickness. I could hear a word or two: "doctor" was the one that stood out—"doctor" then "die" or maybe she said "not die." Josie and Lamar were laughing now and I couldn't make out much more of what my parents were saying. The windows were down, and the curtains were drawn. I could tell that my father was pacing because his voice came and went, and my mother was stationary, probably sitting on the bed. Then my mother let out a mournful, ghostly sound that made me catch my breath. Even Lamar and Josie heard it. Josie looked at me, and then she went back to drying Bingo as if nothing had happened.

But Lamar would not ignore it. "What's wrong with your mama?" he asked me when I came back to the tub.

"Nothing."

"Maybe she hit her foot on something," Josie said.

"Geez, it must have been a Mack truck."

"Well, she has been kinda sick," I said.

"With what?"

I remembered that my father said I shouldn't tell, and technically I hadn't.

"I bet I know what's wrong with her," Lamar said with certainty. He often made pronouncements, and many times he was right, resulting from, he claimed, his superior scientific mind and powers of observation. He wasn't smug in these pronouncements—only certain. "She's having a baby, I'll bet."

"What makes you say that?"

"A girl over at Loveman's had a baby last week and she made a noise like that. Mama said that when a woman has a baby she goes through mood swings—and I bet that's what your mama is having."

"How did you know?" Josie said with mock surprise. One minute she could be just a little girl—more a baby than anything—and the next minute she would be saying something smart-aleck. When she had finished drying Bingo, she gave him a hug. He licked her cheek and then she giggled.

"If you are finished with your chores," Lamar said, "let's collect some specimens for the microscope."

As I started into the house to tell my parents we were going to play, I met my father coming out. At first he walked past me, then he stopped. "What do you want?"

"I was going to ask—"

"Ask *me*," he said in a hard way. Then he softened. "Leave your mama alone, she needs her rest."

"Lamar and I want to go and collect some specimens over to the school playground."

He thought for a moment. "Take your sister with you—and be back in two hours." Then he gave me a playful punch on the shoulders and got into the car and drove away.

4

LAMAR SUGGESTED THAT we sneak into George Ward Park, a whites-only park. A creek ran through it and we might find some frog eggs—if we were lucky, even tadpoles. He had brought a mayonnaise jar along to collect the specimens. I objected to going, not only because it was a whites-only park, but also because the commissioners had closed it and all the white parks to avoid a court order to integrate them. Besides, I had told my father that we would be going to the school.

"Awh, he won't know the difference," Lamar assured me. "We will be back in no time." Lamar had come with a plan in mind. We would avoid the front entrance of the park or any road that went directly into it. Instead, we would sneak through the woods near the creek. Once inside the park, we would stay well away from the playgrounds and ball fields. The plan seemed sound enough to me and, as usual, I followed Lamar. In fact, I was curious about the park. I had heard about large, green ball fields, more magnificent than any we black boys had ever played on. I enjoyed softball (making no distinction in terms, we called it "baseball"), and I had a glove and a bat of my own that I played with at Center Street School. Like many of the boys, I fantasized that I was Jackie Robinson.

We rode our bikes down the path that ran along Fifth Avenue South onto a cutoff that ran along the railroad. Josie rode on my handlebars. She was good at steadying herself and she draped her legs across the front basket. Following the tracks, we went under the bridge at Greensprings Avenue, a busy road and the dividing line between the black and white neighborhoods on the south side. Crossing Greensprings was no big deal. Blacks and whites crossed back and forth all the time, more blacks than whites, the blacks going to work in the white neighborhoods.

The front entrance of the park on Greensprings Avenue was chained off and two "No Trespassing" signs were posted. We turned onto a side street and went uphill along the woods beside the park. The hill was so steep I could not pedal with Josie on the bike. She got down and we walked. About halfway up, we heard a familiar jangling coming toward us over the crest of the hill.

"The Goat Man!" I warned and took a deep breath to hold down panic. He would know that we weren't supposed to be in the white neighborhood and would tell our parents. The Goat Man was Mr. Rodriguez, a vendor, who rode through both the black and white neighborhoods selling items from a cart pulled by a large, shaggy goat named Sue. In the fall he sold hot tamales, which my mother loved. In the spring and summer it was usually Popsicles, but it could just as easily have been boiled peanuts or pickled eggs. More than just the passing vendor, Mr. Rodriguez seemed to know all the children and their parents. At Christmas he would visit my parents.

The visits began when Mr. Rodriguez knocked at the kitchen door and announced he was just poking his head in to say Merry Christmas. He was a tall, yellow man with straight hair, and people said he had some Indian blood in him. Mother said that he was Mexican, and that if he wanted to, he could pass for white. He used to be married to a colored woman and so he went for Negro. Why anybody in his right mind would go for Negro in Birmingham, Father said, was a mystery. "I guess love is the mystery."

How Sue pulled Mr. Rodriguez up the hills was the mystery I puzzled over. He said it was all in planning the route to avoid the steep upgrades and to stay mostly on the streets that ran along the ridges. Mother offered Mr. Rodriguez a glass of eggnog, no liquor in it that time of morning, although Father offered bourbon. Mr. Rodriguez asked Josie if he could have a look at her dolls, and when she brought them to him he'd pat her on the head, and make do over her. "Children are a real blessing," he said. "I don't have any." The way he said "any" would always throw quiet into the room. I wasn't supposed to be paying attention to adult talk, so I pretended to ignore the tension.

Mr. Rodriguez, eggnog on his mustache, cocked his head and stared toward the ceiling. What exactly he was looking at was never clear, and what he saw only the grieving can know. Josie pulled away from him, retreating to where Mother sat. Father, sitting across from Mr. Rodriguez, tried to change the subject. The subject never changed.

"You know, Mr. Burke, I lost my family a few years back. June, seventh, 1948."

"Yes, Mr. Rodriguez, you have told me so." My father rolled his eyes toward Mother, but he spoke sincerely. "I am so sorry for your loss."

"They say that time heals all wounds." Mr. Rodriguez still focused on the ceiling, eyes glassy. "All wounds? I've yet to see a wound that time has healed."

Mother went to the kitchen, Josie tagging behind her, and returned with a plate of cookies that she placed on the coffee table in front of Mr. Rodriguez. She stood a moment, wiping her hands on her apron, looking first at Mr. Rodriguez and then at my father. She seemed deep in thought, as if her voice wasn't her own but one channeling through her. She announced to us all, not just Mr. Rodriguez, "Loss is a part of this world." After a moment, the Goat Man agreed.

I PULLED JOSIE off the road and into the woods, and we ducked. Sue might have seen us, but Mr. Rodriguez passed without noticing. We made sure we were out of sight of the street so no one else would see us.

From the vantage of the hill, we could see about a quarter of the park, across the playground to the picnic area. The creek ran along the bottom of the hill. In the distance, we heard a crowd cheering.

"You said it was closed," I said to Lamar.

He shrugged. "It *is* closed. Maybe they sneaked in, too. Anyway, we're here, now." He reasoned that it would only take a few minutes to run down the hill and scoop up the frog eggs. Already Bingo had started toward the creek, and we laid down our bikes and followed. The creek was about six feet across, with banks about three feet deep, but it contained only a foot or so of slow-running water. Lamar scouted for frog eggs, walking a few yards in each direction. There were no eggs. I leaned over the banks to collect a few stands of algae. The water smelled slightly rotten when I got my nose close to it.

"We should go back, now," I said. "Maybe we can get some tadpoles when we go down to Grandma Pic's place."

Lamar didn't look at me. "I bet there are some a little further down." He knew of a place where the creek made a bend and flattened out. It was next to the softball fields.

"I think there is somebody over there."

"They'll be playing baseball. They probably won't even see us."

I looked at Josie. "If we have to run," I said, "Josie can't run that fast."

"I can, too," Josie said.

"Ain't nobody going to make us run," Lamar said. "Worst is they'll just tell us to leave."

"Maybe we should leave Josie with the bikes."

"I don't want to stay by myself. I'll be scared."

"You'll have Bingo with you."

Lamar started off, following the creek in the direction of the softball fields. I followed and Josie and Bingo followed me. Just as Lamar had said, the banks flattened out next to a marshy field. Since it couldn't be seen from the street, I wondered how he knew about it. "Have you been over here before?"

Lamar gave me a gloating look. "Nah, I just know these things 'cause of my brilliant mind."

"Lie," Josie challenged. "I bet you sneaked in here before."

Lamar confessed. He had never sneaked in, but the year before, the white people his mother worked for had had a picnic there. They had asked his mother to come along to set out the food while the family played softball, and Mrs. Burrell had brought Lamar along. One of the white children had been too young to play ball and Lamar ended up playing with him. One of the things they did was to walk along the creek and look for frogs.

We came to the spot where they had seen tadpoles the year before. Here the water was slightly brackish, a good place for frogs, we knew. Just up the hill from us, just out of sight but well within earshot, was the softball game. When I tiptoed, looking up the hill, I could see the bright hats of the outfielders for one of the teams.

There is a soothing rhythm to a softball game. It's quiet, and the breeze buffets your ears. Then there is the occasional shout of encouragement to the batter, a little grunt and the swish of the pitch and the swing. Strike one! A register of disappointment from some of the onlookers, the wind, a grunt, the pitch and a pop, a rising sound of anticipation from the crowd and then a release of disappointment and claps of glee as the ball goes foul.

All of this was going through my head as we crouched beside the creek. The field had been mowed, so we were hidden only by the crest of the hill. Lamar spotted what we had come for. Just at the edge of the water was what looked to the casual observer like a mound of mud, but to the frog egg hunter a blob of gold. Its bubblewrap texture and its shimmy gave it away. Between the egg mass and us was a yard of muck. Since I was taller, I tried to lean and dip up a jar full of the eggs. As I leaned there was the pop of a ball and the claps and moans of people in the crowd, and suddenly the thud of a ball hitting the ground near us. We froze.

"Awh shit," Lamar said. Out of the corner my eye I saw two white boys run down the hill. One stopped and the other continued running toward us. "Get the eggs," Lamar ordered. He picked up the ball and threw it toward the closest boy. It landed a few feet from him and the boy picked up the ball and started running back to the top of the hill. "Hurry up," Lamar said.

I scooped up some of the eggs, using the lip of the jar to separate a small part of the mass. When I straightened up to go, my shoe stuck in the mud. I sunk in up to my ankle. I tried to pull my foot up and the shoe came off. Then, I almost lost my balance and had to put my socked foot into the ooze to keep from falling. I handed the jar to Lamar and went back for my shoe. Meanwhile Lamar started toward the bicycles. "Go on," I said to Josie. "I'll catch up." But Josie wouldn't leave. She offered me her hand as I got out of the mud and Bingo whimpered and paced back and forth.

I didn't feel the need to hurry, especially with my mud-caked shoe in my hand, but Bingo herded us along as if he knew something we didn't. We hadn't gone far, just managed to get out of the field and into the shade when Bingo turned and barked. Behind us, approaching in a steady pace was a tall white man.

"Wait up." He raised his hand and waved to us.

"Go on and catch up to Lamar," I said to Josie. She refused to leave.

The brim visor of his straw fedora made a stripe of green across the man's eyes and the ridge of his nose, but the face seemed gentle. He jumped a narrow part of the creek and stopped in a patch of sun a few feet away from us. "What are y'all doing over here?" he asked. His voice was pleasant and sophisticated, and I didn't think I had anything to fear from him. I had learned to judge white people by the way they sounded. There was a certain pitch that some of them used, especially the folks from around Hueytown where many Klansmen were said to have lived, that set my nerves on edge. But this man sounded like he was from "over the mountain," the suburbs. No matter what he thought of us, he might put it in a pleasant way.

"We were hunting for some frog eggs."

He raised his eyebrows like he was amused. "Frog eggs? Find any?"

"Yes, sir." I pointed in the direction of the eggs.

He considered the direction, and cleared his throat. "What's your name, boy?" I told him. "This your girlfriend, Walter?"

"No, sir. My sister."

"Does your mama know you are here?"

I hesitated. His tone seemed to have changed. "No, sir."

"Why not?"

"I didn't tell her. She's sick."

"Sick?"

"Yes, sir."

"Tell me something, Walter, how old are you?"

"Eleven."

"Eleven." He looked to one side and let out a sigh. "Eleven years old." His foot kicked a little at the ground.

"Yes, sir."

"Eleven is old enough to know better, Walter. Isn't it?"

My heart was beating fast. I wanted to tell Josie to run, but I knew it wouldn't do any good. Bingo stood beside me, he stiffened, and I slipped my hand inside his collar.

"To know what, sir?"

"I don't like a smart-ass, Walter. So don't bullshit me." His voice was still pleasant, only a little raised. "Are you white, Walter?"

"No, sir."

"What are you?"

"I'm colored."

"Colored?"

"Yes, sir."

"What color are you, Walter?"

I didn't follow his meaning. Colored meant colored—light skinned or dark skinned, though shades were not always a distinction that white people made. I answered the way my father might have. "I'm Negro."

The man looked down at his feet and smiled. When he raised his head again, he had put on a stern look. "What color is a *Negro*, Walter?"

"Light skin, dark skin, medium."

The man clenched his teeth. "I told you not to get smart with me. Do you want me to kick your *Negro* ass into next week?"

I stepped back, pushing Josie behind me with my free hand. "No, sir. I just don't know what you mean." Bingo pulled at the collar. I could hear Josie seesawing from foot to foot on the dry leaves.

The man's body relaxed. He smiled and spoke in a soft, but condescending way. "What color am I, Walter?"

Panic itched inside my chest. I had never told a white person he was white. "White?"

"What is the opposite color of white, Walter?"

"Black."

He sighed. "I didn't think you were dumb. Then what color are you?"

My face flushed hot. In those days we were scolded for calling each other "black." It was considered unbecoming, unflattering, and ugly. If you said "black," it meant "black monkey," "black dog," or "black ape."

"What color are you, Walter?" the man repeated as patiently as any teacher. My lips trembled. I adjusted my hold on Bingo, who was tugging more and more at the collar. "Maybe your little sister can say?"

"She doesn't have to say. I know it. I'm black."

The man looked satisfied. "That's right. That's right, Walter. You are black. Black as tar. A little black Sambo. You know what I'm talking about. And this park is for *white* children. I don't care what you are looking for, don't you bring your black ass back in here until the day you turn white." He paused and looked at Josie in a way that made me want to hit him.

Just then, one of the boys who had chased after the ball ran up. He addressed the man as "doctor" and told him that he was needed at the softball game. I was trembling as Josie and I walked away. I still held onto Bingo's collar and Bingo pulled me up the hill as fast as my weak legs could go. I was angry and ashamed, but also awed. The man was a *doctor*—dressed elegantly, I thought, in a polo shirt, creased khakis, and white-soled deck shoes. I assumed he was a medical doctor, the profession my father had fallen short of, the healing profession that Lamar and I sometimes pretended to practice. There was only one black doctor in our neighborhood, Dr. Sims, and he was a dentist. "Dentists are doctors, too," my father insisted. But the tooth drill did not have the romance of the tongue depressor and stethoscope. Teeth were not tonsils or lungs or hearts.

But there were other "doctors," too, and I pondered whether the man was one of these. In Tittusville, there was Dr. Carrington, who taught English at Miles College. The white man did have some of the mannerisms of a teacher in the way he asked questions, the Socratic method, I learned to call it. But he seemed too confident, too sophisticated, to have been a professor. He could have been a "reverend doctor." We had a number of those in Tittusville—in fact, about half the preachers called themselves "doctors." "Witch doctors" is what my father called some of them. But the white man had cursed, which in my naivete excluded him from being a reverend doctor. He couldn't have been a Dr. Einstein or a Dr. Schweitzer, either. No, I concluded by the time I reached the crest of the hill, he was a medical doctor, the thing I wanted to be when I didn't want to be an astronaut, only I would be the kind who would let children play in a park, regardless of what color they were.

ABOUT HALFWAY HOME, we met my father and Lamar in the car. Lamar had seen the white man approach us and had ridden home to get my father. "Y'all alright?" he asked, as he helped us put the bicycle in the trunk, and broke one of his cardinal rules by letting Bingo get in the backseat with us. Arriving home, he began to give us orders. "Lamar, go on home to your mama. Walter and Josephine, I want to talk to y'all over by the picnic table." Josie said she had to go to the bathroom, so he told her to go, but—"not a word of this to your mama."

Lamar said good-bye and *ahemed*. I knew he wanted to get the full story so he could gossip. I ignored him. He called me. I looked up, but my father said, "Go on home, Lamar. Y'all can talk about it tomorrow."

Even before we got to the picnic table my father was asking me for details. He wanted the story from the beginning. Slowly. He interrupted and asked for more information whenever he felt I hadn't provided enough. Where exactly were we in the park? How far away from the street? How far from the woods? How far from the softball field? I provided the details as best I could and he seemed to have been imagining them as I spoke, getting the lay of the land. It occurred to me that my father had never been in George Ward Park, either, and was curious about what was there. Then he started in on the man. Did the man say his name? Was he the park manager? Did he look like someone in charge or just an average citizen? Had I ever seen him before? What exactly did he say? He allowed me to say the curse words.

Josie, munching on a cookie, joined us. "Where did you get a cookie?" I asked.

"Mama gave it to me."

Daddy looked at Josie suspiciously. "You didn't tell her anything, did you?"

"No, sir. She asked where was I but I told her I had been playing with Lamar." She ate a little piece of cookie. "I didn't lie because we *had* been playing with Lamar."

My father sat down on the picnic table bench and put her on his knee. "I'm not asking you to lie to Mama," he said. "It's just that Mama needs her rest and she doesn't need to be worried about you. If you have a problem, come to Daddy with it. Promise?"

"Yes, sir."

"We want Mama to get well."

No sooner had he spoken than we heard the screen door slam and my mother came out of the back door and started over to us. She looked at me first. "Y'all alright?" Then to my father, "When were you planning on telling me?" She sat, took Josie away from my father, and began to examine her, feeling her legs and arms. "You alright, baby?"

My father started to speak, but she cut him off. "Velma Burrell called here all excited and worried about *my* children. She must have thought I was crazy not to know what happened to my own children. She said Lamar said y'all had been attacked by some white man."

"They weren't attacked," my father said.

"That's what Lamar told her."

My father shook his head and looked at me. "Lamar's not a good scientist."

My mother flashed an angry look at my father. "Everything isn't about *science*. When my children are attacked by some crazy cracker I want to know about it." For a moment, she looked formidable and my father folded his arms and stared at his shoes. "Mrs. Burrell said she was worried because Bull Connor has gone crazy arresting colored people. She said he took fifty or sixty people to jail. Church people. Just threw them in the back of the paddy wagons."

"We weren't attacked," I said. "This ole white man just tried to chase us out of George Ward Park. That's all."

"Did he touch you?"

"I've been through it all with them," Father said.

"Now, *I'm* going through it." Mother repeated the question.

"No ma'am," I answered.

Mother asked Josie the question, with the same emphasis.

"I wouldn't let that ole, nasty man touch me," Josie said. "Bingo would take a big bite out of his butt."

Mother smiled and gave Bingo a pat on the head. "Did Bingo protect you?" There were a few moments of silence, then she commented on the garden, how nice the turned soil looked, and how straight my father had gotten the rows. He didn't acknowledge her compliment. "Why don't y'all run and start your bath," she said, "and maybe Daddy will take you to the movies."

Josie hopped down right away and started toward the house. I moved slowly, pausing to feel the thick tension between my parents.

"Son?" my father asked.

"Can Lamar come, too," I said quickly to cover the reason I had paused.

Father sighed. "Let's leave Lamar out of it this time. I think we have seen enough of him for one day."

My mother held out her hand to me and when I took it she pulled me down and kissed my cheek. "You're my brave boy," she said. "Run along."

I had barely made it to the corner of the house when I heard my father say, "Don't you think I care about my own children?" Mother's reply was sharp. I stood just inside the screen door. I wanted to listen, but I could only hear their tones, cutting and defensive. It made my stomach churn. My mother was sick, so fighting couldn't be good for her, I thought, and yet if she had energy to fight maybe she wasn't so close to dying, and then again, fighting might weaken her, and, too, I knew the whole fight was my fault for going to George Ward Park in the first place.

5

AFTER SUPPER we went to the Carver, a movie house located on Fourth Avenue, the black business district. The Carver was showing *Mysterious Island* and my father said he had heard that it was science fiction—lots of volcanoes and giant squids. His eyes sparkled as he anticipated the movie. Mother shook her head at him and gave him two love taps.

The Carver was one of the larger buildings in the bustling Fourth Avenue district. It was nestled among beauty shops, shoe repair shops, bar and grills, dance clubs, and churches. Around the corner, on Sixteenth Street, was the Booker T. Washington Insurance Company, where Mother worked part-time as a secretary. The company, and the building, too, was owned by Dr. A. G. Gaston, the richest black man in Birmingham, and for all I knew, with the exception of some Yoruba king, the richest Negro in the world. He owned the Gaston Motel, also on Sixteenth Street, the only black-owned motel in the city. He owned a bank, a construction company, a radio station, a funeral home, a cemetery, and most of the rental property in "Negro-zoned" areas of the city. It was joked that if you were a poor black person, you lived and died by A. G. Gaston. You lived in his houses; you listened to his radio station; you paid him burial insurance; and, when you died he buried you in his cemetery. Mother insisted that Dr. Gaston was not just a "nice" man, he was what we children should aspire to be, a credit to his race. And even though he was rich, he hadn't forgotten he was "colored."

"Forgetting you are colored is rather hard to do," my father countered whenever Mother offered her assessment, though, I think, like most black Birminghamians, he admired Dr. Gaston's accomplishments.

In the vicinity of the motel were a number of large churches and, directly across from it, the Sixteenth Street Baptist that had just become the main meeting place of the movement. A large and loosely Romanesque building, its foundation was made of a smoke-colored stone, and the second and third levels of yellow brick. A wide flight of concrete steps led from the street up to a dark portico entrance behind three prominent arches. It was distinguished from the other churches by its twin towers with red-tile domed cupolas. There were prettier churches in the Fourth Avenue district, and, by far, most looked "churchier." Easily, the Sixteenth Street Baptist could have been mistaken for a museum or library, except that on one corner, as if to clarify its purpose, was a blue neon sign with the church's name spelled out in the shape of a cross.

Catty-corner to the church was Kelly Ingram Park, a park for black people, a small patch of sparse woods. Being a "Negro park" and having no facilities more than paths and benches, it was not closed as George Ward was.

As usual, Fourth Avenue was crowded on Saturday, as people from the outlying counties came into town for shopping and entertainment.

We turned onto Sixteenth Street and headed toward the north

side of town, and crossed over Fourth Avenue North where the Carver was located. Mother mentioned to my father that he should have turned. He said he was looking for better parking, but then he passed several good parking spaces, Mother counting them as we passed. Her tone was quizzical, not critical. She knew as I did that he was exploring something. I leaned up in the seat so I could get a better view over my father's shoulder. "Just don't make us late," my mother warned. She pointed to a crowd of people standing on the steps of the Sixteenth Street Baptist and guessed that there was a singing program.

"A mass meeting," my father corrected. He circled the block before confessing that he was looking for Reverend King. I asked how he looked, and began scanning faces in the crowd for one who could possibly be the arch agitator we had heard about on the radio news.

"He's short and black like the rest of them," Mother said with a snap. "Now let's go."

"Aren't you even curious?"

"I'm not curious to see a troublemaker. Sometimes, Carl, you just don't think."

To the contrary, my father was quite a thinking man, but he didn't always think in the practical terms my mother wanted him to—or rather, they didn't think in the same practical terms. Sometimes my father could be very logical, following what he called "a scientific line," other times he was a dreamer—but he dreamt about science. It was at these times that I enjoyed him the most. He became childlike, wide-eyed with excitement as he talked about zoology, astronomy, or physics. It was he who first pointed out frog eggs and newts to me when we were visiting in the country; and he pointed out the seven sisters, and the great nebula.

Mother was practical when it came to running the affairs of the house. Our house was a home of simple, but strictly enforced rules: 1. Work before play; 2. A place for everything and everything in its place; 3. Homework before supper; 4. Come when called; 5. Take all you want, but eat all you take. The list went on and new rules were added as needed. Mother was often called upon to organize events for the PTA and the church, and she bragged that she kept her boss's files immaculately ordered. It didn't take "training," she insisted, to understand her filing system—just common sense.

Because the Carver was a colored movie house, we sat where we wanted. With the exception of the drive-in, my parents wouldn't let us go to the white movie houses, the Alabama and the Ritz, because black people had to sit in the balcony, the buzzard's roost. As for myself, I enjoyed sitting in the balcony, and when Lamar, Josie, and I went to the Carver by ourselves, we chose the balcony. For my parents, the balcony was second class seating whether it was segregated or not. One black actor was in the movie, an actor my parents had never seen before so they made us sit through the closing credits in order to catch his name. They missed it; but Father surmised, "He was no Poitier."

ON THE WAY HOME from the Carver, we passed people coming from the mass meeting. My father saw a man we knew from the barbershop and slowed and rolled down his window. "Hey, Brother Henson," he called to the man. The man greeted him and came to the window. He was dressed in Sunday clothes, a dark suit, an out-of-fashion wide tie, and a fedora. Though the weather was warm, it was usual for men to wear hats or at least to carry them in their hands. There was a hat culture in those days, rules about tipping and removing them, and even about cocking them.

My father wanted to know if King had come to the meeting and the man said he had. The man began to recount what had happened, who had led the singing, and what the inspirational speakers had said. Mother interrupted politely, excusing herself and reminding my father that it was late, but Brother Henson was excited about the meeting and my father wanted to hear him out. Brother Henson held onto the door handle and regaled about the meeting. "Two Kings were up in there, the one we have heard about and his *brother* called 'A.D.' Come a hold of it, A.D. got a church just over in Ensley."

My father said he had never heard either of the Reverends King speak and Brother Henson invited my father to go with him to A.D.'s church.

My mother interrupted again, this time with an impatient sigh so my father said he had to go and get the children to bed. On the way home my parents said nothing, but I could tell from the way my mother had her head turned to the window that she was angry. I could tell my father knew it, too, because he drove stiffly and exactingly, as if any careless swerve or bump would upset a can of wasps.

After Josie and I were in bed, I heard my parents arguing. I couldn't make out their words, only their tones swaying back and forth, rising and falling throughout the house. The tones were rhythmic and tense. As I fell asleep I imagined swordplay, Zorro and Montesoro swashbuckling back and forth, their swords tapping, grating, clanking in a staccato dance across the tiled courtyard. Suddenly there was a sharp cry and my eyes popped open. I couldn't at first think what it might be—a bird? And then I realized it was my mother. Perhaps it was a laugh, just one high syllable of joy, but the sound had heaviness to it and I knew it was sobbing. I got out of the bed and went down the hall and stood outside my parents' bedroom door. I could see light under the door and I heard very plainly now. My father was speaking in a tight, even tone. "I just don't understand why you want to do this to us." It sounded like a line from *The Edge of Night,* the soap opera that Grandma Pic watched, and my first thought was that my mother was leaving. My mother's reply was vague and strange: "It's my body. It's my soul."

I raised my hand to knock, but just then, I heard another sob from my mother, and I opened the door. Mother was in her nightgown, sitting on the side of the bed. She held her palm to one side of her face. My father was standing in front of her in his T-shirt and boxers.

He was leaning toward her a little with his hand on her shoulder. He looked up as I opened the door. His eyes were wide with shiny, full pupils. It was a look I would see on other men before that summer ended. It was a look that would have been easy to describe as fear, but after Vietnam, I would not call it fear—at least it was not fear alone, rather some combination of fear, anger, and frustration. Hope was a part of it, too. For a moment, Father stared at me as if I were a stranger, and then barely parting his lips, he said, "Everything is alright, son. Go on back to bed."

The next morning, Mother was making pancakes when I got in from delivering the papers. She greeted me cheerfully, seeming full of vim. It was hard for me to believe that, as my father claimed, she was dying. I watched her for a moment as she dripped batter into the hot pan, testing the temperature of the oil.

"Go ahead and wash up," she said.

I moved toward the den, toward the washroom, and stopped again. Something in her voice betrayed her cheerfulness, just a short crackle as if she had phlegm in her throat.

"Mama?"

"Go ahead, now."

"But, Mama—"

"What? What do you need? Didn't you hear me say, 'Go wash'? Go on, now." She smiled to reassure me. "Everything is alright."

For a split second I believed her and stepped out of the room, but when I turned and looked back, perhaps to see her smile again, I saw her staring into the frying pan, which sent up a tendril of smoke from the burning batter. She had one hand raised above her head and she seemed to be praying.

Our Sunday mornings were usually relaxed. My father would read the paper in the den and have coffee while Mother listened to gospel on the radio and cooked. Josie and I were expected to eat and get dressed for Sunday school by 9:30. My father would take us to St. Luke's Lutheran, drop us off, and return for the eleven o'clock service.

Mother was deeply religious, but ambiguous about churches. She had grown up a member of Mount Olive Baptist, the same rural church we attended when we visited Grandma Pic and Uncle Reed in Coosada, just outside of Montgomery. Mount Olive, founded by newly freed slaves, was a small church—a white, wooden rectangular structure with a steepled vestibule and no bell in the steeple.

Moving to Birmingham as an adult, Mother explored. It was still a year before she met my father, so the exploration, possibly, had both a religious and a social purpose. Within a ten-minute drive of our house, we could count a dozen churches, all black and about three-quarters of them Baptist. Mother felt something was missing in these "city churches," she told me, but she never made clear what was missing. I assumed, at first, she was comparing them to Mount Olive and from my perspective there was little difference between Mount Olive and the typical Baptist church. The comparative sophistication of the city churches—better-dressed congregation and better-spoken ministers—did not belie their rural roots.

Next, she tried the Methodist churches and then the AMEs and CMEs; then, the Pentecostal, the Bibleway, and the Full Gospel; she even went to a Catholic mass. After nearly two years, she hadn't found whatever it was she was looking for, and the intensity of her search waned. By this time, she had met my father and I was soon on the way. After I was born, she settled on St. Luke's Lutheran because my father was a Lutheran—of sort—and Mother decided that until we children were old enough to make up our own minds about religion, we would be Lutheran.

Though her search had slackened in its intensity, it was never abandoned. When I was ten, Mother began to listen to Reverend A. A. Allen, a radio minister who broadcasted out of Oklahoma. When Allen's crusade came to Fair Park, the state fairground in Birmingham, she wanted to go.

My father dismissed the ministry as "some hillbilly hootenanny," but Mother insisted that either he or I go with her, and he sacrificed me.

The revival meeting was held in a circus tent that had been set up on one end of the fairgrounds. Inside was a wide, low platform and what appeared to be about a thousand folding chairs set up in long rows, and—in violation of Birmingham's "Race Code"—there was no "colored" section. I looked for the colored entrance but Mother walked straight ahead, confident that she was entering at the right place. Later, in his sermon, the reverend clarified his racial philosophy: "Heaven does not have white and colored sections. The soul does not have a color in God's eyes."

At home, later, Mother exclaimed to my father, "True to his word, it was all integrated. Reverend Allen made the point that we were all the same color in God's eyes."

"What color was that?"

"He didn't say."

"Of course, he didn't say 'white.'"

"Maybe we are clear," I said. "Like a spirit."

"'Invisible' is what you mean," my father said with a sneer. "Let's just hope it's invisible to Bull Connor."

To be sure, the Reverend Allen did not have a high standard of earthly integration. He had no black ministers among his staff of attendants, no black musicians among the singers. Though the congregation wasn't divided with a rope, it tended to separate itself.

The service was filled with loud singing, dancing, and speaking in tongues. Reverend Allen said that blessings flowed from heaven through the raised hands. I raised my hands until my arms became exhausted, then felt guilty when I put my arms down.

Mother kept her hands raised during most of the service. She clapped and shouted, but in spite of her involvement she did not reach a charismatic state, "getting happy" we called it. Until the A. A. Allen meeting, I thought only black people got happy. But at A. A. Allen, whites and blacks alike turned over chairs, kicked off their shoes, and ran up and down the aisles as if racing one another— "chasing the devil away," they called it. After the meeting, my father tried to put it into perspective for us. "They were just your white trash and hillbillies. No self-respecting white person would cut up like that."

Toward the end of the service, the ecstasy became even more pronounced. Reverend Allen called people up for prayer and healing. As he prayed and touched them, claiming that the power of God was shooting through him like heat lightning, some went into fits of dancing, some fell down and wallowed on the ground, some simply fell down. Mother was one who simply fell. "Let the Lord have his way," the reverend said.

Often Mother received solicitations in the mail containing prayer cloths. When they first came to the house, I was afraid of the six-inch square of serrated plaid. I treated it like a holy relic, scooping it onto my flattened palm when asked to handle it. My father had a different response. "Not big enough to blow your nose on."

After a while, we got used to seeing them around the house. Eventually they were thrown into the trash can; even Mother admitted they were a gimmick. "But," she insisted, "they make a point."

"That point being?" Father asked.

"There is power in the blood."

SUNDAY AFTERNOON, after I was sure Lamar and Mrs. Burrell were back from church, I went to visit Lamar. We were going to dissect the frog eggs. We sat on the stoop and cut apart the rubbery, slippery blob. Making a clean slice into an egg was difficult because it wouldn't hold still in the tweezers and the scalpel was a little dull. Looking at the eggs through the microscope was the beginning of a way of thinking about how the world was put together. Little things make up bigger things. Cells make up a frog, and people make up a family. Houses make up a neighborhood and neighborhoods a city, and so on.

Mrs. Burrell brought us Kool-Aid and sat down beside us on the stoop. She had her hair nicely pressed and she still wore her makeup from church, but she had changed into a shift and open-toed bedroom slippers. She fanned herself with a church fan that advertised one of Dr. Gaston's funeral homes. She looked at the jar of eggs and grunted. "Lord, y'all better get rid of them things. Don't let them hatch around here and have all them baby frogs crawling all over the place."

"Awh, Mama," Lamar said. "They aren't going to hurt you."

"It's just the thought of all them crawling around." She shuddered. "Anyway. That was what all the trouble was about yesterday? Frog eggs?" She snorted. "That man didn't hurt you, did he, Walter?"

The memory of the tall, white man came back and I had a sharp ache in my stomach. "No ma'am. He just talked kind of rough. He didn't holler or anything—but he cursed."

She shook her head, took a pack of cigarettes out of her pocket, and began to smoke. "I just don't get white people! Cursing in front of children. That's what I call loose morals. Same man probably sitting up in Shiloh Baptist right now talking about loving the Lord. I don't get it. What your daddy do about it?"

"Ma'am?"

"What your daddy fixin' to do about it?"

The question had taken me by surprise. What could my father do about it?

"He didn't whip us."

She leaned back and gave me a look of disbelief. "He'd better not whip you! You ain't done nothing. He ought to be whipping that white man upside the head."

I took a prolonged look in the microscope to avoid engaging her. How could my father even find the man?—and she knew that a colored man didn't go around hitting white men. "Maybe he will go to the police," I said knowing that my parents hadn't brought the matter up again.

Mrs. Burrell chuckled. "Bull Connor's police? Or is there some other kind of police that I don't know about?" She gave me the look of incredulity again, and began a story about a young boy who had been bitten by police dogs. The day before, several preachers had led demonstrators in a march downtown and Bull Connor had sicced the police dogs on them. One boy, a teenager, had been badly attacked by the dogs. "Tore him up!" Mrs. Burrell exclaimed, though she was only repeating what she had heard from someone at church. "Tore off all his clothes and cut him up, too. Those dogs have sharp teeth, and you don't know what kind of disease they are carrying." She folded her arms and sighed. "Negroes are going to have to take things into their own hands if they are ever going to do something."

"Preach it, Mama," Lamar said.

I was surprised by Mrs. Burrell's sudden conversion. Perhaps she had been inspired by the Sunday service. I had heard my father say that her pastor was one of the leaders of the freedom movement, and my mother had called him "just another troublemaker."

"How are we going to do that?" I asked.

She took a drag on her cigarette. "Come to the mass meetings. They'll tell you. I'm fixin' to start going myself—on my day off. Now, I know my old lady," she referred to the woman she worked for, "will have a sure 'nough fit if she knew—that's why I won't tell her a thing. She think she knows all my business anyway. She always talking about how good friends we are. I say to myself, 'If we that good a friends, how come you don't pay me some more?' Did Lamar tell you what she gave me for Christmas?"

"No, ma'am."

"A candle. A raggedy, ole candy-striped candle. What she think I'm going do with that candle? I can get myself one over at Woolworth's if I wanted one. Probably something somebody *gave* her in the first place. A raggedy, ole candle." She looked at me and said emphatically, "All that work I do for her, I wanted me some *money*."

I tolerated her tirade about the candle and brought her back to the subject. "What do they do at a mass meeting?" I told her that we had seen one letting out at Sixteenth Street.

"Well," she admitted, "I don't really know the details. Mother Thompson would know. I just know they are telling folks how to get organized to beat this segregation mess. I'm tired of it. And I don't think you boys need to grow up in it."

"You want to go to one?" Lamar asked me. He had a bright-eyed devilish look on his face, the same look he had when he led us over to George Ward Park.

"I don't know . . . I'll have to—"

"Y'all can go with me one night," Mrs. Burrell interrupted. Without a doubt Lamar was my best friend, and I trusted him. But at that moment I felt set up by him. I felt he and his mother were conspiring to get me to the meetings.

"Y'all will have to go on a weekend 'cause they go on kind of late and there ain't no sense in having to miss school to get your freedom." That much settled, Mrs. Burrell rubbed out her cigarette on the stoop, brushed away the ashes, and palmed the butt. "Walter, go ask your mama. I don't want you to get me in to no trouble with her." She chuckled a little and patted my head.

I DECIDED NOT to mention the mass meeting until supper. Mother helped our plates with potatoes and green beans, and Father put on pieces of fried chicken. Then my father offered my mother a piece of chicken, and she said she wasn't hungry.

"You've got to eat something. You can't go all day without eating."

"I'm not hungry."

My father sighed and looked at the far corner of the room. He spoke in a very quiet measured way. "I'm not asking that you eat a full meal, Clara, I'm just asking that you eat something."

"I don't *care* for anything. I'm fasting."

"Fasting?"

They stared at each other for a few. "Just a wing, then," Mother consented.

My father added a spoonful of potatoes to her plate. He turned to Josie, who was staring at Mother with a quizzical look. "Mama's stomach is a little upset, that's all."

"You're not a doctor," Mother said. "Just remember that."

Father's face flushed, but he controlled himself. "I'm more of one than A. A. Allen."

For about five minutes everybody tried to eat, then my father started to talk about what he had been reading in the newspaper. As if it were a matter of extreme importance, he put down his knife and turned to me. "What did Mrs. Burrell think about the bus strike? Does she have a ride to work?" I was thinking about the mass meeting. "The strike?" he repeated. "Damn, Walter, you deliver the paper, but don't you ever read it?"

"Sometimes."

"If you'd read it you would know what I was talking about. A major event in the city, and you don't even know about it."

"Leave him alone, Carl," my mother said and scratched her hairline at her forehead.

"I just want the boy to be more aware of what's going on around him. For Pete's sake, the whole world is changing. Birmingham, too. We have had a transit strike, and an election this week and we're about to go to war with Russia. I think an eleven-year-old ought to have some cognizance of that."

My father rarely raised his voice to me, and usually only in situations where I knew clearly why. He had never berated me at the kitchen table—that just wasn't done in our house. So, I didn't feel scared for myself; I felt scared for him. Something awful was happening to him and my mother. He wasn't yelling at me, he was yelling at her.

Josie began to cry. "Now look what you've done!" Mother said to my father. I had never heard her sneer before, the words hissing out between clenched teeth. Josie jumped up from the table and ran toward the back of the house, toward her room. Mother balled her paper napkin and threw it in her plate. She stood, glaring at my father, and followed Josie. My father stood, too, first as if he were being polite to a lady, and then as if to follow her. She turned and stopped him with a look. Slowly, he sat back down and looked into his plate.

"That wasn't very scientific," I offered after a minute.

He looked up. I thought he might hit me. A minute or two passed; he spoke quietly, "Your mama and me . . ." He took my hand. "We've been disagreeing about . . . about how she is going to get treated. She doesn't want to use a doctor. She thinks God can heal her."

My attention went to my father's grip on my hand. He was squeezing it and it hurt, but all I could do was to look at our hands. He was making a fist around my palm. My fingers were splayed like one end of a bow tie and were turning purple. My knuckles felt as if they were breaking. But I didn't yell, or as far as I could tell, even grimace, only stared at my father's square fist around my hand as if it were a distant spectacle that had nothing to do with me.

When he relaxed, he put his hand on my shoulder. I didn't move my numb hand but continued to look at it. "Do you understand what I'm trying to tell you?" my father asked. I looked at his face. No tears. Only brightness in his eyes, not fear, not anger.

"A. A. Allen?" I repeated.

He snorted. "'There is power in the blood.'"

I wanted to laugh. "Why?" My voice cracked.

"Religion." He put his elbows on the table and rested his face in his hands. "I really can't tell you. It doesn't make sense."

The day before, he had told me my mother was dying, and she told me she was not. Then, he told me she wanted A. A. Allen to heal her. I felt like laughing, then like screaming, but I sat staring at the roasted drumstick and the mound of lumpy potatoes with margarine beginning to resolidify. I put my hand on his shoulder. "Daddy, we'll just have to be scientific about it."

He didn't look up but spoke through his hands. "This is beyond science. This defies science."

6

L ATER ON THAT NIGHT, I heard Josie crying. She cried softly, and I doubted that my parents heard her in their bedroom on the other end of the house. "Josie, it'll be all right," I said, not loud enough to be overheard. I thought of something that I had heard at Grandma Pic's church that past summer. A revival minister had come from Detroit. A roly-poly, light-skinned man with a happy, gravelly voice, he had said, "By and by. It'll be all right, by and by."

Josie never answered me but continued to sob. About three in the morning, I went to her room. Bingo had already sneaked in, as there was no screen in the window, it being early for mosquitoes. He lay at the foot of the bed and raised his head as I came in. He knew better than to make a sound or he'd be put out. I called softly to Josie but she didn't answer, so I crawled next to her and saw that she was asleep—crying in her sleep. I wondered if I should wake her, but then thought that if I woke her she might never get back to sleep. I put my arm around her and that was how I woke up.

• • •

THE NEXT AFTERNOON, Father explained to me that Mother suffered from a "brain cancer." *A* brain cancer, he emphasized, because there were many types. "We think the kind your mother has is the very bad kind."

"*We* think?" I asked. We were in the yard setting tomato slips. The sun was staying up long enough to allow outdoor work at the end of the day.

"The doctors," he said and looked away. It was not "we" I had meant to emphasize, but "think," so I said it again. "*Think?* Maybe they are not sure?"

"Nobody can be sure about these things." Father did not look up from the hole he had punched in the soil with a masonry trowel rather than a hand spade. "Science isn't that advanced."

"But, Daddy, you said that Mama was fixing to die."

He looked up. "I said she was going to die, and she *is* if she doesn't get treatment." I dropped the tomato shoot I was handing to him. His voice softened. "I know it's not easy to hear, Son. But it's better to face up to these kinds of things. The world isn't easy. It isn't fair. Some things you just have to accept as fact; face up to them because that's the only way you're going to make things better." He picked up the plant I had dropped and buried it up to its leaves, too deep. I recovered enough to follow him down the row, spraying water from the garden hose on the plant after he had set it. "I lost my folks when I was a young age," he continued. "Mommy died when I was nineteen and Pops during my first year at Meharry." His voice was even as he spoke, as if he were merely reciting, but I noticed his body was very tense, more angular than usual. Where his back should have had a bow was straight and where his shoulders should have sloped was hunched—even as he bent forward to lay a plant. I knew that this was how he handled hard things, by getting hard himself, and yet he said "Mommy" and "Pops" as if he were a boy. He had been studying the sciences, first at Hampton Institute and then at Meharry when his parents died, and it seems his emotions were arrested somehow in a scientific mind-set.

"This cancer," he said going back to the subject of my mother, "may cause some . . . well, some mental problems, you see." He looked across his shoulder at me. "Some changes in personality. She might act a little cranky, a little strange."

"Crazy?"

"I wouldn't say crazy. You have to remember she is sick. She has a tumor, a *growth*, in her head. It's putting a lot of pressure on her brain."

My father waited until I had refocused before he reached for the next tomato plant. When he took it his fingertips held onto mine for a moment.

Just a month earlier, Mother had gone to the optometrist for a routine examination. She needed reading glasses. "Uh-uh," the doctor said. He suggested she make an appointment with a doctor at Carraway Methodist Hospital, one of the two main hospitals in the city. It was a segregated hospital and mother didn't like to patronize it. Carraway's "colored" waiting area was a hallway heading to the fire escape on the fifth floor, and people were made to climb the fire escape to get there.

After these trips to the white doctor, Mother refused his treatment. She said she wanted to go to Holy Family so she could at least have a black doctor. Holy Family was segregated, but allowed black doctors to serve black patients. She was not one who believed that black professionals were less expert than whites. To the contrary, she thought, black professionals tended to be better because they had to work so hard to earn their degrees.

TUESDAY, while rolling the papers and still smarting about my father's comment about my not reading, I scanned for news of the day. The bus strike continued. Since we rarely rode the busses, I found it hard to take an interest in the strike. I asked Lamar how his mother was getting to work. Beginning that morning, he told me, she was getting a ride with one of the new preachers, Reverend Timmons, who had come to town with Reverend King. Reverend Timmons had been the guest preacher at the church on Sunday.

I guessed that Mrs. Burrell's newfound enthusiasm for the mass meetings was due to Reverend Timmons, but Lamar denied it. I felt a little devilish. "Oh, I saw the look in your mama's eye when she was talking about those meetings—you sure she's not singing, 'He's so fine, he's gotta be mine.'?" I mimicked the song all the schoolchildren were humming that spring.

"Is not," he declared, and I soon gave up the teasing. Lamar, though, was not one to be bettered, and I could see that he was trying to find something to goad me with all day. "Your mama is so fat she . . . she . . . wears two dresses at the same time." My mama is not fat, I answered nonchalantly. His inability to get a reaction from me spurred him as much as anything and I found it to be great entertainment as well. "Oh yeah, well her teeth are so yellow, they use her spit on popcorn."

That evening rather than riding toward Loveman's Village, he walked his bicycle beside Josie and me, and continued his goading. "Your mama so black she don't make a shadow."

"That's not scientific," I replied.

Josie frowned. "Don't call my mama black."

"Well, she is."

"She's no blacker than you."

"I'm not black." He emphasized by holding out his arm and stroking it. "I'm colored."

"Well, your color is stupid," Josie retorted.

"Don't mind him," I told her.

"What's the matter?" Lamar said, rolling his bike over to me. "You don't like this 'fun' anymore?"

"You've been living in the projects too long," I snapped.

Lamar started to say something back, but I could see I had hurt him, and at the moment I didn't care. I hadn't said anything untrue and he was big enough to take it.

"Oh yeah?" he managed after a moment. "Well, you're not as rich as you think you are. Your mama ain't nothing but a rich man's go-for."

His tone stung me; it stung Josie, too, and she slapped him on his arm. "And yours washes white people's drawers."

Lamar drew back his fist as if to hit Josie and I stepped forward, not saying anything, but letting him know who was bigger.

"Y'all Burkes think y'all are soooo much better than everybody else. But you're nothing but colored." He got on his bike and started away.

"She's a *secretary,* you little black monkey," Josie yelled.

I didn't say a word until we got home, but I knew that before the evening was out, I would have to visit Lamar at Loveman's and make amends.

A half of a peanut butter and jelly sandwich each awaited us. They must have been sitting for hours because they were beginning to dry out in spite of having been wrapped in waxed paper. The cups of milk were warm.

"Mama's home!" Josie said and walked to the back of the house. It was unusual, but not unheard of, for my mother to come home from work early.

"Is she here?" I asked when Josie returned.

Josie drank from the cup of milk. "The door is closed."

I took the cup from her, and got her fresh milk. While Josie ate, I went to my mother's bedroom door and knocked softly. There was no answer. She was asleep, I thought, but still I had to see for sure that she was home. Slowly, I opened the door. The squeak it made I thought would wake her. When I looked in, she was sitting on the bed. She had her nightgown on and was looking straight ahead at the wall. I thought she might be sick and nervously called to her. On my second call, she turned to me. Her eyes seemed sunken and this scared me, but her voice was calming, sweet. "Go away, honey. I'm all right."

I stood in the doorway for a moment longer, hoping that she would say something else, but she turned away and went back to staring at the wall. I took a step into the room. She remained in such deep thought that her aloofness scared me all over again.

Back in the kitchen, Josie and I ate. Just to break the silence, I asked her to start her homework. She said she didn't have any. I knew this couldn't be true and told her she should just do some extra. "I'm fixing to watch TV," she said even though she knew she was not supposed to.

"Mama is *here*," I said, but not even my own voice could convince me.

"I heard you talking to her," Josie said and turned on the TV. "If she doesn't want me to watch TV she can tell me." Our parents were not great fans of TV. We had a stereo set in a large, wood-grained cabinet in the living room. It had a compartment for all of my father's jazz albums, mostly the Nat "King" Cole Trio or Nat "King" Cole by himself. Nat "King" Cole, my father often reminded us, was from Alabama. Our TV was small—convenient for rolling into the closet and out of the way of company. Josie went into the den and plugged in the TV. We could get three channels, and that time of day the choices were between *Yogi Bear, Popeye,* and a science program on the educational channel. The science program caught my eye, but then I felt a twinge of guilt with my mother sitting in the next room, and we flagrantly disregarding her rules. Josie even offered me the science program— something about the solar system, very tempting—but I said no and she turned to *Popeye.* At first she had the volume very low, but during the course of ten minutes she turned it up three times, each time twice as loud, until I was sure that my mother could hear it very well. Josie, sitting on the floor in front of the sofa, fidgeted. She looked at the door that led back to the bedrooms, then at me. For a moment I thought she would break into tears. She got up to turn the TV volume up again, but I stopped her, and I turned off the set. "Josie, Mama is sick. *Sick.*" I took her in my arms. Her little body went limp. "You and me," I said . . . I never finished the sentence.

FATHER WASN'T HOME by five as usual, and Mother was lying on the bed now, asleep I thought, but she called to me.

"Mama's very tired today. Awfully tired. Do you understand?"

I understood "tired" and I understood "sick," but there was something about her detachment that I couldn't understand, something that made her different, not my "mama," but my "mother" as if "mother" denoted only our biological relationship.

Josie came into the bedroom and Mother invited her to sit on the bed, hugged her, and called her a "little peach pit."

"What did you call me that for?"

"I always call you that because you're so suckable. I just want to suck all the sweetness out of you."

Josie looked at me quizzically and smiled, but I remembered the talk about craziness, and when I saw the glassy look in my mother's eye, my stomach turned queasy.

At 6:30, about the time Mother had the TV dinners ready, Father came home. He picked up Josie and swung her around. "How's my baby girl? Looking so cute . . . just as cute as a kitten." He rubbed her nose and Josie started to giggle. Still holding Josie, he patted me on the head, let his hand rest there for a moment, and gently rocked my head back and forth.

For a moment the house was taken over by an infectious playfulness. I let my head wobble in exaggeration to the playful movement of my father's hand. When he stopped I grabbed his hand and put it back. Even my mother smiled. Her lips seemed to take on color for a moment; though her eyes seemed tired, they sparkled, now. "You had a good day," she declared.

My father went over to the cabinet where Mother was taking out silverware. He kissed her, and then the mood of the house changed. I could see anger flush into Mother's face and she turned her head away from my father. The silverware jangled as she shoved the drawer shut and rather than setting the table, she placed the silverware in the middle of it. "Supper's ready," she said. "Sit down and eat."

"Who feels like eating?" my father said, still playful. He danced around with Josie in his arms. "If you ain't got that swang, you ain't got a thang—do-wah do-wah . . ."

"The children haven't eaten." Mother unwrapped the foil from around Josie's dinner. "Put her down."

"Poor baby . . ."

"You're drunk. Put her down."

Father complied, looked sheepish for a moment, and began a fit of apologies. "I just had a drink." He said that he had run into an old friend from the service. They had gone down to the Jockey Boy on Fourth Avenue. In the middle of the explanation, my mother abruptly left the kitchen. "I just had one goddamn drink," he called after her. We heard the bedroom door slam.

My father looked at me. I couldn't tell exactly what he wanted, but the look seemed to be asking for understanding. "I just had a couple of drinks. What's the big deal?" Perhaps he needed me to father him at that moment, to pat his shoulder and say everything would be all right, but something different happened in me. My face felt flush and my eyes teared up. At that moment I saw him as a clown. His clothes didn't seem to fit him. His hair seemed nappy. His expression seemed stupid, and exaggerated. I wanted to ask him why he hadn't come home when expected, especially when Mother was sick. I wanted to ask him how he thought we were supposed to take care of ourselves with Mother sick. I asked him nothing. I turned away, much as my mother had done.

He got silverware for Josie and cut up her food. All the time he kept saying to her what he was doing. "Let Daddy cut your meat. Let Daddy stir your macaroni and cheese. Get it all mixed together—umm, doesn't that look good?"

"I can do it myself," Josie said.

He put down the fork and knife. "I know you can." He sat down and took the foil off of his own meal and stared at it. "Son," he said. I still couldn't look him in the face. "What's the matter? Do you think I let you down? I just had one drink with a friend. *Capeesh?*"

Capeesh? I looked up to see if he was serious. Was he going crazy, too?

"Now go ahead and eat."

I unwrapped the food. I had a ham dinner. "I'm not hungry," I said.

"Now, I don't want to hear that." His voice was suddenly authoritarian. "You sit there and eat." After a moment passed and I hadn't eaten, he offered me his chicken dinner. I declined it.

"Daddy, what's going to happen to us?" I asked.

He answered me very quietly. "How the hell am I supposed to know?" For a moment he seemed so distant that he might as well have had gotten up and left the house.

7

JOSIE AND I listened to our parents' voices coming to us in waves from the back of the house. First came Father's voice, then silence, then Mother's. To take my mind off of them, I asked Josie about her homework.

"Who can do homework with all that yelling?" she said and splattered the mashed potatoes with the tines of her fork.

"They aren't yelling," I said. "Don't tell anybody they're yelling."

"Sounds like yelling to me."

"It's not yelling. And if you're not going to eat, then don't play in your food."

"You can't tell me what to do. And I wasn't playing, either."

"Okay," I said softly, "then just put it in the trash." Though many boys at that age were rough on their siblings, especially their sisters, I was never very hard on Josie. I think my father had a lot to do with my perspective. He admonished me to play "nicely," meaning "gently," with my sister and never to hit a girl. That is what barbarians do.

Even if Father had never admonished me, there was something about Josie that would never have permitted me to hit her; I always saw her as my special charge. In grade school, I held her hand when we crossed busy streets; in high school, I warned other boys not to include her in their locker room talk. Other big brothers have played this role, no doubt, but I felt that she was more than just a little sister, but an aspect of myself, a twin. In her sophomoric way, she gave me confidence; she gave purpose to my actions.

After supper, we tried to do homework in my room, which was the farthest from my parents. Still, we heard them. Josie had math problems to work out and some reading to do. She was a good reader for fourth grade, so we didn't practice reading that night. She fiddled with some of the multiplication and long division problems. Finally, I decided that at least one of us should have homework and did Josie's for her, and got her changed into her pajamas by 8:30. At times the argument between our parents lulled and we thought it was over, then it would swell again. Josie asked if she could sleep in my room, so I let her.

"Say your prayers," I said.

"What for?"

"What do you mean, what for? So you'll go to heaven when you die."

She sat cross-legged on my bed and her lips trembled for a moment. "Well, is Mama going to go to heaven?"

"Yes, Mama *is* going to heaven—but not anytime soon. When she is old. So you pray for her. Pray for Daddy, too."

"I don't want to pray for him."

"Why not?"

Josie didn't speak. Her brow crinkled and she seemed to have been struggling with an idea. Then she got on her knees and began to pray. After a while I got down beside her. I rested my face in my hands and I prayed silently. I asked God to make my mother well, even though I knew that no one who ever had cancer lived long. What is the purpose of prayer, I thought, if some things can't be changed? It seems more like a tease that will ultimately lead to disappointment. Then it struck me that I was praying for the wrong thing. Everything in the future relied on my father. I raised my hands in the style of A. A. Allen and prayed for him.

Some hours after we had gotten in the bed, perhaps about eleven, my father opened the door to my room. He stared in for a while; I imagined he was looking for Josie, who was sleeping on the inside of the bed, against the wall. I did not acknowledge his presence.

Soon after he left, I heard the stereo. Very softly it played my father's favorite Nat "King" Cole LP. As I drifted in and out of sleep, I thought I heard "Sentimental Reasons" over and over again. In my sleep, Nat "King" Cole's soft declaration became my father's: "I love you for sentimental reasons." About midnight, Josie woke me and said she was hungry. I said I would get us some peanut butter sandwiches and sneaked to the kitchen. On the way, I saw my father asleep on the sofa in the den.

AT 6:30 IN the morning, our comet was visible for only a few minutes, before it disappeared behind the skyline. Lamar, in a good mood, seemed to have forgotten about the bad feelings of the previous afternoon. He focused on more exciting news. Reverend Timmons had visited his mother the evening before, inviting her to join the sit-ins at the department stores.

"She's fixing to sit in?" I asked.

"She wanted to," Lamar insisted, "but she needed to go to work— we not having any money and all." He gave me a coy look.

"Lamar," I said, dropping my bale of papers and looking him in the eye, "I didn't mean anything about what I said yesterday. I mean, I didn't mean to hurt your feelings."

"You didn't hurt my feelings," he declared. He sounded like he was about to cry.

"I'm glad. I didn't mean to. I mean we are friends and . . ." I wanted to tell him something that would show just how deep our friendship went. At least that's what I thought I was doing, letting loose the deepest secret in our family. My father had said many times that Lamar had a big mouth and couldn't be trusted to keep anything private. But I saw Lamar as an extension of me, the me I sometimes wished I could be: gregarious where I was withdrawn, inventive where I was dull, playful where I was sullen. But more than that, his hopes were the same as mine. In spite of the differences in our families, we were two boys in the same place. "My mama . . ." I had to catch my breath. Saying it outside of the family suddenly gave it shape and texture it hadn't had before. Just the thought of saying it to Lamar made it solid. It was almost as if I could roll it between my fingers and hand it over to him. "You can't tell this to nobody. Not even your mama. Promise?" I shouldn't have even attempted to get that promise out of him. Lamar told Mrs. Burrell everything. "You have to promise because Daddy said I wasn't supposed to tell you."

"Tell me what?"

"My mama is sick."

"She ain't dying or something, is she?" he asked.

I considered whether I should get mad at his tone, which struck me as flippant, but decided it was just Lamar being himself. How could he have asked any other way than with a smirk? "Yes, she is. She is dying. It's some kind of cancer."

He said nothing, just kept assembling and rolling the papers. When he started to talk again, it was about the Russian moon probe. He had heard on the radio that it was traveling at five thousand miles an hour. That meant it could go across the United States to California and back in one hour. At that rate it would take only two weeks to reach the moon. Two weeks! Can you imagine how far away the moon must be? It still isn't as far away as a planet. It would take a long time to reach a planet. He didn't know how long, but he would have to guess at least a year to get to Venus. That was the closest planet.

I considered telling him to shut up, but I said, "Mars is closer than Venus."

He insisted it wasn't and started to tell me how he knew, and that was what I wanted him to do, to chatter away. He continued the chattering as we delivered the papers, swinging them onto front porches, or thudding them against front doors under car ports—he kept talking, talking about everything except what he somehow couldn't say. I wished I hadn't told him my great secret. It had benefited me nothing. I felt worse than ever about everything and I wanted to tell him to shut up. Finally, I said, "April fools" and laughed.

"April fools on what?" He called from his side of the street and flung a paper at a carport. "Today's not April Fools'. April Fools' ended last week. That makes you the fool."

"It doesn't matter. I fooled you, so it's April Fools' again."

"First point is, you can't fool me when it's not April Fools' and next point, about what?"

Tears came to my eyes. I threw a paper too hard. It missed the doorstep, hit the door with a bang, and bounced into the hedges. It was Dr. Carrington's, the professor's, house so I got off my bike and put the paper in the right place. Lamar waited for me, riding his bike in circles to keep his balance. "About what?" he asked again.

"About my mama. She isn't sick."

He smiled. "I knew it! She's just having a baby, that's all."

"Yes, she's having a baby."

We rode in silence. Lamar looked a little smug, like I hadn't fooled him at all. Suddenly, he turned to me, "Walter?" He waited for me to acknowledge. "I'm glad your mama isn't sick."

"Thank you," I said. I had a very funny feeling and I thought for a moment that it might have been happiness.

· · ·

WHEN WE GOT HOME from school that afternoon, our mother was sitting in the living room, listening to the radio. Her hair was curled and she was dressed in seersucker sheath and had on pearl earrings and a necklace. Dinner was cooked and keeping warm in the oven. When I first saw her, I got the sensation that I was waking up from a dream—a dream in which my mother was dying. She gave us kisses. I was still not quite her height, so I held her around the waist and lay my head against her chest. She had an odd smell, perfumed and medicinal. She patted my head and pushed me away. "Don't get dramatic. Get out of your school clothes."

On the way down the hall to our bedrooms, Josie stopped and I almost stumbled over her. "Oh my God," she said. "I hope Daddy's on time today."

It shouldn't have mattered whether our father was a few minutes late, except that for some reason it mattered to our mother. Perhaps it was her illness that blew the incident into a crisis. Perhaps it was because he had been drinking in the middle of the week when he usually drank only on Sundays. Nonetheless, Josie and I grew more and more anxious as the time went.

We couldn't concentrate on homework. My homework was reading from my history book. Seventh grade history in Alabama meant the history of the War Between the States. What little was mentioned about slavery made it sound mutually beneficial for master and slave. After all, the slave never worried for provisions, always had a home, and was cherished by his master. Masters were never cruel to slaves; it defied logic that a man would cause injury on his own valuable property. In fact, the history book emphasized that some slaves refused to leave their masters when freedom was granted. These were the texts that both white and black students learned from, but luckily for us, in the segregated schools, we had teachers who knew better. After we read a passage, our teacher, Mrs. Griffin, would explain that there was no such thing as a kind slave master. If slaves had it so good, why didn't some of these lazy white people volunteer to be slaves?

Father hadn't come home by the time we had finished homework and Mother sat on the couch, patiently thumbing through a *Jet* magazine. Josie and I went out for a little while and played fetch with Bingo. When we came in, we were very hungry, but still Mother waited. With every passing car, we looked to see if our father had come, while Mother, seemingly unconcerned, creased and thumbed the same magazine. At 6:30, we children went into the living room and sat across from her; the room was saturated with the smell of dinner—one of our favorites—fried chicken and golden corn pudding.

"Mama," Josie complained, "I'm hungry."

"We'll eat as soon as your daddy gets home." Mother looked at the clock, and then she looked at us gravely. "It may be the Lord's will that we might never see him again. We are just poor people, and the Lord is God."

I felt cold for a moment. Had something happened to our father? "But he's just late?"

"Of course he is." She sighed, slapped down the magazine, got up, and went into the kitchen.

As we ate, she stood by the kitchen door and looked out of the screen at the street. Hungry though I was, I found it difficult to swallow the sweet, creamy corn and crispy chicken. I swallowed hard and braved the question I wanted to ask. "Mama, did you and Daddy have a fight?"

She turned in my direction, but it seemed her awareness of me came slowly, as if her spirit had been far away. Reluctantly, she acknowledged what was obvious.

"About what?"

"Nothing that you will understand," she said.

Having been curtly silenced, I looked down at my food. When I looked up again, Mother had turned her face back to the screen door. Suddenly, I feared that I would lose her just then, forever. She would look away and in an instant vanish, sucked through the screen and into the sky by a great vacuum. "Mama!" I said. Mother turned quickly. "Mama, was it about your cancer?"

She folded her arms. "Why do you ask that? That shouldn't worry you."

I swallowed and held back a sudden rush of tears. I wanted to jump up and hug her, but I held on to the bottom of my seat. "It's not fair."

"What's not fair?"

"Everything is not fair." I tried to make sense. "Everything's not fair. The way you don't tell us anything . . . the way—"

"That you're going to die," Josie said blankly.

There was a moment like sighing, except nobody breathed unless it was Josie whose point-blankness had somehow both broken the tension and added to it. Mother came over to the table and stood between the two of us. "Who told you I was going to die?" She smiled, quickly, dully. "Did Carl tell you that?"

"Daddy told us," Josie said.

"Daddy is wrong," Mother said.

"Shut up," I said. "You are lying, Mama. You are wrong. You are going to die. You want to die." I hung my head, ashamed to have spoken this way, afraid of her reaction, but knowing, too, I couldn't go another moment without at least knowing the truth.

Mother stroked Josie on the head. "Did Daddy tell you that, too?"

"Is it true, Mama? Why?"

"It's *not* true, Walter."

I was not looking at her for a long time, but listening to her breathe. Bingo's tail banged the screen door. When I looked up, Mother wasn't looking at me as I expected. She was looking out of the window.

"You deserve the truth, Walter," she said. "You and Josie are so young and I want to protect you from the truth. But I can't. I couldn't from the moment you were born. Life isn't easy, Walter. It's hard in many ways and you will just have to learn how to live with that. Everybody dies."

"I don't care about *everybody*."

"We all are going to die," she said. "It's in the Bible. We die so we can go to be with the Lord—" suddenly she caught the edge of the table as if preventing herself from falling. I jumped in my seat but saw that she had steadied herself. I couldn't tell whether she was dizzy or had simply slipped as she was trying to sit. She smiled as if to assure me, and continued. "But I'm not going to die, now. The Lord promised six score ten, and I believe Him for His word. Daddy is wrong if he says I *want* to die. He has put his faith in man. I'm putting my faith in the Lord. Do you understand?"

"You want to be healed?"

"No." She looked up and then at me. "I *am* healed. I'm trusting the Lord that I *am* healed."

"But suppose the Lord doesn't heal you?" Josie asked. "What are you going to do then?"

"The Lord always keeps his promises." She patted Josie on the head. For a moment my mother took on the aura of Reverend Evans, our pastor, when he offered communion. He opened his hands toward us and spoke in a firm, musical voice as if he were auditioning for sainthood. I had seen the Baptist ministers do this, too, opening wide their arms and looking up toward the ceiling of the church as if in beatific rapture. With the organ moaning in the background, they called out, "Come. Come little children, for Christ said, 'Suffer little children, and forbid them not, to come unto me: for such is the kingdom of heaven.'" We were suffering children, well fed, well clothed and warm, but suffering none the less.

"Are you going to go to A. A. Allen?" I asked.

"Reverend Allen can't heal. He is only God's instrument. I am believing that God has already healed me. That is my faith." She chuckled and stroked Josie's head. "I don't need to go all the way out to Oklahoma when God is everywhere."

I recalled the long line of people who had made pilgrimages to the tent meeting. Some were blind. Others were lame. Some had no obvious disability, but announced a multitude of ailments before Reverend Allen laid hands on them and declared them healed. Their bodies jolted. "Sister, how many fingers am I holding up?" the reverend would demand of a blind person. "Three!" she screamed out and began to dance. "Get up out of that chair," the reverend would command, and an old man would push against the wheelchair's arms but would be unable to stand. "Release him, demon! In the name of Jesus, I curse you, demon. Release this brother in the name and the cleansing blood of the everlasting lamb!" Reverend Allen smacked the old man on the head and the man shook and pushed against the chair. "Stand!" the reverend cried. The chair shot backward from under the man as he jumped to his feet. Surprised that he was standing, the man began to praise and run about, full of vigor. Before he was lost in the crowd, Reverend Allen was laying hands on yet another poor soul.

"I understand that God is everywhere," I said, "but why don't you go to A. A. Allen just to make sure?"

"Don't you trust God to heal me where I stand?"

"Yes."

"Because you *must* trust God. You *must not* doubt God."

"I don't doubt God," Josie said.

We heard our father's car turn into the driveway and we all looked up. "You need a good hair washing," Mother said and made a long stroke across Josie head. She shot a glance toward the door. "Your damn father is home," she said, got up, and went to her bedroom.

8

DEAR MR. AND MRS. JACKSON, *I have heard many stories of miracles since I have been here. There is the one about the GI who was awakened in the middle of the night by his grandmother calling his name. She had been dead about a month, just before he came in-country. He leaves the hooch to take a piss and to ponder what he thought was a dream. He hears the hooch crumble behind him, and explode. You've no doubt heard the one about the guy who was shot in the chest but the medics couldn't find the wound. They tore off his shirt and out falls a pocket Bible, riddled through to the Revelation. Your son even told me one. He was in the bush, lying silently, peacefully, waiting for the dawn, when he felt the muzzle of an AK-47 against his throat. It was an NVA. "Ssssh, black brother," he said, "it not you we want," and moved on. Haywood didn't think it was a miracle. And I no longer hope for such things.*

FATHER PATTED OUR HEADS and asked for Mother when he came in. His touch sent a shiver through me, but I managed to say that she was in her room. I wanted to cry and Josie held her head so close to her plate I thought she was already crying. Couldn't my father see that he hadn't walked into a happy household? Couldn't he see that our plates were full of cold food?

Father didn't go to the bedroom as I expected; he went to the living room and put the Nat "King" Cole Trio on the stereo. The lively combo led by piano and the smooth voice of Cole spread a brightly colored blanket over us. It was a tolerable blanket until my father began to snap his fingers in rhythm. He came back into the kitchen, humming as he lifted the lids on the pans of food. He picked up a chicken wing and began to nibble on it, all the time tapping his feet and swaying to the music. "When you take that Cal-li-forn-ia trip . . ."

"Daddy," I called to him. He didn't seem to hear me. "Daddy . . ."

He turned from the stove. I thought he was responding to me, but he announced, "Those Negroes were *tearing up* downtown today. Did you hear about it?"

"Hear about what?"

"The commotion downtown . . . some of the Reverend King's people were trying to get a little lunch at Pizitz's." He took a plate from the cabinet and began to scoop corn pudding onto it.

I wanted to scold him. "Where have you been?"

"Well, I haven't been sitting at some lunch counter where I'm not wanted—awwwh!" He gave Josie an exaggerated sympathetic look. "Why the long face, baby girl?"

At this point I felt like throwing something at him. I knew he knew why we were sad. Later, I reasoned that he was trying to escape, if only for a moment, from the truth that was all so evident; only, he was the father and there was no escape for him. Children might escape. Children might take flight into some fancy of space travel. But the father, in this case, needed to be sensible. He needed to take charge. If the mother didn't want to go to the doctor, he needed to make her. He needed to be home to cook supper, to make sure that homework was done. He was, after all, half a doctor, and he knew there were procedures for everything whether they had to do with science or not. How many times had he told me that a good scientist saw what was actually there, not what he wanted to see. A good scientist never looked away from the truth. My poor father was beginning to look away.

Suddenly, the music stopped and we heard the piercing scratch of the needle being pushed back and forth across the vinyl. Father froze, his mouth half-open, confused. "Why in the hell did she do that?"

"Don't you know?" Josie yelled at him. "She's sick."

"I know," Father snapped back. He turned away from us and put down the plate with a bang, and swung back around to Josie. "You don't know the half of it, young lady! Your mama isn't just sick—she's *killing* herself. Do you hear that? She's committing *suicide!*"

"Shut up," I said to him. "She'll hear you."

"Don't you tell *me* to shut up!" He stared intently at me; his cheekbones made angles. "Is that what you're afraid of?" he asked loudly. "That *she* will hear me? I want her to hear. She hears everything anyway. Everybody hears everything. Let's not pretend that everything is so hunky-dory." He moved around the table heading toward the back of the house. I got out of my chair to block him. I grabbed him around the waist and tried to push him toward the outside door. He pushed over me, pushing me down between his legs, and dragging me as I held his waist. Suddenly he stopped, and I let go of him and scrambled to my feet. Mother stood in the archway between the den and the back of the house.

"Get out!" she said to my father. "Get out and don't come back until you're sober."

My father stepped back and flared his shoulders. He stared intently at her, and then relaxed. "What a spectacle!"

Mother took a step toward him. "I said, 'Get out.'"

"Not in front of the children," he said.

"You're drunk in front of them."

"I'm not drunk."

"What do *you* call it?"

He looked up toward the ceiling and twisted his mouth. "I call it 'fine and mellow.'"

"Don't mock me."

"You mock yourself." Father hissed the words and drops of spittle flew from his lips. No sooner had the words come out than Mother slapped him on the mouth, and he raised his hand to slap her back. She winced. It happened so quickly that it seemed to have surprised everybody. "I warn you," my father said.

"Just get out of here, Carl."

Father went toward the kitchen door, then turned back. "Y'all children . . . y'all finish eating your supper." He went out and slammed the screen door behind him. We heard the car leave.

Mother made us go back to the table, and she came in and sat with us for a moment, at first just staring, and then speaking softly. "Don't worry, now, okay? Grown-ups get in fights sometimes, just like children do."

"Is Daddy coming back?" Josie asked. Her lip quivered and her eyes were narrow. Mother assured her that our father would be back, and that everything would be normal again.

Father had said more than he knew when he said that everybody could hear us. Not ten minutes after he had left, Mr. Jeters knocked at the kitchen door. Josie and I still sat trying to finish our supper. Mother had gone back to her room so I talked to Mr. Jeters. He made no specific reference to the fight, but casually inquired through the screen door if everything was okay and left. Not five minutes later, Mrs. Jeters came to the door. She was less casual about the situation. In a quiet, persistent way, she indicated to me that she wanted to enter the house. She took note of the uneaten suppers. She made her way to the den and asked if she could see Mother. I told her Mother was not well, and then she asked where my mother was and if she could go to the bedroom and sit with her.

Mother came into the den. She had made herself up, brushed her hair, and refreshed her lipstick. She offered Mrs. Jeters something cold to drink. Mrs. Jeters turned down the offer, as she seemed to study our mother. Mother asked me to go and clean up the kitchen. From the kitchen I heard their pleasant conversation. "Oh, just a spat. You know how that goes," my mother said. Mrs. Jeters made a remark about Mr. Jeters in his youth and both women laughed. Mother walked Mrs. Jeters to the kitchen door and thanked her for coming. She stood a moment while Mrs. Jeters went across the yard to her house. From the kitchen window, I could see Mr. Jeters open the back door for his wife.

Mother came to where I stood at the sink and put her arms around me from behind. "Your father said some cruel things about me. He didn't mean them. He was drunk."

My heart fluttered. To have her voice in my ear, her breath on my neck, and to be able to lean back in her arms ever so slightly made me feel both like a man and a baby. My God, Mama!, I thought. Then, I leaned away from her. "But it's true, isn't it? What he said?"

"He just doesn't understand. I don't expect him to. Or you. It's a trial that the Lord is putting me through, you see. One day it will be over. The Lord will see me through it. He won't give me more than I can bear. When I come out the other end of it . . . well, I will be restored." She turned me around and took my face in her hands. "Do you believe God for his word, my boy?"

"Yes ma'am."

"*Really?*"

I thought about the question. Of course I believed. I had been taught from the moment I was born. As Lutherans, we had had our share of religious training—catechism—and hymns. When we went to church with Grandma Pic, we sang the Baptist hymns; at school, we sang the Negro spirituals. When we stayed with Grandma Pic, she made us recite Bible verses after grace. If we couldn't remember one she would have us say, "For God so loved the world that He sent His only begotten son" or "Suffer little children . . ." Sometimes she would let us get away with a simple "Jesus wept." What did my mother mean when she asked did I "really believe" God's word, as if there were a choice "to believe" and another "to *really* believe"? I hesitated.

She hugged me. "No. You don't *really* believe. If you really believed then you would understand what I'm going through." She pushed me back and held me by the shoulders the way my father often did. "Walter, you have to have faith. Having faith is not easy. Obeying God's will is not easy." She patted my face. Her tone suddenly changed. It was nearly officious. "Thank you for washing up the dishes."

SOMETIME in the night, I got out of the bed to see if my father had come home. I saw no light coming from under my parents' door, and started toward the kitchen to look out of the window for the car. As I started through the den I was startled to hear my mother ask what I needed. A faint light from the Jeterses' porch came in through the window, but I could not see her. Her voice was coming from the direction of the couch, but was she lying or sitting? I told her I was going to get a drink of water, but instead of going to the kitchen, I sat in the chair across from the couch. After a moment, she told me to go back to bed.

"I need to ask you something," I said.

She said nothing, and after a while, I took her silence as permission to speak. "Is Daddy coming home?"

She answered slowly, thoughtfully, "Yes. Don't worry. Because he loves you." She sighed mournfully. In the dimness, I saw that she was not sitting on the sofa, but kneeling before it, as if I had interrupted a prayer. "Your father and I have argued before. We'll get through it," she said with assurance. I started again for the kitchen. "Walter," she said, stopping me. "Will you pray for me?" Something raw and flat in her voice made me afraid. It was as if all the talk of sickness and healing had only been play, a "what-if" game, and now she was ready to peel away the soft skin of the subject and talk about death.

"Pray for what, Mama?" I asked, a quaver in my voice.

"For my soul."

"Mama!" I was trying to get used to the idea that she was getting healed, now she had jumped to the soul, not even to dying, but all the way to the spookiest part of all. The darkness seemed to thicken around me, and I fumbled for the lamp.

"Leave it off," she said. "Come here and kneel with me."

I made a step toward her and stopped. Where was my father? "Walter, you must have faith. It's all you'll have of me, soon."

"Soon."

"Yes," my mother said. "Come here beside me, Son."

I found my way in the dark, felt her hand on my arm, reaching, pulling me down beside her. "Do you want to pray?"

I answered truthfully. "No, ma'am."

"Why not, Walter? Don't you want to pray for your mama?"

"I don't know what to say." Then I blurted, "Mama, aren't you being healed?"

"If God wills it."

"He might not will it?"

"He might not."

"Why?"

"I don't know."

"But why would God heal some people and not you?"

"He has a will known not to man."

"But why?"

"He has a will."

"But why don't you get an operation, Mama?"

She pushed me away and pulled herself up on the sofa and sat.

Her voice seemed colder, more distant. "Listen," she said. "I am obeying the will of God."

"Then why . . . ?" I knew what I wanted to ask. Why pray then? If it was the will of God, what was there to pray for? But I said nothing, only stood in silence for a while, until she ordered me to bed.

I started toward the bedroom, but turned again to her in the darkness. "Mama, what do you want me to pray for?"

"Nothing," she said sharply.

"What, Mama? I'll pray for whatever you want."

"Go to bed, now," she said, her tone softer.

"I just don't know what to pray for, Mama."

"Don't worry about it, Honey." We were quiet. A train rumbled in the distance. Once more, I started away, then she said, "Strength. That's all you can ever pray for, Waltie. Strength to bear God's will."

VERY LATE in the night, the door to my bedroom opened and I saw my father's head silhouetted against the hall light. I sat up.

"Go back to sleep," he said softly.

"Daddy . . ."

"Everything is all right."

"But, Daddy . . ."

"*Shhh.* It's late."

I lay back and watched his shadow flit across the crack of light coming in through the door. He paced, quietly but aimlessly, returning again and again to the hallway, but never going into his bedroom. I thought about getting up and talking to him. I knew the first thing I wanted to say was that I was sorry. Lying there, I found it hard to believe that I had tried to wrestle him—who was, at six two, more than a foot taller than I and easily seventy-five pounds heavier. It was not size, of course, that made the difference; it was that he was my father, the authority to whom I bowed, my protector, my idol. Even at the time of my strongest rebellion against him, of my deepest hatred of him, I admired his elegant swagger, the way he crossed his legs—ankle to knee—the way he wore his hat and raincoat. It was, in fact, my very love of him that made me hold on to his waist in that desperate and foolhardy act of protecting my mother, a mother who had already traveled far beyond my meager ability to protect.

The next morning, Father awoke me just fifteen minutes before I had to be at my route. As I rushed through the house, I saw that again he had spent his night on the den sofa. Thursday went well enough, leftovers and no catastrophes. Father came home on time, and was sober and pleasant, nearly formal to Mother, and she formal in return. After supper we went out to water the tomatoes, and he told me that the brain tumor was making Mother talk crazy. I did not think then that Mother's claim that she was healed could have been a manifestation of her illness. At eleven, healing was as possible to me as science fact. For I had no more hard evidence of the great spot on Jupiter than a fuzzy photo in a science encyclopedia, but I had actually witnessed an A. A. Allen healing.

"She's not acting herself, so you'll have to bear with her." He dragged the hose carelessly and crushed a tomato plant. "This healing business—this A. A. Allen mess—that's not her talking. It's the sickness."

I swallowed hard. I didn't often disagree with him, and I wanted there to be some hope for my mother. "I saw A. A. Allen heal people."

He gave me an admonishing look. "You know better than that, Waltie. Now, I'm not saying that there can't be miracles. I'm just saying you don't find them in a tent show. Did you do any scientific follow-up on those people who were healed? You don't know that they weren't cons—well, maybe they weren't cons, but they were deluded. They just think they were healed." He handed me the hose.

"Maybe if you think it hard enough, it could happen."

"Wishful thinking?"

"You've got to wish for something."

"But wishful thinking doesn't get you anywhere." Father walked away, toward the house, leaving me holding the hose. The water splashed into the garden, making a mud hole at the base of a tomato hill. Suddenly I wanted to cry and I couldn't figure out why until I looked around and saw that I was alone. All of Tittusville seemed hushed, as if every single person had gone away.

ON FRIDAY, Father cooked, and Josie and I marveled and were eager to try his food. Usually, his cooking was relegated to those especially male occasions, Fourth of July barbecues and Christmas Eve oysters, a tradition he had brought with him from Virginia. Father's biscuits and tuna casserole didn't win any awards for presentation. The biscuits were too brown on the bottoms and too white on the tops. The casserole bled a white liquid from its yellow, cheesy crust. Though she did not eat, Mother joined us at the table, poked fun at the food, and laughed. Even so, we loved the supper. We loved it better when Father offered us ice cream for dessert, a fitting consolation for missing Mother's cooking.

But the calm was only a respite. With the easing of the strained formality between them, my parents began to snipe at each other, and it was Mother who set off the first round.

Because it was Friday, we were allowed to watch television, so Josie and I had settled in with *The Rifleman*. My father sat in the living room playing music, Chet Baker, one of the few white musicians he bothered with.

The phone rang. It was Grandma Pic. Mother came into the den and talked to her. I watched her as she spoke, seated on the couch beside the phone table. After the initial hello, she seemed to stiffen. A flatness came to her tone. At first she said, "Yeah, yeah. Yeah, Mama." After a few minutes, she simply nodded rather than answered. After she said good-bye, she sat with the telephone in her lap and stared at *The Rifleman* for a minute. Then she cradled the phone and went into the living room. I heard her talking to Father, but did not pay much attention until she said loudly, "Stop that damn music and listen to me." The music stopped. I had been lying on the floor and I sat up and looked in the direction of the living room. Josie, sitting beside me, did not look, but moved closer to the TV.

"I'm listening," I heard my father say.

"Why did you tell Mama to come here tomorrow?"

"I didn't *tell* her to do anything."

"Well, she and Uncle Reed and the whole bunch of them are coming to 'see about me.' I don't need them to 'see about me.'"

My mother had begun to walk away, back through the den toward the bedroom. "Is Grandma Pic coming?" I asked. For the first time in my life, my mother gave me a cold look, not just the distant looks I had seen earlier. This time it seemed her eyes had scaled over, her shoulders turned from me as if to throw off my question. It was a slight motion, but it seemed to send out a shock wave that pushed me away from her.

Father came after her, passing through the den. "She is your *mother*. Don't you think she ought to know?"

"No! She'll know what I want her to know," my mother answered from the bedroom.

"But, Clara. Baby. Maybe she can help."

"Help? What help do I need from her? I've got all the help I need right here—"

"And what help is that?"

"The help of Jesus Christ, my Lord and savior—"

"Jesus Christ! Jesus Christ!"

Josie moved closer to the TV. "I can't hear." She turned up the volume. The rifleman snapped shut the bolt on his rifle. It was a short, repeating rifle that he wore in a holster strapped to his leg. When he was in a quick draw, he could whip it out like a pistol. In this episode, the rifleman's son was being held hostage by bank robbers.

"Let me alone," Mother said. "I don't need you to tell me what to do—"

"You need somebody—"

"I don't need you—"

"Yes, you do. You need—"

"And I don't need Mama. I don't need everybody poking into my business. It's *my* business, don't you understand?"

"Clara, you are sick. Face it. You are sick and you need help."

"I've got all the help I need."

"Jesus Christ can't help you!"

Mother walked briskly through the den and into the kitchen. I thought she was being chased, but my father had stayed in the bedroom. Mother actually touched the kitchen doorknob before she turned around and came back into the den. "You. You children," she said, breathing hard. "You go on to bed now."

"But *Rifleman* hasn't gone off, yet," Josie said.

Mother switched off the TV. "It's off now."

"Leave the children out of this," Father said, coming into the den. "Let them watch their program." He switched the TV on, but Mother switched it right back off.

"Don't undermine me," she said.

Father's face flushed and he sneered. "You can't be *under*mined."

"Don't mess with me. Don't mess with me, Carl."

Father took her by the shoulders. His tone was even and firm. "Clara, for the hundredth time. I'm not 'messing' with you. I'm not trying to hurt you. I'm not trying to control you—"

"Take your hands off of me."

"Listen." He shook her shoulders slightly. "Just listen, will you?"

She rolled her shoulders. "I said, take your hands—"

He grasped her tighter, shook again. "I'm trying to help you, god-damn it. Let me help you."

She pulled away from him and stepped back. "You can't help yourself, Carl. You can't—you can't even piss in a pot—"

"I can take you to a goddamn doctor. I can do that—"

"Don't say that word—don't say that word to me—"

"Goddamn. Goddamn. Goddamn, Clara. Goddamn!"

"Oh Jesus, Jesus, Jesus, help me." Mother tried to walk past him to the back of the house, but he grabbed her shoulder again. She slapped him. I saw his fist clench. She slapped him again. "Let go of me."

"Let go!" Josie screamed. "Just let go!"

My parents seemed to move in slow motion, he with one hand gripping her arm, trying, it seemed, to pull her toward him in some kind of a jitterbug, and she with her free hand waving back and forth across his face. Then I saw his clenched fist rise, and her face, it seemed, volunteered to meet it. I didn't hear anything, but I saw spittle shoot from her mouth and his fist rose up again. I was lying, as I remember it, but I jumped, jumped for his fist and gripped him somewhere at the elbow and tried to swing down. The momentum of all these motions spun me across the room and sent the back of my head crashing into the pine wall paneling. For a moment things blackened, and then, he, not her, was rubbing my cheeks, calling to me. "Walt. Son. Waltie. Son."

"*I hate you*," I said. My eyes blurred with tears and I tried not to bawl. His large hands gently stroked the back of my head, the same hands that a minute before were striking my mother. When they touched me, I cringed. The idea of those hands was repulsive to me. But when he took them away to begin his stroke again, I craved them. The ache on the back of my head seemed to come in pulses, synchronized with the cringing and craving. My breath synchronized with it. Furthermore, every time I cringed, I hated myself for cringing and when I craved, I hated myself for that.

Then Josie let out a high-pitched scream, similar to the kind of whistle that babies make when they are happy.

"Take your hands off of him," I heard my mother say. Over my father's shoulder, through my blurry eyes, I saw Mother with my baseball bat raised to her shoulder. "Let go of him."

My father stood up and stepped back. "Clara, I'm sorry."

"I want you to get out of here. I mean it, Carl. You get out of here or I'll call the police."

"Clara."

Mother raised the bat as if to strike him. Then defiantly, he kneeled down beside me. He was directly under the raised bat and would have taken a good blow on the head if she had swung it. He put his hands on my shoulders. "I wouldn't hurt you, Son," he said calmly. I knew that he wouldn't. "I . . . don't want any of this to happen. I . . . I want things to be all right." Slowly, he took his hands away and stood up. Eyeing Mother, he walked over to Josie. She shrank. He reached for her and she ran behind Mother. "Josie," he said, "I am not going to hurt you. Daddy wouldn't hurt you."

He looked me in the eye. I don't know what he read in my eyes. Everything I felt was a dizzying tumult. I wanted to shout at him. I wanted to slap him. I wanted my mother to put down my bat. I wanted to listen to music. I wanted to watch television. I wanted to eat supper. I wanted to go to Lamar's house. Finally, my father left. He made an exaggerated effort not to slam the screen door, but he slammed the car door before he gassed out of the driveway.

LATER THAT NIGHT, Josie climbed into my bed. Bingo followed her, curling up at her feet. "Can't you sleep?" I asked her, knowing well the difficulty. I was doing more sleeping in class, cat napping through grammar and history, than I was in the bed. Josie pulled the sheet around her and tucked her little body into mine for warmth. We were quiet for a long time. I was drifting in and out of sleep. It seemed the moment I fell asleep something moved in the room or in my mind, or Bingo or Josie moved, and I was wide awake again. The house seemed spooky, now, with Daddy spending the night away. He had called to say he was at Dr. Gaston's motel.

"Walter," Josie said. I thought she had fallen asleep.

"What?"

"Is Daddy going to jail?"

"No."

"But Mama said she was calling the police—"

"Just to scare him."

She was quiet for a long time and then, "Is Mama going crazy?"

"No."

"She keeps talking crazy."

"About what?"

"About God."

A feeling of dread came to me. "Did she ask you to pray for her?"

"No. She just said that God was using her."

"Don't worry about it," I said after a while. "Mama is sick."

"I guess that's how it feels when you are dying."

"I guess. I guess they are both sick in a way. That's why we have to be good and not to worry about it. Grandma Pic is coming tomorrow. Everything will be all right." I lay there a long time, slowly drifting off and thinking that something needed to happen.

EARLIER THAT NIGHT, soon after my father had driven away, I went into the yard and lay on top of the picnic table. My head no longer hurt where it had been banged, but it was stuffy from crying. Bingo lay beside me and put his head on my chest. High above, even with the backyard lights on, I could make out the great square of Pegasus. I calculated where the Andromeda galaxy was. It was a pinpoint to the naked eye, but if my telescope had been powerful enough, it would have appeared as a great pinwheel of stars.

Though I was not allowed to ride my bike after dark, I thought about riding to Lamar's house. We could look at the stars together and talk about space adventures. Then I thought about riding farther away, to Over the Mountain, to Shades Valley, down Highway 31 to Grandma Pic's in Coosada. The darkness offered many possibilities. Who would know what I did? Who would care? I got my bike from the carport and quietly pushed it to the street. I coasted past the Jeterses and onto the corner at Center Street. Bingo followed. This was the route I took to the school, and I headed that way. The streets were dark in spite of the few streetlights and lights from porches, and from the windows of kitchens and dens. Inside children were doing homework, or settling in the flickering blue light of television for an evening of *The Rifleman* or *Truth or Consequences* or *Amos 'n Andy*. The cool air blew against me as I coasted down the hills or pedaled up, letting the bike go as it pleased, taking the route of least resistance. Finally, I came to the railroad bridge near Greensprings Avenue and stopped: I knew better than to ride into the white neighborhoods, especially after dark.

It took a minute before Bingo, panting, caught up to me. He put his front paws against my stomach, his tail switching crazily, and I patted him.

"Good Bingo. Bingo loves Waltie."

I held onto the bridge railing and took in the view of the downtown skyline. A sliver of moon hung above it. What a picture! I thought. A train track running toward downtown and a pencil line of a moon in the blue-black sky. But what was it a picture of? *Something tremendous must happen.* There was too much tension. The world must explode. I had seen pictures of the atom bomb blowing up Hiroshima, and of tests of H-bombs with their bright stalks rising, mushrooming, and eating up the sky. I knew the Russians had a thousand such bombs pointed at the United States. Somewhere in the Soviet Union, perhaps in a town at the foot of the Ural Mountains, was a silo with a missile pointed at Birmingham. Suppose, just for no good reason, a boy not much older than me pushed a button and let that bomb fly. Suppose, just as I was thinking it, he was walking with his dog and his gun to the silo to push the big, red blinking button.

In thirty minutes, standing on that bridge with the track running to Montgomery in one direction, to downtown in the other, I would see a strange light come up in the sky. At first I would think it was our comet, hanging like a sword over the skyline. One of the four horsemen carries such a sword. But it would move too fast to be a comet, and I would think it was a meteor. It would grow brighter, leaving a fluorescent streak. No, not a meteor. Since I didn't believe in flying saucers—they weren't scientific—I would conclude that it was the missile marked for Birmingham, heading straight in, on course, unstoppable.

What would this matter to me? I was just eleven, born seven years after "the big war," seven years after Hiroshima. And I was black, a colored kid. Colored kids hadn't invented the bombs, even though a colored physicist, I had heard Uncle Reed tell with pride, had helped to build it. Colored couldn't even vote most of the time, so what did we—what did anyone I knew—have to do with a bomb falling from the sky? Yet, for all I cared at that moment, that Russian missile could have been on its way, flaring across Canada and the northern states and arching with ever intensifying grace, ever more beauty, toward Birmingham. As far as I cared, it had already detonated and all that was left to happen was the flash and the rumble.

9

"WE ARE ALREADY DEAD; we just haven't started to stink yet," Vester said. The dawn was a pink fringe along the horizon behind the village, and fog snaked up from the river into the paddies. We heard the roar of a jet and the first of the F-111s passed over Thoybu. The sky filled with trailers from the antiaircraft guns. Two more jets came over, firing missiles. The percussion of the bombs and the shock wave rippled through the mud.

"What the hell are you talking about?" Bright Eyes screamed at him. His face was caked with mud and all I could see of him was the white of his eyes and his teeth. "What the hell——"

"Death, bastard. I'm talking about death. You, me, Mr. Tibbs——we are just as dead as Haywood, I'm telling you——"

"Shut up. I ain't dead. I don't believe that God put me here just to kill me."

"Who said God put you here?"

"What are you trying to say?"

"Who said God put you here? What kind of God would put you *here?*"

"He has a purpose, don't he? He has a purpose unknown to man."

"What kind of purpose is this, I ask you? What kind of goddamn purpose do you see here?"

Kill or be killed, I thought. That is the purpose right now. We had lain all night in the paddy, in the mud. I lay on my poncho to keep me out of the mud, which had become cold as the night wore on. The fighting had continued heavy and all night we had expected close fighting and had our bayonets fixed and ready, but nothing came. Once we had moved up, and I thought we would attack, but we only made it a few yards before the machine gunfire drove us back, back to the very same spot, only Haywood was to my right rather than my left. The good thing was that the mud had kept him cool; his face had been exposed to the sun all the day before and he was bloated, but the mud had kept him cool enough that he hadn't split open. That happens after a few hours in the sun, a split along the jawbone or at the ankles and an ooze of fluid.

Just before dawn, I had been having a dream. In the dream the *rat-pat-pat-pat* of the gunfire was like drums in the distance, the hammering of the thirty-caliber guns, all a distant music. Haywood was in the dream, alive and looking just as good as ever. He had an intent expression, not unpleasant but interested—inquisitive—and I was talking to him. I touched him on the shoulder and I said, "Hey, 'Wood, now you tell me something. You tell me something I want to know. How does it feel? I mean, what is it like?"

He grinned. He was more like Lamar than Haywood. We were lying on our sides in the mud, facing each other. He reached out and touched me in the middle of my chest. Not over my heart, but over my solar plexus, that beautiful, hollow part of the chest. "You already know," he said. "Just think about it."

I thought about my mother and Lamar. "What do I know? I don't know anything."

"You know. You just don't remember."

WE MOVED FORWARD. All I heard was the click and buzz of insects, the squish of the mud, the crunch of the rice stalks beneath our boots. Then Vester stepped on a Betty. He must have felt it slipping from under his toe because he looked at me and said, "I can't believe this shit——"

I WAS FLAT on my back, catching my breath. For a moment everything was blue, very bright, clear, deep sky blue. I felt my face. It was bloody with Vester's blood and bits of his flesh. I wiped furiously at my face and spat out the bits that had gotten on my lips. Bright Eyes was next to me, feeling my legs and arms. "You all right?" he shouted. I sat up for a moment and finished catching my breath. I didn't want to think about anything, but then I decided that I was all right. "I'm all right," I said.

"Can you stand up?"

I stood up.

"You should go to the back." He was still shouting.

I'm all right, I thought. Did I want to look at Vester? Did I even want to ask about Vester? "Vester——?"

"Let's get moving, then." Bright Eyes's lips twitched in an ugly way. "Fugazi."

"Okay," I said. I tried to wipe the blood and fragments of body from my clothes, but I was only smearing it. "Don't you want to look?" I asked myself. "Don't you want to see it?" It was just over to my right. I could sense it there like it had its own gravity, pulling me toward it. I turned to Bright Eyes. His eyes were gray and slightly

ghostly looking. When he was high, especially when we were trip-
ping, his eyes looked like they sparkled.

"All right, then," I said to myself out loud. "Two to go." How did I
feel—or more precisely, how did I not feel? I could not look at Vester,
for looking at him was a part of feeling. I sensed that the main parts
of him, torso and arms, were crumpled in one heap; part of a leg and
booted foot lay a little ways off. I was not looking, but I was seeing it
all, not just Vester, but Haywood a few yards behind him, the expanse
of checkered paddies in different hues of green and fingers of fog, the
breeze moving through the blades of rice like an invisible stream—
and then, like waves over the body of the papa-san. I was seeing it all,
the broad divided river shining like a strip of silver and just up a slope
in front of us, the four clusters of thatched huts and the cratered,
charred, and fuming ground in front of them. There were other bodies, bodies all over the paddies, all over the ridge, in the hooches, in
the forest behind the hooches. I was feeling all of this that I was seeing
and it felt like nothing to me. It didn't matter.

I was like one of those turkey vultures we see in Alabama, buffoon-
ish and hideous, black wings against the bright sky. Looking down, the
earth was neither terrifying nor grand. It was neither sweet nor foul,
even with the stench of a hundred dead people. It merely was the
earth, turning slowly, shapes and colors of no particular value.

By the mid-morning, we had reached the slope just at the edge of
the paddies, just in front of the first cluster of hooches. We had come
that far with only a little resistance. Word came down the line that
the VC had run. It was not unusual for Charlie to put up a good fight
only to fall back just before he got overrun. The whole war was like a
game of hide-and-seek, except with killing. We rested at the base of
the rise. It was good to be under trees, tattered and broken as they
were, and it was good to be on solid ground again.

"Jesus," Bright Eyes said with a sigh, "Jesus, this feels good."

I looked back over the paddies, mottled with sunlight and shadow.
A bird called from the palms and another one darted across toward

the river. "It's beautiful, too," I said. I hadn't forgotten that in the trampled part of the fields lay Haywood and Vester and dozens of others. I could see the purple plume of the Medevac at one edge of the fields, and I could hear sporadic rifle fire and hand grenade explosions.

Bright Eyes was eating. "Yes, it is," he said. "Yes, it is right now. But it ain't as beautiful as back home. I want to go back home. Things will be better back home."

I agreed, but I didn't feel it. I wasn't sure what things would be like at home, "the world," as we called it. I was a short timer, just one hundred and five days and I would go home. I wanted to go home more than anything. Home was sweet and quiet, but home had its dangers, too, especially for black boys.

We both ate for a few minutes. The second lieutenant was the new CO. He told us to move up and clean up the village. It was routine.

"You gonna write to Vester's folks?" Bright Eyes was putting away his rations.

"He didn't ask me to."

"You should anyway."

"I promised Haywood; I didn't promise Vester."

"You still should write."

"Why don't you?"

He moved ahead of me a few paces, but slowed to let me catch up. "I wouldn't know what to say."

"And I do?"

"You know better than me. I mean, you have a way with words. You could've gone to college."

I already felt burdened with Haywood's letter, and had agreed to write it only because we were both from Alabama. Vester was from Detroit. "The army will write it," I said.

"The fucking army! What does the army know about Vester? Vester deserves better than that. You've got to do it."

"Keep cool," I warned. "I haven't got to do a goddamn thing. He was your friend, wasn't he?"

Bright Eyes was quiet for a long time. We ascended the rise to the perimeter of the village. We looked for tunnels and bunkers. When we found one, we'd roll a hand grenade into it and shoot to see if we could flush anyone out. Around us, other GIs were doing the same.

"If I write it," Bright Eyes said, "will you help me?"

I nodded.

"I wouldn't know what to say."

I nodded again.

"Do you really think he was my friend?"

I shot my gun into a bunker even though I knew it was empty. "I guess. You cats did hang together."

"But hanging don't mean he was my friend. Hell, I hang around with a lot of guys and ain't friends with none of them."

"I don't know, Bright Eyes. I can't tell you that."

"Then tell me this. If it happens to me. I mean, if I catch it, will you write a letter for me? Will you promise to do that for me?"

"I'll consider it."

"Consider it? Is that all you would do?"

I took a deep breath and looked at him, right into his gray eyes and light-colored lashes. His face was round and babyish in spite of a wisp of mustache, beard, and cakes of dried mud. He had a slight gap in his front teeth that made him look even more like a boy. He had just turned twenty, was short, and had a well-proportioned build. He was what they might have called "All-American." I was suddenly angry and nearly spat at him.

"I *said*, 'I will consider it.' "

We went into the first cluster of hooches, maybe about fifteen, some of them houses, some of them stables and storage shacks. A dog came out of one house. He was a brown mutt, small and thin, not much taller than my knee. He bared his teeth and barked, and bared his teeth again. I had come to hate dogs, the rubbery, curled lips and yellow teeth.

"Look at the pup," Bright Eyes said to the dog. "Nobody's gone to

106

hurt you." Though it snarled, the dog's tail wagged in frantic spurts in response to Bright Eyes's voice. Bright Eyes started toward the dog as if to pat it. I raised my rifle with one hand and fired. I hit it right in the head and it flipped and was dead. Bright Eyes looked at me and then stared at the dog. I could tell he was angry, but I didn't care. What did it matter? I walked toward the carcass and stepped over it. I told myself to be cool, just step over it as if nothing had happened. Bright Eyes was shaking his head. "You're one sick son of a bitch," he said.

"Somebody 'round here will eat 'im," I said flatly. As I stepped over the dog, I looked down at its fur, the fur on its chest, lighter than its back, and slightly curly. I thought for just a moment of combing my fingers through it. My stomach tightened, and a tight discomfort came in my chest. I fired into the hooch, firing along the roofline as we had been taught to do and waiting for the occupants to run out. No one ran out, so I fired into the sides. The heat from the bullets caused the grass walls to smoke. I stood beside the door, pushed it open with my rifle barrel, threw in a grenade, and covered my ears. No one came out so I took out my Zippo cigarette lighter and held it to the loose grass on the roof. After all the shooting, my chest felt better.

We heard movement behind the hooch, and, rifles ready, we slowly moved around to the side. Sweet grass smoke wafted down, and obscured my view for a moment and then I heard a squeal. It was a pig. I let go with a few pops from my rifle. The pig ran in the direction of the forest. Then we saw a corral with a water buffalo in it. The huge animal stood still and quiet; its big eyes were glassy. Black flies swarmed around its belly, which had been split open so that its intestines hung down like pink and white drapery. Slowly we walked around it. It breathed heavily, but its eyes were not following us. The flies whined and buzzed.

When we had moved a short distance away, Bright Eyes said, "I don't get you, Tibbs. Why are you such a son of a bitch?" I didn't say anything. I didn't feel like a son of a bitch. What would a cracker from Georgia know about what I felt anyway? And what did it matter how I felt—what did anything matter?

Three days later we were back in the hooch at the base camp. Haywood's and Vester's cots were empty, not yet filled by FNGs, "fucking new guys."

Dear Mr. and Mrs. Jackson, was as far as I had gotten with the letter. I sat on my cot with my back against the wall of the hooch and held the tablet against my knee. The blue scrawl was pressed deeply into the lined paper, yet it refused to go farther than the salutation. It refused to tell what had happened. Bright Eyes's tablet lay on his pallet, blank. He had become frustrated and had gone out to see if he could find a girl.

A gecko was in the rafters again, and I lay back on my duffel bag and looked up into the ceiling. I lit a joint and smoked it slowly, taking in deep breaths until it hurt and then letting them out. At first I was thinking about what happened at Thoybu. First Haywood got shot, and then Vester stepped on the mine. Next I shot the dog. It was a mud-colored dog. It was small, and its ribs showed through its fur. It couldn't have belonged to anyone, I was thinking. If I had thought for a moment that it belonged to someone, to some kid, to someone who petted it and played with it, then I wouldn't have killed it.

I wouldn't have killed the dog, I wrote in the letter, *except it was just a mangy dog. It didn't belong to anyone.* Was that reason enough? And Bright Eyes was fixing to pet it. Bright Eyes was getting all soft and sentimental with it. He would have shot down a man in a heartbeat, but he was getting sentimental with a tick-covered mutt. *I wouldn't have killed the mutt, except I wasn't thinking . . . I'm loose.* I tore the paper from the tablet, looked at it, and then tore it into strips.

10

M<small>Y FATHER</small> surprised me as I rolled the papers the morning after his fight with Mother. I was fearful when I saw the blue Fairlaine pull to the curb: I had said I hated him, and now he had come to punish me. He rolled down the car's window and yelled a friendly good morning to Lamar. He joked that he had never seen Lamar in "dawn's early light," and that he found it becoming. Then, more soberly, he called me over to the car.

With Lamar looking on suspiciously, I sat beside my father in the car. He started by asking how I was, then we interrupted each other apologizing. Father put his palm on the back of my head and stroked down to the base of my neck. "Son. You don't have a thing to apologize for. It was my fault. All of it was my fault. Whatever happens to you while you are my child is my fault." He covered his eyes. I thought he might have been crying, but when he took his hands away, his face was dry, worried, but dry. "I had a lot of time to think last night, and . . . I want you and Josie to know that I love you. Whatever happens, both your mama and I love you. But I think . . ." He held his hands out in front of him as if he were trying to shape the air into a ball, trying to explain himself. "I feel it is necessary that I just stay away from your mama for a little while. A couple of days, that's all. I don't want to do it . . . but I think she would like it . . . and I . . . well, I would like it, too. You have to understand, it's so hard——" He looked me in the eyes. "Waltie, it was wrong of me. It's very wrong, I know that. It was a very bad example. And I am not a bad man. I just lost control of myself. I was so *mad* with her." After a pause, he placed his hand on my knee, and offered a faint smile. "I let my emotions get control of me, Son. I wasn't a good scientist."

"You can't always be a good scientist," I offered.

"No. Some things are beyond logic. But that wasn't. That was just wrong."

"But doing right is logical."

He cleared his throat. "Maybe."

On the backseat lay his crisp white shirts and suits, still on their hangers. A suitcase was pushed behind the passenger seat. He told me that he would be staying at Dr. Gaston's motel and gave me the room and phone numbers. You know how to get there? he wanted to know. I knew where it was, though it was not a place I had ever ridden my bike to because it was far outside of Tittusville. He told me which were the best streets for riding the bike, and added, after a pause, that he didn't feel there would be any reason—none at all—to ride the bike downtown. Just one call, and he would come to me. He looked at his hands and let out a chuckle. "You may not believe this, but I love your mama. Don't ever think that I don't. You tell that to Josie." He cleared his throat. "You tell her that I found her in your bed this morning and kissed her. You tell her that Bingo was in there, too." He smiled again. Then his brow furrowed. "I . . . Son, we're all struggling right now. I . . . I . . . don't know when it will end—but it *will* end." He put his hand on the back of my neck again and kissed my forehead. "I'll be around tomorrow to take you to Sunday school." We sat for a moment more, then he indicated Lamar, who had finished with the rolling and was standing beside his bicycle. I got out. Slowly, my father's car pulled away and I felt as if the world had just ended. It was worse in a way than learning that my mother was sick—Mother's sickness was filled with a warm, nauseating emptiness; my father's leaving was cold and hollow and, in spite of his kiss, fearful.

"Your daddy splitting?" Lamar asked.

I felt like killing him. He sounded smug, but when I looked at him, I saw an inquisitive look on his face. "None of your business," I said, got on my bicycle, and started to push off. Lamar grabbed the bike by the back of the seat. He put his hand on my shoulder.

"You can come over to my house—you and Josie both." I nodded my head and smiled. I pushed away again. "Listen," he said, pedaling beside me. "I know your mama is sick for real. I know it wasn't an April fools. My mama talked to our preacher who had talked to your preacher. A lot of people know." He got ahead of me and started the route. I followed and he talked to me from the other side of the street. "Walter, it's hard on a kid. That's what my mama says."

I HAD BARELY gotten in the door, when I heard the toot of a horn and the sound of Uncle Reed's car pulling into the yard. Grandma Pic got out of the car with boxes of food, including sweet potatoes, her favorite. No one would ever accuse her of what she thought was a cardinal sin: "Eating on the sick." Great Uncle Reed came in behind her carrying more boxes. To my surprise, Aunt Bennie and my cousin Vachel from Philadelphia had come, also. Aunt Bennie was laughing as she got out of the car. In the midst of all of our seriousness, only she could get away with laughing. Her laughter was contagious, too. As she came into the kitchen, she gave me a kiss and tug on the ear and exclaimed how I had grown. "You trying to be a skyscraper? Lord knows you've been eating your grits."

Grandma Pic began at once to take over the house. She dropped the boxes on the kitchen table and went immediately to our mother's bedroom. She tapped on the door and, without waiting for an answer, went in. She turned to me, who had followed her. "Go see what I put in the box. Have Bennie serve it up." She gave me an encouraging smile and shut the door firmly. I stood outside the door and listened to her singsong voice. It had the rhythm of a river to it. Thinking about it later, I thought perhaps because Grandma Pic had grown up at the confluence of two rivers, the Coosa and the Alabama, that her voice had taken on the sound of lapping water, a rise and fall that was mostly comforting, but that could slap hard when it wanted to, smooth out, and slap hard again.

First Grandma Pic asked my mother how she felt, then in a scolding slap, she said, "What this I hear you not seeing the doctor?" I couldn't hear the reply, and then Grandma Pic came again, "Clara, baby, you got *two* children. You don't have *no* choice."

At that point Aunt Bennie interrupted my eavesdropping. "*She* in there?" The emphasized "she" was my mother. Aunt Bennie didn't wait for an answer and opened the door. My mother sat up in the bed and Grandma Pic sat at the foot on my father's side and faced her. Mother looked up as Aunt Bennie walked in. Rather than excitement at seeing her sister from out of state, my mother had an expression of dread. Suddenly she stared past Aunt Bennie to me. For a second, I was transfixed by my mother's eyes. I knew from the plastic shine of Mother's eyes that she was beyond reach. The cavalry had come, all guns and horses, but much too late. Suddenly my skin turned cold. My breath seemed to leak out through my ears. I felt dizzy.

"Walter, go along, now," Mother said, sounding like herself. "Walter, go on."

"Poor thing," Aunt Bennie said. She spun me around by my shoulders and slapped my butt to get me going. The door shut behind me.

I sat on my bed for a second, and then Josie and Vachel came in eating some of Grandma Pic's jelly biscuits. Vachel was five, an only child. We considered him a little brother. I told Josie to get dressed, and led Vachel back to the kitchen where Great Uncle Reed was finding pans and preparing to cook breakfast.

Uncle Reed was a lanky, scruffy man with a gentle twinkling eye and a broad smile. Though he was my grandmother's companion, he was, in fact, my mother's uncle, a relationship that seemed odd from the outside, but was accepted within the family. As he cooked, Uncle Reed talked and sang with abandon, not to anyone in particular, but to everyone. He went from subject to subject, sometimes politics, sometimes *The Ed Sullivan Show,* or the weather, or mountains, or animals or ghosts—his repertoire seemed endless—at least one story about any subject and often elaborately constructed.

Uncle Reed was a good cook, and I surprised myself by the amount of breakfast I ate. Vachel claimed he hadn't eaten since the train left Philadelphia the previous afternoon, but Uncle Reed reminded him he had eaten when he and his mother arrived in Montgomery. Nonetheless, he was hungry again. Josie ate as if she hadn't eaten all week. Uncle Reed scraped and put the dishes to the side. He said that Grandma Pic would wash them after she had eaten, but even after an hour the women hadn't come out of the bedroom. Uncle Reed asked about the garden and we showed it to him. It hadn't rained that week, and the ground was dry and the plants were limp, so Uncle Reed instructed us in watering. "Growing a garden will teach you about life," he exclaimed. "If you care about something, you've got to take care of it, keep an eye on it, give it whatever it needs. It's called 'responsibility.' If you love something, you take responsibility for it." His eyes twinkled when he spoke and I could tell he took pride in his pronouncement.

"You ought to have been a preacher," Josie observed and we all laughed.

After the watering, the women still hadn't come out. I happened by the open bedroom window and I could hear their voices. Aunt

Bennie, uncharacteristically tense, was saying, "That doesn't make a grain of sense to me." Though tense, her voice was low, just audible through the window, which she must have been standing near. Mother said something about the Lord's will. I stepped closer, but Uncle Reed saw me. He waved me back to the garden. "How 'bout a ride?" he offered. "I haven't had a good look see at Bombingham since the last time somebody blowed it up." We piled into the car and began to ride.

We rode to Sixth Avenue to look at the bombed-out store. Uncle Reed wanted to look at "Dynamite Hill," but neither of us knew how to get there. Then he had the idea that we should find where they were putting in the new "six-way." He had done roadwork once, and talked about the new kinds of machinery they had to do it with. I knew the general direction of the construction site, the Red Mountain Parkway. When we found the new road it was only a swath of bare red earth cut through the trees. We didn't see any machinery. We drove up Red Mountain and looked at Vulcan, a towering, ungraceful statue of the god of iron. "He ain't got on drawers," Vach exclaimed, pointing to the exposed rump of the god. Indeed, we children found two things remarkable about the statue; that his buttocks were exposed and that the light in his torch, when red, indicated a traffic death. We didn't go inside, this being the white part of town. Instead, we drove to Terminal Station so that Vachel could see the big iron sign, a structure made of a crosshatch of steel girders and cables with the words "Birmingham, the Magic City."

Vachel wanted to know what kind of magic went on in the magic city. Was it like a caped magician pulling rabbits out of his hat and sawing naked women in half? Uncle Reed wondered where he had gotten the notion that naked women were involved in it at all. "Just look at that!" Uncle Reed pointed and slowed before the sign. Behind the sign was the huge, domed terminal building. "Looks like a sultan lives there—and he flies out on a flying carpet. That's how come it's magic."

Uncle Reed suggested that we show Vachel the airport next. I said okay, but Josie said what was on my mind. "Why don't we go see Daddy?" Uncle Reed kept on a minute about new airplanes that didn't have propellers, and I reminded him that they weren't "new" anymore. "They're called 'jets.'"

"Okay, Mr. Smarty Britches. Bet you didn't know they can fly around the world in less than a day." I told him that the Russian Lunik was almost ready to touch down on the dark side of the moon. "Sure 'nough," he said and snorted. "Which hotel is it? Gaston's? I don't know where it is."

It was only a short way from the train station. As we got closer, the street numbers went from high to low, and my heart began to pound. Suppose he wasn't there, I thought. Suppose he didn't want to see us. Uncle Reed looked nervous as he parked the car in the lot of the small, two-story motel. He told us to stay put and he got out and went to the office, located where the building made an angle, the base of an L. I told him what the room number was, but he said he would go to the office, anyway, to see if our father was "available." Uncle Reed took ages in the office and I began to get antsy—a knot in my stomach. Josie asked me to open the car door, and she got out. I didn't say a word to her. I knew exactly what she was thinking. He was our father and we knew where he was, and he would be glad to see us. We climbed the stairwell at the end of the building and went down the balcony until we came to the room. I nodded to Josie to knock, and looked back at the parking lot to see Vachel pointing us out to Uncle Reed. Just then, Father opened the door.

He was dressed in strap undershirt as if he had just gotten up again. He looked surprised for a second and then asked if everything was all right. I said that Uncle Reed was here. He bent down and hugged Josie. "Daddy loves you," he said. He slapped my back and waved down to Uncle Reed.

Uncle Reed looked about the motel room and talked. It reminded him of when he drove a truck out of New York City and occasionally stayed in motel rooms around the East Coast. He laughed at how the motels would advertise that they welcomed colored but when you got into the motel you found they had a special section for colored—even in the North.

"Well, ain't that just the whole country," my father said. He appeared to be distracted. Finally, he asked about our mother. No one really had an answer. Josie just looked blankly. Uncle Reed admitted he hadn't seen her. He shook his head as if some great and unavoidable calamity had taken place. All I could say was that she was the same, though I didn't feel that at all. I found it hard to talk in front of Uncle Reed and Vachel. My mother was changing, and changing everyday so that if you compared her to the mother we had at Christmastime, you wouldn't have known her. My father must have read my thoughts. He patted my head. He put on his shirt and picked up Josie. "Why are we sitting around here on a Saturday? Let's go see what the world is doing."

We walked around Kelly Ingram Park, across the street from the motel. Uncle Reed insisted it was a "colored" park, not a "colored-only" park. Nothing was for "colored only," not even bad luck—but, of course, many things were "white only." My father pointed out the Sixteenth Street Baptist Church to Uncle Reed and told him it was the movement headquarters.

"Agitate, agitate," Uncle Reed said.

"King and his men sleep over at the motel, but they have their big meetings at the church." Father said that Reverend King's room was on the other end of the motel from his. Cars came and went all hours of the night, and preachers in dark suits were always running in and out. Occasionally a white man, a federal man, would go cautiously about. It was funny that you could always tell the federal men by their nervous walk, even before you noticed they were white.

We strolled past the church and down Seventh Avenue, where we ran into a crowd standing along the street that ran up to the city hall. Police cars and paddy wagons blocked off the entrance to the building, and policemen stood in line about halfway up the flight of stairs. At first sight, the situation didn't seem serious. The policemen could have been preparing for a chorus line as easily as a protest march.

"Agitate, agitate," Uncle Reed said again and smiled.

Father stopped. "Maybe we should turn back." He considered for a moment and then, rather than turning around, he took a step in the direction of the crowd. Uncle Reed took a tentative step after Father and broke into a broad grin. "Ain't no harm in just looking," he said.

My father sat Josie on his shoulders and we stood at the back of the crowd, two or three people deep. These people were bystanders who had come, as we had, to look at rather than to participate in the protest. Someone said that King himself was coming to be arrested.

I began to get anxious, not knowing what to expect. It was like a parade in some aspects, with people lining the streets, full of anticipation, only the white-helmeted riot police charged the air with tension. Silently they strutted past us, two abreast, big, angry-looking, and gripping the leashes of German shepherds, as muscular as lions.

Up to that point, it was the "German" in "German shepherd" that threatened me. I had heard postwar propaganda about the evils of German Nazism. Beginning that spring, though, I, like so many black children, would come to see the shepherds as objects of terror. Even now, when one presents its anvil head with the patches of brown on gray to me for a pet, I struggle to suppress a tremble of fear of the black-lipped snarl and sharp, white teeth.

No one in the crowd seemed to pay the policemen or the dogs much attention, and yet the crowd as a whole seemed very much aware of them. The police and dogs were the shepherds and we blacks were the sheep, parting to let the shepherds through and yet seeming to ignore them.

Father pointed out Bull Connor, a squat man wearing a porkpie hat. "I bet he's sore," Uncle Reed said with a slight taunt in his voice. "Got his butt whipped in that election."

Father looked at Uncle Reed. "You talk like you had something to do with it."

"I can't say I got to vote against him, but I *prayed* against him." He shook his head and laughed. "Well, at least I can get some second-hand pleasure out of it."

The crowd seemed to get restless. People complained that marchers were running on "CPT," colored people's time. Someone else joked, that it was colored *preachers'* time. Another supposed that it was part of the ploy to keep the police waiting, off guard and nervous.

We heard a commotion, and then the crowd hushed. For a moment all I heard was the scuffing of feet on the pavement. Then I saw about fifty protesters, dressed in Sunday clothes, walking in unison behind three robed ministers. After a few moments of silence, the crowd began to shout encouragement. Uncle Reed read the placards out aloud: "Khrushchev can eat here, why can't we?" People laughed, sometimes nervously, sometimes celebratory. The marchers began to sing, "Ain't nobody gonna turn me around, turn me around!"

My father had a look of curiosity and expectation, his eyes were wide and his mouth slightly opened. Uncle Reed seemed so delighted he actually clapped his hands and danced a step. Vachel gave him a bewildered look. I had a mixed feeling that ran back and forth between delight and fear. One minute, I felt something terrible would happen, but the next minute, the fear was mitigated by the calm demeanor of the crowd. Suddenly the line stopped. Down the block, in front of city hall, Bull Connor had stepped out to confront the ministers. Bull Connor called to them through a bullhorn, though he was well within speaking distance.

"Oh Lord," Uncle Reed said, "here it comes."

The police began to escort marchers to the paddy wagons. The marchers went along willingly, politely, almost as if the policemen were escorting them across the street. Garbed in gun belt and billy club, all a policeman had to do was to take a demonstrator by the arm or to touch him on the shoulder and the demonstrator went easily to the paddy wagon. Some of the women demonstrators had difficulty stepping into the high backs of the wagons because of their skirts and the policemen braced them by their elbows to help them in. When one paddy wagon was filled, it drove off and the demonstrators and policemen, together, waited patiently for the next one.

"Like lambs to the slaughter," Uncle Reed said.

Though the marchers were quiet, except for an occasional chant, the observers were not. Some yelled at the policemen, but cowardly, from the back of the crowd. When one of the onlookers, mistaken for a marcher, was tapped by a policeman, he resisted going to the paddy wagon, but relented when threatened with a club. A complaint rose from the crowd and then quieted. Then suddenly, a dog lit into a man. Whether he was a bystander or a marcher, I couldn't tell. He was a tall man dressed in good clothes. The dog's growl was shrill but short. The man's pants ripped with a shriek. The crowd swayed as people pushed back from the dog. In a second, I had lost sight of the man and only heard the shouting of the policemen, and the barking and snarls of dogs. With his free hand, my father tugged my shoulder. Uncle Reed had already picked up Vachel, and we made a hasty retreat to the motel.

11

BACK AT THE MOTEL, Father and Uncle Reed talked on the balcony outside the room while we children waited in the car. Father gestured in an agitated way, his hands making shapes in the air. Uncle Reed looked down at his shoes as he played with the wire panels that made up the railing. I imagined that Father was explaining why he had left the house and was beseeching Uncle Reed for help. Finally, Uncle Reed put his hand on Father's shoulder, a rigid but sympathetic gesture. Next, he was bounding down the stairs, and Father was standing alone. He turned and gave a short wave before he went into the room.

We were famished when we got back to the house, and Grandma Pic was slicing country ham and making sandwiches. "Where y'all been?" she demanded when we came into the house.

"We went to see Daddy at a motel," Josie answered. Grandma Pic splattered a dollop of mayonnaise on a slice of light bread and spread it with two swipes of her knife. "Wash up and come eat. Walter, baby." She stopped me but didn't look up. "How your daddy?"

"Fine."

"He say when he coming back?"

"In a couple of days."

"Then what?"

"I don't know."

"He just fixin' to be a man on the loose?"

Uncle Reed interrupted. "I had a good talk with him. He's coming back as soon as Clara says."

"Clara ain't got nothing to do with it. Clara sick."

"He says it's best for the situation that he keeps some distance. Now, he told me plain as day—and I believe him—that he ain't run off. He just put some space between him and Clara."

"Space?"

"So he won't do nothing to her."

"Do? What do you mean *do*?" Grandma Pic stopped making sandwiches and turned, holding the knife, to face Uncle Reed.

"If Clara didn't say, it's not my place," said Uncle Reed.

Grandma Pic studied Uncle Reed. "I see. So, that was what that mark was. He gone back to that again." She turned to me. "Walter, what's been going on here?"

"Nothing." She pointed the knife at me, not so much a threat as to underscore her authority. "They had a fight," I confessed, on the verge of tears.

"He beat her?"

"He told me he smacked her," said Uncle Reed. "He lost his temper with her, that's all. He's sorry."

"He ain't sorry yet." She put down the knife and put a plate of sandwiches on the table. "Y'all eat," she ordered and marched off to the back of the house. Even though Grandma Pic was petite, she seemed much taller than I, much taller even than the lanky Uncle Reed, who was nearly as tall as my father. She came back a moment later with Vachel and Josie in tow, and got us started with lunch. Then she went to the back again. From the kitchen we could hear Grandma Pic's and Mother's pitched voices, exclaiming in angry and in pleading tones.

"Y'all want to hear a story?" Uncle Reed said, trying to draw our attention away from the commotion in the back of the house. "Did I tell you the one about the ghost that live down on the creek behind the house?" No one answered him and he took that as a cue to launch into a story about a man decapitated in a car wreck whose floating head was visible on some moonlit nights. No one was paying attention. No one was eating except Vachel.

After a few minutes, Aunt Bennie came into the kitchen. She leaned against the sink counter and bit into a half of a sandwich. "This here is getting too crazy for me," she said to Uncle Reed. Then, as if to soften her words, "Crazy like Bozo the Clown. You kids like Bozo?"

No one answered, and a moment later, Grandma Pic came into the kitchen. "Every time I turn around, look like somebody trying to drop a bombshell on me. Walter, you all right? You ain't hurt, are you?"

"Ma'am?"

"Clara say Carl flung him against the wall. Say she won't have him back."

"Not in front of the children, Mama," Aunt Bennie said.

"It done happened in front of them. We ain't hiding nothing from them by talking about it in secret."

"They don't want to hear all this."

"Yes we do," Josie said.

"He didn't hurt me," I said. "He didn't mean it."

"Mean it or not, he done it," Grandma Pic said. "And there's just one thing to do now. *I'm staying here.* Clara can't be left alone. Y'all go back and get my things and I'll stay here."

"Don't you think I should have a say in that?" Mother stood in the passage between the kitchen and the den. She had on a gingham shift and a scarf around her head. "It is *my* family, after all."

"You don't want me to stay?" Grandma Pic said, offended.

"I didn't say that, Mother."

"If you don't want me to stay . . . then the children can come down to Coosada with me, if you—"

"I never said I didn't want you to stay, Mother. I'm just saying that I *do* have a say in this."

"What say, Clara? You are sick. You don't have a choice. These children can't raise themselves."

"Why not? We raised ourselves."

"I wouldn't go that far," Aunt Bennie said.

"You wouldn't 'cause *I* raised you."

"Don't you dare!" Grandma Pic said. "I did the best I could in a hard situation—"

"We all did," said Uncle Reed.

"Besides, this is different. You are sick and you got a family. I didn't have nobody until Reed—"

"For the hundredth time—I am not sick."

"What the hell do you call it, then? You can barely get your self out of bed."

"I am not sick. I am *healed.* I believe God for my healing."

"You don't even see that on Billy Graham." Aunt Bennie flicked one nail under the other.

"I don't care what you say. I am trusting the Lord for my healing. If I don't trust the Lord for a healing, I can't have one. And I'm not letting Satan cloud my faith—"

"Now we Satan—"

"Be quiet, Bennie," Grandma Pic said. "Clara, baby, nobody is trying to cloud your faith. We believe in the power of the Lord, too. It's scriptural. But the Lord works in *mysterious* ways—He heals *through* the doctor—that's why He give us all this modern medicine. Now, I believe we must trust Him. We must pray, but we don't tell the Lord what to do. We pray, but we can't depend on Him, not like that. We must pray—but we must *act*."

"Yes, indeed," Uncle Reed said. "That's why they call it the Book of Acts—'cause Apostle Paul had faith, but he also acted."

In its simple way, Grandma Pic's and Uncle Reed's argument made sense to me. I had been following the argument back and forth, turning my head to Grandma Pic and back again to Mother, but now I focused on Mother. I thought now there would be a light of recognition in her face, a sudden submission to the common sense of the argument.

Mother was quiet for a moment. She seemed considering the debate point by point. Then her face tightened. "Is that what happened to Daddy?" she asked. "You trusted and you acted and you see what happened."

"This has nothing to do with Walter Lee!" Grandma Pic shouted.

"You know we did the best we could for your daddy," Uncle Reed said. "You know that, Clara."

"And what good did it do?"

"Don't throw that at me!" Grandma Pic had folded her arms and turned her back to my mother. "What could any of us do? We did all we could. What else could we do? It was just God's will—"

"That's right, Mother, God's will—*God was in it.* God's in everything. If *God* wills it, what can *you* do?"

Grandma Pic seemed stumped, but Aunt Bennie said quietly, "Well, you could see a doctor. That's the least you could do. We did everything for Daddy, but you're not doing a thing for yourself."

"What can a doctor do, Bennie?"

"I don't know, do *I* look like a doctor?"

"A doctor can't do anything because . . . I *have* seen a doctor. More than one for that matter, and they can't do anything because . . . there's nothing to do. It's inoperable."

"Inoperable?" said Grandma Pic. "What does that mean?"

"It means they can't operate on it, Mother."

"I know *what* it means! But what are you *saying* to me, Clara?"

Grandma Pic put her hand to her forehead. "Why are you dropping this bombshell on me? What did I ever do for you to drop this bombshell on me?" Grandma Pic, bursting into tears, pushed Mother aside and went to the back of the house.

"Now, look what you started," Aunt Bennie said to Mother. "Couldn't leave it be, could you, Clara?"

Mother looked down and rubbed her hands together. "I apologize," she said when she looked up again. "I'm under so much stress now. You don't understand how much stress it is. But the Lord is going to see me through it. I believe Him for His word. I believe Him—thank you, Jesus—I trust in Him for my miracle." No one said anything. "Waltie believes me, don't you, Waltie?"

Why did she ask me? I didn't know what to say. She looked like someone who was going crazy, was all I could think. Her eyes were shiny and cold; her hair was tied up in a floral-print scarf; the ends of her mouth strained downward so that her face was an ugly mask of herself. What if I said the wrong thing? What if saying nothing was wrong?

"Leave him out of it," Aunt Bennie said. "He's just a kid; he doesn't know what to believe."

"He's my Waltie!" Mother said. "He's my child, aren't you, Waltie? Don't you belong to Mama?"

"Yes, ma'am."

"What about me?" Josie asked quietly, nearly in tears.

"Oh, yes, yes, yes," Mother said. "You both are mine. You won't leave Mama, will you?"

"No, ma'am."

"I knew you wouldn't. Because you believe. The Bible says that children will believe. And they do." She came to the table and kissed us, first Josie and then me. Her breath was hot and smelled of mucus. After she had gone to the back of the house, I felt like I wanted to throw up.

. . .

ONLY VACHEL seemed to have had an appetite for play. He ran around in circles in the yard, Bingo chasing him, while Josie and I sat like pumpkins on the top of the picnic table. The afternoon was warm, spring had come early. Already dandelions, buttercups, and daffodils grew in patches around the yard.

"What does 'act' mean?" Josie touched me on the knee. She looked bright and brown in the sunlight.

"It means to do something."

"To do what?"

"To do . . . anything."

"That's what I thought it meant." She folded her hands in her lap and looked at them.

The afternoon and evening passed slowly. I felt like a prisoner in my backyard. I was afraid to go inside the house because the constant arguing upset me. I didn't want to play, least of all with Lamar because I might have to explain to him what was going on in the house; besides, Grandma Pic had ordered us not to leave the yard. "Stay in the yard," was her favorite admonition. Part of me wished that we could go live with Grandma Pic. Being bound to the yard mattered little in Coosada, a crossroads in the flood plain of the Alabama River outside of Montgomery. We would have had the free- dom of the expansive yard and fields and the country roads to ride bicycles on, but my gut wouldn't let me feel it. How could I leave my mother when she was sick? "You won't leave Mama, will you?" Mother had asked. Nor could I leave my father; in spite of what Grandma Pic said, he hadn't deserted us—and I knew he wouldn't hurt us. Then it struck me. I would ask Aunt Bennie to stay with us. Josie liked the idea, too. She thought that it would be fun to have Vachel stay, as well. By suppertime, the issue was settled among us children. Until our father returned, which he had said would only be a couple of days, Aunt Bennie would sleep in my room. I would set up the folding cot and sleep in Josie's room. Vachel and Josie would share her bed. All that was left was for us to ask Aunt Bennie.

Supper was ham, biscuits, sweet potatoes, and a hefty serving of strained politeness. We ate in the dining room so everyone could have a place at the table. By this time, Mother had fixed her hair and put on makeup. She looked as well as ever. Uncle Reed said the grace, mumbling in a singsong. It was a dry, thin meal compared to the dinners we usually had when our family gathered. Grandma Pic could turn an ordinary Sunday dinner into a feast, and at the holidays, all the food couldn't fit on the table. There was so much food, and so good, that at the end of the meal, Father would lean back in his chair, rub his stomach, and say, "Piccadilly, my dear, once again, you have gone and outdone yourself. Truly, you have."

As we ate, Josie kept looking at me, and I knew she was waiting for me to ask Aunt Bennie to stay. But every time I cleared my throat and looked at Aunt Bennie, the taut silence among the adults choked me. One word about the situation might cause an explosion, I thought. After supper, as we took our plates to the kitchen, Josie gave me a little kick on the ankle.

"I'm going to ask when the time is right," I assured her.

"They'll be leaving in a minute," she whispered back.

"What are you two whispering about?" Aunt Bennie came into the kitchen with a handful of plates.

"Nothing," I told her.

Josie sighed heavily. "Aunt Bennie, can—"

"Can Vachel spend the night?" I interrupted.

"Lord, no," Aunt Bennie answered. "What y'all gone do with Vachel?"

Grandma Pic came into the kitchen. "I reckon we all be staying the night. Too dark to be driving back now."

"What? Mama, the car got headlights," Aunt Bennie said.

"No need to be driving around at night like a fool if you don't have to—Saturday night, too. And Reed done had a full day. No. There is plenty room for us to put up here for the night."

Grandma Pic was of an old school of thinking that good folks stayed in at night. The dark roads held all manner of dangers, but none worse than drunken white men—Klansmen—and taking a long trip at night on the deserted roads through rural Alabama was an unnecessary risk.

Aunt Bennie resigned herself to the stayover. Mother resigned herself to it, also. She told me to set up the cot in Josie's room and we gave my bed and the den sofa over to our guests.

LATER, I SNEAKED past Grandma Pic and took another nighttime ride to the railroad bridge to look at the skyline. When I returned to the yard, I saw the glow of Uncle Reed's pipe where he sat at the picnic table. He called me over, and I sat on the tabletop beside him. "Where you been riding in the dark, Son?"

"Just around. Thinking."

He grunted. "I reckon, Waltie, you got a right much to think about. I'm sorry, Son. God never did promise us life was going to be easy or make much sense."

The smoke from his pipe smelled like cherries, and sitting with him, quietly at first, breathing in the smoke, made me feel grown up. I bent forward, resting my elbows on my knees, a posture I had seen the men in my family assume. "Uncle Reed," I said slowly, "can you tell me the story of my granddaddy?" After the argument between my mother and grandmother, the story seemed important. It had something to do with why my mother wouldn't see a doctor.

He shifted his position, and seemed to have been debating the request with himself. "Son, it's a kind of rough story. That's why we don't talk about it much."

"But Mama . . . she is mad with Grandma Pic—"

"Your Mama ain't got no right to be mad. Grandma Pic ain't done nothing wrong; we all did what we could." He took a deep breath and I knew the story was coming. "Listen, first, you have to understand. It was rough for colored people. We got it easy now compared to back then. Dr. King and those other Negroes marching and everything— I'm glad they are doing it, but twenty years ago, they couldn't even march in their own backyards. Talk about going to jail for freedom. Shucks. White people would just shoot 'em down in broad daylight. Now, I can tell you about some mean white people—"

"Did Granddaddy kill somebody?"

"As sure as I'm breathing he did not. But you must understand, Son, he didn't have to." He shook his head. "It's a rough story, and I can see now that it ain't over. I can see that it's still in your mama and your grandma, too. I reckon a thing like that don't go away. It just keeps alive from generation to generation. Before it's over, I reckon it'll touch you, too." He smoked his pipe, blowing out a cloud of the fruity smoke. "Your life ain't your own, you see. It's everybody else's life, too. You might think you are in the world all by yourself, struggling and doing and making the best for yourself, but you're not alone. First of all, there is everybody else—how many millions and millions of people?"

"One hundred and eighty million in America," I recited and my stomach knotted. I knew from his serious preamble that it was a difficult story for him.

That so, Mr. Smarty?

"Anyway, you don't breathe this earthly air by yourself. If you did, you wouldn't be breathing it for long. Everybody is hooked up to everybody else in order to get along. Problem is, it's not just the good that you have to deal with, but the bad, too. People can help you, and they can hurt you. People you don't even know can destroy you and that was what happened to your grandfather, my brother." Uncle Reed turned toward me and crossed one hand under one arm while the other held the pipe to his mouth. "It's funny. If we had wanted to go up North—there were good jobs in Detroit and Chicago—but we were comfortable in the South. A colored somebody being comfortable in Old Dixie? People up North laugh at that. It ain't that we like Mr. Jim Crow—but this here is our home. This is where we belong—we the ones that tilled the fields and built up the buildings, just as much as the white man. So folks who say we crazy for staying here, they just don't have any pride in what we done here. And I tell you one thing—most of them will come crawling on back down here, I can see it in their eyes when they come for a visit how much they miss down here. They always talking about country cooking: 'Give me some ham hocks and collards greens.' Can't they cook collards in Detroit? It's not the collards they're craving—it's the whole thing. It's home. It's in their blood." He shifted again and his voice softened. "Anyway, your granddaddy moved up to Birmingham from Coosada and started up at TCI." His voice turned slightly gravelly. "Then one Saturday, a pretty day, Walter Lee was arrested."

12

T HIS IS WHAT Uncle Reed told me.
It began on a Saturday. My mother was in the third grade
and in love with school. She was sitting on the front porch of the
shotgun house they had on Fair Street in Sootville, reading to Aunt
Bennie, who was just about six. The house sat in a dip in the middle of
the street and the chimney stacks of the foundries loomed over it.
The heat had broken and the October afternoon held a hint of the
fall. The crowns of the oaks were blackened, burned by the heat and
smoke. The smell of cabbage, fried pork, and cornbread came from
the kitchens up and down the street.

Mother loved the bold print and sounds of words, Uncle Reed
said. She loved the pictures that went along with the stories, like that
of Little Red Hen and her chicks.

"'Who will help me plant the wheat?'

"'Not I,' said the dog.

"'Not I,' said the pig.

"'Then my chicks and I will plant the wheat,' said Little Red Hen. And they did."

A car stopped in front of the house, and my mother looked up from her book. She recognized the preacher, she later told, but couldn't remember his name. He had a sober look on his face as he stepped from the dusty street onto the porch. She put the book in her lap as the man approached. He smiled. "Is your mama home, little girl?"

Before Mother could answer, she heard Grandma Pic behind her, opening the screen door. "Aft'noon, Reverend Wilcox." Grandma Pic shooed my mother from the chair and offered it to the preacher. The preacher's smile went away. "No'm. This here news is best said standing up."

Grandma Pic stiffened, sighed, and took hold of the children's hands. "Go ahead, Reverend." She was used to hard news, Uncle Reed said, and always took it standing up. Before the preacher had finished, he had taken the chair, but my grandmother and her children remained standing. It was hard for my mother to follow what the preacher was saying, but as she understood it, her father was dead. She told Uncle Reed that her father had been caught by white men and taken to the jail and hanged. She derived this more from the serious tone of the adults and from what she knew of jails. Later, Grandma Pic and Uncle Reed explained that Walter Lee was *not* dead, just under arrest. Then Mother imagined her father in a gang, linked by heavy iron chains to other black men, and forced off to the coal mines. For a few months, Walter Lee had been a miner. Even as a child, Mother talked about the smell of his sweaty clothes, full of oily coal dust, and his blackened skin and red eyes. Later her father had gotten a job in the foundry and was happier.

The story of what happened unfolded slowly. They thought they knew it all after talking to Reverend Wilcox, only to find out there was more to it. Then the sheriff told them part of it. Then someone from the neighborhood who had heard about it from someone else added to it. Even strangers told them about it. Each time they learned more about it, the less clear it all became.

Several months before Walter Lee was arrested, a black man had robbed three sisters from a prominent white family, and killed two of them. In another version of the same story, the robber wasn't a black man but a white man in black face. In this version, the white man, most likely white trash from Hueytown, knew he could get away with anything if he blamed it on a black man. In yet another version, there was a party of black men, rough Negroes from over in Mississippi. They were renegades who roamed the country raping white women and church-going colored women. This was a version from a white man.

For a little while, the white people in Birmingham went crazy, and black people were afraid to leave their neighborhoods, afraid of the white people they worked for, afraid to shop or venture out after dark. This was the time that white men blew up the barbershop in Sootville. It happened at night and no one was in the shop. They had heard the blast: it was near enough that Grandma Pic had come into the front room where the children slept and had taken them to the back bedroom. They had lain on the floor for the rest of the night.

A few nights later there had been shooting. Machine gunfire, Walter Lee had said. *"Poppity pop, poppity pop."* Mother remembered the rhythm of his mimicry and all her life she would say that machine guns said *"poppity pop."* That night, too, they had slept on the floor.

Bombings and shootings were going around in Birmingham in colored neighborhoods. Posses dragged black men from their beds and ransacked their houses, looking for the murderer, or murderers, depending on who was in the posse. Walter Lee said he wished to God that the son of a bitch who killed those white gals would give himself up before somebody else got hurt.

After a few weeks things were quiet again. School started and Mother became absorbed, enraptured by it. According to Uncle Reed, the blackboard was a miraculous invention to her: A great slab of waxy slate on which the teacher wrote sentences, tapping and squeaking the chalk as she went. Mother loved to be called upon to write on the board. She learned to avoid the slick spots where the chalk wouldn't stick. She relished making straight lines and smooth loops. When her letters were not perfect, she insisted on erasing them and beginning again, though the teacher huffed impatiently.

Even before she started first grade, Mother knew all of her alphabets. She did not sing them like the other girls. She could start at any place in the sequence and recite them, and numbers, too. She often got bored reciting numbers, but if asked, she could recite them to a thousand. Her father had taught her. Now in third grade, the teacher gave her books to take home and read. She loved to read because the reading put pictures in her head and took her far away.

That Saturday, her father had gone to a barbershop on Fourth Avenue, a few miles away. Uncle Reed had the only car in the family, so her father had walked. On the way back, a car pulled onto the sidewalk and blocked his progress. A white man jumped out, pistol in hand. The man ordered her father to lie on the bricks and he shouted and kicked at her father while he lay. All her father did was cover his head and cry out, "What I done? What I done?"

Later the police came and took her father to the jail. There he learned that the man, Mr. Williams, was the brother of the sisters who had been killed. The surviving sister had been in the car with him, and had identified Walter Lee as the man who had attacked her.

That was when Walter Lee asked for the preacher.

By the time the preacher arrived, the situation had changed for the better. The sheriff of Jefferson County, where the crime had taken place, told Walter Lee and the preacher that the woman was confused. She's probably not in her right mind after all that had happened to her. Walter Lee did not match the description of the assailant. The assailant was short, stocky, and a very *black,* almost *purple* Nigra, the woman had originally reported. And he spoke with a *northern* accent. "He wasn't from around here." Walter Lee was tall, yellow, and spoke with a swinging lilt that came from high back in his mouth. His was the lilt of the Alabama River licking the mudflats. Walter Lee was as 'Bama as 'Bama could get.

It seemed impossible that the white woman could have made such a misidentification. What could have been in her mind when she saw Walter Lee from her car window, saw him strolling with his long strides, his arms swinging in rhythm, his mouth puckered in a whistle? What could have made her think that she could identify him? Uncle Reed asked. Was it the way the sunlight fell across the bridge of his nose, the way it shone off his freshly pomaded hair? Was it the far-away, dreamy look in his eyes? Walter Lee loved to dream. Did she just want to slap him back to reality?

Or was she deranged? Beaten nearly to death, and barely recovered from gunshot wounds, perhaps she was frightened of everything that moved, especially if it looked like a black man. Perhaps he was the very first black man she had looked at since the incident, or perhaps she just felt a need to get revenge. In her wildness, she didn't care who caught her wrath—just as long as he was black. Since all black people were connected, all from Africa, all knowing one another, or married to one another, then smashing one like a pine beetle would somehow slap at the one who was responsible. Was this what she was thinking?

The preacher assured Grandma Pic that Walter Lee would be released the next day. He said the sheriff thought it best to keep her husband in the jail overnight, in case some of the "county boys" got ideas. As the preacher left, he said that he would drive the family over to the jailhouse after church service.

Uncle Reed didn't attend the Sunday service but said it drew a larger crowd than usual. Reverend Wilcox gave a rousing sermon. He made Grandma Pic and her children sit in the front pew. He compared Walter Lee to Shadrach, Meshach, and Abednego in Nebuchadnezzar's furnace. "Ole King Nebuchadnezzar," he hissed, "was the mightiest of kings, but he was still a man. Man ain't got nothing on

God. Man with all his book learning and inventions can't sway the hand of God. It ain't what man say or do. It's what God say! Ole King say, 'Burn 'em up! Throw 'em into the fiery furnace and burn 'em up.' But it was not in God's plan to scorch his children. He brought 'em out!" Reverend Wilcox came down from the pulpit and stood in front of the family. "Life is a hard trial, sometimes. Sometimes we wonder why God makes it so miserable for us poor colored people. It's hard for us to understand because we are just men, but even if God had not brought his children out of the fiery furnace, even if he had allowed them to be scorched and burned, it would not have been the hand of man that done it, but God's hand! Everything that happens on the face of the earth is in God's plan. God has providence, not man! All we must do is to be faithful. Cast your faith on God, for in Him all things are possible!" The preacher made Grandma Pic and the children stand while he prayed. "Cast your buckets down into the well of the everlasting." Mother did not like standing in front of the congregation. "Daniel was thrown into a den of lions, and didn't the Lord deliver Daniel?" She didn't want people looking at her like she was a circus animal, a trick monkey. "Job was tried, and didn't he come through? And yes, yes, didn't they crucify my Lord?"

After the service, the churchwomen offered Grandma Pic their condolences and patted the children's heads, giving them sad, encouraging looks. My mother didn't want their pity, and when they said that it wasn't God's will to let anything bad happen to her father, she wanted to ask them how they knew. Besides, she reasoned, if it was God's will, what good was praying about it? What good was their pity?

Walter Lee was not released to them when they went to the jail to get him. There was a complication, a policeman said. Later the sheriff told them that it was obvious that Walter Lee was the wrong man, but they couldn't release him as long as Miss Williams was still confused about it. She had been promised a chance, the next day, to identify Walter Lee in a line-up.

The next day, the sheriff brought Walter Lee to an office in the jail building and asked him to stand in front of the great, oaken desk. Walter Lee was nervous, the sheriff later told Grandma Pic and Uncle Reed, but he assured my grandfather that he had nothing to be afraid of. Not only did he not match the description, Preacher Wilcox and a half dozen respectable Nigras had already vouched that he was in Sootville, on the west end of the city, when the murders were taking place on the east side. "Ain't no blood on your hands," the sheriff said and slapped Walter Lee on the back.

A deputy escorted in the brother and sister. They stood side by side. Both were in their twenties and well dressed. My grandfather must have felt the brother study him. The brother's face was lean with handsome cheekbones and his skin had an athletic rouge. He held his body stiffly and pressed his mouth into a thin, lipless line. Uncle Reed saw him at the trial.

The sister, by comparison, was pale. Her eyes were red with black circles underneath, and her lips twitched. She was afraid, my grandfather must have thought, and he must have been afraid, too. *Oh, sweet Jesus, let her have some common sense.* My grandfather closed his eyes and let out his breath. He felt like he had no bones, no shape. Whatever this young woman with the sad, crazy eyes said next would give him his shape. Whatever shape it was, it would be new. Just one word from a girl half his age would determine the rest of his life. But isn't that always the case? If not that thin, frightened, rich girl, then someone else, some other circumstance. From conception, a body's life is determined by happenstance. Some of it makes sense: if you put your finger in a fire, you will be burned. But so much of it depended on what seemed to be coincidence. Suppose he hadn't decided to get a haircut at three o'clock and had gone at four? An hour, ten minutes, just thirty seconds would have made a difference between that particular judgment or not. Or suppose the Sootville barbershop hadn't been bombed and he had gone there, just around the corner, rather than trotting down to the Famous barbershop. Or suppose that black bastard who had killed the girls had not killed them, or had been caught. What if the sisters had taken their picnic stroll at one o'clock rather than noon? Or if they had never been born, then they would never have been murdered, or if they *all* had been murdered, then that slip of a witness wouldn't have stood before him, teetering between reprieve and condemnation. The afternoon of the arrest, my grandfather must have been thinking about the sweetness of the air, how blue the sky was, how the breeze kept the mill smoke away from downtown. It was his first Saturday off in a month, and even though he was poor and a Negro in Jim Crow's South, he couldn't have imagined a more perfect day. He had had a haircut and a nip of rye, and he felt good about himself as he strolled along. When that car slowed and the young white woman pointed at him, he ought to have been afraid. It was rare, and almost always meant trouble, to be pointed at by a white person, especially a woman. But he strode on, his thoughts returning to the pleasures of the day until he met the car again.

The next moment, his eyes still closed, Walter Lee felt something punch him in the chest. He fell backward, over the great desk. Then there was a sting in his arm and another one in his hand as he brought it up in surprise. By the time he realized he was bleeding, the policeman had wrestled the gun away from the brother. The brother spat at Walter Lee. "You killed my sisters," he said, his mouth distorted. "Just little girls! What did they ever do to you?" Veins bulged in his temples. He wrestled with the policeman, trying to get at Walter Lee.

When Walter Lee caught his breath, his chest gurgled and blood gushed into his mouth. He looked at the sister. She hadn't moved; she looked confused.

IT WAS LONG after dark before the sheriff of Jefferson County came to the front of the shotgun on Fair Street. Mother thought he was bringing her father home. In the two days since the arrest, all the black people had been saying what a good man the sheriff was. In his sermon, Reverend Wilcox had marveled at the good treatment the sheriff had given them. He was living proof that all white people weren't bad.

The sheriff took off his hat and fingered it nervously as he stood on the porch and talked to the family. He insisted that everything would be all right, an overture to soften the blow of the news he brought. "The good news is he ain't dead."

The sheriff took them to Holy Family Hospital. Mother sat for hours in the wooden chairs in the colored area. Grandma Pic was rolling her hands, one over the other. She didn't wring them, but rubbed dry skin over dry skin. My mother watched, hypnotized by the movement of one hand over and under the other. The hands were waves at the ocean, Mother must have thought, though she had never seen the ocean. Yet, the hands sounded like waves at the ocean as the callused skin rasped across knuckles, the sound coming and going, and the hands coming and going, and the time passing.

Mother's back began to ache and she stood up and stretched. At the end of the room was a nurses' station. The nurse wore a white habit that seemed bilious and luminous. Was she an angel?

Mother's back straightened. She held her chin the way she had been told a princess would. She looked at Grandma Pic, whose eyes were closed and whose hands still moved around each other. Aunt Bennie was asleep across two chairs. Slowly, Mother walked toward the nurses' station. Uncle Reed said she walked like royalty. She placed her hands in front of her solar plexus, fingers gripping fingers. When she got to the nurses' station, she stood and waited until the nurse looked at her. The nun said nothing and Mother, very calmly and properly, making sure every word was enunciated, every letter clipped, asked, "May I, please, see my father's corpse."

The nurse looked perplexed, then laughed.

• • •

THE BASEMENT WARD where Walter Lee lay was dark and foul. The beds were occupied with men who stared at the family with dull eyes. One may have made an attempt at a nod, but no one spoke. Mother walked the length of the room before she got to her father's bed. Next to him was a burned man. He smelled of burned flesh and antiseptics.

Again, Mother thought her father was dead, but as Grandma Pic began to tend him, Mother realized he was only asleep. He had a sheet pulled up to his clavicle and tucked under his armpits. His bandaged arms lay on top of the sheets. When he opened his eyes, he seemed to see Mother first, and reached for her. She jumped away, her heart pounding, but he took her hand and pulled her toward him. "You my little peach pit," he said, "so sweet and suckable." No one wept. Soon a nun came in and asked them to leave.

For six weeks, Walter Lee fought infection and pneumonia. When he was strong enough, he was taken back to jail to await trial. He was held under very tight security, now, because rumor had it that he had raped the woman who accused him, though rape had never been a part of the original charge.

A few years earlier, a black man from near Sootville had been accused of raping a white woman. He had been her yard worker. They said when the woman brought him sweet tea and biscuits, he threw her into a pile of shrubbery clippings and ravaged her. Had the woman's husband not come home just then, the yard worker might have killed her. The yard worker got away, and there was a manhunt. Black men simply disappeared. A wife might call northern relatives with the hope that her man had suddenly run north, but she got no relief. When she asked around the pool halls and barbershops if the missing man had a mistress, someone he had taken off with, she got no relief. No one dragged the Cahaba or Black Warrior or Coosa for them, though skulls and leg bones washed up on the riverbanks from time to time.

Mother didn't see her father again until his trial. She sat in the gallery of the Jefferson County Courthouse, overlooking the court-room full of Birmingham's finest white men. They dressed in seer-sucker and held straw fedoras in their hands between their legs or capped on their knees. The few white women in attendance were clustered around the accuser. They mopped her face, fanned her, and raised glasses of water to her lips. The prosecutors sprawled at a table in front of the young woman. One smoked a cigarette, flicking the ash on the courtroom floor. Her father, the only dark-skinned per-son on the floor, sat stiffly at the defense's table. Walter Lee seemed to lean to the side where he had been shot, as if a rib had been taken out.

Her father's lawyer was a Jew, a lawyer for the ILD, the Interna-tional Labor Defense, and that worried the family. The sheriff called the ILD a bunch of "red troublemakers." Hiring them was a surefire way to get the jury to vote guilty. He advised the family to seek the mercy of the court. Grandma Pic, Uncle Reed, and Reverend Wilcox had debated whether the ILD would do more to harm than to help the case. Uncle Reed prevailed. He said the court was already in the pocket of the rich white folks. They all went to the same churches, and parties, and they were all married to one another. At least with the ILD, the truth would be told. The truth, Grandma Pic said, was that Walter Lee was damned either way. "He could have Jesus for a lawyer. . . ."

My mother heard her father as he testified, his voice was strained but soft, saying where he had been on the day of the murders and say-ing he knew nothing about them. He made such good sense to my mother; he sounded so truthful. It *was* the truth. How could any one of the men on the jury not believe him? Mother took her hand away from Grandma Pic, and rested it in her lap. She stared down into the courtroom, not looking at Walter Lee because she didn't have a good view of him, but looking at the jurors, their blank faces and placid hands. She couldn't tell what they were thinking, or if they were thinking at all. Would just one of them have the courage to stand up and say, "It's obvious that this man is innocent"? She stared, but what she saw was the deep hole her father was sliding into; he was already over the rim, and even though a thousand spectators stood looking into that hole with her, not one of them would reach out to him. This is what it is like to be a Negro, she thought. A Negro's lot in life is to be black. Black, black, black. Being so black, a Negro could only depend on God, and if God couldn't help him, then nothing could. God help my father, she prayed. God. God. God have mercy.

The family had come home during the recess. They expected the jury to be out for hours, perhaps even days. But twenty minutes after they got home, the sheriff knocked and stood on the front porch of the little wooden shack. Grandma Pic met him in the door. My mother and Aunt Bennie stood behind her. Aunt Bennie held on to the back of Grandma Pic's wrap-around apron. Even before the sheriff spoke, Mother heard what he had to say. It was a voice in her head, a white man's voice, calm and official, but genuinely full of regret. "Guilty and the sentence is death."

Later, the sheriff petitioned the governor. He collected signatures from several prominent white men, explaining that a mistake had been made. The petition said that Walter Lee was a good Negro, never a troublemaker. It noted his alibis and said that Miss Williams was probably still in shock from her brutal attack. It noted that Walter Lee had already suffered from having been shot by Mr. Williams in a fit of grief. Several months after the trial, the sheriff came again to the house to announce that the governor had looked favorably upon the petition. He had commuted the death sentence to life in prison. "Some justice, in the end."

Grandma Pic profusely thanked the sheriff, and he left seeming satisfied that he had done all a good white man could do. But when she shut the door on him, Grandma Pic cursed him. She said the justice was worse than death. Why not just kill the man outright and get it over with? "Gracious Lord," she said, "I wish he was dead." Three years later, Walter Lee died of pneumonia. By the time the family was notified, the state had already buried him.

13

AFTER HEARING Uncle Reed's story, I lay on the cot in Josie's room, unable to sleep. The house filled with various rhythms of sleep; both Grandma Pic and Uncle Reed snored, hers a wheeze and his a grunt. They had opened the den couch into a sleeper. First thing in the morning, they and Vachel would leave. Aunt Bennie had taken my bed, and Vachel, refusing to sleep with her, had curled up next to Josie.

I told Josie the story. I kept thinking she had fallen asleep. Then she complained that Vachel was taking all of the covers. By the time I finished the story, I was sure both she and Vachel were asleep. How could I blame them? Even as close to me as the story was, it seemed that it could only have happened to someone far away and unrelated to me. It happened to dangerous black men, to those who raped white women, or who acted uppity or sassed white people. Since Walter Lee hadn't been one of those, it couldn't have happened to him.

But it had happened so he must have done something wrong,

something to trigger it. Perhaps he had looked at Miss Williams in the wrong way, meeting her eye for a second too long. Or perhaps, as Uncle Reed said, he had walked too proudly that day, lost in a daydream; he had forgotten how a Negro should walk in downtown. He had held his head too high, or had walked a little too easy. His eyes were soft with daydreams.

Or maybe he had just been unlucky. He was Negro, so he didn't have much luck to begin with, and somehow he used up what little he had. He had lost favor with God—indeed, that was what it meant when your luck ran out. God controlled everything, so God controlled luck. Walter Lee had become unlucky; he had become cursed. He was Negro. He was the cursed of Ham. So was I. So was my poor mother. My limbs ached. How do you come out from under a curse?

Out of the blue, Josie spoke. "Waltie, I asked Aunt Bennie to stay."

"Why? I was going to do that."

"I know. But I asked her. Someone has to take care of us."

BECAUSE HIS MOTHER had insisted, Lamar and I rushed through our Sunday delivery, and it was Monday before I got a chance to tell him about the march I had witnessed. By then he had a march story of his own. I heard it during our route, and I heard it again and again during the course of the school day as he told it in the back of the classroom, on the playground, in the hallway, in the boys' room, and finally, in front of Mrs. Griffin's class. Mrs. Griffin tried to turn it into a lesson, occasionally stopping Lamar to correct his elocution and grammar.

Each time Lamar told his story, the march seemed to grow. He incorporated what bits he knew of my own story into his in a fairly seamless integration. Hearing his story grow, it occurred to me that I should discredit him—call him a fibber—but each time I heard the story, I reentered the excitement and wonder of the march: the trample of feet on the pavement, the shouts of encouragement, the singing, the bark and snarl of the dogs.

Lamar had witnessed the Sunday march in which three famous preachers had been arrested. He lavished details about how the preachers were dressed, each wearing a billowing, black robe, a crisp clerical collar, and a long, red-trimmed stole on which were embroidered golden crosses. Even in the swelter, these ministers emanated an air of cool. To Lamar they seemed to float above the pavement. He couldn't see their feet actually touch the ground, but only the swaying hems of their robes as they moved down the street. They seemed indifferent to the dogs. When the dogs nipped at the folds in the robes, the ministers whipped the material away from the foam-spitting mouths as if they were flagging capes in front of mad bulls. For a while there was a graceful Spanish dance between the proud ministers and the dogs, so enraged they stood on their hind legs and strained their leashes. Then, in a furious second, the tides turned. Four or five dogs, Lamar wasn't sure, were loosened on the ministers, tearing the robes to shreds, practically undressing the men with their teeth. The ministers held onto their dignity by standing still and straight as the dogs stripped them down to tatters of underclothes. Miraculously, the dogs drew no blood, but a bystander wasn't as lucky. A young man moved to interfere, and drew what appeared at first to be a pistol. The dogs bowled him over, and the policemen let them sink teeth into his arms and legs and stomach. Later, they saw he had been holding a wooden crucifix.

AUNT BENNIE had snacks waiting for us when we came home after school. She had taken off from her job at the factory in Philadelphia, but she said she could get it back in the fall. The factory often laid her off, anyway, so she was used to going months at a time without work.

During such times she would take on day work. These jobs didn't pay as well as the factory but they kept money coming in. Already she had found a cleaning job in Birmingham. She had been hired to work Wednesdays and Saturdays for the wife of one of the mill big shots. This way she could work and still be able to look after my mother. It was easy work, she declared. The old woman just wanted to be sure she had help on the days when her staff was off; the regular staff would have already done the hard work. Aunt Bennie said her job was mostly just to talk and kowtow to "her new Miss Queen." Her assessment of the new "work woman" was that she was "not too bad."

She was a typical old, rich woman, according to Aunt Bennie. She lived in a dreamworld of women's clubs and other overly important social activities. "The woman has never read a newspaper in her life so there is no danger that I might have to talk about something that would get me fired."

As we snacked and Aunt Bennie joked about her new boss, I realized what I liked so much about her. Aunt Bennie had a smaller frame and darker complexion than my mother; still, they shared facial features and mannerisms so much so that even strangers would recognize them as sisters. The big difference was that Aunt Bennie was not as sober as my mother. She had an easy slouch about her that allowed her to get close without making me feel she was on top of me. She laughed a lot, and enjoyed "putting on." She made funny faces and mocked people with ease. She would even mock a person while that person was listening, but it was done in such a way that the person usually ended up laughing at himself.

After the snack, Josie went to do her homework. I stayed behind in the kitchen and joked with Aunt Bennie. I was trying to figure out a way to ask her about my mother. I was quiet for just a moment, and Aunt Bennie tapped me on the head. "Now loverboy, what's on your mind?"

"I . . ."

"I *what*?" She pulled her glasses down on her nose and looked at me like an old schoolteacher. "What do you want to know?"

It was not so much that I had a question as it was that I wanted some comfort, some sign that everything would be all right. "I . . ."

"Well, whatever it is, it ain't your business," Aunt Bennie said quickly, but in a light tone. She turned away from me and busied herself wiping the counter. Then she turned back. "Contrary to popular thought, life *is* a bed of roses, but roses are full of thorns, you know, and sometimes you get stuck." She sat down at the table. "You need to go ahead and enjoy your mother while you can and enjoy her for who she is. You might not understand all that she is doing, but at some point, if you don't let her be herself, you are going to miss what little time you have with her." It was strange to hear Aunt Bennie talk this way, seriously, philosophically. I expected that, at any second, she would undermine the gravity of her talk with a joke. "Even them ole, rich white people, as easy as they got it, they got a few thorns, too."

"But why? Why can't life——"

"'Cause Eve bit the apple, I guess. That's just the way things are. But listen, what I'm telling you is that it ain't all bad. You just got to look for the good in it."

"What's good about Mama being sick?"

"Poor baby," she said. It felt very genuine, not sarcastic. "I can't think of a thing that's good about it. And probably there *is* nothing good about it. All I'm saying is that life ain't all bad. It's got its ups and its downs. You got to enjoy the ups and get over the downs." She paused and looked toward the ceiling. "You know, I lost my father at an early age."

"I know."

"You know it all? Who told you?"

"Uncle Reed."

"*Nobody* knows it all. Not even poor daddy. It's a story that's too damn big to tell every detail. But then, I guess, every story is. The world was just full of stories like it. Especially about colored people. White people die in car wrecks and go down on the *Titanic*. Colored people got to watch out for those things, too, and more. We got to watch out for the race accident.

"The difference between Clara and me is that I can take what joy I can out of it, and she can't take anything but the sorrow. That's not to say that I'm not sorry. All I'm saying is that I feel grateful that I knew my father and that I have fond memories of him. All Clara remembers is losing him." Aunt Bennie got up from the table and went back to the sink. "You know you were named for him. You look like him, too."

THE NEXT AFTERNOON, Mrs. Burrell met us at the schoolhouse. She was riding in a new Dodge Dart with a man she introduced as her friend, Reverend Timmons. Reverend Timmons was from Atlanta and was helping with the movement, she said, and beamed. Reverend Timmons was a stocky, dark man with a balding head. He wore a white shirt and black tie and smelled of spicy cologne. He gave us a hearty handshake and invited us into his car. Mrs. Burrell said that she was on her way to our house with a box of food so that our mother wouldn't have to cook supper with all that was going on. When she added "with all that was going on," I knew she was talking about my father's leaving. Josie said that she would walk home with Bingo, but Mrs. Burrell insisted that Josie ride. Bingo would find his way home.

We sat in the backseat and I reached behind Josie, sitting between us, and pinched Lamar on his butt. He gave me a frown and mouthed that he hadn't told anything. I guessed then that the word was getting around in Tittusville about my family, that my parents were fighting on top of my mother's sickness. Now the good reverend had come to rescue our souls, I thought. I envisioned Josie and myself in a church orphanage, or worse, as wards of the state—but I reminded myself that my father was just downtown and all I needed to do was to call him.

Almost as if he had been reading my mind, the Reverend Timmons asked if we children had heard of the afterschool workshops that the movement was having for children and said we should ask our mother if we could come.

Mrs. Burrell turned to me with a big red smile. "You remember I told you about them. I'm going to let Lamar go and it would be *nice* if you all could go together." She was gushing, and I thought she was putting on for the reverend. The reverend went on about the workshops—how they taught about the history of Negro people and true Christian values, not the hypocrisy that the white preachers taught. I wondered if he meant our Lutheran preacher, Reverend Evans, or white preachers in general. I interrupted him to point out our street and house.

Mrs. Burrell asked the reverend and Lamar to stay in the car while she went inside. She stood in the den and "yoo-hooed" for my mother. Aunt Bennie wasn't at home, so I went back and tapped on the bedroom door. Mother appeared to be asleep, but just as I started to leave, she beckoned me over to her. Was it Velma Burrell? she wanted to know, and what did she want? I told her about the food. When Mother came into the den, she wore a scarf around her head and a little lipstick.

"I hope you don't mind," Mrs. Burrell started apologetically. "I heard you were a little under the weather so I made you a little supper. Least you won't have to cook one night—I know how it is when you aren't feeling well and I remember how good you were to me when I had my little operation last year." Mrs. Burrell seemed nervous and talked very quickly, her hands motioning at the cardboard box full of food. Finally my mother touched her on the arm, and smiled. Her voice was hoarse, but she said she appreciated the food. She invited Mrs. Burrell to sit down, but Mrs. Burrell said that she had someone waiting—and blushed.

"Is it a beau?" Mother asked.

"Well . . . we just met, really," Mrs. Burrell said. "He is from over in Atlanta." She said "Atlanta" as if it were an exotic country on the other side of the world.

Mother said to invite him in, so I went to the car and told the reverend and Lamar to come in. My mother asked me to pour sweet tea for them, but Mrs. Burrell and the reverend insisted that they were just dropping in and didn't intend to stay longer than it took to say "hello."

The reverend mentioned the workshops he was on his way to conduct. Lamar was going to start that afternoon and it would be nice if she would send Josie and me.

My mother thanked him. She gave him a full, gracious smile that seemed to indicate more than pleasant refusal. Josie was too young, she said, and I was needed around the house.

Reverend Timmons leaned forward, resting his elbows on his knees and rubbing his hands together. He looked like he was relishing a chance to persuade Mother. "Change," he said, "begins at home. We have to be courageous enough to let our children learn about their past so that they might change their future."

Mother listened a while, and slowly the smile she tried to hold weakened and faded to a dull, impatient look.

"I think we ought to be going on," Mrs. Burrell announced and stood.

The reverend didn't stand. "You know, too many of our people are just content to let things stay the way they are. The rest are just afraid of change. Rather keep on shuffling and scraping than to stand up for ourselves. Some of us get a little bit, get a nice house and a car and forget about the ones we left behind."

"Is that so?" Mother said, "Which one are you?"

The reverend seemed shaken up for a moment, but then he got back on track in spite of Mrs. Burrell signaling him again. "I'm for change, Mrs. Burke. Change and justice. You know, we have too many comfortable Negroes in this town—too many people like A. G. Gaston who are just happy to see the Negro stay put because he can get rich off of the white man's inequity—"

"Reverend," my mother said, "Dr. Gaston is my *employer*. If you think so lowly of him, it's because you don't know anything about his own struggles. He is a fine example of just the kind of courage you are talking about. Now, if you are going to talk so disrespectfully, you'll have to do it in the street. Not in my house."

"I do respect your house, Mrs. Burke," Reverend Timmons said with a nod of his head. "All I'm saying is that Gaston could be doing more for his people than he's doing."

"Like what? Don't go acting like Dr. Gaston's white. He's as colored as the rest of us. White people tell him where to live just like they do you. Just because he got money, don't mean the KKK wouldn't lynch him in a heartbeat, and get away with it, too."

"All the more, he should be with us."

"I never heard he wasn't with us—" Mother stopped herself— "with you, Reverend Timmons. I don't know of a Negro who isn't for rights."

"Neither do I, Mrs. Burke, but that doesn't mean they got the spirit to do something about it."

Mother's arms crossed around her stiff body. "Don't talk to me about spirit—"

"All I'm saying is that you know a tree by its fruits and a man without conviction has dead spirit."

"Are you calling me a dead spirit?"

"Politics always do get folks into trouble." Mrs. Burrell gripped Reverend Timmons by the shirtsleeve and pulled him to standing. "Child, I'm glad you feeling better. Now, you give me a call anytime you need something. You want me to watch the children or something? You just give me a call—okay?"

Mother thanked Mrs. Burrell. She started to get out of her chair, stopped, and smiled weakly before she tried again. I came to her side, and she took my hand and pulled herself up. She stood by the screen door while Mrs. Burrell and the reverend left and then she turned. "How dare that man talk about Dr. Gaston . . . *he's* driving a brand-new car." She began to take the food out of the box. She smelled the plate of fried chicken that Mrs. Burrell had wrapped in waxed paper. "Smells good." She took down plates and glasses and began to serve us the food. When we were seated and eating, she sat with us.

THE NEXT MORNING on our paper run, Lamar talked excitedly about the workshop. There had been a large group of children and they had met at St. James's Baptist Church. At first they sang hymns and read from the Bible just like Sunday school. Then they pledged allegiance to the flag just like daily school, but unlike daily school, the teachers, all of whom were preachers of one kind or another, explained to them what the words meant. They especially talked about freedom and liberty for all. "'For all' meant Negroes too," Lamar inflected the way he had heard the preachers do. "The law says that we are just as equal as the white man. But the 'white power structure' wants to throw us back into slavery." Throughout our route, Lamar mimicked the rhetoric of the workshop. We were to say "Negro," not "colored," he admonished me. "Everybody—even white people—have a color."

"So why not call everybody 'colored'?" I really didn't want to know the answer, but only asked to say something. I was still thinking about my mother and Walter Lee. For some reason the story of Mother asking to see her father's corpse bothered me. That the nurse laughed bothered me. That Uncle Reed said that my mother took on "proper talk" like she was a lawyer bothered me. I had seen my mother speak to sales clerks in just that way, crisp, distant, and cool. I knew what she thought of them when she spoke that way.

Lamar had no answer about the color question, so he ignored it and kept talking about the workshops. Finally, I asked him about the frog eggs in order to get him to talk about something else.

AFTER SCHOOL, Aunt Bennie allowed Josie and me to visit Lamar. Lamar let himself in on the days his mother worked. Even before the bus strike, she rarely got home before school let out. Now, with Reverend Timmons picking her up, she was often later than she had been when she searched for rides.

Lamar offered us peanut butter crackers and Kool-Aid. Even though Aunt Bennie had warned us not to eat anything before supper, Josie and I took a cracker—after all, we had also been admonished to be polite. After eating, we set up the microscope to look at the frog eggs. The moment we unlatched the shed door where Lamar stored the jar of eggs, we smelled the odor. Lamar took the jar and placed it on the grass in front of the shed. It was half full of syrupy rot.

"Not very scientific," I said. Lamar shrugged, and Josie backed away. She looked like she was about to faint. Lamar pretended to throw the eggs at her and she screamed. He laughed. I touched her on the shoulder. She was cold. "It's making her sick."

Lamar apologized and returned the jar back to the shed. He said he would look at it later. When Josie felt a little better, we walked home. Just before we turned the corner at Tenth Street she told me that it wasn't the smell that had made her sick. It was that it reminded her of something she had overheard Aunt Bennie tell Grandma Pic. She heard that our mother's cells had gone rotten.

"Mama's cells aren't rotten," I said.

"But that's what cancer is—it's when your cells start to rot."

I let my palm rest on her head as we walked along. "Aunt Bennie was probably joking."

Josie seemed relieved, then confused. "Aunt Bennie didn't look like she was joking."

I patted her head and pulled her over to me and gave her an awkward hug. "Sometimes it's hard to tell when Aunt Bennie is teasing. It's her trademark."

That evening, our father came. Josie and I were in her room doing homework when we heard the familiar sound of his car. It sounded so familiar that, at first, I hardly gave it a thought. Bingo, who was spending more and more time indoors, perked up, hopped on the bed, put his face through the window, and wagged his tail. Josie looked at me with wide eyes and we both ran to the kitchen door.

Father brought in three large shopping bags, hugged us, and gave each of us a bag. In mine was an Easter suit, complete with shirt and clip-on tie.

"Oh, Lord," Aunt Bennie said, "you haven't been breaking that boycott, have you? These race folks will kick your butt if you've been doing that."

Our father rolled his eyes. "I slipped down to Montgomery. Couldn't let my children go raggedy, now could I?"

When we had gotten dressed in the new clothes we came back to the kitchen where our father and Aunt Bennie were having a cup of coffee. Our father adjusted the clip-on tie and spun me around. "We'll get you some new shoes," he said, "when this boycott dies down."

Josie's present was a pink dress with so many ruffles and bows I wondered if she would be able to sit down in it. Aunt Bennie ran her finger around the waist, checking for fit. She shook her head. "Lord, Carl, the poor girl looks like an airplane."

"I love it, Daddy," Josie said. She tried to hug him without crushing the ruffles. Then we went to show Mother.

Mother looked up from reading the Bible and smiled when she saw us. She asked for the overhead light to be turned on. Then she asked us to model for her, walk forward, turn, and walk back. "You look, smashing!" she declared with a British accent. "Simply smashing."

My father stood in the doorway and chuckled. Mother acknowledged him with a quiet "hi." My body stiffened. I wasn't sure if I should let him into the bedroom. Should I throw him out?

"You got the pills?" she asked.

"Gave them to Bennie."

She thanked him, her tone neither welcoming nor dismissive. Without moving from the doorway, Father asked Josie to take the third shopping bag to Mother. I helped Mother take a box from it, which she sat on her lap and untied while expectation built in the room. Aunt Bennie brushed past my father and sat on the foot of the bed. Out of the box came a smart-looking pillbox hat, pink with a green veil. Mother held it up, and turned it back and forth.

"Ahh, put it on," Aunt Bennie said impatiently, and took the hat from my mother and arranged it on her head. "Go get a hand mirror," she order my father. He came with the mirror, bringing it to Mother's bedside and holding it for her to look at.

"You look beautiful," Father said, his voice soft.

"Like an angel," Josie said.

Josie and I were standing behind our father as he held the mirror. A moment of suspense passed, and then Mother took hold of our father's hand and moved the mirror back and forth so she could view the hat at different angles. "It's sweet," she said. "Very sweet of you." Her eyes filled with tears; she still held our father's hand and looked at him. "You've got to give me a little more time."

"You don't have much time." Father's voice was firm, suddenly he choked. "Let's make the best of it."

At that moment I imagined the bedroom as a throne room. Mother sat on the throne, a queen receiving a tribute of peace from a rebellious subject. Were I chief counselor, I would have bent forward and whispered to the queen to accept the gift, to make peace. But I, as son in a dispute between parents, was frozen, afraid to move.

Mother's reaction was quick, surprisingly so, given the deliberateness with which she had been moving. She plucked the hat off of her head and put it on Aunt Bennie. "Where will I wear it? Besides, it looks better on Bennie." My knees wobbled. Josie looked as if she were in a prayerful trance. Her lips pushed together, she stared straight ahead, with one hand inside the other, held against her heart.

"But Mama . . ." I said, "you could wear it to . . . you could just *wear* it."

Aunt Bennie took off the hat and rubbed the veil between her fingers. "It's such a nice hat. But it's not my style, Clara . . . and it looks so good on you." She put the hat back on Mother and tried to arrange it, but Mother took it off and placed it on the bed. "Well," Aunt Bennie said, "I'll put it up for you." But she didn't move to pick up the hat.

I turned to my father, who was still kneeling beside the bed. His expression was blank, and he was staring at Mother. She avoided his stare. "Daddy will take you some place," I said. "Maybe on a date."

"Maybe to Joy Young's." Josie named Birmingham's Chinese restaurant, a place open to black patrons.

Father stood up and dropped the mirror on the bed beside the hat. His face was flushed and he spoke stiffly. "Put the hat away then." He started out of the room.

"Carl," Mother called after him. "In due time."

He turned. His lips were tight. He nodded and left.

TWO DAYS LATER was Good Friday and there was no school. After I had delivered the papers and had breakfast, Aunt Bennie assigned chores to Josie and me. I watered the garden, which was looking pitiful because the weather had been dry and hot, and we hadn't been watering it.

After chores, I went to Loveman's Village to visit Lamar. I asked him if he had studied the frog eggs under the microscope, and he began to deliver a pontification about chickens and snakes that bore eggs and snakes that bore live young and the difference between mammals and reptiles. Finally I told him to shut up since he obviously hadn't learned anything about frog reproduction. He gave me a sly look and said he knew more than I knew about reproduction—and he didn't mean frogs. He knew how babies were made—and not that eugenics crap—and further, he had recently witnessed the procedure in action.

"What do you mean?"

He looked sheepish. "My mama and her boyfriend."

"Reverend Timmons! He's a preacher. He ain't supposed to be reproducing or anything like that."

"He was a man before he was a preacher," Lamar said. "Anyway, Mama said a man and a woman have needs and besides, what she is doing is not wrong since she and Reverend Timmons will be getting engaged." I shrugged. It was hard for me to imagine ministers doing the things ministers were always hollering at other people about not doing. But if I thought about Reverend Timmons as a man, a mere man, it made sense. Mrs. Burrell was an attractive woman, and even I had felt those "needs," as Mrs. Burrell had called them. I imagined that adults must have felt the need ten or twenty times greater than a boy, and if that were so, then it was no wonder half of them were crazy. Jesus, I thought, we don't have a whole lot to look forward to in this world—working everyday, and trying to satisfy that urge every night. And on top of it, people were always saying one thing to each other and doing another. Reverend Timmons was of the group that said you shouldn't be doing anything about the urge, and now I find out he was running around doing something about it with Mrs. Burrell; and my parents, who were married, should have been doing it, and they were living in different parts of town.

I WENT HOME to tell Aunt Bennie I was going to ride around with Lamar. Aunt Bennie and Josie were gone. Grocery shopping, I assumed. Though many of the grocery stores had bad reputations when it came to treating blacks fairly, there was no boycott on grocery stores. People needed food more than they needed clothes. At any rate, there were a couple of small stores that were owned by blacks and at least one white-owned market that advertised "Every customer is important."

I knocked quietly at my mother's door; it was ajar. I heard the hum of the oscillating fan and the rustle of the Bible pages as the breeze swept back and forth. My mother was propped up on the pillows and looked asleep. I called to her quietly, and seeing that she remained still, I tiptoed closer to her. It did not occur to me that she might be dead; rather, it seemed that an angelic sleep had come over her, that she was restful and perhaps even happy at that moment. Her face moved a little, not a twitch, but a soft smooth movement, nearly a smile.

On the nightstand was a tray with a pitcher of iced water, a glass, and a small brown pill bottle. I read the label and understood that these were painkillers. These were the pills my father had brought when he had brought the hat. I rolled the bottle between my fingers, looking at the round tablets inside. Father had driven all the way to Montgomery for that hat, and she had tried to give it away. She had almost made him cry. Now she was peacefully sleeping on the pills he had brought her. If she wanted to die, why should she die so peacefully? I slipped the bottle into my pocket. Doing so gave me a cold satisfaction.

I hid the bottle in the secret place in my closet, a gap between the baseboard and the wall that could be found only when crawling on hands and knees, looking, as I had been when I discovered it, for lost socks.

Meeting Lamar outside the kitchen door, I felt exposed, as if he could see that I harbored a secret, darker than Cain's, for Cain only killed his brother. I tired to cover with a smile, but I felt he could see through me, so I turned away from him for a moment.

"What did she say?" he asked as if expecting bad news.

"She said it was okay." I swallowed, and took a deep breath, trying to act normal.

"Then why don't you look happy?" He backed away from the subject, "Oh . . . I guess she's not doing so well."

"She's sleep."

He looked puzzled again, and I realized my mistake. We said nothing and rode toward downtown.

THE GASTON MOTEL was a four-mile ride, but once we got our pedaling rhythm the trip went quickly. We rode down Center Street to Sixth Avenue South and followed it most of the way. We passed Ollie's, a big barbecue restaurant, shaped like a flying saucer. A sign on top advertised "The World's Best BBQ." I always wanted to taste the world's best barbecue and was amazed that we had it right in Birmingham. Lamar said it was just a ploy. *He* was amazed that white people could cook barbecue at all, much less cook it better than colored people. But there was no way of comparing, since colored weren't allowed to eat at Ollie's, not even at the back door.

Sweaty and panting, we parked the bikes near my father's car. I hesitated a moment, thinking that I might be in trouble because I didn't have my mother's permission, but I decided that my father would be happy to see me, after all. I knocked twice on his door, and there was no answer. Peeking through the blinds into his room I saw little.

"Why don't you get someone at the desk to let you in?" Lamar suggested. "You're his son, that's all you have to tell them."

I decided against it. I was afraid that my father might indeed be inside. "If he left his car," I thought out aloud, "he's not gone far. We will just wait."

We waited about twenty minutes, leaning over the iron balcony railing and enjoying the shade until a commotion on the bottom level attracted our attention. We identified the men as preachers by their black suits and white shirts. But two in the group wore work shirts and blue jeans; Lamar recognized one of them as Reverend

King. He had seen Reverend King's picture at the workshops. King had a worried, serious look about him. It was hard to believe that he was the man that everyone was talking about. The white people had made him out to be a devil, a troublemaker, a Communist. Some of the blacks thought the same. Others saw him as a savior, practically divine. To me he looked very ordinary. A short, stocky, dark man. Many of the others looked more to my liking for a hero, looked more like they could have been on TV. The group hurried into the church across the street.

I knocked again at my father's door. Lamar said that my father was probably getting some lunch, so we decided to ride around and see if he was at any of the lunch places along Fourth Avenue. We looked through the windows of every place that advertised food—Fried Chicken, Bar-B-Que, Meat and Three, Burgers and Shakes—but we didn't see him. We had been away for an hour, and I thought Aunt Bennie might be getting worried, so I suggested that we head home.

No sooner had we rounded the corner than we came face to face with the preachers leading a line of marchers. A crowd of bystanders milled around them. Policemen marched in front of the demonstrators, some walking backward to keep an eye on them; others walking with dogs to shepherd them; still others on motorcycles zipping back and forth, creating a ruckus in what was otherwise a sober display of hand clapping and shouts of encouragement. Reporters with TV and still cameras followed along, too. Lamar said that we should cross the street so that we could get in range of the TV cameras. We could see ourselves on TV.

"Yeah," I said, "your mama will see you, too, and knock your head in."

"Your mama would knock you, but mine would be proud of me."

He started across the street and I followed. Suddenly the parade made a turn and everything went into confusion. The white people, the policemen and reporters, were heading down Seventh Avenue toward the courthouse, but the marchers went in the other direction, toward Fifth Avenue. The policemen scrambled after the marchers, shouting orders and revving their motorcycles. Lamar and I found ourselves in the middle of the rush. We straddled our bicycles as the men pushed around us. Suddenly, I felt the hot breath of a dog against my leg. I froze. The dog snarled and snapped its jaws an inch from my leg. The officer who held the dog gave me a mean look; even so, I could tell he was only trying to scare me. He yanked the dog's leash and rushed by.

Rather than following the marchers, we rode around the courthouse and tried to intercept them. Then, we found ourselves behind the police barricades. Since we could see the marchers from there, we did not dare to get closer. Suddenly, without the fanfare of a speech, a white man, we assumed a policeman, stepped up to Reverend King and caught him by the back of his belt and pushed him toward a paddy wagon. Reverend King did not fight back in spite of the indignant way the man pulled his pants into his crotch and Spanish walked him. The other man in jeans, Reverend Abernathy (I learned later), was treated in much the same—if not a more indignant—manner. The policeman who arrested him bunched Reverend Abernathy's shirt in his fist and used the shirt like a leash.

Lamar and I watched quietly while the protesters allowed themselves to be escorted to the paddy wagons. A policeman noticed us and asked us if we wanted a ride to jail. We said "no sir," and he told us to "skee-daddle." We rode all the way back to Center Street before we stopped to catch our breaths. Lamar said he just couldn't wait to tell his mother and Reverend Timmons. I knew I couldn't tell anyone.

"Listen," I said, "don't tell your mama because she might tell my mama, and I didn't tell my mama where I was going."

Lamar gave me a sanctimonious look that made me want to slap him. "You didn't tell your mama? You told me you did."

"Well, I lied."

"I tell my mama everything I do."

"Well, I don't."

"Well, I don't have to, if that's what you mean."

"No, that's not what I mean." I pushed off on my bike. "I mean, I wish I could."

14

WHEN I RETURNED from downtown, Aunt Bennie was preparing to cook a small ham. Josie sat at the table, making a clumsy effort at scraping potatoes, and Bingo sat under the table, attentive to the peels as they fell. I started to tell Aunt Bennie that my parents didn't allow Bingo in the house, but I decided to give him a break, and patted his head. He wagged his tail happily. The scene struck me as comfortable, but strange. This was no longer my mother's kitchen, a thought that made me miss her suddenly. I sneaked to her bedroom door and I saw her lying in the bed, her hair moving in the breeze from the fan. She seemed to be restful, and I noticed that the water pitcher and glass sat on the tray, apparently undisturbed.

Because she had to work the next day, Saturday, Aunt Bennie cooked and put away food for us to eat. Then she took us in the car to Palmer's BBQ, a black-owned restaurant, where we got hot dogs and pork barbecue. Even though it was good, I thought about Ollie's and wondered how much better the "World's Best BBQ" would be. After Palmer's, she took us to Dairy Dip. I told her that my mother never allowed us to eat at Dairy Dip because we were made to order at the back door. Mother preferred Diary Frost on Eighth Avenue. Aunt Bennie said since we were at the Dairy Dip, we would go ahead and "get a dip at the Dip." I wanted the ice cream badly, and had never tried Dairy Dip's, so I decided not to protest. Josie, on the other hand, said that she didn't want any.

"Why not? Aren't you the one who is always wanting ice cream?" Aunt Bennie asked.

"I know," Josie spoke softly. "But, not here."

"Ice cream is ice cream," Aunt Bennie said as she got out of the car. I saw the sign that said "colored" with an arrow pointing around back.

"Mama wouldn't like it if we ate here," Josie told Aunt Bennie through the window.

Aunt Bennie patted Josie on the head. She considered, and then she frowned. "Who wants to eat ole Jim Crow's ice cream anyway?" We got back in the car and on the way home we stopped at Mr. Lee's grocery store and Aunt Bennie bought a carton of Neopolitan ice cream. She joked that it was integrated ice cream: "Even got some Indian blood in it."

When she was scooping out cones for us, I thought about the idea of blood in the ice cream. The swirls of vanilla and chocolate seemed appetizing, but the strawberry, the Indian blood, looked raw to me. I kept thinking about what must be going on in my mother's body. I nibbled at the cone, and Aunt Bennie asked if it was all right.

"I just don't want the strawberry," I said.

She rolled her eyes. When Aunt Bennie rolled her eyes I never felt admonished; it was just another playful face. "Y'all some choicey children," she declared. She scooped me another cone with just vanilla and chocolate. I didn't enjoy it, but I managed to eat it.

After eating the ice cream, Aunt Bennie sent us to our rooms while she watched TV. She was watching *The Edge of Night,* which she said was not a children's story. An hour or so later, I heard my mother and Aunt Bennie talking. My mother said something about pain and I knew she had discovered that her pills were missing. Aunt Bennie declared that the pills were on the stand just a minute ago. She went through a series of questions: When was the last time you took one? When was the last time you remember seeing the bottle? I moved to the door of Josie's room, but not into the hall. My mother was having trouble remembering exactly when she last saw the pills. She said she had gotten up a couple of times during the afternoon, but she couldn't remember if she had taken a pill or not. Aunt Bennie searched Mother's bedroom and bathroom. She surmised that my mother had mislaid them. "For the time being," she said, "take some aspirin."

"Aspirin?" Mother sounded insulted. "I need *pills.* Call Carl. Tell him to get me some more."

"You know the doctor won't allow that! They are very particular about giving out pain medicine."

"Call Carl."

Aunt Bennie dialed the phone and asked to be connected to Mr. Burke's room. Then she talked to the operator again, leaving a message. "He isn't there," she reported to mother. "Probably out getting sloshed."

"Oh God," my mother said. "Bennie, I need those pills."

I DREAMED THAT my mother was drying up like a plant. Her features wilted and she begged me for water. I stood next to her bed in a garden plot and held a hose from which water spilled. All she wanted was a spray of water, a little water, she said, and she would spring back to life. I teased her with the hose, bringing it near, and taking it away, letting the clear, cool water waste. "It's God's will. It's God's will."

During a period between nightmares, I heard Mother talking plaintively with Aunt Bennie. Once or twice she moaned, sending a shiver through me. I wanted to get up and get the pills for her, but I knew I couldn't explain why I had taken them. I felt very mean and it occurred to me, again, that I was murdering my own mother. But not even this thought made me get the pills. For one thing, Aunt Bennie was sleeping in my bedroom, and I didn't think I could sneak the pills out without her knowing. For another, I seemed paralyzed. I said to myself, Get up and help your mother. Get her pills for her. But I didn't move and then I dreamed she was wilting, crying, melting, and when I awoke I heard her soft moans.

In the morning, Mother seemed to have been sleeping quietly, and I felt better. Maybe she really didn't need the pills after all. Maybe stealing the pills was a good deed. If my mother didn't have the pills and the pain was bad, she would realize she needed the operation. If the pain were bad, she would call for my father to come home.

When I came back from the paper route, Aunt Bennie, looking like she hadn't slept, was already dressed for work. She was on the phone to the motel trying to locate my father. She asked me if I had seen the pills. The lie slipped out easily. "What pills?" I asked. She explained, and sent me to search. She kept repeating that my mother must have mislaid the pills.

Mother's room had a faint odor that I couldn't quite place. Even though Aunt Bennie took pains to see that Mother was bathed every day, her lying in the heat day after day must have caused the odor. Yet, the smell was not quite like body odor, nor was it like medicine. It was the smell of something old and earthen. The window was open and the fan bathed my sleeping mother in the cool morning air. Still, the odor. Was the smell that of my mother's cancer, the smell of death? The thought made the hair on my neck stand.

I went through the motions in Mother's room. I scanned among her bottles of perfume, opened and closed drawers in her vanity, looked among my father's colognes and shave creams. All the time, I was waiting for Aunt Bennie to go to work. Once she was gone, I would return the medicine. Then I would say that I found it someplace that Mother must have dropped it.

Aunt Bennie was considering canceling work, though it was only her second day. After a while, she decided that it was an easy job and if she lost the day she might lose the job. She gave me her work number and told me to keep calling my father. "If worse comes to worst," she said, "call the funeral home." In those days, the funeral home offered ambulance service.

Mother woke up before Aunt Bennie left. She said that she was better and would call her doctor later to get a new prescription. Hearing this, I didn't have to risk exposing myself by pretending to find the medicine. My mother would get a new bottle and if I wanted to, a mean part of me thought, I could take that one, too.

With my conscience eased and Aunt Bennie at work, I went about taking care of the house. Aunt Bennie had given us a list of Saturday chores: clean up Josie's room, take out the garbage, wash the dishes, give Bingo a bath, water the garden. I thought I would cut the grass, as well. This was usually my father's job, but since he wasn't around, I felt that I needed to be the man of the house.

I was not allowed to use the gas mower, only the push mower, but I decided if no one was around to tell me what to do, I would use the gas mower. After all, it was more efficient and more fun than the other. I pulled the mower out of the storage shed and tried to crank it. I fiddled with the clutch, setting and resetting it, and pulled and pulled on the crank rope, but I could not get enough torque to get it to turn over. From time to time it sent out a series of loud pops. Josie came out and told me that Mother had said to leave it alone, that our father would be coming to cut the grass. I stood a foot or so away from the machine. Why was it doing this to me? Why wouldn't things go smoothly? All I had asked of it was to do what it was made to do. I kicked it. It hurt my toe a little, but I kicked it again. The spark plug broke off. I looked at Josie; she looked a little surprised and grinned.

I called the motel several times but couldn't reach my father. Apparently Aunt Bennie had been calling, too, because the operator told me she had sent someone to his room to knock at his door, and he wasn't in. I asked if his car were there, and described it. The operator left the line for a moment and came back and said she didn't see it in the parking lot, but it could have been on the street.

This concerned me since I hadn't heard from our father since he came with the presents. When I told Mother he couldn't be reached, she seemed angry more than concerned. She asked for the phone, tried to dial it, and then had me dial her doctor's number. She reached the nurse and explained her problem. The nurse said the regular doctor was on vacation until Monday, but she would have his substitute call later.

It was early in the afternoon before the substitute doctor called back. He wanted to speak to our father. I told the doctor our father wasn't home, and he said to have him call. I wanted the doctor to talk to Mother, and he agreed. It was a short conversation, with her saying "yes, sir" and "no, sir" and then hanging up with a look of disgust on her face. "What does he think, that I'm a addict? I would be dead if I had taken all those pills this soon."

A little later, I went quietly into my mother's room, ready to put the pills back, but then I saw the hat my father had given her sitting on the chair next to her bed. It looked like a layer of pink wedding cake, except for the green veil. I stood a moment too long looking at it and Mother asked me what was wrong.

"Nothing," I said, startled. I thought that she would see the bulge of the pill bottle in my pocket. "I was just checking up on you."

"You're sweet." She reached out for me, and I took her hand. Suddenly, I felt liquid, and I froze. Part of me wanted to melt in my mother's arms. With her warm hand in mine, she seemed to pull me back into childhood. I resisted that maternal gravity, and twisted away from my mother as she pulled me toward her for a kiss. I couldn't let her see the pill bottle, bulging like a stone in my front pocket. Resist though I did, I bent. Her breath smelled stale—it was the smell that permeated the room. The kiss was brief, on the cheek, and then she fell back on the bed, her eyes closed. I sat on the bed beside her. I liked her like this, so much warmer and closer without the medicine.

When Aunt Bennie came home, she called the doctor again. Hand on hip, she began, as she would later say, "to lay into him." Somehow a compromise was reached. The doctor would make a prescription for a milder painkiller, which we could pick up that evening, but the original prescription would have to wait until the regular doctor returned.

I rode with Aunt Bennie to pick up the prescription. On the way, she was silent and serious. "Lord," she said after we had gotten the prescription, just four little pills in the bottle, "why do things have to be so hard?" She looked at me, her eyes wide and tired. She didn't say anything about Eve biting an apple.

Aunt Bennie had a heavy foot; the storefronts zipped by. In the blur of the buildings and the weeds turning into bloom—dandelion and fleabane—I began to see a picture of how things were. Perhaps it was the first step in understanding something about my mother. She didn't deserve what she was getting. But life doesn't give you what you deserve; it just gives without rhyme or reason.

"A cancer can happen to anybody," I said, thinking aloud. Aunt Bennie grunted uncommittedly. Of course, it wasn't just happening to anybody; it was happening to *my* mother and I wanted it to be happening for some reason. "It has to do with Granddaddy," I said.

"What?"

"The cancer."

Aunt Bennie pursed her lips and grunted again. "That makes about as much sense as people on the moon."

"Not the cancer," I said, "but not getting it operated on. That has a lot to do with what happened to Granddaddy."

Aunt Bennie slowed the car and looked at me. "What makes you say that? What happened to Daddy has nothing to do with cancer. That was a bunch of prejudiced white people on a rampage. You have no right to talk because you don't know. They were like a pack of wild dogs! Animals!" Her sudden anger surprised me and I was quiet for a few moments.

"That's not the way I meant it." I took a moment to form my thoughts, and Aunt Bennie waited. "I mean, Mama doesn't think she can do anything about it, so she doesn't even try."

"Maybe she can't do anything about it. You can run away from Jim Crow. At least, you don't have to stay here. But, cancer, you can't run away from it, honey."

What little I knew about the North at that time painted it as a haven for black people, but I had also heard about vast ghettos where black people lived in roach-infested tenements. How much of an escape was that? "Aunt Bennie," I ventured boldly just as she turned the car into the driveway, "maybe she can't run away, but she can *try* to do something. Don't you think? Don't you think she should try?"

Aunt Bennie sighed. "Yes, I do, Waltie. If it was me I would be fighting it with all my might. But for some people fighting is a luxury they can't afford."

"You mean we don't have the money." I was excited because I thought we could get the money somehow. "We can borrow it from Dr. Gaston."

"It's not money. Lord knows it's not that easy."

THAT NIGHT Mother rested easier, but still moaned occasionally and talked to Aunt Bennie in tight, complaining tones. I had carried the pills around with me all that day, even when we went to pick up the substitute medicine. When I dressed for bed, I slipped the pills inside my tennis shoe, put a sock in the shoe, and put the shoes under the bed. I had decided now the best thing to do was to throw the pills into the garbage at school when I went to assemble the morning paper.

That night, again, I dreamed about my mother. In this dream Mother and I were walking beside a river, perhaps the Coosa, which Uncle Reed claimed was the liquid part of our blood. Mother slipped from the bank and reached for me as she was falling. It was the same way she had reached for me that morning, not reaching out for rescue, but reaching to pull me toward her. Only in the dream I didn't want to go to her. I didn't want to fall into the river, churning with slow, oily waves. Nonetheless, I reached for her—I couldn't help myself. I was reaching, but I was pulling away, too. I was trying to catch her, and trying to keep a foothold on the bank. The soft dirt gave way.

The next morning, I got to the school earlier than Lamar, determined to throw the pills away. I lifted the lid on the garbage can and held the bottle above the refuge. Just as I let it drop, I saw my mother's name on the bottle. It was too much like throwing her away, so I picked it out of the trash and put it back in my pocket.

When I got back from the route, I quickly hid the pills in my sneakers, and got into my Easter suit. Josie was already dressed and eating breakfast. After breakfast, Mother inspected us and said how wonderful we looked. She gave each of us a kiss and told us to be good in church. Then we went into the den to wait for our father. An hour passed. Aunt Bennie called the motel. This time Father answered and Aunt Bennie caustically reminded him that he had "some duties to take care of." He arrived a half hour after the phone call. Aunt Bennie was livid. She barely let him into his own house, guarding the kitchen door. He pushed by her.

"Where have you been *hiding* yourself?" Aunt Bennie asked. "We had an emergency here. We could all be *dead* and you were nowhere to be found."

"What emergency?"

Aunt Bennie explained about the pills. My father started to the bedroom, genuinely concerned, but Aunt Bennie only let him go as far as the den. "She's asleep for the first time this morning." Then Aunt Bennie placed a hand on her hip and turned with an accusatory tone to Daddy. "She's been in horrible pain—*you know.*"

My father glanced at the ceiling, something he did when he was mad, and then back at Aunt Bennie. "Well, she didn't expect to die without having any pain, did she?"

"I don't know what she expects." Aunt Bennie shook her finger. "Apparently, nothing from you. Just tell me where I might find you the next time your family needs you. The Jockey Boy? The Cotton Club? Or are you the type that hangs around in alleys?"

"That's not fair, Bennie."

"Nothing is fair; but it's true."

My father walked back into the kitchen and sat at the table. A minute passed and Aunt Bennie followed him. She didn't say anything, and he said, "Bennie, I don't know what to do. This thing is driving me crazy."

"You're not the only one." She nodded toward me standing in the doorway. "What about your children?"

THE CHURCH SERVICE had already begun when we walked in. Reverend Evans and one of the elders were reading the Scripture. Reverend Evans moved in quick, officious measures—very different from the deliberate swaying of Grandma Pic's black preacher. The black Lutherans liked the service to move quickly and to be done promptly so that we could be on our way in a little over an hour. They liked the clean ritual of the Lutherans. Aunt Bennie once said she didn't think Lutherans were right in the head to like those German hymns. There was no spirit in them, no clapping during the service, no answering the preacher—when the message got to you— "and the *message* would have to get to you because that German *music* never would." My mother had argued that there was more than one way to worship God. Some people liked to knock off their hats and get sweaty; others liked a quiet contemplation. No one way was better than the other and as far as she was concerned, quiet contemplation made people take church seriously. Father said if people wanted to dance around, they could go to a club.

The Easter message was none too original. Reverend Evans talked about resurrection—the resurrection of Christ and the many different ways in which dead things come to life again. He likened resurrection to the rejuvenation of a dry lawn. When the drought has killed the grass, the roots are dormant until water—the baptism—comes and nurtures the lawn. The lawn becomes green again. Then came the radical part of his sermon, tailor-made for the audience—the congregation knew what he meant, though he wouldn't say it directly. "Even a large city can be dead and dry in its spirit. The nurturing rains will come—sometimes as a great storm—and after the thunder and lightning—after the tumble and turmoil—a new beginning will come." This seemed to please many of the people in the service and they nodded their heads.

My father's attention was elsewhere. He fidgeted. When the Communion tray came, I had to nudge him to take the wafer and glass. When it was time to eat and drink, he was a little behind the group.

HOME AGAIN, we changed our clothes and Aunt Bennie put out our Easter meal. I could tell she was still angry with my father, but she invited him to stay for the supper. She said it in such a way as to make it sound as if it was his duty to eat Easter supper with his children. Aunt Bennie had set the table in the dining room. She also said that she would move my mother to the table—but Mother said that she wasn't very hungry and it hurt too much to move. I started to feel guilty again about the pills that now I had hidden in my church shoes. Aunt Bennie set a beautiful table, using the good china. She served the ham with pineapple slices and mashed sweet potatoes and fresh baked rolls—but not as light and buttery as my mother's.

Father called me from his place at the head of the table. Josie sat next to him. Aunt Bennie had a place across from Josie. My place was beside Josie. The foot of the table was empty. I couldn't even go into the dining room because my mother's absence at the table sickened me.

Why was I, her only son, torturing her so? I didn't think that the pills would bring her to the table. They would put her to sleep, take her away from us. But hadn't I tortured her enough, and for what? I couldn't say.

My father called to me that the food was getting cold. I called back to get started, that I needed to go to the bathroom. I heard him begin the dinner prayer and I went into Josie's room and got the pills out of my shoe.

My mother seemed asleep. I decided that I would simply place the pill bottle on her dresser, among her perfume bottles. If it wasn't found in an hour or so, then I would conveniently find it. The adults would think that they simply overlooked the pills among the other bottles. I walked quietly past the bed to the dresser where Mother had a silver tray with a dozen or so perfume bottles on it.

I kept one eye on my mother as I took the pill bottle out of my pocket and placed it on the tray. I stood for a moment, examining my handiwork. The scheme seemed plausible, and I felt pleased for a second. Then I saw my reflection in the dresser mirror, a skinny, brown wretch, not a child, but a hooligan. I began to sneak away.

"What's that?" I heard my mother say.

"Just me."

"I know it's you. What are you doing sneaking around in here, honey?"

"Nothing."

"What were you doing on my dresser?"

"Just looking."

"Looking at what?"

"Nothing."

"Come here," she said. Her tone was quiet, and I came over to her bedside, my defenses down. She slapped my face. The strike came with such swiftness that it seemed to have surprised both of us. "Walter, I never thought you would lie to me."

"I didn't lie."

"Why did you take my pills?"

"I didn't . . ."

Her eyes glared. "Walter. Do you know what you have done to me?"

I couldn't look at her. My face felt bloated and my nose stopped up. I wiped my hand across my eyes. *Yes. Yes.* I realized what I had done to her. I had no explanation. I tried to speak, "Mama . . . Mama, what about me?"

"You? You aren't in any pain." She scoffed, and her eyes wandered away from me, looking at something out of the window. "Listen," she said, turning back and reaching for me. I did not come closer. "Listen, I may only have a month to live, *but I'm still your mother.*"

Now it felt as if I had been slapped again. A month. The end was so near. Somehow knowing she was dying and not knowing when, I could have the illusion that she were dying no faster than anyone else, the illusion that the end was far off no matter how clearly it was in view. To place a measure on the distance, a month, a few weeks, before my next birthday, and to hear it from her own lips, overwhelmed me. Up to this point my mother had denied the inevitable that my father had announced and Aunt Bennie had hinted at. She had said she was *not* going to die, and now, stripped of deceit by her own anger, she had told the truth. My body seemed to spin as a sweet, slow vertigo gripped me. I may have passed out. I found myself on my knees trying to catch my breath.

· · · ·

LOSS IS A PART of this world, dear Mr. and Mrs. Jackson, and losing a mother, or losing a son, is the deepest loss you will ever feel. All this other carnage, these bits of arms and legs that lay scattered over the bush, is just craziness. Craziness. But the mother, the child, that is the unspeakable one. It is the one that can cause you to lose yourself if you aren't careful.

AUNT BENNIE came in. I said nothing, managed to stand, and went to my room—the one I was letting Aunt Bennie stay in—and slammed the door.

Aunt Bennie was not pleased to have her supper ruined, and in spite of profuse apologies from my father, she continued to complain, walking back and forth between the kitchen, the dining room, and the den where I sat with my father. It was only when my father said that he would take me with him for the night that Aunt Bennie stopped complaining about me. Now she was concerned that I would be staying in a downtown motel with "race men." The KKK, she asserted, could set it on fire.

"And me?" my father asked. His mockery was jocular. "You would let the KKK burn *me* up?"

Aunt Bennie pursed her lips and turned her face away from him, dismissing him. I told her I wanted to spend the night with my father. And then, Josie said she wanted to, as well.

"Not on my life!" Aunt Bennie shook her head vigorously. What kind of parent would let a little girl spend a night in a motel? Father said Josie could stay if she wanted to; after all, we were his children, not Aunt Bennie's.

Aunt Bennie tried to wake my mother but it was too late. Mother had taken the pills. Aunt Bennie moved away from the bed and declared that if Father took us to the motel that she would pack up and return to Philadelphia.

"And abandon your sister?" my father shot at her.

"You did," she shot back, but he ignored her and tiptoed to my mother's bed and kneeled down beside her. He put his face next to her and seemed to whisper to her. He kissed her. The mood of the house calmed as if some love charm had been thrown on us. We, including Aunt Bennie, who had been rampaging a moment before, were suddenly transfixed by my father's kiss, by love's mysterious power to transcend the ruckus. When he stood, he seemed to notice that we were staring at him, and he smiled and told Josie and me to get our clothes—just pajamas and toothbrushes—we would be back first thing in the morning.

JOSIE AND I had never spent a night in a motel, so we tried out everything in the small, plain room. We amused ourselves for a few moments with the venetian blinds, and then with bouncing on the bed. Our father told us to put on our pajamas and he stepped out onto the balcony. Josie wanted to use the bathroom first. She unpacked the paper sack that Aunt Bennie had put her things in, and very carefully placed her brush and comb and toothbrush in a line on the sink counter before she began her shower. I peeked through the blinds at our father. He was leaning on his elbows on the balcony railing and smoking a cigarette. I had never seen him smoke. He looked over his shoulder at me. My first impulse was to hide, but I didn't move. I figured he was my father and I could look at him if I wanted. He stared back for a moment, smiled, and waved me onto the balcony.

"I guess you think we adults are pretty nuts," he said and dragged on the cigarette. I was amazed that he smoked so well, as if he had been doing it all his life. "Well, Son, one day I hope you'll understand that life has its ups and its downs, and it can get pretty . . . darn . . . confusing." He dragged again. The butt glowed orange in the twilight. Around us the air was damp and cool, and the evening was blue with haze. I mimicked his posture against the railing. After a moment, he let out a long stream of smoke, and I took a deep breath to draw it in. It smelled sweet, but it tickled my throat and made my eyes water. "Smoke bothering you?"

"No, sir."

"I think I know why you did what you did to your mother. I might have done the same thing if I thought I could get away with it. It's so damn aggravating."

"Yes, sir."

He sighed and rested the hand with the cigarette on my shoulder for a second. "It's a terrible thing to say. . . ." He stopped talking and I thought he had dropped the thought. When he spoke again, his voice was strained, as if he were making himself say the words. "It's terrible, but maybe it's for the best. Go ahead and get it over with." He crushed the cigarette butt out on the railing and flicked it into the parking lot below. "We don't know what's going through her mind. She's probably as afraid about it as we are. Damn. More afraid. I guess we've got to let her handle it her way."

We were quiet for a bit. I wanted to say a lot of things, but I couldn't think of a way to say any of it. I wanted to say I didn't know why I took the pills; and I wanted to say I didn't want my mother to die; I wanted to say that I wanted my father to keep talking; I wanted to ask him if I could have a cigarette. Josie came out on the balcony, dressed in pajamas and robe. "Look at all the lights!" she cried and stood on the foot rail, pulling herself up on the railing so swiftly that my father grabbed the back of her collar. From the balcony we could see the lights of most of the high-rises in Birmingham, the Cabana Hotel, the City Federal Bank Building, and the Alabama Power Building with the golden Goddess of Electricity on top. Our father pointed out Vulcan on top of Red Mountain in the distance. Vulcan's torchlight was green. It was one of the tallest statues in the world, Father said. "Also, one of the ugliest." He lit up another cigarette. Josie gave him a strange look and asked the question I had been wanting to ask. "Daddy, where did you learn to smoke?"

He picked her up in his arms and nuzzled her. "My honey chile," he said, "you don't know everything there is to know about yo' daddy. B'lieve it or not, yo' daddy was grown before you were born."

After I had showered, we sat on the bed a while and listened to the radio. It was WENN, which was located just down the street. It played a mixture of popular songs, mostly rhythm and blues. We sang along with the songs we knew, "Blueberry Hill," "Hit the Road, Jack," or the very popular, "He's So Fine." Whenever a jazzier tune came on, my father got excited. "Listen to that backbeat," he proclaimed when Dinah Washington came on, "Listen to that horn!" when he heard Lena Horne. "She's a Georgia girl, you know."

Eventually, he declared "lights out" and he tucked us into the bed, Josie in the middle and me on the outside. He sat in the chair, in the dark, and looked out of the window into the parking lot. I watched him a while, and though he made a sad sight, I felt comfortable being with him. Gradually, I fell asleep. Very late in the night, I woke up and saw that my father was gone. I sat up in the bed hoping to see a light in the bathroom or a cigarette glow on the balcony. From the balcony I saw that the car was still where he had parked it. Back in the bed, I lay awake for a time, thinking that he must have just gone to the motel office, or just around the corner—perhaps for cigarettes. I fell asleep again, but was awakened when I heard my father come back into the room. At first, I thought he must have been out for only a few minutes, but as I watched my father walk unsteadily across the room, I realized that much more time had passed. He stood a long time by the dresser, holding onto it. Then he progressed toward the bathroom, balancing with one hand on the wall. He shut the bathroom door and turned on the light. I fell asleep and was awakened by him again. He had been sitting in the chair by the window, apparently asleep, and had rolled out of the chair onto the floor. I called to him, but he did not answer.

·   ·   ·

THE NEXT DAY, we attended our first workshop at St. James's Baptist Church. It was Aunt Bennie's idea. We had come in from school and were snacking. She asked if we wanted to go and play with Lamar. I explained that he would be going to the workshop at 4:30. She looked as if she were considering. She knew that my mother objected to the workshops. Father, on the other hand, had said he thought it might be all right to go once a week to learn something about "Negro history"; after all, that was a part of our education, too. Aunt Bennie had disagreed with our father to his face, but when he was not present, she had said that our mother was too protective.

After our snack, she asked again about the workshops. This time, I mentioned that Reverend Timmons would be leading that day's workshop. She grunted. I couldn't tell if she approved of him or not. Then she said quietly, "Y'all got to promise two things. One: you get to your homework the minute you get back; and, two: your mama, she doesn't have to know."

Josie cheered and Aunt Bennie hushed her.

Aunt Bennie didn't say so, but I suspected she wanted us to go to the workshops to divert our attention away from Mother's illness. The workshops, we didn't know then, would divert us, temporarily, but they would also lead us on a path that would bring us face to face with every strength and frailty in both of our parents.

15

THE GECKO CAUGHT a beetle and crunched it. Bits of wing and exoskeleton floated down from the rafters. The lizard was the color of a lime and a good size for a gecko, nearly as long as my hand. After its meal, it seemed to sleep.

I had written another first line of the letter to Haywood's parents and scratched it out. It had said, *I'm writing with bad news,* but I had no news for them. What, indeed, could I tell them that they didn't already know? Would they want to know that the bullet had hit Haywood above the brow rather than in the throat? Would they want to know that he had fallen backward rather than facedown? What difference would the details make for them? Should I tell them a story, something that would make them feel better about having a dead son? What would that be? *Dear Mr. and Mrs. Whatever Your Name, As you well know, since you are Negroes, life is an illusion of comfort, prosperity, and happiness. Negroes know this because we have no choice but to know it. We rise early to a bright sun warming the green lawns and say, "Thank God for this beautiful day." We happily delude ourselves that the sun is not a fireball sputtering in a cold vacuum and life on this rocky earth is not an accident. That the pink azaleas and snowy dogwoods that decorate the lawn are something more than weeds sprung from a sludge of a trillion dead things, and that soon those beautiful blossoms, too, will be sucked by parasites, withered and rotted. We say, "Thank God," because we want to believe that God is good and all things happen according to His will. That He is righteousness and righteousness is never a wrong, and that we poor sons of Ham have been wronged, miserably wronged, but that it is right in the long view. We are happy, believing this. Happy, happy. We want to be happy—we need to be happy—for just a few moments each morning before we step into the streets and become Negroes.*

Haywood was a Negro, blacker than Ham. Now, dear parents, he is as dead as ham. Dead, blackened ham.

Are you surprised? Your beautiful ham, full of muscle, good humor, and wit, has had a bullet riddle his brains? Dead as a door nail. Dead meat. It's no tragedy. Even now, a lizard is crunching up something that was once alive. Well, it's a tragedy to the bug! Don't you believe me? You say you believe your life is one happy bug adventure? Who told you that? You fools! Who ever told you to hope for anything? Some preacher? The Reverend Ike? The Reverend A. A .A. Or maybe the Reverend King, King, King?

No. King knew better. King knew better.

I put a big "X" across the page, and started again.

Dear Mr. and Mrs. Jackson, My name is Walter Lee Burke, and I was Haywood's friend from Birmingham. Once Haywood asked me to tell him about Birmingham, about the marches, and I regret that I did not. To tell the truth, I did not know what to say. To tell the truth, I do not know what to say now. Maybe I will tell you the truth if you want to hear it. And that is that I am not very happy and I am scared. So were Haywood and everybody else. I would like to say that we were heroes somehow, but honestly, we are just average guys. We just get along from moment to moment, doing the best we can and trying to remember to do the right things we were taught to do in school and in church. But we forget. The times are very hard, right now, and in hard times it is easy to forget. When you forget, you become loose and lost and you do things you regret. When I was little I studied in a civil rights workshop and I heard Reverend King speak. I, more than most, ought to know right from wrong, and yet, you must understand, please, that I am so scared and weak.

THE WORKSHOP HAD BEGUN by the time we arrived. Lamar's relationship with Reverend Timmons meant that he was a preacher's kid, a position, or rather a *condition,* that suited him. He would have to come early to church and stay late. He would have to lead children's services. He would have to sit in the front pews and look alert. But being the center of attention would please him. He was already beginning to play the role. As the expectations for his own standard of behavior rose, so did his expectations for Josie and me. When we slipped into the pew beside him, he gave me an admonishing look; and, when we rose to sing "The Star Spangled Banner" and the Negro national anthem, "Lift Every Voice," he gave me a grin.

I was surprised to see that there were quite a few children in the church. Many of them, having come directly from school, still carried their schoolbooks and lunch boxes. They were mostly teenagers, but some of the children were very young, six- or seven-year-olds.

The reverend talked about Crispus Attucks—the first man to die for American Independence—"and a Negro, too." He talked about the Civil War and how Negroes fought to preserve the Union. He went on for a great long time about the soldiers of World War I and II. On this subject he got quiet and personal and he nearly brought me to tears. He talked about his own father who fought in France in the Great War, "the war that was supposed to save democracy," and then, nearly weeping, he talked about his brother who had been killed in France in World War II. As he talked, I remembered that my own father had seen service in World War II, though it was something he never talked about. Reverend Timmons went on in some detail about the loss of his brother. How his brother had volunteered for the army, and had trained in a segregated unit in Fort McClellan. How he went off to war to fight Hitler. Reverend Timmons made this sound as if his brother and Hitler had fought hand to hand.

"Then why," he cried, "oh why, can we not find freedom at home?" He paused and looked about the sanctuary and pointed to a student.

"Do you know who Kelly Ingram Park is named for?"

The student didn't know. Kelly Ingram was the first man from Birmingham to die in World War I. He was a white man and the black park was named for him. "Now, does anyone know the name of the first Birminghamian to die in World War Two?" No one knew. "Of course not, because he was *Negro*. His name was Julius Ellsberry. He died at Pearl Harbor, and we have asked that the city name a park in his honor. And we have asked. And we have asked. And we have asked, again." He seemed to wind down, shaking his head and walking around in front of the pulpit. Then suddenly he sprang toward the pews, jabbing the air with his finger. "Negroes are equal when the white man wants us to die," he declared. "We are equal when he wants us to work for nothing. We are equal when we invent something he wants. We are equal when we entertain him with song and dance. But when it comes to voting—ooooh! When it comes to the paycheck . . . when it comes to a good house . . . when it comes to the good job . . . even when it comes to getting a park named for us." He shrugged in mock puzzlement. "We ain't equal no more."

Though I knew that my father and other black men had fought in the world wars, I had never imagined them doing it. I had never thought of them as heroes. In the family album there was a picture of my father in uniform, but I never connected him with the heroics of the war. I had seen war movies about heroes like Audie Murphy, but never had I seen a black man in a fighting uniform, with helmet and gunbelt. I had seen *From Here to Eternity*, but I had never known that black men had died at Pearl Harbor; I didn't even think blacks were allowed into Pearl Harbor. Nowhere in our history books did I see a

black soldier. Or on television. Or on statues. And yet, Reverend Timmons said that "Negro men" had fought in the world wars, and in
Korea, and in all the wars, even before the American Revolution.
They hadn't just been potato peelers; they had been soldiers, and my
own father had been one of them.

I felt proud of their accomplishments, but also an uneasiness that
it didn't matter what black people did for America, we would always
be segregated. I had learned in school about the ideals of the Declaration of Independence and the Constitution, the freedoms of religion,
speech, and assembly and so on. At that time, the ideal that was most
disturbing to me was the pursuit of happiness. I couldn't have articu-
lated it, but I knew that even though my parents and my teachers
said that any boy in America could grow up to be president, in their
truest hearts, they didn't mean me. Even more disturbing was that I
knew I could never be an air force pilot or an astronaut. It would be
hard enough just to be a regular scientist, much less a space adven-
turer.

"We cook the food that white people eat," Reverend Timmons
declared. "We put our hands in it and mix the burger meat." He mimicked mixing hamburger. "Put in a little chopped onion and celery.
Throw in a few breadcrumbs and stir it around with our fingers. Then
pinch out a ball of that meat and pat it into a cake." He stopped and
smiled. "Am I making anybody hungry?" The audience laughed. "We
butter the toast with our hands, and assemble the sandwiches—and
yet, when it comes to sitting with a white person at a lunch counter,
the city of Birmingham says, 'You ain't equal.'"

Reverend Timmons came nearer the pews. He looked in our direction, at Lamar, and spoke quietly. "White people trust our mothers to
take care of their children. They trust our mothers to cook and feed
their little babies. They trust them to look after the little children to
make sure they don't play too roughly or fall into any danger. They
trust our mothers to iron and clean and run their households without

setting the houses on fire." By this time, Lamar's chin was beginning to quiver, and as I looked at him my sinuses burned and I gritted my teeth. "They trust our mothers to shop at the curb market and bring home the correct change. They trust our mothers to cook supper for them without poisoning them—and they love what our mothers cook as much as we do. They would still be eating milk toast and Welsh rabbit or whatever you call it—that old moldy bread and cheese—if it wasn't for Negro women cooking good fried chicken and okra and tomatoes. But when your mother wants to try on a hat at Pizitz's or Kress's or Woolworth's, she ain't equal!"

Then Reverend Timmons touched Lamar on his shoulder. "Tell me, son, is your mama equal?"

Lamar's voice was choked off and he sniffed loudly. "Yes, sir," he managed to say.

"My God, she is!" Reverend Timmons said. "She is, because she is, somebody!" He moved down the aisle to the next pew and touched a teenage girl on her hand. He invited her to stand up. He complimented her looks, saying he bet she had boys lined up around the block on Saturday night. There were giggles. Then his tone changed and there was silence. "What about your mother? Is she equal to a white woman?"

"Yes," the girl said with a confident toss of her head.

"You aren't just saying that?"

"No. She is."

"What proof do you have?"

The girl looked perplexed and slightly embarrassed. She didn't answer.

"Do you need proof?"

"No, sir."

"Then how do you know?"

"Because I know—"

"Who told you so?"

"Nobody had to tell me—"

"My God! Nobody had to tell you! Because you know! Deep down in your heart, you know." He moved farther down the aisle. "You don't need proof of it. Because God gave you the proof. God made you. You are somebody! That's proof enough!"

By now some of the teenagers were standing and clapping. Others were shouting in agreement with Reverend Timmons. "Say it loudly," Reverend Timmons said. "I am equal!"

We began to repeat after him. "I am equal! I am somebody!" Soon the shouting became a raucous, rhythmic chanting. Some of the teenagers began singing the chant to the tune of "He's So Fine." "I'm so fine, equal rights gotta be mine all mine." Others danced in the aisles and Reverend Timmons encouraged them, laughing and clapping and praising Jesus.

After about ten minutes, he quieted the students and began speaking in a more officious tone. "I don't need to explain to you the importance of our nonviolent, direct-action campaign. We are asking those of you who are old enough, to come out and march with us and to go to jail for your freedom. And the younger ones, we ask that you encourage your parents to come out and support our efforts." It stung me when he said to encourage our parents. I knew my parents would never march. I looked at Josie. Her face seemed to have a light behind it. She smiled at me and slipped her hand in mine. By the time Reverend Timmons dismissed the meeting, we were well on our way to becoming "race men."

OVER THE NEXT WEEK, Lamar, Josie, and I attended three more workshops. Since it was taboo to talk about the workshops at school (not all of our teachers were sympathetic and those who were could get into trouble with the school board), we and the other children from our school who attended the workshops created a secret band, winking and nodding in recognition of one another. Someone might sing a verse of a workshop song—"Ain't nobody gonna turn me around," or "This little light of mine"—and another might pick up a tune and carry it along. Since these were also songs that we sang at church and school, we were above suspicion. Someone might imitate—with deference—even if it was funny to us, a gesture that Reverend Timmons might have used, shrugging his shoulders and rolling his eyes and asking, "We ain't equal?" and another might echo him from the other side of the playground.

ONE WORKSHOP was led by Reverend Bevel, a maniacally energetic man whom we thought to be both hilarious and stylish. He wore a skullcap, much like a yarmulke, on his shaven head. Though no boy ever expressed a wish for the bald head (we were nearly bald, anyway, as close cutting was the fashion of the day), we often talked about getting a skullcap. Some even went so far as to modify and wear their nylon stocking caps, sleeping caps used to flatten their hair overnight. The teachers strongly disapproved.

Reverend Bevel spoke about the contradictions most black children grew up with. At the same time that our parents and teachers told us we were as good, as smart, and as handsome as white children, they also told us that in order to be good, we had to be *like* white children. Good, in those days, meant being white—straight hair was "good" hair, "light" skin was good, and "proper" talking meant sounding white. But in the same breath, we were told that white people were unfair and mean. They were hypocrites. Never a week passed in which we didn't hear stories about white people calling blacks names, or spitting on us, or refusing to serve us.

Listening to Reverend Bevel, I realized that these ironies had less to do with my black skin, my thick lips, my kinky hair, or with the curse of Ham. Where in the Bible did God ever curse Ham? Ham was cursed by his own father, not by God. And as far as we could tell from the storybook pictures, it was one white man cursing another. The curse had more to do with greed and fear than with God. We were the white man's cheap labor. He told us we were worthless and all the time he worked us to death. Jim Crow isn't God's will, it's man's will, and man's will can be changed.

One morning, soon after we began the workshops, Lamar was laughing at a film we had seen about a lunch counter sit-in in Nashville. In the film, college students sat at stools at a lunch counter in a dime store. The white waitresses stood behind the counter with their arms folded, refusing to take the students' orders. Behind the students was a group of white people, teenagers and older. One white man poured sugar from a sugar pitcher on a woman's head. He let the sugar drain out into a pile, like a cone of sand in the bottom of an hourglass. The woman sat very still and let the sugar pile up on her head and sprinkle around her shoulders. Later in the film, the white people shoved and beat the students.

"I know it ain't supposed to be funny," Lamar was saying, "but did you see that little pile of sugar on her head. It looked like a little hat she was wearing."

"It did look funny," I agreed, but I was thinking about the expression on the girl's face. It was a look of contradictions, intense and vacant, as if she were willing herself away from what was happening. I imagined that it was the expression I had seen on my mother's face, but it was not. Mother's expression was more vacant.

"What would you do if somebody dumped something on your head like that?" Lamar asked.

"I don't know. I guess I would be nonviolent."

"Me, too." Lamar tossed a paper that landed just under Mrs. Rucker's carport in front of her door. "Bull's-eye." He looked at me for acknowledgment of his feat. "What would you do if they were going to lynch you? You wouldn't act nonviolent then."

"That's stupid. Who's going to act nonviolent when they are going to lynch you? You can't act nonviolent. You can't act no way. If they are going to lynch you, you've got to run if you can."

"I'd shoot them," he said.

"No, you wouldn't."

"Why wouldn't I? If somebody's going to shoot me——"

"There are too many of them."

"Are not."

"Why do you think we have to fight for our rights, stupid? It's because there are more of them than us."

Lamar threw a paper hard. It slammed against the front door of the Carrington house.

"Mrs. Carrington is gone get you for that."

"I don't care."

"You better care or the newspaper ain't gone to pay you. White people are everywhere and everywhere you go you are just going to be colored to them. And there's always going to be more of them than of us."

He was quiet for a moment. "If the KKK tried to lynch me, I would run away to New York City."

"So what? The KKK can go to New York City."

"But they can't go to Africa."

I didn't know enough about Africa to dispute him. "You look like an African anyway——"

"Shut up," he said.

"You started it. You look like a monkey——"

"So do you. With them big ears. You look like a gorilla." He made an ape sound. "You look like Cheetah. Where Tarzan, Cheetah? Hey, Cheetah, you want a banana? You ain't nothing but a big, black monkey." His words came so easily and so fast that I felt my cheeks burning. I knew I wasn't a monkey, but his words didn't just mean that I looked like a monkey. He meant that I was stupid, worthless, and I realized that I didn't have to hear that. I shoved him; he teetered, stopped his bicycle, and almost fell.

"Damn, Waltie, can't you take a joke?"

"It's not a joke! This race shit is not a joke. And I'll kill you if you say it is."

He looked shocked for a moment. "You started it."

I had stopped and faced him. I breathed hard and tried to cap my temper. "Yeah," I confessed, 'I'm stupid for starting it. But it ain't funny. It never was."

16

DURING THAT WEEK after Easter, things seemed to pick up for us children. Between delivering the paper, going to school and the workshops and doing homework, Josie and I were too busy "to mope," as Aunt Bennie called it. Mother seemed to have forgotten that I had stolen her medicine. She slept most of the time and when she wasn't asleep she was drowsy. There was only a short period just after school when she was alert. During those times, she walked slowly into the kitchen and sat at the table with us while we snacked. She never ate with us. Even the smell of the food made her nauseous. Aunt Bennie joked that her cooking couldn't be that bad.

We were careful to contain our excitement about the workshops, in order to keep the secret from Mother. We limited our conversation to what was going on at school, all the time fidgeting and eyeballing the clock because we only had an hour between the time school ended and the workshops began. As I think back on it, my mother probably knew we were up to something, but was too weak and unfocused to interrogate us. When Josie looked at the clock, Mother looked at it, too, and then back at Josie with a quizzical look. Josie ignored the look, and so did I. It gave me a dirty feeling to be deceiving my mother, but I wanted to go to the workshops and I knew that she wouldn't allow it.

ON SATURDAY, Lamar invited me to go with him and his mother to Terminal Station to see Reverend Timmons off to New York City to help raise money for the movement. Neither Lamar nor I had ever been inside Terminal Station, so we looked upon it as an adventure.

From the outside, the classical, domed structure looked imposing enough, but walking into the cavernous interior gave me a chill. The sunlight was muted, and fell in shafts from windows along the base of the high dome. I imagined that I was walking into a temple, and I could tell from his expression that Lamar must have felt the same way. By contrast, Reverend Timmons and Mrs. Burrell seemed to pay little attention to the building. They worried about the schedule board and the ticket prices, reading and rereading the board to make sure they were looking for the correct train. The station smelled of leather and floor wax. Around us milled people dressed in good clothes and women wearing strong perfumes and hats.

After the adults had gotten the tickets, we sat in the colored waiting area. Lamar and I sat a little ways apart from Mrs. Burrell and the reverend. "They don't want us to hear what they are talking about," Lamar said. He feigned not caring, but he kept glancing across his shoulder to see what the adults were doing. I was looking around at the various travelers. Though they were well dressed, they weren't the rich people I expected to see. On the colored side of the waiting room, I didn't expect to see wealthy people, but my movie watching had led me to expect that the white travelers would be wearing furs and diamonds and carrying Pomeranians in their arms. Only once did I see someone who suggested the movies. She was a smartly dressed, older white woman with a black porter trotting behind her.

Then, across the way from us, I noticed a young black woman. She was dressed very neatly, a pleated skirt and collared sleeveless blouse. Her hair was short and pressed in a style copied after Jackie Kennedy. She sat rather primly, her sandaled feet together, and she seemed totally absorbed in a book. I wondered what the subject of the book was. From the distance it did not seem to be a romance novel as it had no colorful cover with a passionately entwined couple; rather, it had a dull cover that made it appear to be a serious book. It seemed thick and heavy, and I imagined that the woman was a college student. Suddenly, I had a rush that flushed me from toe to head. At the time I couldn't put a name on the rush, now I would call it a sexual rush. But even then, in my adolescent mind, I knew that something remarkable and unscientific was occurring. I wanted to be close to that woman. I wanted to read over her shoulder, to smell the scent of her hair, to smell the dab of perfume on her neck. Who was she? What did she know? It was the first time I remember making a more or less conscious link between sexual desire and book knowledge. Such a young woman would become a central image of my maturing imagination, beautiful, smart with science, sophisticated—not unlike my mother, and yet the essence of nonmotherliness.

Just as my flush was subsiding, Lamar noticed the woman. His hand came down on my knee with a steadiness, and then he said, "Uhh-oh." Hardly had the admonishment cleared his lips, when a white man approached the young woman, and now I noticed what I hadn't before: she was sitting on the wrong side of the rope; she was sitting on the white side.

Because the station was noisy, I couldn't hear the conversation between the man, who looked like a manager, and the woman. The man's face was red, and he bent toward the woman with his chin stuck out. The young woman recoiled. She felt around her seat for her bag, grasped the handle, but couldn't move because the man was leaning over her. I imagined that he was calling her names because she looked like she would burst into tears. A few of the white customers stopped to look at the scene; they jerked, recoiled in sync with the young woman.

Reverend Timmons came behind us and spoke quietly. "Steady, boys, steady. If I walk out, you follow me."

There was no need for us to leave. The situation defused quickly, as the man stood back and gave the young woman enough room to flee. A moment later, people turned back to their private concerns, some laughing, others shaking their heads. She was a demonstrator, someone in the colored section said disparagingly. Another disagreed. No. She was a northerner and didn't know any better.

I looked at Reverend Timmons, his dark, round face full of relief. Why hadn't he helped her? He was always saying we needed to go to jail for our rights, but he had told us to follow him if he walked out.

He patted my shoulder. "We live to fight another day." He went back to where Mrs. Burrell sat and took her hand.

Lamar let go of my leg. "She ought to have known not to do that. Look at the sign." He nodded his head toward the sign that prominently pointed out white and colored waiting areas. "She must not have been able to read or something."

Where the young woman had sat remained empty, except for the book lying on the chair. Suddenly, I wanted the book. I wanted to read it, to ponder what she had pondered. Perhaps I could find the woman and return the book, and we would sit and talk about all the complicated information it must have contained. I watched the book and waited for a chance when I could spring away from the colored section and snatch it. I pointed it out to Lamar.

"Don't mean she can read. Lots of people have books," he said.

"Don't you want to see what it is?"

Lamar looked interested. He looked over his shoulder at his mother, and then gave me a look that dared me to go and get it. Just as I was about to accept the dare, a white man, about the same age as the woman, came along and picked it up. Out of my earshot, he seemed to ask the people around if it belonged to them. Someone must have told him what had happened for he moved awkwardly for a moment, seesawing with indecision. Then in a graceful, angular stride he took the book to the wastebasket. A moment later, Reverend Timmons's train was called.

"Come on, y'all. Come see the train," Mrs. Burrell called to us as if we were babies. We had seen trains before, but we followed the adults downstairs to the platform and to the colored-only coaches. We shook hands with Reverend Timmons and he gave Mrs. Burrell a kiss on the lips. She seemed embarrassed. She made us wait until the train pulled out of the station.

On the way back upstairs and through the terminal, Lamar suddenly took a detour. Quickly, with an intent look on his face, he walked through the white waiting area. Mrs. Burrell did not see him as she focused straight ahead, negotiating her way through the crowded station. In just a moment, Lamar was at my side again, smiling. He held the book to show it to me, but when I reached for it, he snatched it back, making clear that it now belonged to him. The book was *Leaves of Grass* by Walt Whitman. When I asked my father to explain it to me, he said it was poetry that college students studied. I readily accepted the explanation since neither Lamar nor I could make much sense of it.

ALTHOUGH THE HOUSE was quiet when I came back from the train station, I did not think anything was wrong until I peeked into Mother's room. The covers were thrown back from the bed and her gown lay on the floor. I called her name, and there was no answer. For a moment I stood and listened. Through the window, I could hear birds chirping and squirrels barking, and the faraway voices of neighbors going about their Saturday business. Inside seemed hollow, and suddenly as cavernous and dim as Terminal Station.

On the kitchen table was a note from Aunt Bennie to me. It said that Mother was at the hospital, and that I was to wait until my father came to get me. In a few minutes, I heard his car in the driveway, and ran out to meet him. I wanted to hug him, but he didn't get out of the car. He asked me to shut up the house—we didn't lock up in those days—and to get in the car with him.

"Your mother is in the hospital," he said matter of fact, but his eyelids fluttered and I knew he was upset.

Josie was asleep on the couch in the waiting room, her head in Aunt Bennie's lap. Father took her into his lap. She squirmed, but settled into the crook in his arm. He and Aunt Bennie talked about my mother's condition. Aunt Bennie whispered that Mother had been in a lot of pain and the medicine didn't seem to do any good. Then she began to spit up blood. That was when Aunt Bennie first said she would take Mother to the hospital, but my mother refused to go. When you are sick, Mother said, who wants to be reminded that you are being treated second class. It was not until she passed out that Aunt Bennie called the ambulance.

My father spoke in his normal voice. "Goddamnit," he said, "she is going to get an operation. That's all." Aunt Bennie's look seemed to upset him. "What?" he said. "Don't tell me you are going to support her in this foolishness. Bennie, be reasonable."

"It's too late to be reasonable," Aunt Bennie said. Her face began to jump around as she fought to hold back her tears. "The doctor said it's too late. *Didn't you know?* All we can do now is to make her comfortable. You did know, didn't you?"

Father put his face against Josie as he rocked her. He looked sunken.

"Carl, you did know, didn't you? She did tell you."

Father said nothing.

"Lord, I can't believe—"

"Yes, Bennie." Father raised up and cut Aunt Bennie with a look. "What do you think? Of course she told me. Why wouldn't she have?" His lips trembled and he looked angry and ashamed.

I felt my face getting jumpy like Aunt Bennie's, but I managed to hold everything down.

THERE WAS A great deal of excitement at next Wednesday's workshop because a demonstrator, William Moore, had been killed just outside of Birmingham. The excitement was particularly poignant because Moore was a postman, a federal employee, and a white man. Black men were killed all the time in the South, Reverend Timmons, recently returned from New York, reminded us. Some we hear about in the Negro newspapers because they are lynched by mobs, but many just disappear until someone draws a bucket of bones from the bottom of a well. But the murder of a white man was sure to get the attention of the television people. The reverends gave a lesson about all the people who had died for "the cause." At the end of the lecture, Reverend Bevels invited us to stay for the mass meeting. I thought we should go home, but many of the children agreed to stay, and Lamar and Josie wanted to stay, as well. Since Reverend Timmons was taking us home, anyway, we didn't have much choice.

By six o'clock, the church was packed with adults. Though we children had seats near the front, we were squeezed into the pews. Several preachers talked and led songs before Reverend Shuttlesworth gave the main talk. Though I had heard Reverend Shuttlesworth's name mentioned at the dinner table by my father and Uncle Reed, I had never seen him in person. He had been the leader of the civil rights movement in Birmingham for as long as I had known. He was a dark, wiry, energetic man. He bounced and raised on his toes and clapped and sang and got the crowd into a very good mood. In spite of the fact that this was a serious meeting and somewhat dangerous because the police detectives were sitting in the back of the church taking notes, the preachers kept the mood upbeat. They joked back and forth with one another and made jokes about Bull Connor and Governor George Wallace.

A commotion from behind got my attention. People were standing in the aisles so I couldn't see all the way to the back of the church. A white man was causing the disturbance. At first I thought he was a policeman, but I saw that he was a fireman wearing a formal uniform, epaulets and badges. He was yelling that the building was too full and that the meeting had to come to an end because we were breaking the fire code.

Rather than dismissing the meeting, Reverend Shuttlesworth seemed amused. He sauntered back and forth on the podium, and made jocular gestures that made the crowd roar with laughter. I lost sight of the fireman as the crowd jostled, but it was apparent from the actions of Reverend Shuttlesworth and the crowd that the fireman was frustrated.

"I'll have you arrested for contempt," the fireman threatened.

Shuttlesworth shrugged and made a face of mock fear. Then he laughed and spoke into the microphone. His voice boomed over the crowed and drowned out the strained voice of the fireman. "That's your prerogative, Chief," he said. "But now, you wouldn't want all these Negroes here to come down to the contempt trial and have to use the whites-only water fountains at city hall? Now would you?"

The crowd laughed with growing hilarity. At first I was not certain whether to laugh. I looked at Josie, who seemed in a limbo, as well. We took our cue from Reverend Shuttlesworth, the little man with the booming voice, unafraid and frisky. We began to laugh and jeer the fireman. "Yeah," I heard myself saying, "we will drink your white water." Josie repeated it after me. The laughter had an infectious power, more powerfully entertaining than any cartoon slapstick at the movies, more powerfully infectious than any canned laughter from a sitcom. It was laughter that filled me up, tickled me under the ribs, bubbled up deep in my lungs, convulsed my stomach muscles, and spilled out of my mouth in chest-clenching heaves. Josie's little body swayed with laughter. Her mouth was wide and her eyes shut tight and her voice was loud. The laughter seemed to rush out of her like music from a horn. I was suddenly outside of myself, witnessing myself laughing and enjoying the laughter. It seemed the laughter was solid, something we could fall back into like a room full of feather pillows, something that held us up, while we let our bodies go limp, while we let down our guard, while we let ourselves feel invigorated and rested and alive.

I could not see what happened to the fire chief, but I imagined he left in disgrace. Nonetheless, the mood changed when other preachers gave tribute to William Moore. They spoke so eloquently that people wept. I put my arm around Josie's shoulder, and she looked at me and smiled. It was a smile so much like our mother's that I had the feeling she was my mother for a moment, that Josie was the older and I the younger.

Then Reverend King came to the pulpit. I hadn't thought much about him in the week or so since his arrest, but caught up in the mood of the meeting, I was elated to see him free and jumped from my seat and applauded. In my mind his return from jail was no less a triumph than Shadrach, Meshach, and Abednego's emergence from the furnace.

When the cheering died down, Reverend King spoke in a swaying voice, as much singing as speaking. At first, I wasn't listening to his words as much as I was feeling them, feeling them sing and hum, and then an abrupt silence came. Reverend King called for volunteers to go to jail. No one went forth on the first call. He explained his strategy, that in order to win our rights we had to show that we were willing to fill the jails. Without volunteers to fill the jails no one would believe that we wanted our rights. A few people went up. The other preachers clapped and sang out praises when a volunteer went, but hardly anyone in the audience clapped. The preachers cajoled, joked, encouraged. Finally, a high school student went forward. "Praise God," someone on the podium said. Then another student went up. Suddenly, I had an impulse to move, to go to the front. It felt like a calling, a voice in my head repeating all that I had heard in the workshop and all that I had heard in the meeting. But I was also called by the feeling of the laughter, the lightness, the feeling that I had nothing to fear, that life in all its monstrous writhing was nothing at all to worry about, rather something to banter with, something to challenge. I felt myself moving, but simultaneously I was being pushed as Josie squeezed past me. My hand automatically went into hers and we walked up to the front of the church. "Lord have mercy," I heard one of the preachers say. "Look at our children. They know what they want. They know they want their freedom." More children came forward, including Lamar, until among the twenty or so volunteers stood ten children.

Reverend King spoke very sympathetically to us. He said he deeply appreciated our willingness to suffer for our freedom. He hoped that our shining examples would inspire our parents to our noble cause. But, he said, we should take our seats. The cause was important, but it was not so desperate as to send children to jail.

We didn't move. None other than _Reverend King_ had told us to take our seats, and still we didn't move. I thought about my mother, and I knew she couldn't be here, and my father—I didn't think he would volunteer, so I would have to stand for them. I said to Josie that she should take her seat. She stared straight ahead. I said again for her to sit down, and she looked at me, a sparkle of defiance in her eyes and I knew that as long as I stood, she would stand with me. Even if I sat down, she might remain standing. No matter how Reverend King entreated us, we would not sit down.

DEAR MR. AND MRS. JACKSON, *Reverend King is dead. He had a dream. Now I am dead. I had a dream, too. It was a dream deeply rooted . . . deeply rooted in the human dream. I had a dream that one day I would rise up above the ground in a space capsule. That one day, I would look down on the earth, spinning blue and brown below me, spinning softly, slowly, spinning blue. I had a dream one day.*

17

OUR MOTHER didn't have the energy to get mad with us the next morning when Aunt Bennie, in a confessional mode, marched us in front of her and described the worry we had caused her. At first, Mother had a trace of a smile, but as she came to understand that we had been out of the house until after ten o'clock without permission and at a race meeting to boot, she lost her smile and shut her eyes. "Well . . . you're okay. That's the important thing." The old Mother would have pitched a fit, but the new Mother, assured that we were safe, slipped into a placid somnambulism. It seemed that a new order of rules had come to the house.

Some years later, I decided that there are but a handful of rules that determine everything moral in life and death. These are the same rules regardless of religion. In fact, it is better to profess no religion and adhere only to a few choice principles that, unfortunately, guarantee nothing in the way of happiness and might even increase life's hardship. I cannot catalog these principles. I cannot make a list of commandments or beatitudes. Every case is different. Everyone must make his own list. But, for me, every one of the rules is concerned with love, however it is defined. Love is very complicated. It resists analysis. It cannot be counted or counted upon. It presents unsolvable problems that, nonetheless, are solved everyday, though rarely solved neatly and often with ambiguity.

Many times I would forget my rules—they are not easy to keep in mind because there are no timetables of love. Love has no factors: A mother times a father equals what? A sister divided by a brother is what? And when the whole world goes crazy, then what? What do you do when the world divides itself into black and white, free and red? Where do you stand? When you are chased by dogs and beaten down with clubs, how many times do you turn the other cheek? When your friends are shot and blown up to chunks, how do you love? These are more than just questions. They are our daily bread. How can you love without hating a little?

Even drugged, Mother could not come to a truce with my father. When Aunt Bennie mentioned that my father had called and he wanted to come over, Mother's eyes fired. In a weak, gravelly voice she said that she would call him when she wanted him, not the other way around.

Father lectured to me on the telephone about responsibility when he learned we had stayed at the meeting. School, he said, was my ticket out of Birmingham, not demonstrating in the streets. In a flash of anger, he asked if I had been thinking about endangering my little sister. Then he grounded us.

Aunt Bennie scoffed when I told her what our punishment was. She said Father had better come home and supervise—but then, immediately, she reinforced him. I knew that the punishment was not enforceable—Josie and I would go where we wanted. Aunt Bennie's authority lacked whip and snap, and with our mother sick, and our father in a motel, there was no one to restrain us. In fact, our neighbors felt so much sympathy for us that they practically melted when they encountered us.

School and homework held us in check for the rest of the week, but on Saturday we decided to go with Lamar to the Carver Theater to see the new Tarzan movie. I asked Aunt Bennie, and Josie gave her a pitiful look and complained that it wasn't our fault that Reverend Timmons hadn't brought us home. Aunt Bennie sighed and said to ask Mother. I knew Mother was likely to be asleep, but I went to her room anyway. To my surprise, she seemed awake. I told her that we would be going to the movies. She smiled so vacantly that I repeated myself. A few moments later, Lamar and I set off on our bikes with Josie on my handlebars and Bingo running beside.

The boycott of the white stores didn't affect Fourth Avenue, where black people came to get their hair fixed and to be entertained. People were dressed up, some especially sporty, wearing narrow-legged pants, half boots, and porkpies with feathers. Some men wore conks with scarves tied around them. The women preferred flaring skirts made of shiny materials, and some wore the heavy mascara made popular by girl groups like the Vandellas. We called it the "Motown look."

The woman who took the tickets at the Carver knew my mother. She asked how Mother was, and then she refused to take our money. Now we had extra money to buy Sugar Babies, popcorn, and grape Nehis. Bingo waited outside, settled beside our bicycles in one corner of the Carver's alcove. A Tarzan movie starred Mike Henry, a new actor. Unlike movies that came on television starring Johnny Weismuller, this movie was in color. We thought the new Tarzan "was stronger"—had a better physique than the old—and he was educated. He used good grammar. He understood the modern world. He could use a gun as easily as a knife. In many ways, the Mike Henry Tarzan was more like James Bond than Tarzan, despite his running around in a loincloth. He seemed to treat the natives with a respect the old Tarzan didn't have. A native porter could fall off of a cliff, and the old Tarzan would only be concerned that the supplies were lost. The new Tarzan killed plenty of natives, but they were bad natives. On the other hand, he had friends among the good natives. Lamar said the new Tarzan was a race man. We left the movie with a very good feeling that Tarzan had taken up the cause.

After the movie, we started home, rolling our bikes at our side. Soon we became aware of chanting and sirens in the distance.

"It's the demonstration," Lamar told us.

I remembered my father's lecture about responsibility and I worried that he would see us, but the worry evaporated in a flash and a pang when I thought of Father lying on the floor in boozy slumber. I should have insisted that we go home, but with workshop rhetoric in my head, I led as we returned our bikes to the Carver's alcove and walked in the direction of the demonstration.

"What if we get arrested?" Lamar said.

"That's what we're suppose to do," Josie said. She had a determined look on her face, hardened by a tense jawbone. Her eyes were narrow.

"We will just look today," I decided. "We can march and look, but we won't go to jail until we can tell somebody."

"Ahhh," Lamar said with some bravado now that he thought we wouldn't be going to jail. "You're just scared to go to jail, that's all."

"And what about you?" Josie came back.

"I ain't crazy," Lamar said with a good-natured laugh. "Besides, they won't arrest kids."

As we drew closer to the commotion we found ourselves at the rear of a large crowd of spectators. Many of the spectators were people we had seen earlier on Fourth Avenue, dressed in shiny suits and dresses. It was difficult for us to see what was happening at the front of the crowd, though we could hear people singing "This Little Light of Mine."

Suddenly the crowd shifted, everyone stepping back at once. Almost immediately I lost sight of Josie, as a wave of people swept around us. I couldn't see what had caused the crowd to move, but the confusion and alarm suggested it was dangerous. I caught a glimpse of Josie as adults, not looking at their feet, were bumping into her, throwing her off balance. Then I saw a flash of Bingo's tail and I knew he was beside her. I made my way to her and picked her up. Suddenly an elbow hit my eye and I dropped Josie. I caught her hand as she stumbled. I picked her up again. Bingo yelped and I saw that a man's foot had kicked him.

When we got clear of the crowd, I could see the police restraining huge German shepherds. The police were big men, but even in their uniforms, they didn't impress me. There was a time when the uniform of a Birmingham cop would have made me freeze in my tracks, but after the workshops, after the laughter at the mass meetings, I simply saw them as white men bearing the countenance of someone doing a dirty job. The dogs, however, were a different story. For one thing, stories had been circulating already about the ferocity of the dogs. It was told how the razor-sharp teeth could bite through a leg with one snap. Police dog. A curious and dangerous animal, like a rattlesnake or a grizzly bear, but it was not one that acted out of instinct; rather, it had been trained to hate "nigras." You didn't have to do anything wrong, you only had to be black, and you were subject to its attack.

I held tightly to Josie's hand, but I had lost sight of Lamar. I thought he had gone back to the bicycles, as his strategy was always to make a hasty retreat. Josie, in turn, held onto Bingo's collar and the three of us pushed through the crowd of adults. They were jeering as the police arrested a man. The dogs had shred the man's pants.

We made our way to the rear of the crowd and around the next block, heading in the direction of the Carver. The block was lined with automobiles but it was nightmarishly empty of people. Josie pulled her hand away from mine, and we walked hurriedly. Then, suddenly, Bingo's ears pricked and the hair on his back bristled. He stopped and leaned in the direction we were heading and barked and snarled.

"What's the matter, Bingo?" Josie asked. No sooner had she spoken than a stallion of a police dog emerged from behind a van. She screamed and held Bingo's collar. A policeman came around the van, holding the dog by a leash. The police dog stood stiff and snarled.

"You children go on," the policeman said.

I took Bingo's collar away from Josie and started to drag him across the street. He relented and we moved into the middle of the street, then he stiffened again as the police dog, still leashed, came around the van the other way. The dog's lips were drawn back, and his growl rumbled. Bingo returned the growl, and the dogs leaned toward one each other, neck hairs spiked and teeth bared. The shepherd was twice Bingo's size and I could see right away that it would make short work of him. But Bingo showed no fear. He had braced his back legs and had gotten pretty ugly. The policeman waved us on again, and as he did so, his dog made a lurch. The policeman stamped his foot and made as if to chase Bingo. Bingo stood his ground. The shepherd was much closer now, having pulled himself toward the middle of the street. I slapped Bingo on the nose. I felt terrible doing it because he made a high-pitched yelp and put down his head. Josie kicked me. "You don't have to—" she said. The shepherd made another lurch. I looked up, and as I did I felt my hand slip from Bingo's collar.

The two dogs met chest to chest like wrestlers; there was a whirlwind of ferocity as their bodies twisted and spun around one another. Paws scratched on the asphalt. Bingo yelped and then there was quiet. Fur floated in the air.

Josie screamed and turned her face to me. The policeman came from in between the cars with a stick, but he didn't need to use it. His dog came back to him when he called it. Josie turned away from me now and took a step toward Bingo. Bingo's bloody chest heaved and then he was still.

Now, Josie's face was full of questions. I couldn't move for a moment before I went over to Bingo, and felt his chest. His fur was warm and wet. Josie stood beside me, looking intently at Bingo. She didn't touch him, only repeated his name, each time more like a question. The police came over and asked, "Is he dead?"

I nodded.

"I'm sorry, son." I looked up at the man. I thought he might yell at us, but now he stooped and put his hand on Josie's head, not to pet her but to rest it there. I felt a strange, hot tremble when I saw the man's big, white hand on my sister's head. She seemed indifferent to the hand. Again her face was hard, her teeth were grinding. Slowly I stood. The policeman was big, as big as a TV wrestler. I slapped his hand off of Josie's head. "Why couldn't you . . . ? Why did you . . . ?" was all I managed to get out.

"Look, children—" he said.

"You killed Bingo!" Josie said. She twirled to face the man. "You killed him!"

"Little girl, I didn't kill anything."

"Yes, you did!" Josie's shoulders flared back and I thought she might attack the policeman.

"Let's go, Josie," I said. I picked up Bingo, cradled him in my arms the way I had sometimes done with Josie, and started toward the Carver. "Let me give you a ride," the policeman said, but we ignored him.

LAMAR WAS WAITING for us at the Carver. He wanted to know what had happened, but we couldn't tell him. Strangers stopped us to ask what had happened, and slowly we were able just to say a police dog had killed Bingo. We could barely open our mouths to breathe. We went by the motel to find our father, but he wasn't there. So I carried Bingo, and Josie and Lamar pushed the bikes as we started toward home in the hot afternoon. After about a mile, a man in a truck stopped and asked if we needed help. I told him we didn't, but he insisted that we get on the truck bed, and he took us home.

Aunt Bennie cursed and called the policeman names until Josie asked her to be quiet. Then our aunt had an odd expression, embarrassment, I think. She told us to get cleaned up and we would bury Bingo. She and I dug the grave in the soft dirt next to the garden. With mattock and shovel we dug down to where the ground turned rocky. When everything was ready, we buried him.

18

AUNT BENNIE insisted that it wouldn't be much of a funeral if there were no funeral repast. No one felt like eating, but we sat at the table anyway. Mother sat with us, smiling again. It was not a real smile, and I wished that she would stop it.

After lunch, Mother asked if I would walk her back to her room. Tenderly, I put my arm around her waist. I tried to be gentle, to let her lean on me and to hold her at the same time. She smelled bad and her arms were just bones and soft skin. Part of me wanted to push her away. She was more like an elderly stranger than my mother. Another part of me wanted to give her a hard hug and cry on her shoulder. These impulses fought inside of me, but I was successful in not allowing either to win.

Lying in the bed, she patted the sheets near her side, inviting me to come and sit by her before she took her medicine again. Josie came in, sat with us, and held Mother's hand.

"My poor children," Mother said. "This won't go on forever." I knew what she meant, and suddenly a rock-hard lump came in my throat and made it impossible for me to swallow.

"Yes it can," Josie said. Mother turned her face away from us. We waited while she struggled not to cry. I looked out of the window at the sunlight on the lawn. The lawn needed cutting; the garden was wilted. Bingo's grave was a mound topped by a small bouquet of Mrs. Jeters's azaleas.

When mother was composed again, she continued, "I don't want to leave you, but what can I do?"

"You can have an operation," I said.

"You are like your daddy for the world. Just a scientist!" She rested for a few minutes. "Even the doctor said the operation wouldn't save me, Waltie."

"It would give you a chance," I said.

"Waltie, honey, I know what you're going through. I would give anything not to have you go through it. I went through it, too. With my father." We could hear Aunt Bennie in the kitchen washing the dishes. "I think it's easier to die than to go through what you are going through. You get used to dying, and you know it's going to end, but the hoping, maintaining all that hope, is so hard." She began telling us the story of Walter Lee's arrest. "I hoped and prayed, and prayed and hoped. The preacher said, 'Let God's will be done,' and I prayed that God's will would be done. And it was." She rested a moment. "That's the funny part of it. God's will must always be done, but you pray for it, too. I prayed they would let you go."

"Who, Mama?"

She dropped Josie's hand and took mine, and looked into my face. Her eyes seemed alive, now, but focused beyond me, and I knew she was talking to my grandfather. I was not afraid: rather, I thought the situation strange and sad and I took a firmer grip on her hand.

"They say you the wrong man, but they keep you anyway. I pray they don't lynch you. They don't, but they shoot you. I pray you don't die in the hospital. You don't, but they take you to the courthouse. I pray you get off. The damn sheriff of Jefferson County say you innocent and still they condemn you to the chair. I pray, God, don't electrocute my daddy. He my daddy!"

Josie patted her head, and smoothed back her hair, and she came back to us.

"That was the only prayer He answered. Let him rot in the jailhouse." She focused on me. "So Waltie, what's the answer? I want you to pray. But don't *hope* for things. Just trust that God's will is God's will. That's what faith is. Trust, but not hope."

"But, Mama, don't you hope for us? Don't you hope for the better?"

"Hope is a delusion. Something to keep folks down. You keep hoping for the better, but it doesn't get better. But they keep telling you to hope for it. You spend all your life wasting your time hoping. That's why I like working for Dr. Gaston—because he *is* colored, and I never had to worry about being colored. We never saw any white people, so we were just who we were. We didn't have to pretend one way or the other. No delusions about 'overcoming.' What was, was what was. You see, I'm really more scientific than your father. He is still hoping for an operation to save me. He's even hoping for some operation to save colored people. *Doctor* Martin Luther King! But I've learned to accept things as they are because things just go on like they do. It's God's will. You've got to be realistic about God's will."

I couldn't grasp all of what she meant, but she seemed brave, and I thought that she, not my father, was correct. She was the more scientific because science meant accepting facts.

"But you *could* still have an operation," Josie said.

"No, peach pit."

"You haven't even tried."

Mother's smile was slightly condescending. "This is not like homework, child." She paused again and I realized now that her pauses were crests in her pain. I got a pill, put it in her mouth, and helped her drink a glass of water. Soon, I could see relief bloom in her face. Then I was sorry, more than ever, that I had once deprived her of that relief.

THE NEXT MORNING, when I came home from delivering the newspapers, my father surprised me. He was turning into the driveway, earlier than usual, coming to take us to Sunday school. He called out a greeting as I put away my bike, and he strolled toward me with a big smile. Closer, the smile seemed waxen, and his walk stiff and as angular as a gunfighter.

"Wait up," he called. I waited at the kitchen door, my hand on the handle. When he reached me, he patted my head. "How's my boy?"

I wanted to say, "I'm not your boy," but I said, "Okay," and opened the door. "Daddy's here!" I called more like a warning than an announcement.

"Look what the cat drugged in," Aunt Bennie said. She was cooking breakfast, standing in her robe and slippers, her hair in curlers. "You're on time for a change."

"God bless you, too, Benita. How are things here?"

Aunt Bennie sighed and cracked an egg on the edge of a bowl. "It's your house, don't you know?"

Father stood patiently and looked around the room. "How's Josie?" he asked me.

"She's okay."

"And your mama?"

"She's okay, too," Aunt Bennie answered. "Children haven't had their breakfast yet. Why don't you just sit in the den and wait for them?"

"Bennie," my father said, "I know I haven't been here, but that's not my fault."

"Whose fault is it then?" Aunt Bennie told me to run along and get ready. I started away, but stopped. "I have a family of my own to worry about," she said, "but I'm here for my sister. The least you could do—"

"I'm sorry, Bennie," my father said. "If it's money . . ." He pulled out his wallet. His hands shook.

"Money, Carl? You know better than that. Your family needs *you*. You don't have the luxury of cooling your heels at the swank Gaston Motel while your wife is dying and your kids are running wild."

"Running wild. Who's running wild?"

Aunt Bennie put down the spatula and took the pan of eggs off of the eye. She wiped her hands on the apron and turned to face my father. Her voice was a sharp whisper. "'Running wild' may be an exaggeration, but these kids need you."

My father stepped toward me, a threat in his posture, something I had seen in him when he had fought with my mother. "Walter," he said. "Who is running wild?"

"Nobody," I said.

Aunt Bennie moved behind him. "I said I exaggerated, Carl; *nobody* is running wild. Your children need you. You need to be here for them. You need to act like a father."

He turned to her. "I don't need *this*. *This* is what I don't need. *You* don't tell *me* how *I'm* acting." He turned to me again. "Walter, when haven't *I* acted like a father? Aren't I a good father to you?"

"I didn't mean it that way," Bennie said. "I just meant that the children need you at this time. I can't be their daddy, Carl. I can't do everything."

I stepped backward into the den. Father stepped toward me. Aunt Bennie followed. Josie came in the den from the bedrooms. My father's tone changed. "Hi, sweet pea."

Josie burst into tears and ran to him. "Bingo got killed."

"Bingo got killed?" My father picked Josie up and looked at me. "What happened?"

"Dog fight," I said.

"What dog?"

I didn't want to say, but Josie said, "A police dog."

"A police dog? How did a police dog . . . ? Where did this happen?"

"It happened downtown," Aunt Bennie said. "They went to the movies and that's where it happened."

"You let them go by themselves?"

"I let them? What do you mean, 'I let them'?"

"I mean, if you aren't watching my children any better than——"

"Shut up!" Aunt Bennie stamped her foot. "Carl, I don't get you. What has happened to you? Have you let liquor rot your brain? Think about it." She pointed two fingers to her head like she was pointing a gun. "Just think about it? Where were you yesterday? Which bar were you in when your children needed you?"

We looked at my father, as if he were about to provide an answer to a perplexing mystery. His face seemed to fumble, lips trying to make words, and words seeming to fall off his chin. I looked as long as I could and turned away, only to come face to face with a bony, fiery-eyed apparition of my mother.

"Get out," she said hoarsely.

My father's fumbling stopped and he faced her, a little surprised. "Clara, baby . . ." His voice seemed full of wooing. "Baby——"

"Don't you criticize Bennie when you haven't been here."

Father raised his hands. "How do you expect me to be here? You—— I'm trying to do what you want me to!"

"You don't even *know* what I want. You don't even . . ." Mother's voice drained to a whisper.

Father spoke evenly, but firmly. "Clara, how can I know? How can I figure this out?"

Mother turned her back to him and started toward the bedroom. She braced herself against the doorjamb and looked as if she might fall. Father beat me to her. He held her under her arm. For a moment she let him hold her, then she shrugged and pushed his hand away. "Walter." I took her by the elbow.

After we got mother back to bed, Aunt Bennie went on the offensive. She ordered my father out of the house. At first he dared her, spreading his legs apart as if to challenge her to move him. He shook his head and lowered it. "This doesn't make sense. You are just as crazy as she is."

"I didn't *beat* nobody," Aunt Bennie said. "Is that what you mean by crazy?"

"Bennie . . ." Father raised his hands in defeat and went out the house. I followed him.

"Go on back in. Go on and take care of your mother. I guess you're the man in the house now."

"Don't go, Daddy."

"You make one mistake, one time—"

"Don't go, Daddy." He had been away for three weeks.

He laughed. "Do you see me going any place? I have no place to go, Son. Where am I going to go?" He got into the car and started it. For a moment, he just sat and looked at his lap, as if praying. Then he looked up and smiled, crisp and lovely, as if nothing were the matter.

ON WEDNESDAY MORNING Reverend Timmons sent word by Lamar that we should return to the workshops. "I told him that your daddy had put a curfew on you," Lamar explained as he banded the newspapers, "but Reverend said that the workshops were more important than a curfew. He said you have a higher authority to answer to than your 'earthly father.'"

I stopped rolling the papers and stared up at the stars. With the springtime change, the mornings had become dark again.

I wanted to go to the workshops, but I also wanted to obey my father. Already, Father thought that I was irresponsible, that I had endangered Josie, and that it was my fault that Bingo had gotten killed. "Reverend didn't say that."

"He did, too," Lamar said. "He didn't tell me to *tell* you he said it, but he said it. He told me to tell you that you are a child of God and that as a child of the living God you had to make the right stand. He said it was good to obey your earthly father because the Bible says to honor your mother and your father, but sometimes you got to step out by faith alone."

"What did he mean by 'faith alone'? Not to obey my father?"

"He didn't say what he meant. He just said to tell you that."

I imagined the way my father looked when he left the house that Sunday morning, how he hung his head and looked at his lap. If Reverend Timmons had heard the dry chuckle my father had made, more a clucking in his throat than a chuckle, then he wouldn't tell me to disobey him. He would see that "stepping out alone" wouldn't be right. "Tell him no. Josie and I aren't coming to any more workshops."

Lamar snorted. "And may I ask why?"

"No, you may not." I loaded the papers into the bicycle racks. "Josie said that since our father had put us on curfew and since we had already disobeyed it, that it would make him feel very bad if we disobeyed him again."

"So what does she know?"

I could have hit him, but I got on my bicycle and delivered the papers and didn't say anything else to him that morning. Still, Reverend Timmons's message troubled me. What did he mean by stepping out by faith alone? It seemed that any way I stepped, it was by faith—and alone. It seemed that everyone was stepping by faith alone all the time. Mother wouldn't get an operation because of faith alone and Father wanted her to get the operation because of faith alone. Anything anyone did, after all, was done on some kind of faith. When Lamar and I flung our newspapers, we had the faith that they would land, because as crazy as things were getting, there was not one reason that they shouldn't fly off into space. Having faith, after all, wasn't the problem; the problem was what to have faith in. If I went to the workshops I had the faith that we would get our freedom, and that kind of faith involved having hope. It involved dreaming for something better, and that was not my mother's faith.

• • •

THE NEXT MORNING, Wednesday, Lamar met me on the way to the school to roll the newspapers. "I couldn't wait to tell you, and Mama said it was too late to call last night," he said breathlessly, not even a "hello" first. "You want to march?" His eyes were bright, picking up the porch lights along Center Street. "Not just see one. Be in one?"

"Who's going to let you be in one?" I asked. I remembered how we were told to sit down when we had volunteered. "Reverend King said that children couldn't march." I got off my bike at Center Street School and began to cut the twine on the stacks of papers that had been tossed on the lawn for us.

"He's changed his mind. He said it is all right for kids if they want to. But you have to be baptized."

"Why?"

"Because you have to be called by God. W.W. said if you're baptized nothing will happen to you."

I thought about Grandpa Willie Lee. He must have been baptized. "Bullshit," I said.

"Shit? What you say 'shit' for? You don't cuss."

"I do now."

"What got you started? Just because I mentioned you had to be baptized, you got to go and act like you're not."

"I'm not baptized. I'm *christened.*"

"It doesn't matter. Mama said it's all the same in God's eyes. But don't say anything about the marches. Loose lips sink ships is what W.W. said." He said "W.W." like it was a new word.

"W.W.? Who the hell is W.W.?"

Lamar pursed his lips and scratched behind his ear. "That's what Reverend told me to call him." A smile stretched across his face. "He and Mama are getting very close."

"Close?"

"Staying over close."

I worked fast at bundling my papers and putting them in the bike's basket.

"Staying over . . ." Lamar repeated.

"I heard you."

"I might be getting a daddy."

I mounted my bicycle, kicked up the kickstand, and stood strad-dling it while I waited for him. The air was cool, a little damp. I looked at Lamar standing in a patch of light from inside the school. You might be better off without a daddy, I started to say, but stopped before the thought formed breath. What was the use? He'd find out before long, and there was nothing I or he could do about it. I looked at Lamar and then at the dawn. The astronauts Glenn, Grissom, and Schirra circled and circled the world, but what was this world in the sea of stars? Even as high as they were, they hadn't gone a thousandth of the way to the moon. They were specks. What influence has a speck on the current of the universe? And a colored speck? Forget the thought. Every little river in the state of Alabama, in any southern state, could spit up a colored man any day of the week. And what could a colored boy do, if a man couldn't do a thing? The universe was wide and it was pretty to look at, but it ran a course all its own, and that was just the way things were.

AT SCHOOL during recess, Josie approached me on the softball field. Usually she played with the girls by the swings and only rarely acknowledged her relation to me.

"What's the matter?" I asked. I was playing in the center field, but had to cover right field, too, because the boy who was playing there didn't have a glove.

"Nothing's the matter," she said. Suddenly I wanted to hug her she looked so pitiful, my little sister, looking like an old woman. She slipped a folded leaflet into my free hand. "Keep this for me. But don't open it. It's one of those party invitations that's going around and Mrs. Buford will get you if you have one." I slipped the paper in my pocket, heard the crack of ball and bat, and looked up. It was foul. When I looked again at Josie, she was already heading back to her sorority at the swings.

I forgot about the leaflet and didn't read it until we were walking home from school. It was the first day since Bingo died that Josie hadn't mentioned him, so I tried to keep her mind on the leaflet. She took the leaflet away from me and began to skip while reading it aloud. It read, "Come to the big party." It urged us to leave school at noon on Thursday, the next day, and to meet at the sixteenth Street Baptist Church for a big march. It said that we should come regardless of what our parents or teachers said.

I took the leaflet from Josie and considered the information. Getting to the church wouldn't be a problem, since I had ridden to the Gaston Motel and the Carver Theater, and I knew exactly where the church was. The problem was that the church was just down the street from the Gaston Motel, and I worried that Father would see us. The larger concern, that the objective of the march was to get arrested and to go to jail, did not bother me until later.

"So what if he sees us?" Josie answered with a smirk. "At lunchtime he'll be at school. At least he's supposed to."

I wondered for a moment if my father was even working anymore. Maybe he spent both night and day in the bars. I reasoned that he was too much of a scientist not to make an appearance at work. If he were showing up at work, then he would probably have seen the leaflets. "He's going to know about it," I said.

Josie stopped and gave me an emphatically exasperated look. "So what? He'll think it's just for high school students, since that's what they keep saying—it's just for high school students, but elementary kids can come if we're baptized. Anyway, we're not baptized, so he won't think that we would be going."

"*We're* not going," I decided.

Josie stopped. She waited until I stopped and turned toward her. "*I'm* going." It was part challenge and part plea. I stared at her for a moment, giving her my best stern look. Almost immediately I felt my resolve crumble and I knew then that I would be going to the march. But for the life of me, I couldn't see Josie marching, hardly waist high to an adult. It was difficult enough when the crowd lurched the last time when we were only bystanders. To put Josie in the middle of a rushing crowd would be more than irresponsible; it would be just plain criminal.

Her face was set with such glossy rigidity that I knew there was nothing I could do short of tying her up to prevent her from going. "We'll see," I said.

"No, we won't see." She didn't follow when I started walking again; I stopped.

"You could get hurt."

"I know."

"I mean you could get hurt real bad," I said.

"I know. Like Bingo."

I sighed.

She rolled her eyes. "Be scientific, for Pete's sake. What are the chances?"

"There's nothing scientific about this. You *could* get hurt. What the hell do you think all those German shepherds and policemen are there for?" She maintained the determined look. "Josie, you are too small. A big crowd will just push you down. You can't outrun the dogs if they chased you."

"Neither can you."

"Besides, you don't want to go to jail."

"Neither do you."

"Damn right. Who said I was going?"

"I *know* you are. You've got to go because Daddy isn't going—and don't say 'damn' to me, I'm not a bitch."

She surprised me. "Whoever said you were a bitch? Where did you even learn that word?"

"For Pete's sake, I've got ears. And nobody *said* I was a bitch. I'm just telling you, I'm not a bitch, so don't talk to me like one."

I put a hand on her shoulder, then the other thing she had said struck me. "Did you say 'Daddy'? What do you mean about Daddy?"

She started to walk. "Daddy would do this if he wasn't—you know . . . sick."

"Daddy isn't sick . . . he's . . ." How could I say "a drunk" to my little sister?

She helped me. "Sick. He's sick because Mama is sick. He's sick because he doesn't want her to be sick, and because he's scared."

"Scared?"

"Can't you see it? In his eyes? Every time he looks at Mama in the bed. Every time he walks in that room, he's scared."

I supposed I had seen it, but didn't want to believe it. Mostly my father had a calming influence on me. When I was in his presence, even when I had fought him, I saw him as the strong one, the one who could, who would eventually set things right. "Aren't you scared, too?"

"I was," Josie said. "But then Bingo got killed. Now I'm mad."

"Mad?"

She looked up at me, her face in a pout. Then she giggled. "Real mad." It was an odd giggle, thrown off as if some other voice possessed her. Her eyes showed none of the mirth her voice suggested. Her pupils were beads. They ought to have been in a robin's head. She had bags under her eyes, too. I stopped her and pulled her into my arms. "Josie, you don't have to be mad. Everything will be all right. I swear, eventually everything will be okay."

She wrestled from my embrace and started up the driveway to the house. "Not if we don't *do something*."

19

JOSIE SNEAKED the radio into the bedroom and turned on Tall Paul's show for more information about the march. Aunt Bennie came in and asked if we were finished with homework. She had had a long day at work, she said. Her work woman had hosted a club luncheon, and "those old hankty biddies nearly worked me to death. 'Be-nee-ta'," she mocked "'bring the may-on-naise for the sandwiches—oh, Be-nee-ta, this isn't the may-on-naise—I meant the salad dressing, the Blue Bonnet with the nice flavor.' Why didn't she say Blue Bonnet the first time? Am I supposed to be able to read her mind? And then had the nerve to tell the other women: 'She's not my *regular* girl—my regular girl knows what I mean.'" Aunt Bennie said that these women set themselves up as the "good white element" of Birmingham. They thought it was such a shame that Bull Connor was running around with police dogs. But on the other hand, if the colored preachers would just stick to preaching and stop all the marching, they said, then Bull Connor wouldn't have to act up. The preachers were just adding fuel to Bull Connor's fire. If they didn't watch out, Bull Connor's element would be in charge and then where would colored people be? Aunt Bennie grunted and shook her head. "Those old biddies don't know a thing. A atom bomb could go off in their backyard and they wouldn't know it."

We listened politely to Aunt Bennie's rant, and then Josie explained that she had finished her lessons and wanted to hear "He's So Fine" by the Chiffons. Josie looked so innocent when she asked, "Aunt Bennie, have you heard it?"

Aunt Bennie sat down next to Josie who was lying across the bed, looking down at her schoolbooks in a neat stack on the floor. She patted Josie's head. "No, sweetheart." She seemed pleased that Josie had an interest in the music. "I haven't heard it, but when it comes on, call me."

In between the songs, Tall Paul repeated what the leaflet had said, "Kids, there's gonna be a big party at the park. Bring your toothbrushes because lunch will be served. Don't miss it, now." When "He's So Fine" came on, Josie turned it up and called Aunt Bennie. Aunt Bennie listened for a minute, and then she did a little step, trying to imitate the twist.

"Lord," she said, "I'll throw my back out after carrying all them heavy trays." She asked Josie to turn the music down. The song ended and Tall Paul mentioned the party again. Josie and I looked at each other, anticipating Aunt Bennie's reaction. "Party," she snorted, "that's the last thing I want to go to. Might have to work!"

That night Josie and I made a plan. I would take my bicycle to school and leave it out front. At recess, we would meet by the corner of the school building near the swings and ride down to the church. But in the morning when I was delivering the papers, Lamar told me his plan. He was simply not showing up to school. He had talked with his mother about going to the march and she and "W.W." had decided that he was old enough. Reverend Timmons would drive him there. I said that Josie and I should ride along with him. He was thoughtful for a moment and slowly told me that he had already asked his mother if we could come along. She had said no. She knew that our mother hadn't approved of our going to the workshops and certainly wouldn't approve of our participating in a march. Mrs. Burrell was not willing to risk other people's children. I decided that we would have to meet Lamar at the church.

Josie was eating breakfast by the time I got in from delivering the papers. Aunt Bennie sat with her at the table, having a cup of coffee and offering me scrambled eggs and bacon. I handed her the paper. She turned immediately to The Money Column, her favorite section. Josie and I ate in silence, occasionally looking up at each other. We gave no sign of excitement, no sign that today would be anything but a usual school day until Josie got up from the table.

"What have you got on, girl?" Aunt Bennie asked. Josie was wearing the dress our father had given her for Easter. "Lord," Aunt Bennie said, "how did I miss that? Go put on your school jumper, girl. You don't need to be seen in public in that."

"I want to wear it. I've only worn it one time."

"If you're lucky, it'll be the only time. Now, go put on something you can play in."

Josie went back to change. I met her in the room. "Why did you put that thing on?" I whispered. "You can't march in it." She was in her panties, pulling her jumper over her head. "I just wanted to look nice, for Pete's sake."

"You need to be comfortable," I said. I gave her some candy bars. "Put these in your pocket in case you get hungry. And be sure to bring a washcloth, a comb and your toothbrush." She already had those things, items we had learned from the workshops that we would need in jail.

The morning classes went along as usual; there were few absences—Lamar's absence being notable because he was so talkative. At recess, I went out on the softball field as usual, and when I saw

Josie's play group come out, I made an excuse to go to the bathroom and started toward the front of the school where my bicycle was parked. Mrs. Buford, the principal, was standing guard at the front of the building. This was unusual, and could only have been because of the leaflets. In her white blouse, black skirt, and high heel shoes she looked like a sentinel with a yardstick for a weapon, and glasses on a glittering chain for decorations. She paced in front of the school, from one corner to the next. Josie came up behind me, and we hid behind a boxwood next to the bike rack.

"When the bell rings," I said to Josie, "she'll have to go in. Then we will make a dash for it." But when the bell rang, Mrs. Buford looked at her watch, and continued her patrol. Then Mr. Edwards, the assistant principal, came out and replaced her.

"Maybe we should go back," I whispered to Josie who waited quietly. She had sat down under the boxwood and slipped into her patient, quiet mood.

"Just wait," she said, "he can't stay out here forever. He has to go in and watch that rambunctious class of his."

Mr. Edwards looked in our direction with such intensity that I thought he had seen me peeking at him, then he turned to go in. I wasted no time, and went to the bike rack. I was quick with the combination lock and was just about to release the chain when I heard Mr. Edwards clearing his throat. I continued to undo the chain, all the time trying to think of an excuse. He told me to hold it just where I was, and he began asking questions about where I should be. He knew very well where I should have been, and no doubt Mrs. Buford had already reported me missing, for then he asked, "And where, may I ask, is Miss Josephine?"

Josie gave herself up, and we were marched before Mrs. Buford. She gave us a stern look over the top of her half glasses, and then asked us to sit down. I hadn't had many trips to her office, but I knew that being asked to sit was not a regular part of the routine. More than likely a child was asked to bend over in order to receive a half dozen whacks from her well-worn paddle. She surprised us again by asking us how our mother was rather than launching into a reprimand.

I hesitated. "She is not very good."

"Not very *well.* I'm sorry to hear it. Very sorry, indeed." Mrs. Buford took her glasses from her nose and folded them on the chain and let them lie against her chest. "Don't answer me if you don't want to," she said softly, "but has she long?"

Josie and I looked at each other. How could we not answer her, whether we wanted to or not? I stumbled on the words at first; tears welling up, I said, "No, ma'am."

"I'm very, very sorry," she said. "I lost my mother when I was young, too. Not as young as you, but it is never easy to lose a mother, no matter what your age. Everybody loses someone at some point in time. The important thing is not to lose yourself. Children, I know you look upon me as a principal, but you may also look upon me as a friend. If you need to talk . . . or if you just want to come over to my house—my children are all in college but I have a TV and lots of books and toys—you can come anytime. I don't live far. How does that sound?"

"Okay," I said.

"And you, Josie? How about you?"

Josie kept her head lowered. "Okay."

Mrs. Buford slipped her fingers together hand in hand and placed them on her ordered desk. "Now," she asked, her voice no longer soft, "do you children know the meaning of the word 'truancy'?"

The change was so abrupt that I felt betrayed. One moment she was inviting us to befriend her, and the next she was being a principal. "'Truancy,' I said, "is when you skip school."

"Yes, it is, and it is illegal in the state of Alabama." Her tone changed again. "You all were going down to the march, weren't you? To the so-called big party? You were trying to join your little friend Mr. Burrell, weren't you?"

"Yes, ma'am."

"As an employee of the city of Birmingham, a trustee of her public schools, you know I can't allow you to do that. Don't you?"

I started to say, 'Yes ma'am" but Josie cut me off. She had held her head down and avoided looking at Mrs. Buford until this point. "Why not?" she asked. "You ought to let the whole school go."

Mrs. Buford sat back in her chair and she flipped open her glasses. "Ought I?"

"She didn't mean any disrespect," I said.

"None taken," answered Mrs. Buford. She leaned forward again and spoke quietly. "Frankly, children, I agree with you—and I witnessed your display at the meeting last week. But you know it is harder for an adult than for a child. Your father works for the school system, too. What does he think?"

"What do you mean?"

"Is he letting his students march? Is he encouraging you?"

I answered slowly. "He hasn't told me what his students are doing, but he is all for us getting our freedom."

"Does he want you—look at you, Josie, you're not four feet tall—he's not in favor of you marching. And with your mother sick? I can't believe it. Besides, there *is* his job. That's another thing we worry about."

"If Daddy can't march, and we can't march, then who can march?" Josie asked.

"I'm not opposed to the march, mind you," Mrs. Buford said. "I'm just saying we have things to consider. Besides, there are some few people who *can* march. People who don't have public jobs." There was silence, I wondered for a moment what she would do to us. Call our mother? Our father? Paddle us? "But again," she said, changing her tone once more, "I can't tell you what to do. That's between you and your parents. But I do have a responsibility to you. I'm not letting you leave from these premises. If you wish to be truant, you'll have to do it from home."

• • •

THE PHONE RANG the moment we walked in the house. Aunt Bennie picked it up, and I could tell right away that she was alarmed. "No. No," she said, "the children just came in from school—they're right here." She handed the phone to me. It was Mrs. Burrell. She was upset, but controlled. She said she had half expected us to have gone to the march. I couldn't tell her in front of Aunt Bennie that we had tried, only that we didn't have permission.

Mrs. Burrell seemed giddy as she began to tell me what had happened to Lamar. She, Reverend Timmons, and Lamar had driven down to the Sixteenth Street Baptist Church where she and Reverend Timmons had helped organize the children for the march. "It was a glorious success," she declared.

The children had sung the songs we learned in the workshop, and the preachers had come out and lectured to them, told them to be brave and that no matter what happened to them it wouldn't be as bad as not fighting Jim Crow. Sometimes you had to go to jail in order to live in freedom. "There must have been over one thousand children," she said, with pride. "And Lamar was right up in there with them. Right up front."

"One thousand!" I repeated. That seemed like every black child in Birmingham and I felt as if I had missed out on the most important event of my life—and all because of that bald-headed Mr. Edwards.

"Lamar was in the third group to march out. I believe they caught the police off guard. They didn't know what to make of so many marchers at one time." She said that Lamar's group took advantage of the surprise and got around the police barricade and headed toward city hall. As the police scrambled to catch up, the children held up signs that read SEGREGATION IS A SIN. Mrs. Burrell laughed nervously. "Seems like more than anything they didn't want nobody to read those signs." No sooner had the police caught up with Lamar's group than another group of children came out of the church, and another after them. "The police were dumfounded!" she said. She didn't see any more of Lamar from her perch on the church's portico, but she knew he had been arrested. "I just wish he had his friend in there with him," she said, a little strain in her voice. "I would feel better about it."

At that point, I nearly confessed that we had tried to march, but Aunt Bennie hadn't moved since she had handed me the phone. I felt very much as if I had let Lamar down. "You can always count on me," I told Mrs. Burrell.

"I know that, baby," she said. She had gone to the jailhouse that afternoon, but had not been allowed to see Lamar. The policemen claimed they were still processing the demonstrators and then a judge would have to set bail. After all, they had broken a court-ordered injunction against marching. "I knew he was going to be arrested, but I didn't know how I was going to feel until it happened. W.W. said this is the colored version of summer camp," she joked, but her tone undermined the humor.

AUNT BENNIE wanted every detail, and later Mother asked me to come in to her room and to tell her what had happened to Lamar. "I'm glad you are too smart to go following him. Jail won't look good on your record," she said. My father called after supper. "Listen, Son, it is very important that you don't get involved in that tomfoolery. It could ruin what chances you have. It's dangerous—and not just in the way you think. Lamar may think it's a great adventure to go off to jail, but he has probably damaged whatever little chance he had to complete his schooling. No telling what the school board will do to him—he'll be lucky if they don't expel him. And I don't mean *suspend*, Son. I mean *expel* him. Permanently. And with a jail record he can kiss college good-bye."

"He was just trying to get his freedom, Daddy. I mean, what good is college if you don't have any freedom—"

My father's heavy sigh interrupted me. "You don't become a scientist in jail, Walter. Be practical. You've got too much to live for than to throw it away for nothing."

After lights out, I lay in the bed listening to Josie's breathing. It was deep and even and I thought she had fallen asleep very easily, considering all the excitement. Then she said, "I miss Bingo."

"So do I."

"Walter?" Her voice was musical in the darkness. "Are we going to try again tomorrow?"

"I don't know. I don't think so."

"I think I will. Because I think if I don't I will just cry. I don't want to start crying because if I do I don't think I'll ever stop."

I sat up on the cot. Jesus, I thought, we had been sliding into a deep well since Mother got sick. I couldn't imagine what was at the bottom, but I doubted it was water. At the top, at least, was a dim ring of light, some small bit of hope, a promise, but we had to climb to it.

I lay down again. "Let's sleep," I said. "I've got to do the whole paper route tomorrow. And then we'll go."

20

THE NEXT MORNING, Friday, we set off for school with Aunt Bennie's admonishment to "come directly home" ringing in our ears. When we were out of sight of the house, Josie asked if we could go back. She had left something behind, she said—but we would have to sneak it. Since we weren't going to go to school, we had plenty of time, but I worried that one of our neighbors would see us.

"Just tell them I forgot my homework," Josie insisted, but still didn't tell me what it was she had forgotten. We went around the block and came to the house from the direction of the backyard. Josie asked me to stop just behind Mrs. Jeters's azaleas, and she sneaked into the yard to Bingo's dog house, took out a paper sack, and ran back.

"What's in the sack?"

She smiled. It was a smile that lifted my spirits for I saw in her the old Josie, full of play. "My dress!" she said with a nod. "If I'm going to get arrested, I'm going to look good!"

"For Peter's sake! That's a church dress—you can't march in it. You need—"

"I need this dress," she said. "Daddy gave it to me for Easter, and this may be the only other chance I ever get to wear it."

I gave up. She climbed onto the handlebars, put her feet in the basket. We put the dress and the books on the side baskets and set on our familiar route down Sixth Avenue to the Sixteenth Street Baptist church.

We arrived very early for the march, but Reverend Timmons was already at the church. "Well, well, well," he cried out and welcomed us with hugs. "What took you two so long?"

Quickly we explained our previous failed attempt. He patted Josie on the head. "I'm proud, so proud." We registered and were told what group we would be in. More children began to come in and soon, even early in the morning, the church filled up. Josie went to the girls' room and changed into the dress. She did not give up all practicality to fashion, however, as she kept on her Buster Brown shoes, soft play shoes suitable for walking and running.

The Sixteenth Street Baptist was a cathedral compared to St. Luke's Lutheran. The red-carpeted sanctuary, with pews arranged in a semicircle, could hold over a thousand people. Above the pews snaked a balcony, supported by metal poles. The balcony, a modern addition, clashed with the nineteenth-century interior and cut up the view of the story-tall stained glass windows, one on each side. Narrow stairs rose six feet to the pulpit, where a couple of simple rail chairs undermined the grandeur of the church. Since Father had often called Sixteenth Street Baptist the "rich colored folks church," I assumed the simplicity was by design. Behind and above the pulpit was a choir stand, and behind and above it was a silver pipe organ. The effect of the pulpit was that I kept looking up, farther and farther, until I was looking above my head at the ceiling, three stories up. A rectangular skylight of yellow stained glass dominated the ceiling. At each corner of the skylight, like an angel on a string, hung a spidery chandelier. I hadn't been in many big churches, so the grandeur of it awed me, but something I was amiss, as well. Later I learned that, though it was the staging ground for the marches, the church's middle-class congregation reluctantly welcomed the civil rights workers and was often at odds with Reverend Shuttlesworth's poorer congregation.

Josie and I sat next to the window portraying Jesus knocking at Mary's door. By summer's end, that window would become a symbol of Klan violence. Just under the window, a bomb would kill four girls, but at that time, as I gazed upon the face of Christ, I wouldn't have guessed about the bloodshed to come. Christ was robed and caped; he carried a staff in one hand and with the other he knocked at a heavy, arched door. He was the barefoot shepherd calling upon the faithful. He had a kind, expectant look on his face. My stomach quivered. Looking upon the face, backlit by the daylight, I told myself that Josie and I were answering His call. Christ was knocking at *our* door. He didn't say, "Trust, but do not hope." He said, "Trust and dream. Be not afraid, and hope." Behind Christ, past the corner of the house, was a landscape of fields and distant mountains, the Promised Land. The light played through the colored glass, sparkling blues, pinks, and yellows.

ABOUT NOON, Reverend King himself came into the church. He spoke encouragingly, and then another reverend told us to get into our groups, about fifty per group. Because we had gotten to the church early, Josie and I were in the first group. We lined up two by two, facing the front door. Older children were placed in front and behind us. The adults hushed us, and someone swung the double doors open. Sunlight streamed in.

Slowly the line moved forward. I squeezed Josie's hand. My heart pounded. It was like going on stage. I remembered the PTA plays, when I waited outside the cafeteria where the plays were held, my stomach knotting, pains shooting through my abdomen and down my legs.

As we moved toward the sunlight, I saw the tops of trees across the street and the blue sky. I saw the roofline of downtown, but I could not see the crowd that awaited us until I was on the church's portico. Most were black, the usual bystanders, but there were also many white reporters. People cheered as we started down the steps. Josie looked at me with a condescending frown. "If they can look, why can't they march?"

I don't know, I thought. I did not feel badly toward them. I felt raised above them.

We began to sing as we had been instructed. The song was one word, a fortifying chant of "freedom" sang in the tune of the old benediction, "Amen."

When we were halfway down the stairs, I saw the policemen and firemen, a line of uniformed and helmeted men making a human bulwark. Behind them were fire trucks, ambulances, police cruisers with flashing red lights and, of all things—this struck me as funny— school busses and paddy wagons, together.

As planned, the line turned away from the police and started around the park. Both adults and children were in the park, cheering, clapping, and shouting encouragement. I realized that some of the bystanders were parents of the children who were marching. By allowing their children to march, the parents were able to keep their jobs while sacrificing a son or daughter to fill Bull Connor's jail. Realizing this put to order what Josie and I were doing. Since our mother couldn't march, and our father worked for the city, we could take their places. Where was Father? Could he be among the cheering parents? That time on a Friday afternoon, he would have been in the lunchroom of the high school monitoring the behavior of the few students who had gone to school that day.

When we had marched two blocks, reaching the far side of the park, on the catty-corner from the church, the line stopped abruptly.

A policeman in a fancy uniform stepped in front of the line and raised his hands. We demonstrators stopped singing but the crowd of onlookers jeered. We had been told in the workshops to expect an officer to tell us we were in violation of the marching injunction and to threaten us with arrest. The officer said nothing about arrest. He ordered us to disperse. He pointed over his shoulders at the fire trucks and said that if we didn't disperse, we were fixing to get wet.

The threat seemed insubstantial: We were fixing to get wet? Here we had been bolstering ourselves for one of the worse fates that could befall a southern black of any dignity—a jail term—and the best threat the policeman could make was "You are fixing to get wet"?

We started to march again, but the policemen held the line so we stood and sang, waiting for them to begin arresting us. Suddenly, there was a roar of surprise and screams as a cloud of fog rolled around us. Demonstrators and bystanders alike were soaked. Then, as if to taunt us, a fire truck let out a blast from its horn.

This first volley, I later found out, was from a fogging nozzle, a low-pressure spray meant to dampen our dignity. Up until then, the students, especially the young women, had looked crisp in their school blouses and skirts and their neatly fixed hair. Drenched, the hair lay limp around their faces and their clothes were soaked through, bras visible beneath the cotton tops. Josie's ruffles hung limp. Because her hair was braided, the water did not have the same undignified effect as it had on the hairstyles of the older girls with curled hair or the few guys who had conks. Josie brushed her bangs out of her eyes with her free hand.

Our line broke as people tried to get out of the way of the mist. Some ran and hid behind trees or cars. The others of us retreated about half a block and began to reform. We started to sing, and taking courage, we advanced toward the policemen.

When the fog cleared, it was evident that the next blast of water would do more damage than just get us wet. The firemen took the front line of defense and crouched behind what appeared to be machine guns on tripods. I had seen the machine guns used in World War II on television, and these "monitor guns" looked like those World War II guns. The monitor gun joined together two fire hoses, doubling the pressure and distance of the stream of water. At full force, the water could loosen bricks in mortar and strip bark from trees. If any in our group, or in the group of bystanders, knew what was about to happen, he gave no sign of it; rather, some jeered the policemen, daring them to spray us.

With a roar and scour, a stream of water so pressurized it looked like a white metal rod whipped over our heads. I wanted to run. I realized that something terrible and unexpected was happening. There would be no friendly arrests, no exasperated policemen helping young women into the paddy wagons. I wished Josie had stayed home. The line broke again, and the marchers fled along with the bystanders. I pulled Josie as I ran. Her toes skimmed the top of the ground as she tried to keep her balance and find footing. Inside the park, we took shelter behind an oak. I sat with my back to the tree and put Josie in my lap. The tree was just as wide as my back, and my shoulders were exposed as I huddled around the hard-breathing Josie. "Uh-oh," she said, and I heard what she heard. Even among the chaos of screams and trampling feet and sirens and horns, we heard the scouring of the water. It seemed to run as if along a fuse line across the grass. I turned to see it churning up the ground, creating a muddy explosion as it came toward the tree. Suddenly it hit the tree with a blast. We were showered with water and chips of bark, but the stream had not hit us directly. It turned with a malicious whip to a boy running past the tree. It lashed him in the ribs and sent him tumbling heels over head. He lay a moment in the mud, and, bent double holding his side, limped a few steps before the stream tripped him again.

Josie wanted to get up, whether to help the boy or to run, I don't know, but I held onto her and tried to tuck her under me. Her fingers dug into my arm. Across the park we saw some of the children dancing, playing hide-and-seek with the jets and taunting the firemen. It was a dangerous game of tag, because the pressured hoses could have broken ribs and arms or given them concussions if it hit them in their heads. Even so, the dancing was joyous, so pure and daunting that Josie and I relaxed and laughed. I was tempted to abandon our safe place and join them, but I worried about Josie. I looked around the tree for the position of the hoses and saw that they were no longer pointed in our direction. I also saw that more demonstrators were filing out of the church. They went in a direction away from the park, circumventing the chaos. I pointed them out to Josie. They were about a block away, and I said we should make a run for that group. On my mark, we stood and, hand in hand, ran, dodging behind trees.

Suddenly we were surrounded by bystanders mounting a retaliation. In the workshops we had been taught to be passive, to cooperate when arrested. If beaten we were to cover our heads but we weren't to strike back. The bystanders had made no such commitment. A barrage of bottles, rocks, and bricks were hurled at the firemen. As I feared, the bystanders attracted the water.

The boy in front of us was hit squarely in the back as he tried to duck the jet. The pressure picked him up and bowed him, as if he were a sail caught in a gust of wind. His arms flailed like a rag doll as he flew forward through the air. Then he flipped and fell with a splat on the muddy ground. I pushed Josie down and lay on top of her. The stream whipped above us like a mad, flexing tail, and then it went in another direction.

We made it to the edge of the park before we had our next encounter with the water. Across the park, I saw a fireman, dressed in the traditional slicker and fireman's hat, dragging a hose into position. Seeing him strengthened the notion that *human beings* were controlling the hoses. Before it was more like a freakish natural disaster, something mindless and heartless. The fireman aimed at us and I saw the stream coming, coming as if it moved in its own time, a spotlight at first, then suddenly a shining rod telescoping toward us. I looked for cover, but nothing was near. Cars parked along the street were too far. The water whooshed over our heads and hit the ground a few feet beyond us. Then it traced its path, beating up the ground as it came back. First I felt the droplets needling my back and then the full force, like a blunt hammer. It was not so painful as it was numbing. It pushed against my back, pushed me against Josie, and forced the breath from the both of us. I tried to get a foothold, but the mud was too slippery and the force too great for me to stand. Josie was trying to scramble from under me, but I held onto her.

Suddenly the water stopped, and I thought the stream had been redirected, but the sound of the water was still just behind us and the spray drenched us. "Get up, and stay low," I told Josie. We crawled a little ways before the pressure flattened us again. Then, as if it had played with us enough, the stream went in another direction and we ran to the shelter of the parked cars.

Behind us bodies and swaying ropes of glittering water went back and forth. In one part of the park, a group huddled, making a turtle shell of their backs as the water hammered at them. Another group charged like a cavalry and pitched bricks and stones at the firemen. In yet another place, a teenage boy demonstrated a version of the twist. He jumped to the right or left to get out of harm's way, taunting, twisting his hips, swinging his arms, and turning his taunt into joyous rebellion.

Josie stood in between the parked cars and wiped water out of her face. She tried to straighten her dress.

"Are you cold?" I asked.

She rolled her eyes. "No, I'm *wet*. If they had told me they were going to spray us, I would have worn my bathing suit." We laughed. The skin on my back burned where the water had hit me. Later my back and ribs would be sore, but then I felt a jittery levity, a clear-minded drunkenness, strong as a bull. I could do anything. Shout. Pitch a stone. Shake my tail at the policemen. They had no power over me. Nothing they could do would stop me from marching. Josie and I shook ourselves as dry as we could, and strutted toward the group of demonstrators at the end of the block.

We had marched about a half block with our new group before the line halted and collapsed. I heard snarling and understood, even before I saw the frightened children running past us, that the dogs were coming, the muscular German shepherds straining at their leashes.

Josie held out her arms to me and I picked her up, not feeling her weight, and ran for a storefront door. I tried the door, but it was locked. The crowd rushed past us, and then came the dogs. They appeared to be passing us by, when one turned its nose toward us, sniffing the air. Josie screamed, not so much out of fear as rage. I knew what she was thinking: Here is Bingo's killer.

"Y'all come out of there," the policeman ordered. I didn't move, but pushed Josie behind me and squeezed us against the door. The policeman ordered again, sounding like somebody's father. "Didn't you hear me say to come out of there?" But how could we come out with the dog just a foot away? The dog pulled at the leash so hard it stood on its hind legs. I could see teats on its belly. Terror broke in my gut. A bitch. A bitch would tear us to shreds. I could smell her hot breath when she shook her salvia-splattered muzzle. The policeman cursed and called us names. I don't know what made me speak, but I suddenly thought, I can't let him just call us names. He can threaten us, he could hit us with the billy stick, but I'd be damned if I'd let him call us names.

"There's no need for that!" I screamed at the man. "I'm an American citizen!" How pathetic! My fist clenched, I lunged at the dog, lunged as if to strike her on the nose. One good blow on the nose ought to send her whimpering. My strike missed, and before I knew it I was tumbling back, the furry head and hot breath against my stomach. Reflexively, I sucked in my abdomen and I landed hard on my back. The sky and buildings spun, and I heard Josie scream and I tried to sit up. The dog was inches away, its body fully stretched toward me as it struggled against its leash. I was attached to the dog by a strip of my shirt that had torn away from my belly and chest and caught on its teeth.

"Run!" I yelled to Josie, and to my relief, she darted around the dog. It lunged toward her, and I kicked it, landing a blow on the side of its mouth. The kick brought the dog's attention back to me and more name calling from the policeman.

21

A BRICK SMACKED the sidewalk just at the policeman's heel. He turned, pulling the dog with him. Hands grasped and pulled me to my feet. I slapped at them, trying to get away, until I realized they were black hands. A woman put her arm around my shoulder and pulled me along with the crowd.

When my senses cleared I began to look for Josie. Time had become stretched out and I had no sense of how long it had been since she had run. I asked the woman who was guiding me if she had seen my sister—the little girl in the pink dress. She hadn't. She insisted that I should stay with her, that she would guide me to safety, but I pulled away. She beckoned for me to follow. She was a young woman, slim and attractive. I wanted to follow, but out of a boyish interest more than a concern for my safety. When I didn't follow, she waved "bye-bye," with a small gesture, and moved into the crowd.

I thought Josie would have gone back to the bicycle, so I made my way behind the church where we had left it, far out of reach of the fire hoses and, I hoped, the dogs. Behind the church, just two blocks away from the park, was peaceful. Except for an occasional wet or bloody person, the people I encountered there seemed oblivious to the demonstration.

The bicycle was still in its place, chained to a parking meter, but Josie had not been there. Was she hurt? Did a dog get her? I felt like crying, but told myself to be scientific. Science would work for me. Where would she know to go? First, she would go to where we had started, the church. Since she wasn't by the bicycle, and I hadn't seen her on the way over, she might have gone inside the church. That's where I would look next. Then she might go to the Carver; it was a familiar place and the ticket woman knew our mother. A slim possibility, I thought, but she might go to the motel to look for our father, though he would have been in school that time of day.

Systematically, I began my search. Inside the church were hundreds of children still waiting to march. The preachers were holding them back, letting one group go at a time in an attempt to keep the police off guard. I scanned the crowd from the balcony. No Josie. Could she have taken off the dress? I went to the pew where we had sat earlier and found the shopping bag with her jumper. Then I pedaled to the theater. It was closed. I doubled back in the direction of the motel, but I didn't get far before I saw the police line. An armored car was parked behind the fire trucks, and I knew that was Bull Connor's headquarters. I didn't think Josie could have gotten through that line, but I couldn't go home until I had looked. I took the long way around, riding several blocks on a parallel street, and then several blocks past the police blockade and approached the motel from behind. I went to my father's room. He wasn't in, nor was there a sign that Josie had been there. I went to the front desk and asked if anyone had seen her. No one had. My stomach seemed bottomless. I felt weak and sat on the stairs leading up to my father's room. How could I tell my parents that I had lost Josie? We were supposed to have been arrested, carted away to jail with the other children. No one said that the police would hammer us with water, sic dogs on us, and beat us with clubs. I hadn't seen any arrests, but then the possibility that the policemen themselves could be Josie's saviors was my only hope. Suddenly a bright thought occurred. She could have walked home. I might catch up to her before she got home.

AUNT BENNIE was in the kitchen when I came in. I took a deep breath before she turned around from the counter where she was making a snack. She was smiling when she turned, and I thought for just a moment that Josie might have made it home. Then I saw the smile freeze and Aunt Bennie's expression slowly changed to puzzlement. "What happened to you?" Her head crooked to one side.

"I—"

"Where's Josie?"

"I don't know."

"You—what happened!" she shouted. She came over and grabbed me by the shoulder and pulled me into the middle of the kitchen. She looked outside as if looking for someone chasing me. Again she asked what had happened, but before I could answer she was asking another question. "Where have you been? Don't tell me you've been downtown. Don't tell me . . ."

She pushed me into a chair, took a deep breath, and regained her calm. "Take your time, and tell me what happened." I told her. She paced toward my mother's bedroom and came back. She picked up the telephone to call my father. Since it was only 3:30, she called him at the high school. She paced back and forth through the den while she waited for him to come to the phone.

My mother called to me from the bedroom. Somehow, even in her weakened, drugged condition, she sensed something was wrong. When I went in she was sitting on the side of the bed. She reached out for me. I was afraid to get close, afraid she might hit me, but she pulled my head against her chest. "What's going on? What's happened to Josie?"

"I don't know, I think she's gotten arrested."

"Arrested? Arrested? Who would arrest her?"

"In the demonstrations."

"In the demonstrations?" she looked puzzled and then angry. "What were you doing at the demonstrations? We don't go to demonstrations. We don't do things like that. We aren't like that." She slapped me on the shoulder and then she pushed me away, a weak slap, more of a brush of her hand, but the impact of it couldn't have hit me harder if she had punched me in the mouth. Her eyes were fierce and her mouth had tightened to a pinch. "You are worse than your father," she said. "If anything happens to her, I'll never forgive you."

"Mama!" My breath caught on the word. My head felt like it would explode in a splatter of tears and snot. I sniffed deeply, growling, and held back the tears. "Mama." Suddenly I felt exhausted. My shoulders and chest slumped. Where was my father? Why was my mother blaming me? What did she care anyway? "What do you care anyway?" I said.

Slowly, Mother got up from the bed and came toward me. At first she looked like she might hug me, but then her hand came against my ear with a pop. "You will never know! You will never know how I feel."

"I don't care how you feel. You don't care about us. Why don't you just go ahead and die, for Pete's sake?"

I turned to run, but Aunt Bennie blocked the door. I tried to push by her, but she pushed me back into the room. I ran to a corner and turned my face away from them. After three or four minutes, I heard the bed squeak as Mother sat down.

Mother talked to Aunt Bennie. "Did you call the police?"

"Carl is doing that. He is going to try to find her at the jail, he said.

But I am going to go out and look. She just might be wandering around, you know. Walter can come with me."

"No." Mother spoke firmly. "Walter is staying with me. You go and look."

The next hour and a half passed with not so much as a word between my mother and me. We hardly moved. We had listened to Aunt Bennie crank the car and drive away. The house was silent. The entire neighborhood seemed silent. My mother sat on the edge of the bed, her hands on her knees, bracing her weight. At times she looked asleep, but then she would let out a long breath and move slightly in a way that suggested she was thinking. I sat in the corner with nothing but thoughts of Josie in jail to occupy my mind.

The afternoon became evening and the sun cast a sharp angle of shadow across the room. My mother was sitting in the shade and I in the sun. In the shade, Mother's arms looked thin and soft, her skin so loose it looked like part of her nightgown. Slowly the line of shade was making its way across the room to me, as if it were the hand of a gigantic clock, the clock of shadows. How could I have said to my mother "just to go ahead and die," when I knew that all that day and all that week and for all the month before, dying was all she had been doing? If the shadow that touched my mother was the clock hand of death, then it was already halfway to me. Softly, I called to her.

"Yes, Walter." She did not look at me. Her voice was tight.

"Mama, I'm sorry about what I said."

"I know you are." She was silent for a moment. "Come here." Her voice weakened; she looked up. "Sit with me."

I moved to the bed and sat close, but not touching. Breathing deeply, I tried to adjust to the smell of urine, which seemed to permeate her bed. "Mama," I offered brightly, "they'll find Josie. She won't be hurt. She wanted to go to jail. They were just putting them on busses and besides, there were a lot of other children her age—"

"Please. Don't talk like that."

"Like what?"

"Like it is all right."

"I know it's not all right, but—"

"It's God's will."

I was puzzled. "If it's not all right, how can it be God's will?" She didn't answer so I asked again.

"You won't understand. The world is not scientific. There is not a simple explanation for everything. You have to have faith. You have to believe that things happen because God wills it."

"I believe in God's will."

"No, you don't." She placed her hands in her lap. "Neither you nor Josie. That's why Josie is where she is now. You don't have faith in God's will." Her tone suggested finality, an immutable judgment.

"I never told you but many years ago, my daddy went to jail."

"You told me."

Mother cocked her head. "Who told you? Carl? What business had he to tell you that? That's not the kind of thing we talk about."

"It should have been, Mama. You and Daddy should have told us a long time ago."

"We would have when you needed to know." She focused on me. "How did it make you feel?"

I thought for a moment. It was a story of long ago, like a story of slavery, and yet I knew it had happened to my own grandfather. It had deprived me of ever knowing him, not just because of his early death, but because no one talked about him. "It made me feel . . . *mad,* I guess."

Mother sighed. "I wish I could feel angry about it. But feeling angry doesn't do any good. Nothing does. Grandma Pic told us to forget about it. To go on and do the best we could, and she was right because it was God's will. We forgot about Daddy. We forgot about him so much, we even forgot we had a mother. After Pic took up with Uncle Reed, we stopped calling her Mama for a while. Just 'Pic.' We became motherless because we didn't have a father. I suppose it was easier to pretend we never had a father than to live with what happened to him. You just can't fight God's will. They say that colored people suffer under the curse of Ham. It's in the Scripture somewhere. I've been trying to find it. Every time, I'm just about to find it, I fall asleep." Her voice went up into a rhetorical pitch, half-mocking. "Poor, poor Negro. Catch a Negro by the toe; if he hollers let him go." She laughed. "My dear boy, Waltie . . . I don't want to die, but the doctor said there was nothing to do—it was inoperable from the beginning. It would have been just a waste of time. Just like when we tried to save Daddy. Your father is full of dreams. I dream, too. I want you' to grow up. Become a doctor or a scientist. Marry a nice girl. Have some children. I dream, Waltie. I dream for you. But what's the use? It is better not to dream."

"Everybody has got to dream, Mama."

"Other people dream. Well . . . some people can afford to dream. They are the lucky ones." Her voice cracked. "It's not that I don't dream. . . ."

I swallowed hard. "What, Mama? Tell me about your dream, Mama?"

She said nothing for a while. "It's too late. Too late."

"Tell me, Mama. You always said dreams could come true."

She smiled and shook her head. "Did I? Dreams can come true, if God says so."

"But He does say so, Mama. You've got to have hope."

"Hope. I have hope, Waltie. But it just doesn't do any good, so I rely on Him."

Her eyes fluttered from exhaustion and she wasn't making good sense, yet she had an authority that came from what was happening to her. Authority that came because she was my mother. It was so frustrating that I wanted to take her by her frail shoulders and shake her. But how can you shake your mother?

Mother slept for a short while before the telephone rang and we both jumped. It was Mrs. Burrell. "Y'all missing someone?" she asked. She sounded like she was teasing me. "They have her over at Fair Park. In the Four-H dormitories." She chuckled. "We integrated something in Birmingham."

I told Mother and watched her eyes brighten. "Ask her if she has a car," Mother said. Mrs. Burrell didn't. Then my mother took the phone. "Did you see her?" My mother's voice was edged with sarcasm. "How could she be all right on a fairground? She's just a little girl. Where's your preacher friend? Well . . . thank you." She hung up and asked me to dial the school number for Father. He had already left. I called the motel. He wasn't there. "He's probably gone to the police station," I assured Mother. "He'll know where she is."

Mother was looking out of the window to see if Mr. Jeters was home. No car was under the carport. She told me to see if our other neighbors, anybody around the block, had a car. I rode around the block on my bicycle. It was Friday afternoon. Most people were doing grocery shopping or still at work. Only Mr. Rucker's car was parked under the port, but when I knocked at the door, no one came.

When I returned, my mother was getting dressed. She had her back to me and asked me to zip up her shift. She moved stiffly, but purposefully. I asked her if she wanted to take some medicine. "Call the cab company," she said. I looked up the number and phoned. At least an hour, I was told. The busses were still on strike and it was shift change so a lot of people were going to and from work. "Call another one," Mother said. "A *white* one." I did. An hour and a half at least. I called another. They didn't pick up in Tittusville.

"Aunt Bennie might be back in a few minutes."

"Might be a few, or it might not be. I don't want to wait. I don't want Josie in anybody's jail."

"Mama, you'll have to wait."

She gave me a stubborn look, the look Josie had taken from her. "You've got your damn bicycle, haven't you?"

"How are you going to ride?"

"How do you ride Josie?"

"On the handle bars, Mama. That's not going to work."

"I'm not that heavy, you can—I want to get Josie!" We had moved to the den and she sat on the sofa and slumped. "You are always talking about doing something, aren't you? Well, do this." She looked softly at me. "Please, I don't want my baby in that place."

I took her hand. "I promise. I will get Josie back." Mother squeezed my hand, holding me back just a moment before she let go.

THE FIRST HALF MILE along Center Street and Sixth Avenue went easily, the ground was level and I was able to ride fast. When I came to Elmwood Cemetery, I had to decide which way to go. The fairgrounds were on the other side of the large cemetery. The cemetery was restricted and I didn't want to risk cutting through. The distance around on Montevallo and Lomb streets would have added two miles, but there was the possibility of meeting someone I knew.

Then I heard a familiar tinkling in the distance. I strained for a moment to make sure I had heard it. I laughed. It was Suc and Mr. Rodriguez, the Goat Man.

22

AT FAIR PARK, Mr. Rodriguez and I saw dozens of boys penned in the open stalls where prize cattle and pigs were kept during the fair days. They waved and shouted to us from behind chain link as we passed. A few adults were on the outside of the pens, talking through the fence and tossing blankets and food over. I saw a boy I knew from the workshop and went to the fence and asked him if he had seen Josie. She was wearing a pink dress, I told him. The girls were being kept in the dormitories on the far side of the stalls, he said. He was hungry. I passed him the candy bars I had intended to eat during my own incarceration. Other boys shouted to Mr. Rodriguez to give them tamales. He looked as if he might, but then he shook his head and stared straight ahead.

Taking my cue from Mr. Rodriguez, I approached the lone officer who stood behind the barred window of a brick ticket booth near the gate. At first I stumbled over my words, then I managed to ask if I could get Josie out of jail. The officer looked at Mr. Rodriguez and made a sucking sound on his teeth. He asked Mr. Rodriguez if he had release papers. Without the papers, no one could be released. Mr. Rodriguez looked at me.

"My mother gave me money," I explained. I had a hundred dollars, five twenties, more money than I had ever carried before. Little did I know that the bail was actually five hundred dollars.

Though it was apparent that the officer had heard me, he waited until Mr. Rodriguez reported what I had said. Then the officer said that probably a hundred like us had come up to him just since lunchtime—all wanting him to let go of this or that one. If it were up to him, he would let them go. He didn't see the reason to lock up little children. But he did have a job to do and he had to see papers before he could let anybody loose. Go downtown and get the bail papers.

"We can't buy them here?" Mr. Rodriguez asked.

"Does this look like downtown?" the officer said. "You get your papers downtown."

Mr. Rodriguez ran his fingers through his hair. "Now looka here, this boy has got a sick mother and she needs her daughter with her. We can get those papers later, and there is no need to hold a child."

The officer stepped from the booth and studied Mr. Rodriguez. "Even if you was the governor, I wouldn't let go this gal without papers." He shook his head and smiled as if congratulating himself. "No, sir. Not even for the governor."

"I've got the money," I said. I reached in my pocket.

"But you don't have the papers."

"Can we just see the little girl, then?" Mr. Rodriguez asked. "See if she needs anything."

The officer wiped his brow and considered. He was a heavy-set man, a big belly and fat chest. He had a familiar, cherubic face.

"No," he said again. "You get the release papers, signed and sealed, before I let you see anybody. That's the law and the law is the law."

"She is just a little girl, not even ten years old."

"Do I look like I care how old somebody is?"

Mr. Rodriguez's voice was sharp. "No, you don't."

The officer looked beyond Mr. Rodriguez, looked to one side and then the other. "If she's old enough to break the law in Birmingham, then she's old enough to serve time. I don't know what you people think. You must think you make the laws. Now, mind you, I don't have anything in the world against you. I don't care if you want to take our seats on the busses or to eat in our restaurants. I don't care if you want to go to school with our children or even live in our section. I believe in live and let alone. But my job says, you got to have papers."

"All right," Mr. Rodriguez said. "We'll get the damn papers."

"You do that."

We started back to the goat cart when suddenly Mr. Rodriguez's face turned red and he turned back to the officer. "This boy's mama is on her death bed. She needs her girl with her now. Won't you at least have some compassion?"

"I'm not a doctor," the officer said.

"You're a fascist!

The officer pulled up his belt and put his hands on his hips; he seemed to expand. "Are you calling *me* a Kraut? I know you're not calling me a Kraut. You don't know who you're talking to, to be calling somebody a Kraut! I'm a *veteran!* Third army, under General George Patton." The man jabbed Mr. Rodriguez on the shoulder with his index finger. "I took a bullet at the Maginot line! I saw my best friend go up in fireball! White men died so that these pickaninnies could tear up Birmingham."

"Well, ain't that the way it's supposed to be——"

"Don't tell me what's supposed to be—go tend your goats. Go on back to Greece or It'ly or wherever you come from—telling *me* what's supposed to be. If it weren't for American boys like me, you would be eating sauerkraut this minute."

"I happen to like sauerkraut, you goddamn, ignorant peckerwood!" Mr. Rodriguez turned sideways to the officer.

"Peckerwood?" the officer said. "And I didn't call you nothin'." His face stiffened and reddened.

The two men stood within arm's length of each other, but not looking at each other. I have no doubt, though, that each man sensed even the slightest movement, the slightest breath, perhaps even the body heat of the other. Then Mr. Rodriguez strode back to the wagon. "We'll have to go and get a permit or whatever he needs," he said to me. "You, not being the parent, will probably have to get your daddy to go." He looked at the children who stood behind the fence as if surveying for Josie.

"The girls aren't here," I said and indicated the 4-H buildings on the far side of the grounds.

"Good thing, too. It looks like rain." Sure enough, the sky had clouded over and a slight, damp breeze had begun to circulate. He boarded his wagon and turned Sue around.

I mounted my bike and glanced over my shoulder at the policeman. He was ignoring us, and then he looked up, hearing the sound of my father's car.

Father got out of the car and walked over to me. His stride was easy, confident. "I'm here," he said. His voice soothed me. He straightened himself and looked ahead at the officer. He stepped forward, putting a hand on Mr. Rodriguez's shoulder as he passed. My father didn't say anything to the officer, but pulled a paper out of his breast pocket and held it out to him. I dropped my bicycle and ran to stand beside him.

"What can I do for you?" the officer said.

Father teetered a little, shifted his weight from one foot to the other. He seemed to have been walking a tight rope, and then he stood tall. Unlike Mr. Rodriguez, my father was dressed in suit and tie, the clothes he wore to school. He was also taller than Mr. Rodriguez, and a few inches taller than the officer. Lean and broad shouldered, he looked capable of overpowering the stocky officer. His features blended in the evening's long shadows, unlike the white man's face, which, facing the sun, was shiny.

His eyes in a squint, the officer took the paper, studied it, and walked to the window of the ticket booth. "Do you know what your friend called me?" the officer said and nodded toward Mr. Rodriguez.

My father shook his head.

"I don't understand all those head butts and hand signals you people use. Speak up when I talk to you."

My father's chest went out. "No, sir," he said, "what did he call you?"

The officer studied my father. "Are you a preacher?"

"I'm a teacher."

The officer circled over the paper with a pen and made a small check. His hand waved back and forth, but he did no more writing. "Just as bad. Maybe even worse. Your damn preachers just want the money, but some of your teachers, you just think you're plain uppity. I can't stand uppity. White or colored, mind you, or whatever your friend calls himself. I just can't stand it. Uppity, smart alecks. Preachers and teachers. Look at this!" He pointed to the pens of boys. "What do you call this? We've treated you decent. Why can't you just leave well enough be? You're going to push and push and push until you push us right over the edge. And then what?"

"I don't know," Father answered distantly.

"You do know, too. You want me to *give* you everything I have, right? What do you want? You want my job? You want my house? You can have the busses. You have the restaurants, if that's all you want. I ain't got no use for restaurants, anyway. Hell, half of the cooks are colored so I don't see the difference. But my job. You want my job? You want my house? Is that it?"

"I've got my own house—"

"You want to come live with me? You want my wife? Is that it?" He clucked his tongue. "You can have her, if that's what you want! Sassy wench. Running loose all over Hueytown with a bunch of drunks and me standing up here guarding a bunch of—" He slammed his palm against the link gate. "If that's what you want, you can have it."

"That's not what I want," my father said calmly.

"Everybody wants something. Do you know what I want?"

Father held my shoulder, pushing me slightly behind him.

"Well—"

"No, sir. I hadn't considered—"

"Damn right you haven't. Who cares about a peckerwood? Right? Just as long as *you* get what *you* want. Don't you know that I have given blood for this country? But who cares about that?"

"Look, I've given you the papers—"

"Even my wife says I'm spoiled. I tell her about what happened to my friend and she says I'm spoiled."

"You're not spoiled."

"What do you know about it? Your friend called me an ugly name. I hadn't called him nothin', and he had to call me something. I wasn't raised to call people names. My mama said that we were all the same in God's eyes. White and colored. But she was wrong. She went to her grave with nothing but the pine box she was buried in."

"Well, what in God's name do you want?"

The officer was abruptly silent.

"You wanted me to ask you, now what do you want?" my father said.

The officer seemed to consider. "Nothing. I don't know what I want. I want what you want; that's what I want."

"Officer." My father's hands opened in an elegant gesture. "I don't want to cause you any trouble—"

"You don't cause me trouble. You see, I would have to have— what do you call it? Compassion." He sneered at Mr. Rodriguez. "You think a man can't have compassion because he's white? All I got is compassion." The release order slipped from his hand. He fumbled trying to catch it, but it fluttered on the ground.

"For Pete's sake!" my father said. He bent at the knee as if to reach for the paper, but came back to his full height. In the next instant, the officer and I both bent for the paper, stopping and starting when we thought the other would reach for it. Then Father caught my shoulder and pulled me straight. The officer straightened and squared his shoulders. The colored layers of the paper rustled at our feet.

"Don't get proud on me," the officer said.

My father's hands came together in a plea, and his knees bent again. "She's just a little girl, that's all. Don't you have a little girl—some children."

"I'm just doing my duty, here. I don't want to see you beg. But it wouldn't break my heart to see a sharp dressed man like you pick up that paper or two."

My father let his arms fall to his side.

The officer shook his head and smirked. "Just what I thought. Uppity colored man afraid of getting his knees dusty. But the peckerwood, he'll do it for you."

"I didn't say those things. I have respected you." Father looked away from the officer, at the horizon, at the sunset just above the mountains. I thought that he should not pick up the paper. The officer had dropped it, and besides, my father had everything to prove by standing. Maybe he was a Negro, but he was smarter than the white man. He had been to college, and to medical school. So what if he was a teacher? That was better than what the white man was. Besides, Josie would be all right. She wouldn't want him to pick up the paper. No white man could order our father around.

"Listen," Mr. Rodriguez said to the officer, "I take it all back. I didn't mean those things. I apologize to you. I was just upset, flustered. I forgot my place. And Mr. Burke . . . he's not like me. He doesn't think the way I think. He's a gentleman."

"Now, I've heard everything," the officer said. "A gentleman, too. A colored gentleman. I've heard of a English gentleman, but never have I heard of a colored gentleman."

"You are just doing this because you can," said Mr. Rodriguez. "Just because you can."

The officer looked at him and smiled. He seemed about to relent. He nodded. "I'm not doing anything."

"Why should I have to beg you?" my father asked.

"You don't have to do anything for me," the officer said, "because you don't *deserve* to do anything for me. This is my country, not yours. In my country, I have done for you. I fought a war for this country. I took a bullet for you, and what have you done but complain? I lost my buddy for you. My buddy was burnt up to a black crisp. Burnt up just as black as any one of you. I took a bullet at the Maginot line. Then my buddy caught on fire like an ole truck tire. When I think about it, it gets me in a deal where I can't think straight."

"I know." My father's voice was quiet and deep.

The officer stared a moment and shook his head. "*You* don't know."

"I do know. I was infantry, too."

"You don't know a goddamn thing."

"Three hundred seventieth Infantry, Ninety-second Division, Fort—"

"You don't know a goddamn thing—"

"I was infantry," my father said and smiled.

The officer's face was blank. I couldn't tell what he thought, but I thought he must get Josie now. A soldier for a soldier.

Then the officer smiled, too. "You may have been infantry, but you were shining shoes."

"I crossed the Moselle."

"You were shining shoes."

"I was infantry. I was in action."

"I took a goddamn *bullet!*" the officer said. "What did you take?"

"Nothing."

"You're a goddamn liar. I was on the Maginot line. I crossed the Moselle River. I can't count the number of boys I saw killed and maimed and every goddamn one of them was *white.*"

"I was infantry."

The officer spat. The spittle splattered under my father's left eye and dribbled down his cheek. "Don't belittle the name of those boys with your lies."

Father made a sudden move with his hands. They got no higher than his waist before he stopped, fist balled, and pushed his hands against his side. In a moment, his hands relaxed; he did not wipe his face. "All right," he quietly said, "I was not there."

"You weren't even shining shoes, were you?"

Father looked up at the sky. "No, I wasn't even shining shoes."

"You were sucking on watermelons in Mississippi, weren't you?"

"I was sucking on watermelons."

"White boys dying by the truck load, and you were sucking on watermelons in Mississippi."

My father said nothing.

"Wasn't that the way it was?"

"That was the way it was."

For a moment the whole world was silent as it reordered itself. Then, I screamed. "*He was, too! He was infantry!*"

My father put his hand over my mouth. "I wasn't even there," he said. "I wasn't anywhere."

The officer stuck out his chest, put a thumb in his belt, and studied Father for a moment. Then he shook his head and started to bend to scoop up the paper. Suddenly, Father dropped to his knees and reached the paper first. Then he held it up to the white man. "I'm sorry for your trouble."

The officer shifted uncomfortably, pulled at his belt, touched his gun, then his mouth. He took a step back from my father and took the paper. "Get up." Father's head went down, chin to his chest. His shoulders trembled. "Look," the officer said. "I didn't mean it like that. Get up. I understand you just want your little girl. Now, get up."

I tried to pull Father up and some of the boys called from the pens for him to stand, but he would not.

"I didn't mean it *that* way. I lost myself, see? My wife says I get too worked up about that war. *Get up.* C'mon, now. Get up from there." He waited and looked about nervously. "Suit yourself, then." He went away hurriedly.

Again, I tried to make my father stand. His shoulders shook and he put his hands over his eyes. My face burned, and I looked away. I kept looking at the horizon, at the pretty colors behind the mountains. Mr. Rodriguez was looking away, too, but neither of us could keep looking away.

AUNT BENNIE ran out of the house when Father got home with Josie and me. In a flurry of excitement and questions, she grabbed Josie in her arms and felt her as if checking for broken bones. Mother came to the kitchen door, and as I crossed the driveway, I caught an exchange between her and my father. She nodded to him, a nod of gratitude, and he nodded back.

Then Father called to me. His eyes didn't meet mine. "You look out for . . ." he started as I approached the car. "I'll see you tomorrow." Then, as if to reestablish our connection, and perhaps his authority, he added, "Son." I wanted to say to him that I understood why he had gotten on his knees in front of the police officer. But I had no words for him. I wished I could have asked him something about science. Science had always been the net over which we could toss our affections. But there was no science for what had happened.

As I watched him drive away from the house, I resolved that I would never do what he had done, never fall down to that level. No matter what the reason, I would never stoop before a white man like that. Now, I had more reason than ever to join in the very next demonstration, and in spite of the worry I knew it would cause my parents, to go to jail.

23

AFTER THE HOUSE settled down that evening, I took a ride around the neighborhood. Several groups of men with hunting rifles sat on their porches watching, looking out for troublemakers, specifically the Klan. I had never heard of a porch watch in Tittusville. In North Birmingham, especially after Reverend Shuttlesworth's house was bombed, men did the watches regularly. But Tittusville was a quiet neighborhood, not known for activism, so the general feeling was that the Klan wouldn't bother us. Whenever I encountered a group on watch, they shouted, "Who goes there," or some other challenge. When I told them where I lived, they'd say, "Go on home, boy," or "It's past your bedtime, son." Somehow they didn't understand that it was kids, even younger than I, who were filling the jails at that very moment. As much as anything, the movement had become a children's crusade. We were doing what the adults wouldn't do, or couldn't do. We were looking out for ourselves and for our future.

I left the first two watches as soon as I was told to, but at the third, I recognized several of the men, including Mr. Jeters, and I lingered and listened to them talk.

Much of the talk concerned bombings and lynching in Birmingham's past. I knew from Uncle Reed that Birmingham, indeed, all of Alabama and the South, had a violent history when it came to black people. But I had not heard the particular stories that the men told, stories about lynchings, castrations, police shootings, and bombings. The men did not doubt that Bull Connor was behind much of the violence. They noted that Reverend Shuttlesworth had asked Bull Connor to protect the Freedom Riders when they had come through Birmingham a couple of years earlier, and instead Connor had allowed the demonstrators to be beaten by a mob in the middle of downtown in broad daylight. There had been over fifty bombings of black people's houses or churches in the city in just ten years and no one had ever been arrested; no one had even been accused.

"That's because Bull set them bombs himself," one man insisted. He was Mr. Brown, who ran a curb market on Sixth Avenue. He had said he knew someone who had actually seen Bull Connor at a Klan rally. The other men laughed.

"Who do you know who has been to a Klan rally—and lived to tell about?"

"Colored go all the time," Mr. Brown defended himself. "To spy on them."

"S-sure 'nough," Mr. Jeters agreed. Later, I learned there was some legitimacy to their claim. Black people often sneaked around the periphery of Klan rallies in order to send warning if the mob was getting out of hand. The rallies were part family gathering, part political rally, part church revival, and part lynch mob. Even if the general meeting just espoused the usual diatribe against race mixing, you could never tell when a smaller group, drunk with both liquor and rhetoric, might drive off to have "some fun" at the expense of a colored person. This is what had happened to Judge Aaron, the man who was castrated and left for dead about five years earlier.

"Where did he go?" Mr. Brown wondered aloud. The other three men speculated that Aaron had gone to live with northern relatives, but no one knew for sure.

"Shame, shame," Mr. Jeters complained, "N-Negro can't live in his own home." He lit a pipe and leaned back in the porch swing. "Can't even walk down the street without worrying about some low-life c-c-cracker cutting off your manhood."

Mr. Brown chuckled, and one of the others let out a guffaw and shook his head. "It ain't funny," the man said. "But it's just the way you said it, Jeters."

"It ain't just your poor white crackers," Mr. Brown said. "It's every white son of a bitch around here. I don't care if it's Mayor Boutwell or the head of TCI."

"It's George Wallace, too," one of the men said of the governor.

"Hell, that ain't saying nothing," Mr. Brown said. "Wallace is the most crackerfied thing up in there."

"H-how you figure that?"

"Just look at him with that slicked-back hair and them turned-up lips—like a ole boar pig. If that ain't a cracker to look at him, I don't know what is."

"God said don't judge a book by its looks," one of the men said. "But then he done done plenty, too."

"H-he talk plenty."

"That's all he have to do. He talk and they walk—and that son of a bitch would never have been elected if he hadn't got Big Jim Folsom drunk on TV. Looka here, Jeters . . ." Mr. Brown paused and took on a serious look. "You are an educated man. You can't have me believe you don't know that Wallace and some of these so-called Big Mules couldn't put a stop to this mess in a minute. Alabama got a governor. We got a legislature. We got a judiciary. We got your good white citizens—journalists, ministers, schoolteachers, and businessmen. They can tell us where to live. They tell us where to work. They can tell us where to drink water and even where to take a piss. And they got rules for their own kind, too. They even tell you what position you can take with your wife and they can lock up your ass if they catch you doing something else. So now if all these good white people allowed a colored man to get his nuts cut off, it's because they wanted it to happen."

"They just don't give a shit," one man said.

"They're greedy, that's what."

"The love of money . . ."

"What makes the world so damn wretched—just one thing—*greed*. All other calamity is natural."

The men were quiet, shaking their heads and smoking and considering Mr. Brown's profundity.

"I-it's cowardice, too," Mr. Jeters said. "They don't have the courage to stand up against it, because it takes courage, too. It takes courage not to do wrong and most of them—your average white—he don't do no more than just go along—"

"Well, ain't that enough?"

"B-but it takes a brave one to stand against what's going on and you don't have too many of them—"

"Ain't a single one, if you ask me."

"A-and it takes a hell of a someone to lead the people right—"

"And we ain't seen one of them since—"

"R-Roosevelt—"

"Roosevelt? Hell. Since Lincoln," Mr. Brown said. "If it wasn't since Christ Jesus."

The men laughed.

Usually, I wouldn't have presumed to do more than listen to older men talk. But I felt I had earned the right to say something on the subject of the race struggle. I was, by my actions that day, a bona fide race man. I had no pronouncement to offer, not even to repeat some phrase from Reverends Timmons or Bevel. I didn't really want to talk about the march because I didn't want to tell about Josie's arrest. I knew my mother wouldn't want Mr. Jeters knowing about it. Then it struck me that I did have something to say, a story about my own suffering at the hands of whites. I cleared my throat and waited until Mr. Jeters looked up at me. "Mr. Jeters, do you remember what happened to my granddaddy?"

"Y-your granddaddy? Who would that be?"

"Walter Lee Williams."

The men looked puzzled. "I can't recall that name," Mr. Brown said. One of the other men thought he had known a Walter Williams who had worked at the Schloss furnace, but that man had died before he had any children, much less grandchildren.

"Well, what happened to him?" Mr. Brown asked.

The story rushed through my mind, but I couldn't get it started. It was tied up in the sound of Great Uncle Reed's voice, and I couldn't make it my own.

"Was he the one they lynched over in Bessemer?"

"The one they lynched for wearing his army uniform? Say he was courting a white girl."

"Say he raped her."

"They always claiming rape—look sideways at a white gal and she raped. Got the most tender virginity in the world, listen to them. Come near six feet to them and they raped." The men laughed.

"Yeah," I said quietly, unable to continue, "I think that was him."

AFTER DELIVERING the papers the next morning, I had a tough decision to make. I knew my parents didn't want me near the demonstrations, but I felt it was necessary to go. How could I not go as long as Lamar was in jail? And given the fervor of Reverend Timmons, Lamar might never get out. How could I sit still knowing that my own little sister had been penned up like a pig and my father had to beg on his knees to get her released? Besides, something had awakened in Birmingham and I wanted to be a part of it. All that morning, I saw my grown-up neighbors rising early to cut their lawns and water their gardens, and just before noon passing by my house dressed in Sunday clothes and serious looks. Wearing Sunday clothes on a Saturday afternoon usually meant a funeral, but no one wore black—even though it was the death of something.

After lunch I tried to sneak away, but Aunt Bennie had a close eye on us. Poor Josie could barely leave her room without being questioned. "You want to go to jail?" Aunt Bennie said to her only half teasing. "I'll treat you like jail."

Aunt Bennie kept giving me chores, things to keep me in or near the house. Eventually she needed me to run to Mr. Lee's corner store. She gave me a cock of her head. "I reckon I can trust you to ride around the block without getting into any trouble, can't I?"

When I got to Mr. Lee's store, I saw a carload of people heading toward downtown, toward the demonstrations. Something enchanted me about the four people, two men in ties and two women in crisp dresses. The only clue that this wasn't a shopping trip was that they were wearing tennis shoes. My body tingled. Just thinking about the sirens, the hoses, the big, bull-faced policemen with their clubs—even the dogs—was exciting. It was a game, a challenge, and I was itching for it.

On the other hand, I knew Aunt Bennie was depending on me. My mother hadn't awakened for the day. Aunt Bennie said she had been in pain all night and was exhausted, too. So I knew just a little trip to the store and coming home without worrying Aunt Bennie was important.

Mr. Lee was sitting behind the counter when I went into the store. He was a lean, light-skinned man, about seventy. Although the store was a narrow shotgun with a counter at the front and one aisle of goods, it was said that it had made Mr. Lee one of the wealthiest men in Tittusville. His was one of only a few neighborhood stores, and because many blacks despised the treatment they received in the white-owned stores, they would pay Mr. Lee the few cents more he charged for goods.

"Everybody and his brother is headed downtown today," he announced to me as I put the baking soda Aunt Bennie needed on the counter. "Marching for their freedom. They gone have to do more than march to get free. All them chillun getting locked up! Saddest thing I heard. What y'all gone do with a record? Won't be able to get a job emptying the trash." I had heard him speak before, but not directly to me, about colored people getting rights. There could be no progress without wealth. Get rich and then get free. "Nobody listens to a poor man— and a poor black man can't even take a piss without asking the boss." He counted out my change and leaned across the counter. "So where you gone be if you got your tail on a chain gang?"

Rather than discourage me, Mr. Lee's admonition clinched my decision to make a detour. I wouldn't join in the demonstrations but just watch from the distance and return quickly. At the most, it would take me thirty minutes.

THE POLICEMEN and firemen had cordoned off the park, and bottled up the demonstrators around Sixteenth Street Baptist. It was difficult to get close for the number of people. Demonstrating had become popular. Still, many of the people were spectators, standing along the side of the park across from the church, as if they thought the policemen would care that they weren't demonstrators.

I made a wide berth around the police line and ended up in the vicinity of the courthouse. Then I saw what was happening. The demonstrators weren't meeting at the church where the police expected them, but were meeting in alleys and alcoves, or just hopping out of cars that stopped in front of the buildings they wanted to picket. While Bull Connor had arrayed his army in a blockade of the church, the preachers had never allowed themselves to be trapped, and were already behind the enemy lines. In groups of three or four, they headed toward the city government buildings with picket signs they had hidden under their jackets and skirts.

Only a few policemen were guarding the public buildings, and most of them seemed to have been inside city hall. They came rushing out to confront the demonstrators. For the first time, up close, I saw the archenemy himself, Bull Connor. Bull Connor looked much less like a bull than he did a hog. The man who ran down the stairs at city hall, frantically waving his hands, was red-faced and fat. He ordered his men to arrest the demonstrators. Bystanders like myself retreated with remarkable swiftness, while the police pounded the demonstrators with clubs, tore their signs from their hands, and pushed them up the stairs into the buildings.

No sooner had the first demonstrators been rounded up than a woman and a little girl who had been standing nearby walked to the bottom stairs. They kneeled and folded their hands in prayer. Their action surprised me; it brought a sudden lull to the frantic moment. It was a beautiful, gracious sight and I wished the woman were my mother. Mother and Josie and me and my father, too, like an idealized family on a church fan, neat clothes and groomed hair, kneeling in front of city hall, daring Bull Connor to interrupt our prayers.

A moment later, the Bull responded. He ordered the police to drag the woman to her feet. They jerked the girl from the pavement; her feet pedaled the air. Then Bull Connor stood on the portico, surveying the spectators. With a sweep of his hand, he ordered us all arrested. Someone shouted that she was an innocent bystander. Bull Connor shouted back that no Negro in Birmingham was innocent. I thought about Aunt Bennie's baking soda, and hightailed it home.

24

INSTEAD OF GOING to church on Sunday morning, Father and I worked in the yard. We trimmed the hedges, mowed the grass, and weeded the flower bed and garden. I thought my father would complain that I hadn't been doing all I could around the house, but he was sullen and pensive. After we finished the work, we sat at the picnic table and drank sweet tea. He lit a cigarette, the first time I had ever seen him smoke at home. "Son, I owe you an apology," he said, seemingly out of the blue. I tensed, thinking that he would talk about what happened at Fair Park. "I've preached to you about being responsible, but I haven't been very responsible to you, have I?" He dragged on the cigarette. "Just look at the those tomatoes, so yellow and limp. Come summer, we'll be lucky if they make it, and your mama loves tomatoes so much. But the blame lies with me. I'm the father here, and I guess I just haven't been thinking straight."

"That's all right," I said, relieved we were talking about tomatoes. "I am here. I can water them."

"It takes more than just water. It takes being here, Waltie. And it's not your problem. It's mine. I owe it to you. You don't owe me anything. The garden is my garden, and the house is my house, and you all, all of you, are my family." He was not looking at me, but his voice was so sincere it seemed to cut right into me, making me feel warm inside. Even sitting, he seemed towering, too tall for me to see over.

"Daddy, does this mean you're coming back?"

He sighed out a breath of smoke, looked down at his shoes, and shook his head. "One day. Soon, I hope. It's up to your mother."

"When you come back, things will be different."

He looked at me to ascertain my meaning. "Yes." His voice deepened with melancholy.

"I don't mean just about Mama," I asserted. "I mean, I will be more responsible, too."

He rubbed my head and chuckled. "Growing up, hey? You don't have to worry about more responsibility. Just what we talked about. Just finish being a kid."

"But I'm not just a kid, and even if I am, I want to be in the marches. I want to fight for our rights."

He put out his cigarette on the tabletop and put the butt back into the cigarette package. "You and Josie don't need to worry about that."

"Somebody has to worry about it."

"Worrying is for me to do."

I snorted sarcastically.

"You think I don't worry about things like that, Mr. Big Pants?"

"No, sir."

"Son, I'm thirty-eight years old. Before you were born I had already lived more than twice as long as you have now. Don't presume you know everything about me."

I accepted his rebuff with humility, but the humility turned false and I kicked at the ground.

"Son." My father took out another cigarette. "I confess, I had my day, too. Just after the war, I marched with Reverend Ware and the veterans to get our voting rights. We dressed out in our uniforms, and paraded down to the courthouse. They gave us a test on the U.S. Constitution that we had to pass in order to vote." He lit the cigarette. "You could fight all right without passing a damn test, but you couldn't vote unless you could recite the preamble and name all the amendments. I had finished college, and I thought I was ready for that. It didn't matter. They didn't want us to vote."

I hadn't heard this story and it was difficult to picture my father as a race man. "You gave up," I said sharply.

He studied me, then blew smoke at his feet. "I didn't give up. I met your mother. We had you. My priorities changed." He dropped the cigarette, still long, and crushed it against the dry grass. "Negroes have more to worry about than just getting our freedom."

"Like what?" He didn't answer. "Like what, Daddy? What could be better than being free?"

"Eating."

My throat went tight. Freedom wasn't a matter of convenience, I wanted to argue as I had heard Reverend Timmons do. Freedom is God-given. We shouldn't have to wait until it was practical for rich, white men to give it to us. But I couldn't argue with him; I had seen him on his knees, begging for my sister, and that thought made my heart pound. In one stroke, my heart opened to him; how much more could he have loved Josie than at the moment his knees slapped down in the dust? In the next stroke, my heart closed to him; was there a more shameful moment in life?

WHEN THE SUN got hot, we went indoors and my father sat in the den. He asked Aunt Bennie if he could talk to Mother—he didn't want to disturb her if she was asleep. I wanted to say, "She ain't Aunt Bennie's wife," but only shook my head. Aunt Bennie said Mother was asleep.

Josie came in and crawled into my father's lap, and he held her like a baby. "My, my," he said, and looked at me, not at her. "My little baby is a jail bird."

"Am not," Josie said.

My father stopped the teasing. Instead, he said to me, "You know, I am counting on you."

"Why are you counting on him?" Josie asked.

"Because he is older."

"You can count on me, too."

"Well, I do, sweet pea."

"What about yourself?" Josie said. It was a remark that ought to have been cutting, but Josie said it with the innocence of a ripe plum—sweet and juicy. Aunt Bennie stepped into the room just then, and I could see that she wanted to add a bit of tartness to the remark. She didn't say anything, but gave my father a haughty look as if to say she had told him so. My father got up as if he were going to leave. On one hand, because I felt he blamed me for Josie's going to jail, I didn't care if he left; on the other hand, I didn't want him to leave. I went to the stereo. Father was always so fussy about his albums that no one dared to touch them, so when I opened the stereo I saw that the Nat "King" Cole album he had been playing when Mother kicked him out was still on the turntable. I started the music. It stopped him. He stood for a moment to listen, and then smiled. The song was "Sentimental Reasons," a soothing, mellow love song. He sat down again, and began to sway with Josie in his arms. Even Aunt Bennie's scowl disappeared. Then I heard Mother call him, just a hoarse whisper: "Carl."

Father put Josie down and went to Mother's room. Josie came to me and put her arms around my waist and we danced around in a clumsy twirl. Our jubilation was short-lived, however. In less than ten minutes, the time it took Nat "King" Cole to finish two more numbers, our father came back to the den. He seemed nervous, upset, but he smiled and patted Josie's head as he went out.

. . .

THE FOLLOWING WEEK brought more demonstrations, but Josie and I stayed away from the marches. Lamar, too, released on bond, seemed less eager to join them. Three nights in jail had satisfied his curiosity. Mrs. Burrell said it was somebody else's turn, and I wondered if she meant me. I would march again, soon enough, I reasoned, but for now I had nothing to feel ashamed about. I had put myself on the line. I had been hit in the back by a hundred pounds of water, and I had had my shirt torn off by a dog. Besides, the jails were still filled to capacity because many of the parents couldn't afford bail money. To make things worse, there had been a couple of stormy nights, and the children at the fairgrounds were getting sick from standing in the rain.

At school we weren't allowed to talk about the demonstrations or our jailed classmates. We were told not to identify ourselves as having participated in the demonstrations because, in the eyes of the school board, demonstrators were criminals and could be expelled. Principal Buford gave Josie and me a wink and a pat. She was glad to see us back in school she said, and she never asked us where we had been. Though we didn't talk about it, it was obvious that many of the students were protesting. Built on a side of a ridge, Center Street School had two levels. The classrooms on the lower level, first through third grades, were nearly as busy as usual, but the upper level classrooms, where the fourth, fifth, and sixth graders studied, practically echoed from the emptiness. At recess, there weren't enough of us to play softball.

WHEN JOSIE AND I got home on Thursday afternoon, Aunt Bennie was talking on the telephone, pacing back and forth in the den. I could tell she was talking to a doctor by the deferential way in which she spoke. She gave me a wide-eyed look that alarmed me. I dropped my books and ran to my mother's bedroom. Josie was just a step behind me and ran into my back when I stopped at the door. Mother lay still, her face placid, the way I had grown accustomed to seeing her. But something was different. I thought she was dead. After a moment, Josie moved around me and walked up to the bed. Mother opened her eyes and she tried to speak, but her voice faltered. Soon she lost focus and drifted back into sleep.

When Aunt Bennie finished talking on the phone, she sat down on the sofa and bent double. I went over to her and sat beside her. I put my hand on her back. When she stopped crying, she told us that the doctor said that we could bring Mother to the hospital if we wanted to, but there was nothing he could do for her but to make her comfortable, and we could do that at home. She sat up and shook her head. "I'm losing my sister." She held her arms out for Josie and for me. "We are losing her, my dear sister."

We sat together for about ten minutes, a warm, damp huddle. Then it was time for more phone calls: Grandma Pic and Uncle Reed, first. She tried to call my father at the high school, and not reaching him there, left a message for him at the motel. After supper, she tried twice again to call my father. About twilight, I went out into the yard. The stars were faint and there was a breeze that promised rain. I got on my bike and rode toward the railroad bridge. I passed by men on a porch watch. They waved to me and someone made a joke. "You haven't seen any Klan in the neighborhood have you, boy?" Soon, I realized I was riding downtown to find my father.

My father wasn't in the motel room so I rode around Fourth Avenue, peeking into the windows of restaurants and bars. If he were drinking, I made myself think, he would be in a bar. I couldn't bear to think of my father sitting on a corner or in an alleyway. Finally, I saw him sitting in the paperbag brown light of the Jockey Boy restaurant. He was sitting at the bar with other men, yet he seemed to be sitting apart from them, his body turned away just a little. He laughed with them, but his mouth opened later than the others and he seemed less amused. I wanted to go into the bar and yell at him, remind him that he had two children and a sick wife. Then I suddenly felt fearful for him. He looked sad, lost. Could I tell him that my mother was dying? I pedaled away, as fast and as hard as I could.

25

I GOT UP and searched Bright Eyes's locker for whiskey. Wild Turkey was what I was looking for, but he had a bottle of Jack Black and that was good enough. I drank from the bottle. He wouldn't mind. He drank on me when he wanted to. The white boy, the little rabbit. I didn't mind him, but there was always going to be that problem between us: He was white. In the field, that meant nothing. He was a GI. He died as easily as I died. But in camp he was a rabbit. A peckerwood. A likeable peckerwood, but a peckerwood just the same.

I took a deep draft of the whiskey and felt it burn me from lips to stomach. I couldn't help but to grin. I filled my mouth, swallowed again, and laughed. The laugh caught in the back of my throat and I snorted whiskey out of my nose.

Something is loose in me. Maybe it has been for a long time. When I was born, I was very happy because I didn't know anything. Then my mother started to die and I was scared. After that Reverend King came to Birmingham, and I thought I knew something. I thought I was somebody. But since then, every part of me has become loose. The part that dreams is loose. The part that dreams is lost.

I started to tear out the page from the tablet to crumble the letter, but I stopped. I stared at it. The letters were blocky, all caps, my handwriting, but vaguely unlike my writing. Too impressed into the page. "No," I said, "it was not the dreaming part." I sipped from Bright Eyes's bottle, picked up the pen, and wrote again. *Yes, I think it was the dream I lost because I lost faith. You can't dream without faith. You can't even nightmare.*

I WAS SURPRISED to see Lamar at school on Friday morning since two hours earlier, while delivering the papers, he swore that he would be at the demonstrations again. Now, he told me, the demonstrations were over.

"What do you mean, over?" I asked as we walked into our nearly empty classroom. About twenty of the thirty children were absent.

"W.W. says it's over. They are going to announce it later today."

Still, the magnitude of the statement escaped me. The demonstrations were over, but did that mean that segregation was over? If that were true, then what would happen? "Do you mean we won?" I asked. Mrs. Griffin shushed me and asked one of the girls to lead the pledge of allegiance.

"I guess," Lamar whispered. "But W.W. wasn't sure. All he knew was that we weren't suppose to march." Mrs. Griffin tapped Lamar's shoulder with the end of her yardstick. "But the marches are over," Lamar pleaded before she could strike him.

"It's about time," she said and withdrew the yardstick. "Maybe now we can get back to the business of school." She nodded to the girl to continue the pledge.

"But we won!" Lamar interrupted. "I *think* we won."

Mrs. Griffin was still for a second, then she asked us to take our seats though we still had the last phrase of the pledge to recite. "It doesn't matter who won. Nothing's changed in the classroom." Lamar was about to protest, but Mrs. Griffin slapped the yardstick against his desk and silenced him. "Now, who will lead us in 'Lift Every Voice'?"

At recess, we heard from one of the younger children that her brother who had been imprisoned at the fairgrounds was released; all the children were being released. But no one knew whether we had won. After recess, as the children queued into the classroom, I saw Mrs. Buford. I thought she might be able to tell me something. She seemed very cheerful, but when I tried to speak to her, she patted my head and pushed me back into the line.

When the school bell rang announcing the end of the school day, Lamar leapt from his seat and rushed toward home with promises that he would call as soon as he had the details. Later, he would tell me he had forgotten to call. For me, the clanging school bell brought new apprehension. What had happened to my mother? Neither Josie nor I rushed home. Taking our time seemed to prolong any bad news.

Our father called that night; Aunt Bennie answered. "What do you mean, 'How bad is it?'? It's bad is all you need to know. How am I supposed to know if she wants you to come? I don't know what she wants. All I know is—well, Carl, come when you want to. Just take your time." Aunt Bennie slammed the phone down.

"Is Daddy coming?" Josie asked.

Aunt Bennie patted her head. "There's no need for him to come tonight. Mama's all right for tonight. He'll come tomorrow."

I went outside and sat on the picnic table. More than anything, I wanted my father to be with me. In spite of his flaws, his weaknesses, I needed to feel the solidity of his presence. The world had been spinning hard, it seemed, since that day that I learned that my mother was dying. The family had been spinning and the town had been spinning and now things were slowing down. Things were about to stop, I thought. Sometimes when things stop spinning they fall. I suddenly had the feeling that I was about to fall. My stomach ached and I doubled over, head to knees. The air was sweet and thick, and the ground kept flipping over my head. "Father, father, father," I said. "Daddy, where are you?"

ON SATURDAY MORNING, Mother was sitting up in her bed and smiling. If not for her thin body, we could have fooled ourselves into thinking she had miraculously recovered. She asked that we sit with her, and so Josie and I spent most of Saturday sitting in our mother's bedroom, chatting with her, remembering old games and jokes.

After supper, though, we saw that the old wives' tale about finding strength just before death had validity. When we went back into Mother's room she lay with her head hanging over the side of the bed, as if she had been sitting and had collapsed. Josie screamed. I ran to Mother and took hold of her. She opened her eyes, but seemed disorientated. I helped her to lie down and she said for me to give her a kiss. I kissed her on the cheek, and she clutched me, held me, let out a deep breath against my ear. She did the same to Josie. "Now, son, go and get your father." My heart felt like it had popped open. Was she saying she was ready to die?

Aunt Bennie wanted to call the ambulance, but Mother said no. She wanted to be at home. She wanted my father, so we called the motel for him. There was no answer. Desperate, Aunt Bennie said she would just start calling bars, and I suggested that she call the Jockey Boy. The man at the Jockey Boy said he knew our father but that he usually didn't show up until later.

SHORTLY AFTER TEN, Mother began talking to herself in a hoarse whisper. When we put our ears close to her mouth we heard her say something about "Daddy."

"Oh Jesus," Aunt Bennie said and wrung her hands. "She's talking to Daddy. She is passing. She's seeing Daddy! He's come for her."

I looked around the room, imaging the grandfather I had never seen in life was there. Where was Mother looking? Her eyes seemed unfocused. Perhaps the spirit was everywhere in the room, filling it like the air.

. Of all of us, Josie seemed the calmest. She was already in her pajamas so she crawled into the bed next to Mother and lay in a little ball, close but not touching. At times I thought Josie was asleep, but she was awake, quiet and listening.

I had to do something so I went outside and got on my bike and began to ride. Something was amiss in the neighborhood. The men sitting on porch watch were agitated. One actually cocked his pistol as I surprised him rounding the corner. Cars sped down the streets, and I heard shouting at a distance. I stopped at Mr. Brown's porch watch where I learned that the KKK had bombed the house of Reverend King's brother, A.D. They were trying to kill Reverend King and thought he was staying with his brother. No one had been hurt, but the bomb had made a hole so big a Mack truck could drive through it. Everyone was running off to see the hole.

I thought about going to see the big hole, too, but just as suddenly, I had a need to find my father. I needed to tell him about Mother. She wanted to see him. She was dying, and she wanted to see him. I wanted Mama to see him, too. And I knew that he would want to see her. I turned my bike toward downtown, away from where everyone was heading to see the bomb, and started down the dark streets. If Mama died and Daddy wasn't there, I wouldn't know what to do.

Just as I got to Fourth Avenue, a block from the park, the air quivered and the ground rumbled. My first thought was that a train was coming, but an invisible one with no engine and no clanking boxcars, but just rumble. Then I heard shouts and screams. People rushed into the streets with frightened looks. A bomb! In a few minutes I realized the bomb had gone off at Dr. Gaston's motel.

I could only think of Father as I rode toward the motel, dodging through hundreds of people who were pouring out of the bars and dancehalls. In the strobe of ambulance and police lights, I made out a hole the size and shape of an arched doorway on one side of the motel office. I felt a degree of relief. My father's room was on the other side. As I headed toward his room, I saw his car, debris-covered and dented. Again, I was afraid for him, and hoped, for the first time, that he was in a bar rather than the room. The motel rooms were dark, because the electricity had been damaged, so I couldn't tell by the lights if he was in. The only hope I had was that the end of the motel where my father's room was located seemed undamaged. I ran up the stairs and tried the door to his room. It was locked. I banged on it with my fist. Kicked it. Father must have been out, I thought. Thank you, Jesus, he must be in a bar. I kept banging on the door until a fireman startled me. I didn't know whether to run or not. He ordered me away from the building. "It's sealed off," he said.

"This is my father's room."

The fireman hesitated. Then he knocked on the door. "Ain't nobody in there."

"He might be drunk."

The fireman took a step back from the door, raised his booted foot, and kicked at the latch. It took three hard kicks to break the door. It swung open to an empty room.

"Thank you," I said and ran.

A MEAN CROWD had gathered outside the motel and in the park as the bars and supper clubs emptied. People in party clothes, some still carrying drinks, milled through the streets. "An eye for an eye," a man growled through cupped hands. A woman screamed, "Let's blow up something of theirs!"

I made my way to the Jockey Boy, pushing rather than riding my bicycle through the crowd. When I got to the restaurant, I looked through the window and saw Father sitting alone at the bar. Propping the bike against the wall, I took a deep breath and pushed my way past the spectators who blocked the door. No one noticed me; the few people who remained at their tables or at the bar were focused on their drinks. Everyone else watched the street. I stood beside my father and I steadied myself on a stool. Slowly, he looked up at me, and without my having to say a thing, and without surprise at seeing me, he nodded an acknowledgment of why I had come. Tired and sad, his resignation was so complete that I felt like an angel of death. Not a mere bearer of bad news, but the very agent who brought on the event. Trembling, I wanted him to hold me in his arms, but I realized that, just then, I was more powerful than he.

"Son?" he said at last.

"Mama . . ." I choked, not just because of the news, but because of what the news had already done to him. I couldn't say what I had come to say without first saying what I thought he needed me to say. In spite of all that had happened, his leaving the family, his hitting my mother, his begging on his knees in front of the officer—I loved him. But the words were impossible to say. Even under these circumstances, when I doubted that we would live through the next moment, I simply couldn't say the thing the boy, the boy-man, needed to say.

Father was no help, either. He turned away when I said "Mama." He looked at the mirror behind the bar, took a drag on his cigarette, and crushed it out before he turned back to me. Then he put his hand on my shoulder. The power I thought I had over him vanished. With his touch, I spoke my news. "Mama said to come home now."

He continued to hold his hand on my shoulder and I repeated the message. Then he took out his wallet and put money on the bar, and we started toward the door.

We were only outside a moment when we saw that the crowd had become violent. People threw bottles as they retreated from a cohort of policemen. Two men in front of us pried bricks from the sidewalks and hurled them at the policemen. The policemen, in turn, clubbed through the crowd with nightsticks, and the police dogs shredded party dresses.

The firemen were trying to set up the monitor guns, but the bombardment of bricks prevented them. Above the roar of the crowd I could hear the preachers screaming through megaphones, entreating the crowd to disperse orderly.

My father decided we should walk to the motel and get the car. Pushing my bicycle, I followed him as he squeezed around the onlookers at the periphery of the fighting. The crowd jostled us, and on several occasions I was pushed down and my father pulled me up. He said that I should take the bike back to the bar and leave it, but I didn't want to.

When we got to the motel, we ran into a faceoff between the policemen and the crowd. A preacher, who, I surmised, was A. D. King, reasoned with the crowd. He told the people about the bombing at his house, and assured the people that Reverend King was in Atlanta with his family. He insisted that the people go home. "Why should we go home?" a woman near me yelled. "*They* bomb us, and *we* have to go home!"

My father went to a policeman and explained that he needed to get into the parking lot to get his car. Seeing my father with the policeman gave me the jitters. Would he beg again? The policeman said no one was allowed in the lot, and my father turned away without another word. "Well, Son," he said. "I guess we'll have to walk."

We started away from the police lines when we heard singing. The singing seemed to ease the people. For a few minutes, everything went smoothly, everyone walking in the same direction. Then there was an unexpected jostling. Someone pushed me from behind and I fell again. My father pulled me up, but a wave of people crashed over

my bicycle and pushed against us, shoving us along, farther and farther from the bicycle, which I could mark by the rapid it caused in
the rush of people. We were pushed a half block away before the press
of the crowd eased. "Dogs," a man said with disgust. He was a young
man dressed in a porkpie hat and a Motown suit. But there were
more than just dogs. People ran by us with blood streaming from
their heads. Then we noticed small groups, mostly of young men,
throwing bricks in the direction from which they were running.
Again, a great shove came. We found shelter with a group in the
alcove under the marquee of the Carver Theater as a phalanx of state
troopers, not city policemen, shoved past us. This was how our governor answered the end of the demonstrations. The state troopers
were dressed like combat soldiers, helmets, boots, and flack jackets.
They had dogs, and billy clubs, and something I had never seen until
then, carbines. When a dog attacked, the troopers let the leashes go
slack and let the dogs maul the victims. When someone did not move
fast enough, they *thonk*ed his head with the clubs. The whacking,
thumping, and cracking sounded like a parade of out-of-tune drums.
"Ain't this some shit?" the man in the Motown suit said as he joined
us under the marquee. "I ain't fixin' to take this."

Suddenly there was a *whoosh*. A building about a half block away
went up in a blaze. "The food store," the Motown man exclaimed.
"The damn food store. What the hell . . . ?" The firelight trimmed the
streetscape in flickering orange. It reflected from the faces of the people, eyes wide with fear or narrow with rage. It reflected from the
golden eagle insignia on the helmets of the troopers. The helmets
shaded the troopers' eyes; all that could be seen of their faces were
their tight lips and teeth. The fire spread quickly to other buildings,
or perhaps other buildings were set afire; at any rate, panic was on
two fronts as the troopers pushed the crowd toward the burning
buildings. A woman in nightclothes, having been chased from bed by
the flames, joined us under the marquee. "What's going on?" she

asked my father. When he didn't answer, she turned to the Motown man. "They trying to kill us all," he said.

Now the center of the melee was right in front of us, people running first one way and then in the other as the troopers trapped and beat them. Then, as if they were on the end of a flickering whip, the troopers turned on us. "Get indoors," they ordered. "Get your black ass off the street." They kicked and swung the clubs and let the dogs bite arms and legs. The Motown man sprung like a cat onto the back of a trooper. He raked the trooper with a glinting switchblade, slicing into the trooper's shoulder. As if with one mind, five troopers turned on the Motown man, hammering and hammering him with their clubs. "You'll kill him!" my father screamed, and started toward them. I grabbed at my father, caught his belt, but he had already drawn the attention of the troopers. The fury turned on my father and me. Father spun around, pushed me into the corner of the alcove, and lay on me. I could feel the clubbing reverberate through his body, a torrent coming down on him. He tensed, groaned. I heard him loose his breath as the air was knocked from him. The attack was brief and furious, a dozen strong blows. My father lay still and the fury moved on.

We remained hunched in the alcove for twenty minutes as Father recovered. The only way I knew he was conscious was by the tension in his body. After a while we stood up. He took my hand. We went through the alleys, until we were away from downtown. As we went, I felt my father grow tall again; elegance came back into his frame.

WHEN WE GOT HOME, Aunt Bennie looked like she was going to scold us, until she saw the blood on the back of my father's head. She called to Grandma Pic and Uncle Reed, who had just come in from Coosada. As I told what had happened, Aunt Bennie tried to attend Father, but he pushed her away and went into the bedroom where Josie lay beside my mother. At first he stood and looked at her.

Slowly, she reached out to him. They held hands. It seemed that a silent conversation was occurring between them, one that we onlookers would never understand. Father got down on his knees and whispered into her ear. She smiled, faintly but genuinely. He remained on his knees for most of an hour, talking softly and singing Nat "King" Cole songs.

26

WHERE WERE YOU *when President Kennedy died? What were you doing? I was somewhere in Birmingham that day. I was somewhere all over Birmingham, in a hundred different pieces. I was loose. By that time, I was already loose.*

The summer after my mother died, there were four police murders, two KKK bombings, and a riot in Birmingham. Even so, the summer passed idly for us children. Because I had lost my bicycle, I had to give up the paper route. Because of the marches, we had fallen behind in school, so Father made us stay home and study. Occasionally, I played with Lamar. We talked about science, watched television, played with the microscope, and even sneaked into George Ward Park, ignoring the "No Trespassing" signs. The white softball teams ignored the signs, too, but no one chased us away.

The city was implementing desegregation, but the changes came slowly, so slowly it seemed that nothing really changed. A few race men dared to break the segregation patterns, and when they did, we heard stories: black people who went to eat at the white lunch counters were served, but only in certain areas of the counter; or served on paper plates rather than on china. It was rumored that some restaurants had special food for black people, dog meat in the hamburger, urine in the ice tea, and "blackbird stew."

The board of education called for limited integration of the schools, just five black students from the entire city would go to select white schools. They chose the smartest among the black students, all high school students and all from the "best colored" families. The tension about the schools continued to build, and soon after the school year started, a bomb went off at the house of the lawyer who represented the integrationists. We felt the blast in Tittusville, two and half miles away. People rioted after the bombing. The police killed one man. Twenty more went to the hospital.

The first three weeks of school went by quickly. Josie and I were happy to be back in school. It gave us something to do, for one thing. For another, we had been threatened with expulsion because of our participation in the marches; and for a third, Aunt Bennie had offered to take us to Philadelphia. By then, we had had enough of Aunt Bennie.

One Sunday in mid-September, I had gone to church with Lamar. Our father had taken Josie to St. Luke's Lutheran. Lamar and I were playing around on the church grounds after Sunday school. Lamar was talking about going to the moon. He said that the Apollo program would put men on the moon in five years. I told him I thought the Russians would get there first and set up a colony under a plastic dome. We had seen the concept in the movie Forbidden Planet.

We continued this banter, standing a little to the outside of the group of adults. Suddenly we felt the ground shake. "Earthquake," Lamar said and gave me a look so serious I mocked him. The adults looked wary. One of the deacons ordered us to get into the church. "It was a bomb," I whispered what was obvious to Lamar. We were amused more than frightened by the excitement.

At the beginning of the service, the minister made the announcement that the Sixteenth Street Baptist had been bombed. He paused. There was loss of life, he said. A groan went up from the congregation. "How many?" somebody asked from the deacon's pews. The preacher shook his head. At this time, he did not have authoritative information, he said. But he had heard that about twenty were badly hurt. He took a breath. Four killed. Four little girls. I thought about Josie, but I knew she was at a different place, a safe church.

After church, I went home with Lamar and changed into a set of his play clothes, short pants since my legs were longer than his. Mrs. Burrell asked me to call my father and tell him I was all right. I told him I would stay with Lamar and come home after supper.

Lamar and I decided to sneak and look at the bomb damage. Since I weighed more, I pedaled while Lamar perched like a parrot on the handlebars. He was jabbering all the way, but in the breeze and with the effort and rhythm of the pedaling to keep me busy, I let his words float by. I heard a truck turn the corner behind me, accelerate, and pass us. A Confederate flag flapped from the aerial of the truck, and two white teenagers sat on the back. My stomach knotted. Something told me to ditch the bike, to throw it down. But I kept my rhythm; I kept the bike steady. Why run? They were just two white boys on a truck. Besides we were close to home, not yet outside of Tittusville. Then I saw a glint in the hands of one of the boys. It seemed, and now this could just be a trick of memory, that I saw very clearly the boy's face. Call it "All-American," if you want. He was lean and freckled and not at all mean-looking. But he had a strange look in his face. What emotion was it? Hatred? I have named it variously. From time to time, I think it was merely curiosity—the same curiosity that had sent Lamar and me out on our adventures. At other times, I call it confusion, a spinning in the head that made him act without thinking. Then again, could it have been hope? That same thing my mother warned me against. Could he have been trying to fulfill a dream impressed upon him by his minister, or his Scout master, or Governor Wallace— some dream of a world in which he might be happy and secure. I know the dream.

The boy pointed at us.

Lamar shoved against my shoulder, causing me to swerve the bike and run it over the curb. I yelled at him to sit up, stupid, but he had fallen limp, his face was looking up into mine and his eyes were losing light. The bike fell on the sidewalk, my right leg momentarily trapped under it. Lamar lay partially on my shoulder. Blood pumped from his neck.

After I saw the blood, things went loose. I remember sunlight on the dry grass. The smell of diesel in the air. The whistle of a bird.

I stood up, letting Lamar's head roll against the sidewalk. His eyes fluttered and closed. His mouth opened. The fountain at his neck stopped. I shook him.

The shirt I wore, Lamar's, had a ring of his blood on it. My hands were bloody. A fly lit on my arms. I started walking, holding my hands out from my sides. It seemed I walked for a long time, in many different directions at once. People ran toward me, then past me. They were all around me, shaking me. I remember the blue sky, bright and empty of everything.

THIS WORLD IS *full of loss. But you never get used to it. People keep coming in and going out. What does it all mean? It's got to mean something, don't you think? One thing it meant was that I got the book that Lamar took out of the trash basket at Terminal Station. Mrs. Burrell said I could have the microscope, too. I gave it to Josie. She claims it helped her become an "A" science student. The problem with loss is you gain something from it, but it's never the same as what you had. The loss of my mother gave me a father who drank too much, and the loss of Lamar gave me a book of poetry I couldn't understand.*

I dreamed in a dream I saw a city.
I dreamed it was the new city of friends.
Nothing was greater there than love.
It was seen every hour.
In the actions of the men of that city
And in all their looks and words.

Let me tell you about the actions of men.

After my mother died, my father promised my sister and me a dog. He never got it for us. He promised us a trip to Washington, D.C., but he never took us. Josie said the promises were enough, something to hope for. But they were not. Some days Father sat in our living room from morning until midnight listening to jazz records and drinking and never coming out to eat. At times he and I went

months without saying a word to each other. I was always on the
out of high school. My sister pitied me, but even she lost patience.
Bennie came to my defense, blaming my father. One day my fat
and said, "You might as well join the military. You'll be drafted anyway and
you'll never get into a college with those grades." We were standing in our
kitchen. I believe I had a cigarette, which I stubbed out in the sink. I didn't say
anything to him and walked out of the door. That was at ten o'clock in the morn-
ing. When I came back that afternoon, I was in the army. My sister said that the
news made my father cry. I told her I was happy he had cried. You might have
guessed, I was far, far from it.

When I lost Lamar, I lost the moon; I lost the stars. What did it matter to be
the first Negro in space? What did it matter if we became doctors, or famous sci-
entists? The immutable fact was that we were Negroes and being Negro tethered
us to the earth. It seemed to me that my mother was right, after all. Trust, but do
not hope. To hope will only set you up for disappointment.

WHAT WERE YOU doing when Reverend King died? Where were you standing
then? I was all over town. Loose as a goose on a string.

VESTER SAID I was cool, when I shot that papa-san. But I was loose. I saw
him long before Haywood pointed him out. He was wearing the black pajamas,
and he was running away, so I said to myself, I can shoot him, if I want. It would
be all right. I couldn't see him, but my heart told me he was an old man. My
heart said, What if he was a VC? He was just an old man. A man out tending
his crops. A man just strolling along, minding his business, thinking about the
blueness of the sky and the warm way the sun lay on the rice. That was when I
decided to shoot him. Who was he to enjoy the sun, when Lamar was dead?
Wouldn't it be God's will if the bullet struck him or not? Then, I decided to
ignore him; let someone else take him down. But next, as if destined, Haywood
pointed him out to me and I put him in my sight.

Did I always do what Haywood told me? I didn't tell him about the marches and Birmingham, and I should have, dear Mr. and Mrs. Jackson, that was what he needed to know about more than anything. That there was a time when we dreamed and hoped.

JUST THEN A FLY lit on my forehead and I wiped at it. Suddenly, I felt fly-covered, the way the buffalo's intestines we saw later were, a buzzing swarm of flies covering me like fur. I wiped again at my head, and saw that except for the gnats that were always there, my head was clear. The papa-san was tugging at the mud, swinging his arms widely to give him momentum as he ran across the paddy. Sweat ran into my eyes. I wanted to take off my helmet and wipe my palm over my hair and forehead. I thought the papa-san was becoming a mirage, first visible, and then shimmering away. He ran, gangly, as if threads held his joints together. He swung his arms widely, made exaggerated steps. His movements were becoming gibberish. He wobbled. His gestures teetered, chattered. He was more a monkey than a man. A black monkey. A little black monkey.

I squeezed off a round or two. When I saw him go down, I thought, That's the way it's supposed to happen. That was just God's will. The insects were buzzing around my head again; they were in my ears buzzing and there was a big throb in my chest, and my stomach crunched into a knot.

DEAR MR. AND MRS. JACKSON, what brought me here? I wasn't raised this way, and I have been in the civil rights workshops with Reverend King. I know better. What a murderer I have become. I don't feel like a murderer, though. I don't feel like anything, but scared. And I think I know how those firemen in Birmingham felt, and I think I know how Mr. Williams who shot my grandfather felt, and I think I know how those boys who shot Lamar felt—but, no. I don't know because they had never been to a civil rights workshop. They had never heard Reverend King. I have a dream that one day every valley shall be engulfed, every hill shall be exalted, and every mountain shall be made low, the *rough places will be made plains and the crooked places will be made straight, and the glory of the Lord shall be revealed and all flesh shall see it together.*

I LAY WITH my eyes closed. I could see flashes and streaks of light against the blackness. I thought, I will never write this letter. It's a letter that can't be written. I felt myself drift.

WHERE WAS I when Haywood died? I was right by his side.

A CURRENT of dream took me and I was floating. I was looking down on the blue orb of Earth from space. *Apollo 11* rocked like a cradle. Moonlight flooded the cabin. Lamar smiled at me. His grin was practically goofy. Didn't I tell you, Waltie? Didn't I say we would be the first?

WHERE WERE YOU when Lamar died? I was right by his side. Right by his side, then I ran. Why did you run? I was scared. And you aren't scared to go to the moon?

From the space capsule, we saw the paddies outside of Thoybu, the thatched roofs of the hooches, the river snaking through the green canopy. The capsule began to descend; the navigational jets roared on. Down, down it came toward some place, toward Alabama. And then I was in Coosada, of all places. Coosada.

And where were you when your mother died? Lord, lord, where were you then. I was standing by her side. Yes, I was right by her si?

• • •

WE HAD BEEN CRYING all morning and neither Josie nor I wanted to go to Mother's funeral. It was hot that afternoon and my Easter suit was scratchy. The hearse met us in front of Grandma Pic's house. I remember walking by the hearse and seeing the coffin through the rear window. It's a space capsule, I told myself. Inside there were oxygen and lights and radar screens and radios, compasses, and the excitement of taking an exotic journey.

On the way to the church, we rode behind the hearse in the undertaker's limousine. I remember my father's face looked bruised and he moved his neck stiffly from the billy club beating. I remember how the white policeman stopped traffic at the one intersection in Coosada to let the procession pass. The policeman took off his hat as the hearse passed, and some of the white men on the sidewalk, turning, looking with curious faces, did likewise.

The countryside had been baked by drought. The crops were stunted and brown and the plowed areas had a dead color as if the red soil had been dusted with talc. I had the sensation, sitting in quiet numbness with my family, that we were moving through a dreamscape, not nightmarish, but visionary. Something about the place was also like something about every place I had ever been or would ever go. The scientists tell us that the entire universe was in one place at the beginning, and so, all of it was right here on the roadside on the way to my mother's funeral. What was the difference, after all, between a crossroads like Coosada and a hamlet like Thoybu? Between Birmingham and Da Nang? Are they not just places full of people, and the people full of hopes and struggles? Here a field, there a paddy; here peanuts, there rice; here a church, there a temple. We are always ready, are we not, to point out the obvious differences? But just below the surface—or maybe just on top of it, visible to those who would see it, invisible to those who would not—is the incontrovertible proof that the world is a tumultuous place and every soul in it suffers.

JACKSON, Dear Mrs. Burrell, Dear Daddy, that
ally learned. Everybody suffers. Suffering
ss can't always do that. What we learn

from suffering, from grief, is what every other person is learning. It's human compassion, like no other. I forgot about compassion. When Haywood asked me to tell him about Birmingham, I should have told him about compassion.

THE PREACHER WAS ROTUND, *darkly complected, with a cap of tight, dingy wool for hair. He used country grammar and a country whine that I didn't pay attention to at first. But then his rhythms began to take on the life of a song. His voice reverberated in major and minor keys. He was preaching about death. He said that no one escaped it. He said that it was written. He said that it was the contract we had made with God so that our lives would have purpose. We did not want death. No man wanted to die. Longevity had its place. But death was the price of being human. He looked directly at Josie and me. "We love Mama," he said. "Mama brought us into this world. Mama nurtured us and fed us. We don't want Mama to go—but Mama's got to go. Mama's got to go. We all got to go, sometime." Around me, I heard sniffles, throat clearing; the church had a hot, snotty smell. But I no longer felt like crying. I was tired and hot, and I wanted it all to be over.*

When the preacher sat down, a small, olive-colored woman with her hair pulled into a beehive stood up in the choir stand. She sang in a clear, sweet voice without accompaniment. It was a voice more jazz than gospel, cool and slightly sophisticated. I looked at my father, who had closed his eyes.

"Leaning. Leaning. Leaning on the everlasting arms!"

Someone in the congregation let out a sorrowful moan. There was more sniffling. I felt the humidity rise, and my scratchy suit became more uncomfortable. It was as if I were being tortured in every way possible and I thought, Fine, then—I'll just have to suffer. Mama had suffered. Oh, my God why? How can we survive beyond this hour?

The officious-looking undertakers, their faces unaffected by the proceedings, adjusted the flower spray and unlatched the coffin. It opened with a hiss, and I knew I did not want to look. I had been looking at my mother when she died, when tension left her face, and I imagined her spirit leaked out of her open mouth.

What a look of release! How calm and free her face became. How beautiful. And I did not think I could look at her again. Yet, when the lid was propped open and the undertaker stepped aside, I craned to see her stiff-lipped, beautiful corpse. Father was attempting to stand while holding Josie, who had gone limp on his shoulder. Aunt Bennie cried out, "My poor sister!" Grandma Pic sobbed. Uncle Reed cried silently. Vachel looked stunned. Father was still trying to stand up; it seemed an interminable process. Dear Mr. and Mrs. Jackson, I was trying to stand up beside him.

About the Author

Anthony Grooms was educated at the College of William and Mary and at George Mason University. He is the author of *Ice Poems* and *Trouble No More: Stories* and is the winner of the 1996 Lillian Smith Award. As a writer, teacher, and arts administrator, he has won awards from the National Endowment for the Arts, the Bread Loaf Writers' Conference, and the City of Atlanta Bureau of Cultural Affairs. He is currently the Professor of Creative Writing at Kennesaw State University in Georgia, and lives in Atlanta with his wife, Pamela B. Jackson.

- What happened with Lena?
- Letters?
- workin idea that paper about.